GOOD FOR NOTHING

GOOD FOR NOTHING

BRANDON GRAHAM

SKYSCRAPER

Published by Skyscraper Publications Limited
Talton Edge, Newbold on Stour, Warwickshire CV37 8TR
www.skyscraperpublications.com
First published 2014
Copyright © 2014 Brandon Graham

Designed and typeset by Mary Neal Meador
Printed and bound by CPI Group (UK) Ltd, Croydon, CR0 4YY
ISBN-13: 978-0-955-1810-7-8

Dedicated to the memory of my friends

Leslie Anne Hamilton,

Brian C. Gwaltney,

and

John Lynch

GOOD FOR NOTHING

A SERIES OF RASH DECISIONS

For the hundredth time in ten minutes, Flip cinches the terry cloth belt of his forest green bathrobe. This frustrates him, so he cranks it down tight. He's convinced his belt is mocking him.

He'd considered changing into his grubby clothes before starting this chore, but he knew none of his clothes would come close to fitting. He and his body are not on speaking terms. He has gained two or three pounds a week for at least the past eight months. He'd always been prone, since he was a little boy, to seeking comfort in food, especially during stressful times. For him, comfort food was aptly named. Food was the only thing he'd found comfort in for some time, even before he was fired. It'd gotten so bad that he only felt comfortable wearing his Tabasco-bottle boxer shorts and threadbare bathrobe, both of which were Christmas gifts from his wife, Lynn. He's aware things can't continue like this. Given another year like the last one, a group of firemen with chainsaws and block and tackle will be needed to hoist him from his bedroom. Assuming his entire family isn't living on the street by then.

Flip takes a wide stance and leans awkwardly over the paint can he's just placed on the old sheet he's using as a drop cloth. He breathes heavily at the mild exertion. His gut forces the belt loose again and his robe hangs open at his sides, like impotent wings, revealing his corpulent, furry mid-section. *Ignore it.* He leans his weight on the paint can for balance and gazes down his torso.

What the hell happened? His chest is loose and covered with coarse silver hair, like he's been dipped in honey and rolled in steel wool. His gut is enormous. In this position, it sways a little. He sucks in his abdomen with no visible effect. His skin is sallow and blotched. He thinks it's irritated by his own perspiration and imagines it would be tender to the touch. He lets a hand brush along his clammy skin, and his index finger plumbs the depths of his belly button, finds crusty dead skin around the edges. *I should moisturize.*

He stretches to pick up a putty knife and wiggles the tip around the gummy perimeter of the paint lid. Slowly the lid begins to pry loose. He levers it harder. The putty knife slips and the sharp point painfully gouges a sliver of flesh from the heel of his left hand.

"That figures!" His voice rises to a squeal. He flaps his hand, sucks at the wound, dances clumsily in place and flaps his hand a little more. He looks at the flesh divot hanging by a thread of skin and his blood welling up thick and red. He pumps his fingers and watches the blood gather in a widening pool in the palm of his hand, obscuring the crescent shape of his life line and making his fate line unclear. He tips his hand and lets the blood run over his wrist and drip to the floor. He looks down to see red soaking into the carpet, just beyond the edge of the drop cloth he'd been aiming for.

"Shit," he says. He wraps his hand in a rag Lynn left out for him, ties it off, using his teeth to tighten the knot. He rushes a second rag into the hall bathroom and wets it in the sink.

Earlier that morning Flip had been happy to hear his wife calling his name.

"Flip," she said, "Flip. You need to wake up." In his dreamy stupor, her voice moved to him in a husky, warm whisper laced with the promise of gentle caresses and moist, meaningful kisses. He often dreamed of her, and of them together; of the places they'd travelled, of times they'd made love.

When she called to him, he was with her in the south of France, a little coastal village on the Mediterranean. All day they casually walked from one vineyard wine-tasting to another, stopping at lunch to sip café au lait and then again at dinner to dine on fresh Provençal seafood stew, followed by more local wine.

They lingered in town long after midnight, unwilling to return to the hotel. In the early morning hours they walked barefoot on the beach, their toes working into the sand as the foamy surf rose and fell. In a secluded spot they spread a blanket they purchased from a tourist stall and let their warm, tan bodies glide together. Her sandy foot ran along the sides of his calves, pulling the hair. It hurt. But they were intoxicated, drunk on one another, on life. A part of his mind knew that Sara was conceived that night, conceived out of a mix of love, wine and lustful abandon.

"Flip," she called again. "Get up."

As he half-woke from his reverie, he wanted to hold Lynn and tell her how much he loved her, breathe her in and hold her essence deep in his lungs. He reached for her and his hand came down on the empty pizza box he'd been sleeping beside.

"Flip!"

His eyes creaked open and it became clear Lynn was not interested in losing herself in his embrace.

"Will you wake the hell up? It's nearly ten o'clock. Dylan got me up at five-thirty because he needed me to wipe his butt. I've been up ever since. Sara has a stomach bug, again, and is in one of her moods. Again. Or should I say still. I am this close to throttling her." She stood in the doorway of what used to be their bedroom. She didn't come in and didn't bother to uncross her arms to gesture when she said the words, *this close*. Months earlier she'd started sleeping in the guest room in the extension and had slowly been moving all her belongings to that end of the house.

"Okay. Sorry. Hey baby. I guess I was up late again," he said. Flip had slept slumped awkwardly across the duvet, his neck torqued at a painful angle and his head propped on the crunched pillows he'd stuffed behind him as he watched the Tarzan Theater Movie Marathon the night before. He'd slept in his robe again. "Yesterday was a stressful day," he added.

The truth was, the previous day Flip had only ventured out of the bedroom long enough to take delivery of his Pizza Pizza; then he'd returned to the serious business of flipping channels. It was the only thing he felt good about doing.

He couldn't stand to be out during the day, was afraid he would catch a glimpse of his likeness in a mirror or a window. Or worse yet, in the eyes of strangers who would look at him with disgust or pity or avoid looking at him at all. He preferred low light and cool dark places. His life had become a pathetic parable of alienation, a self-imposed banishment. Being alone made him feel simultaneously liberated and isolated. He missed his old life, but this was all he felt capable of handling.

"Do you remember three weeks ago when I asked you to please paint the office?" She didn't wait for a reply. "Do you remember that you said 'Sure honey. No prob.' and then you proceeded to do nothing?"

"Um-yeah," he said. He tried to sit up. His body ached and his head throbbed painfully. He reached behind his neck and rubbed at a tender protrusion at the top of his spine, under his shaggy hairline. He wondered if he had herniated a disk.

"Well, two weeks ago, in an effort to encourage you, and not to nag or be impatient – God forbid I sound unsupportive – I paid Sara and her boyfriend to help me move the furniture away from the walls, to make it easy for you to get to everything. Do you remember that?" He remembered. He shifted around some more on the bed and pulled the TV remote out from the small of his back.

"Did you really need to pay Sara and her boyfriend?" he asked, trying to degrade the momentum of her rant.

"Well, yes."

"Did they ask you to pay them or did you volunteer to pay them?" He rubbed a hand across his throat; it was like sandpaper with damp strips where his flesh had folded while he slept.

"What does it matter? I volunteered to pay them. I needed the help."

"Yeah, but Sara lives here, rent free. I'd think that she could help without you needing to pay her . . . she is a member of this family. Family. That's the definition of family. You do things for each other because they need doing. And also the boy, What's-His-Face, should have refused to take your money. If he wants to be welcome in this house he should act like family. I would have refused the money if I were in that situation. It's not right. Doesn't he have any pride?" Flip's bladder felt as if it might let go without permission. He tried to find a position that would ease the pressure.

Lynn said nothing. Instead she re-folded her arms under her large, tired-looking bosom and made her lips tight. She tilted her head as if to say *All good points. But I find them somewhat ironic given your current situation.* He knew she was right. He had known how she would respond as he spoke. They had been married a long time. That was another of his problems: he lacked the capacity to self-edit. Sometimes it was as if his mouth was subjected to more gravity than the rest of his body. He couldn't stop himself. Words just fell out.

"My situation is completely different," he said weakly.

"So the room has been ready for weeks," she ignored him and got back to her original point. "But apparently the task of gathering the painting supplies was too taxing for you because all you've been doing is dicking around the house. The kids are back in school. I've picked up more hours at work. So I know it wasn't fear of interruption." She paused to give him a chance to argue. He had nothing to say.

"So last weekend, in a final effort to make it as easy for you as I can, short of moving your body through the motions needed to paint a room, I bought a new roller pad and paint tray; I bought masking tape and a new angle brush. I dug out old sheets and rags and I even found the leftover paint from remodelling and I placed them all in the office."

"I told you thank you," he said. He jerked his open robe closed over his lap and adjusted the belt yet again.

"Yes. I know you told me '*thank you*.' It was the most you'd said to me in weeks so I remember that you said '*thank you*.'" Her voice was getting progressively higher. He knew this as a bad sign.

"I've been having a tough time," he explained.

"Really? Have you? I hadn't noticed. Oh wait – is that the reason you've been completely useless for the past . . . what is it now? Six months? More than that – over half a year. Because you had a touch of the blues? Flip – grow a pair, will you? Your family needs you to snap out of it." She hissed the last few words at him, an attempt to yell quietly. She didn't like the kids to hear them disagree. As if the kids hadn't already noticed their marriage was circling the toilet. If he honestly assessed the state of their relationship, he would have to say Lynn only stayed with him out of a kind of sentiment, the same sort of sentiment she felt for the wretchedly misshapen and dangerously sharp, gaudy, and globular coil-pot Sara had made in first grade art class; a Mother's Day gift. *I am just a cracked pot she keeps because it would break some emotional contract to get rid of me.* But he tried not to think about things like that.

"What do you want me to do? No one is hiring right now. I've networked and put in my application and paid for resumé services and called in old favours. I contacted three headhunters. I don't know what else to do. The market is bad. No one is hiring right now. My hands are tied. We are upside down on our mortgage, so we can't afford to sell. We have no equity, which means no down payment on a new home. My old buddies over at McCorkle-Smithe have stopped returning my calls. I think I've been blackballed. It's not my fault." He rocked his body a few times before managing to swing his legs over the side of the bed. He didn't look at her as he spoke. He noticed he was wearing only one black sock. "I looked through the want ads yesterday," he lied. "And there was nothing new. I've applied for everything."

"Do you understand that we are putting the house up for sale next week? We have an open house in nine days. If we can't sell the house on our own, we will likely go into foreclosure, file for bankruptcy, piss off our friends and neighbours by bringing property values down, be the subject of whispers and gossip and ridicule. That room has to be painted so we can move the furniture back. It's not been fun trying to pay bills with the office torn apart, by the way. But I didn't nag you about it, did I? No. I did not. I worked with the situation. I did not blame the inconvenience on you. I ignored it. Because, let's face it, complaining about it would do no good." In spite of her intentions, the volume of her monologue was escalating. She took a deep breath. Flip looked at the bathroom door. God, he needed to piss. He glanced at the gnarled stub of pizza crust in the box beside him and wanted to eat it, but he let it alone. That faint flicker of self-control felt like a small victory, as if he'd accomplished something for the day. Now he could take it easy.

Then Lynn regrouped and made another verbal pass. "Your legs still work," she quietly hissed at him, gesturing toward his massive pale thighs. "The downturn in the economy hasn't crippled you has it? You can still do some dishes or laundry can't you? You could help the kids with homework or pick Dylan up from school. You could get outside and mow the yard so we don't have to hire that pothead from next door." Flip was certain the yard work comment was her way of calling him fat, telling him he needed the exercise. The fact was she was so sickened by him she had moved out of their room. She said it was his snoring, but he knew it was disgust. Or she was withholding sex as a way of teaching him a lesson: sex is for men with income, for closers. As if they were characters in a Mamet play.

"That 'pothead' is named Kev and he is not a pothead. He's a drummer. I shook his hand and said he could have our business. I can't go back on a deal." His heart wasn't in the rebuttal, and even as he spoke he was aware Lynn knew he hadn't actually paid Kev in a month.

She gave up on hissing, threw her hands up and started screaming. "Fuck it! Look, I've made arrangements for Mom and me to take the kids to the amusement park for the day, so you can crawl out of your cave and do this one fucking thing for your family. Do it. Don't do it. Let your conscience be your guide. But if you don't get it done, you need to find somewhere else to be." She turned and scrambled down the steps and yelled for the kids.

"I understand," he said to no one. He sat on the edge of the bed, gnawing on pizza crust and feeling defeated. He listened to his family tramp across the kitchen floor and head out of the back door. He heard the garage door lift and the sliding door on the minivan slam closed. He heard his family drive away. And still he sat; until finally he wiggled his foot out of the unmated sock and moved his aching body into the bathroom to take a badly-needed leak.

"Dab don't rub. Dab don't rub," he tells himself as he leans over the bloody carpet stain. Lynn takes housework seriously. And with the house going on the market, the room needs to look impeccable when he's done. He's determined not to cock this up. *Lynn is right. I've been worthless.*

He sees this project as one little baby step that could be the first move toward some kind of personal redemption.

When it comes to painting, Flip has a system. First he uses a four-inch angle brush to cut-in along the ceiling and down the corners as far as he can reach; then, cut-in along the baseboards and up the corners as far as he can reach. Finally, he slowly rolls the spaces between. He doesn't use masking tape. He considers it a waste of time, and he regrets that with their finances so tight, Lynn wasted money on unnecessary supplies. One just needs to go slow and steady.

It feels good to have a plan. He is directed and motivated; once he has a plan, successful implementation is a foregone conclusion. *I've earned a break.*

Food sounds good, but he's determined that tomorrow he'll wake up lighter than this morning. So he walks to the kitchen and looks for something healthy. The fruit basket only has bananas, and bananas aren't his favourite. He looks in the pantry for cereal. Lynn's Special K seems like the best choice. He goes for a heaping handful of Lucky Charms instead. He likes to let the chalky, desiccated little marshmallows swell with moisture in his mouth before chomping into them.

The Chocolate Chip Cookie Dough ice cream beckons to him from the freezer, but he ignores it. He's proud of his will-power. He figures that since he's only had a little cereal he deserves to reward himself with a beer while he paints. It's early to be drinking but he doesn't have to drive anywhere. Besides, drinking beer and manual labour go hand in hand. It's the one useful thing his father ever taught him.

He twists the cap off a Sam Adams and winces at the twinge of pain as the teeth along the cap's edge catch on the makeshift bandage wrapped around his palm. He shakes the cap loose and meanders back into the office.

He takes stock of the job ahead. He imagines Lynn's glee when she gets home and sees what a great job he's done: the room looking fresh and crisp, all the furniture moved back in place. Dylan will tell him how good it looks, hopping up to hug his leg, like a koala clinging to the trunk of a tree. Sara will give him a rare smile and Lynn will kiss him, for the first time in a long time. Hell, maybe she will even invite him down to her new bedroom where they can screw as loudly as they want. *Yes, this office will be my fresh start.*

The room had been his gym before the remodel, and Lynn's craft room, back when they liked one another's company. It's smallish for a bedroom but plenty big for an office. Sara and that weasel she is dating had moved the desk, filing cabinets, and bookcases haphazardly into the middle of the room. So first things first: get a screwdriver and take the faceplates off the sockets and switches.

He takes a long swig of beer and sets it on the top shelf of one of the bookcases. He cinches the belt of his robe again as he returns from the kitchen with a screwdriver and starts on the switch plate next to the door. He places the screws and plate on the desk and begins to crawl around the room and take off socket covers. His robe falls open and is in the way again, so Flip shucks it off and whips it onto the desk. The robe's belt smacks his beer and the bottle glugs its contents onto the top shelf of books. Flip stands frozen, watching the foamy liquid do its damage.

"Perfect," he says. He picks up the bottle and pitches it in the kitchen garbage. He considers recycling, but the bin is in the mudroom and he doesn't have the energy. *Next time.* He comes back with a roll of paper towels and sops up all he can. The books will always smell like beer.

In a fit, he clears the whole shelf with one sweep of his arm. An oversized, hardbound, self-help tome his wife had recently purchased for him falls, corner first, directly on top of his bare foot. He hops around among the damp books.

"Fuck fuck fuck fuck," he says. He is pretty sure he's broken a bone.

He limps over to the socket he already started, hunkers down on all fours, and continues his circuit of the room. He notices a sour smell and wonders if there's another dead mouse in the wall. Then he realizes the smell is coming from him. *I'll have to take a shower when I'm done, so as to better charm my wife.*

When he's finished with the sockets he goes out to the garage to find his paint pot. When he takes the steps down he feels the fat bobbing up and down the trunk of his body, driving his bare feet hard into the gritty cement slab. He can't find what he's looking for among the kids' toys, bikes and garden tools. Lynn must have thrown it out, not knowing it is the perfect tool for this specific job. In the kitchen he finds a piece of Lynn's Tupperware that will do the trick. He'll have to be sure and dispose of the evidence before she gets home. Otherwise she'll be pissed. She loves her Tupperware.

He pours paint into the bowl. The paint is a warm beige; a little too pink. Flip tries to read the label, but the printing is covered with drizzles. He decides to call the colour *Caucasian*. He sets the bowl down and comes back a minute later with a step stool. He grabs his angle brush and stands on the stool. He dabs the tip of his brush in the paint and wipes it on the edge of the bowl. He feels cold. *I'm standing around in my boxer shorts for Christ's sake.* He heads down the hall to turn off the air conditioning.

He's still thirsty, and he spilled his beer, so he decides it'd be a good time to go ahead and get another drink. He goes in the kitchen and works his way through the last Sam Adams. From where he stands he can see Kev and Kev's girlfriend lying out on the deck next door. They are shielding their eyes with bent arms and squinting at one another as they talk and laugh. The muscles of their firm little abdomens pop as they giggle. Flip absently picks something hard out of his belly button as he downs the beer.

Back in the office Flip mounts the stool, brush in hand, and lays the first line of flesh-coloured paint along the top of the wall. He steps down, nudges the stool along and steps back up. About halfway around the room, his neck and shoulders start cramping up on him. He rubs the sore spot at the base of his skull. *Herniated disk.* He's sure of it.

He needs to take something or he'll get a raging headache. He leaves the paint on the desk with the brush balanced carefully across the mouth of the bowl. In the hall linen closet he fishes through half-empty prescription bottles until he finds the muscle relaxant he'd been prescribed when he hurt his lower back the year before. He thinks it's a good idea to take it with alcohol, just to get the full effect. He drags a kitchen chair over and rummages in the half-cabinet over the fridge until he finds some whisky they'd used for Irish coffee at their annual neighbourhood Christmas gala. He pops the pill and knocks back a mouthful of whisky. He screws the lid back on, but leaves the bottle out, just in case his neck and shoulders keep hurting.

In the office he finds the brush has fallen off the rim of the bowl and is leaving a huge paint blob on Lynn's desk. Flip leans over to grab the damp cloth he'd used on the bloodstain and his boxer shorts tear in the back. He feels his cool, damp, fleshy ass through the rip with the tips of his fingers.

"Damn it all," he says. He snags the rag and wipes at the paint. Most of it comes up, but the wood grain has soaked up the pink hue and it won't come out no matter how hard he scrubs. *There's no way Lynn will miss this.* He gives up.

Flip stands on the stool and finishes painting around the edges of the ceiling. When he's done, he stands back to evaluate, and determines he's done a decent job; could have been steadier, but not bad. He's feeling light-headed from the paint fumes, or the drugs and booze. He sets the bowl and brush down and snaps on the ceiling fan, watches the dusty wooden blades slowly rotate and pick up speed. He'll give it a few minutes to air out before he gets back to work.

His neck still hurts. He rubs it, tries to pop it, and stretches it from side to side and front to back. In the bathroom he looks through the cabinet for aspirin. He finds sleeping pills, Pepto Bismol, and sun-screen. He considers searching through the linen closet again, but decides more whisky will be as good as aspirin. After dosing himself thoroughly and pouring more paint in his bowl, he starts cutting-in along the baseboards.

As he leans over with his rump in the air he feels a draught. It's his favourite pair of boxer shorts too. Now he'll have to sew them. He wants to ask Lynn to do it for him, but doubts she'd be receptive. Maybe after she sees the room and he sexes her up good. She is always more agreeable after sex. Christmas night was the last time he'd got laid, and nearly the last time Lynn had been agreeable. But he can't blame her. The rug had been jerked out from under them.

Last Christmas, he'd orchestrated events so that Lynn would open her gift from him last.

"What's this?" she said, giving the small box a little shake.

"Don't know. It's from Santa," Flip answered. He looked over and grinned at Dylan, winked at Sara. The kids both smiled back.

"How did Santa know I liked small presents?" she asked.

"Don't get too excited. It might be a lump of coal."

"I doubt that," she said, as she tore the little silver bow from the top and went at the silver paper. "I've been a very good girl this year."

"Maybe Santa saves the best gifts for bad girls," he joked, allowing a slightly lascivious sneer to creep into the comment.

"Gross," Sara said, as she pushed her folded hand into another new, bright bracelet.

"What's gross?" Dylan stopped pretend-flying his new Transformer long enough to participate in the exchange.

"Dad's being a perv with Mom," she explained.

"Gross," Dylan agreed, nodding his little head earnestly. "What's a perv?"

"Don't listen to your sister, Dyl. Just play with your robot," Flip said.

Lynn pulled the little black, felt box out and held it close to her face, so she could be the first to peer inside. She pulled up the hinged lid and gasped. Then she licked the ring on her right hand, giving Flip a suggestive glance, and slid it off. She slipped the new ring on and held her hand out as far as she could, to take a good look at it, twisting it slightly to let the Christmas lights catch in the facets of the jewel. "I love it," she said. She crawled over and knocked Flip onto his back as she hugged him and planted wet smackers all over his face. "Careful with the back," he said. "It might have some work to do later. If you know what I mean," he said quietly.

"Gross," Sara had said.

Flip finishes cutting-in around the baseboards and working the corners without incident. He stands and stretches his lower back; it still aches. He surveys the room. *Looking pretty good.*

In the kitchen he twists the lid off the whisky and takes a long swig. *The hard part is done. It's all downhill from here.* The clock on the microwave reads 3:30. It had taken longer than he thought. *There's no rushing perfection.*

He fills the paint tray, gets the roller ready and starts rolling the walls. The saturated fibres of the roller pad make a wet whirr, like surf slipping back into the sea. He's cold again. He turns the ceiling fan off and watches to see that the blades are actually slowing, walks back and steps right in the middle of the full paint tray. He lifts his cold, slippery foot and dangles it over the drop cloth. Tendrils of flesh-toned paint create an instant action painting as he rattles his dripping foot on his swollen ankle. He loses his balance and steps right on the frantic design he'd just made, slides along in the paint slick. His other foot moves to keep him from falling and steps onto the paint roller, it shifts and crushes under his weight, pitching him, gut first, onto the paint tray. He lies there a long time with most of the air knocked out of him. He can smell the whisky on his own stale breath as he exhales into the drop cloth.

The paint tray has cut his side. He worries he's broken a rib. He gets up on all fours and looks under himself as the paint drools from his soft, sagging belly. His skin is pale and stark against the vivid pink smear. He backs himself onto his feet, and after two failed attempts, he stands. Cold paint slowly rolls over the front of his boxer shorts. This frustrates him. *At least I won't need to sew them.*

The baseboard is splashed with pink, the rug is soaking up pink paint, and his torso is dripping paint onto the tops of his hairy toes and yellowed toenails. It looks like the slaughter scene from a slasher film, only in anaemic, pastel tones. *This is horrible.*

This was what he was afraid of; it's exactly why he'd avoided this job for weeks. Disaster is an inevitable outcome of everything he tries to do lately. *I'm cursed.*

Flip reaches back to steady himself against the desk. His hand comes down on the round-bottomed Tupperware bowl; the bowl tips up and pours paint on the top of Lynn's desk.

"Oh no." He kneels where he is. His knees just give up and he dry sobs into his hands for a long, long time, the edge of his bandaged hand leaving smears of paint along the stubble of his unshaven face.

When Flip is bored with sobbing, he forms a new plan. First, he marches into the kitchen with his body still dripping paint and takes long pulls of whisky. After a few minutes he begins to feel courageous. He drains the bottle and throws it in the sink. He makes his way into the bathroom and washes down the bottle of sleeping pills with Pepto Bismol. It tastes worse than he imagined possible. He doesn't want that to be the last thing he ever tastes, so he goes to the freezer, digs around and stands over the sink, pounding down Chocolate Chip Cookie Dough ice cream with an oversized serving spoon as fast as he can. His stomach doesn't seem too happy about it. He pats his fat chest a few times, and belches long and loud.

He realizes he's drunk when he opens his mouth wide and pokes himself in the left eye with a spoon full of ice cream. He wipes off his eyelashes and keeps at it, one eye closed, because he likes to finish what he's started. Eventually he polishes it off and leaves the carton and spoon in the sink. As he stumbles away, his belly smears paint along the edge of the counter and the doorjamb.

In the office he finds the belt of his robe and makes a noose in one end. It eats up over half of the belt's length. But it should still work. His paint-spattered toes find purchase on the middle shelf of a bookcase and he teeters there drunkenly, periodically throwing his arms out for balance as he tries to loop the other end of the belt over the motor of the ceiling fan. When he's satisfied with his work, he sticks his head through the noose and tightens it.

I'm ready, he tells himself.

He doesn't know the proper protocol, but he assumes he should leave a note. He doesn't know what to say and *Sorry* is all that comes to his foggy brain. It would be a lot of effort to go and write a note that only says, *Sorry. Is it really worth it? Can't I just blow it off? I'm beat.* Finally he realizes it will be inconsiderate to his family not to attempt to explain his actions, so he digs his fingers into the knot and manages to loosen it. He loses his balance, and the bookcase half-full of self-help books tumbles onto the floor where they join their beer-soaked brethren.

He dangles there, looking up the short piece of terry cloth toward the ceiling fan. He's shocked the fall hasn't broken his neck; in fact it has made his neck feel better. *Not a herniated disk after all. What a relief.*

He's surprised he can still breathe and that the tips of his toes just touch the floor, though his foot throbs from where the book crushed it. He worries at the way the fan is cocked sideways over his head. What if it falls and gives him a nasty concussion?

Then he hears the garage door opening. His ass is cold. How embarrassing would it be for his family to find him hanging there, dead, with his boxer shorts ripped?

He tries to reach around and close the gap in his shorts. The movement causes Flip to twist slowly, like a grotesque, sad-hobo ballerina *en pointe*, and as he does, his eyes drift around the paint-drenched room, at the pink carpet and baseboards, at the trail of spatters and footprints leading in and out of the room, and at the half-painted walls.

House keys rattle and the voices of his bickering children come to him. He hears his mother-in-law's voice too. He thinks of the whisky bottle, the ice cream carton, and the stench of beer. As the door opens, his eyes finally rest on Lynn's desk and her Tupperware bowl.

"Oh shit," he thinks. He reflexively reaches to tighten the belt around his bare middle and realizes he's hanging from it, by his neck.

"Oh shit," he says again. Then he tries as hard as he can to be dead.

A SUPPOSED SOURCE OF HELPFUL ADVICE

Flip's nose is runny and he's convinced he's allergic to some spore that has leached its way through the floor from the flower shop below. He swipes his nose with the side of his hand and snorts. Then he wipes his hand on his XXXL Hawaiian shirt. It's new. One of the purchases Lynn made on the way home from the amusement park. He's also wearing new khaki shorts from the Big and Tall men's store. The clothes make him feel short, broad, and lush, like a tropical cinderblock.

Flip looks over at Lynn. She's snapping the pages of an *Architectural Digest* at the opposite side of the tiny waiting room. He coughs, clears his throat, and snorts again. Lynn refuses to glance in his direction. He drops a copy of *Golf Digest* on the side table and cruises the room looking for Kleenex. There are none. There are six chairs, two sets of three different styles of mid-century modern classics. He doesn't know the names of the designers, but he's sure they are European. Each set of similar designs has different colours and patterns. The effect, Flip is sure, is supposed to be eclectic and casual, yet sophisticated. Flip finds it obvious, trendy and pretentious; but to each his own.

"What kind of shrink doesn't supply his clients with Kleenex?" he asks rhetorically.

Lynn looks at him out of the top of her eyes. Flip takes her glare as encouragement.

"I mean, don't you think with all the blubbering that goes on in this type of place he should have Kleenex everywhere? I think it shows a lack of consideration if not a lack of professionalism."

Lynn licks a fingertip and snaps a page. She exhales heavily and concentrates on reading an ad for designer replacement windows.

The "he" Flip is referring to is Dr. Hawkins. Flip has a deep dislike for Dr. Scruffy Face already. On the day of *the recent unpleasantness*, as Flip likes to think of it, after the ambulance arrived, Flip was rushed to the emergency room at St. Elizabeth's. His stomach was emptied with a combination of ipecac, liquid charcoal plunged through a nose tube directly to his stomach, and some kind of medicine that emptied his bowels in a horrible and violent black-licorice-smelling eruption. While it turned out to be an effective hangover cure, he wouldn't recommend it.

Then, because he was deemed a threat to himself, his wrists and ankles were strapped to bedrails and he was kept under observation overnight and into the next morning. The doctor took his sweet time getting there for the mandatory psychological assessment.

"Your last twenty hours or so have been rather eventful," the doctor had said as he looked through Flip's chart.

"Yes," Flip replied. The doctor didn't introduce himself or shake Flip's hand. Flip chose to feel insulted. Plus the doctor was fit, youngish and fashionably unshaven. This pissed Flip off.

"So, let's talk about what happened," the doctor said. Then he stood patiently. Flip thought of waiting him out, but realized it would only prolong his stay. So he spoke up, with feigned earnestness.

"Yesterday, I woke up with a headache and took some medicine. Then I had a couple of drinks. I guess there was a bad reaction. That's all, just a flukey thing. I won't do that again, I can tell you." Flip tried to gesture; his wrists tugged against the straps, the metal buckle tapped against the bed rails.

"Well, that's good to hear," said the doctor. He made some notes, dropped a fancy pen in the pocket of his casually-rumpled lab coat and tucked the clipboard under one arm. "Listen. I need to ask you some questions," he said as he started unstrapping Flip's left wrist. "I just want you to be honest with me. Then we can see about getting you out of here." The doctor circled around the foot of Flip's hospital bed and unstrapped the right side restraint. Once Flip's hands were loose the doctor reached over and pumped Flip's hand once, hard and firm. Flip missed the doctor's grip and ended up getting his fingers squeezed. "I'm Doctor Hawkins. Good to meet you."

"Doc. I appreciate your concern. But I'm super good. This is embarrassing. And I'm tired and hungry. Also my side itches 'cause I scraped it up, my foot is bruised, my palm itches and my ass is raw from the concoction they poured down me. I need to get home. I want a shower and a change of clothes. So if you could just, you know, hurry the hell up. Not to be rude, but I've been waiting here, tied up like a criminal, forever. I think those straps gave me a rash," he said rubbing his wrists. Flip had more to say and Dr. Hawkins just let him talk himself out. "I would like to get home, be with my family. I don't feel right here, with all these bright lights and strangers. I need my wife and kids with me. I need to be home," he said finally.

"As I said, Mr. Mellis, you need to answer my questions. You need to be frank and honest and thorough. After that we can talk about going home." Dr. Hawkins pinned Flip with his disarmingly clear blue eyes. Then he said, "If it helps, I just spoke to

Lynn in the waiting room." He called her Lynn as if they were old friends. "She has a suitcase for you. She says the kids are with her mother. It's fortunate your mother-in-law is around to help; a stroke of good fortune, don't you think? Everyone is fine. Lynn can come see you as soon as we are done here." When he finished speaking, the doctor scuffed his chin and looked thoughtfully at Flip's chart again. He un-pocketed his pen and jotted down a quick note. Then he said, "Mr. Mellis. I need to understand how you ended up trying to hang yourself."

Flip stared at the doctor. "Fuck you. Fuck you very much for all your concern. This is America. I have my rights. I am an American. So take your list of questions, ball it up real tight and then ram it up your nosey, fresh-out-of-the-fraternity, blue-blood, silver-spoon ass." Flip was disappointed his insult had spun out of control. But still, he was proud of the effort. That would make the fucking jerk back off.

But, instead of backing off, the doctor leaned in close and said, "I don't think you understand your situation. You are under my care. If I think you are likely to attempt suicide again, then I will have you committed to an institution." His breath smelled delightful. *Fucker.* "If you are confrontational, I will keep you here for another twenty-four hours. If you just piss me off, I might have you sedated." He smiled a tiny, mirthless grin that showed his pointed canines. "The way you just abruptly changed your demeanour from pleasant and persuasive to aggressive and abrasive could be characterized as a violent and erratic mood swing." The doctor just let that hang there for a long moment. "Unless you want to start again," he said.

"Well that is some bullshit, because I'm fine. I am not a criminal. I have rights. I'm fine. I'm getting out of here and going home." Flip heaved himself into a sitting position.

Dr. Hawkins put his hand on Flip's chest and pushed him back in the bed. "You're wrong, Mr. Mellis. You may not be a criminal. But you have no rights. You gave up your rights when you stuck your head in that noose and tried to hang yourself. I will strap you down and leave you here until a space opens at a long-term mental health facility. Unless you think you can cooperate with me. Fully." He paused to let that sink in. "I ask questions, you answer them. It takes as long as it takes. You cooperate and maybe you get to go home." The doctor didn't remove his hand from Flip's chest. Flip tried to sit up again, but couldn't budge. Clearly the doctor worked out. Then he said, "Now. Do you understand the situation?"

Flip longed to mouth off some more. But he had finally replied, "Yes sir," very respectfully.

That was nearly twenty-four hours ago. It had taken until this morning to get his discharge papers processed, which meant he had spent two nights away from home. Lynn had rushed him straight to this appointment after he had slipped into his new clothes.

A door to the waiting room opens and Dr. Hawkins is standing there. "Hello," he says. "Mr. Mellis," he nods once to Flip. "And Ms. Mellis," He nods again in Lynn's direction. He doesn't say *Mrs. Mellis*. He says *Ms. Mellis*. He gives her a slight smile. "Why don't you come in and let's get started." He is dressed in slim slacks and a tailored sport jacket all in soothing earth tones. His stubble is exactly the same length as it had been at the hospital. His hair is wavy and thick and slightly unkempt in a devil-may-care, rough-and-ready-way that Flip pulled off once when he was twenty-two, but has never been able to replicate. Dr. Hawkins continues to hold the door. Lynn stands quickly from her pale yellow fibreglass chair, flashes her long legs as she crosses the room and passes by the doctor closer than seems necessary. He smiles at her again and watches her after she passes.

"You should have some Kleenex in this place," Flip says. He wipes his drippy nose on his rashy wrist. Then he says, "Nice chairs," and knocks shoulders with the doctor on the way through the door. He remembers too late that he bruises like a banana. *I'll be sore later.* He notices, grudgingly, that the doctor still smells terrific. *What a complete ass.*

Dr. Hawkins' office looks like a page from a designer catalogue. At the far end of the room there's a big blond wood desk with chrome legs, Danish modern, flanked by many framed diplomas and tasteful black and white photos, displayed on a rich, warm, burnt-cinnamon accent wall that Flip is certain is meant to be both masculine and calming.

There are matching bookcases thoughtfully decorated with a mix of scholarly texts, popular literature, stacks of magazines and symmetrically arranged and colour-coordinated art objects. They take their seats in surprisingly comfortable leather club chairs, placed in a circle and arranged equidistant. They are identical in size, but in three different colours, and with the seat cushions mixed up. Either the good doctor has too much time on his hands, has hired an interior decorator, or is gay. Flip's wishful prediction: gay with an interior designer boyfriend.

Dr. Hawkins crosses his legs at the knee and bobs his long, zipper-booted foot casually. "So, I would like to do this in two parts. First, though, how are you feeling today, Mr. Mellis? Are you all set now, with your facial tissues?"

"Great. I'm good," Flip says. His ass barely fits between the arms of the chair, and he's holding a square box of Kleenex on what remains of his lap. He straightens the tails of his Hawaiian shirt where they fall across the front of his pleated khaki shorts.

"Well good," the doctor says. He nods thoughtfully and makes notes in a black folder with his fancy pen. He shakes the expensive-looking watch on his wrist and checks it, then makes more notes. He looks at Lynn. "Is that true, Ms Mellis? Is Flip feeling great?"

"No," she says, "He needs help. He won't talk to me about what happened. We haven't been talking for months. He is all bottled up, clenched tight like a fist; emotionally speaking." Lynn looks stiff, formal; she's talking in her forced-calm voice.

"Why are you asking *her* how *I* feel? I just told you I feel great. Know why? 'Cause I feel great, that's why. I have had a good mornin . . . ah . . ." Flip opens his mouth, closes his eyes and sprays a fine mist of snot and saliva from his mouth and nose. The sound he makes is like a mighty battle yawp. He knocks the box of Kleenex into the centre of their circle.

"Sorry," he says. "That one snuck up on me." He stands, pushing hard on the arms of the chair to get himself up. The chair squeezes his hips for a moment, finally releasing him. He bends deep at the knees, and scoops up the Kleenex.

"I have allergies. I bet that happens a lot. You know, when you put your office above a flower shop." Then he wedges his ass back in place and honks his nose more loudly than intended. The doctor and Lynn sit quietly waiting for him to settle, as if he's a toddler telling a joke with no punchline. "As I was saying, I have had a great morning," Flip continues. "I'm feeling good. I think things are really turning around." The doctor makes a note on his pad and underlines it, taps out an exclamation mark, nods as he does it. Flip pinches the damp Kleenex in his fingers, not sure where to put it.

"Okay, Mr. Mellis. Let me get back to what I started to say a moment ago. I would like to do this in two parts. First, I want to talk with both of you. I want to be certain you and Ms. Mellis are practicing good communication strategies, I want to understand the conditions you will be returning to. Then, I will speak with you alone, Mr. Mellis." He turns to Lynn. "Ms. Mellis?" he smiles encouragingly. "May I call you Lynn?"

"Of course," she says. She smiles shyly in return. Flip thinks she actually bats her eyes, but the fucking calming low light makes it hard to tell.

"Hey," he says. "Not to interrupt, but do you have someplace I can dispose of this?" He indicates the Kleenex with a twitch of his head and a presentational gesture.

Dr. Hawkins waits for two deep breaths. "Are you sure you didn't mean to interrupt, Mr. Mellis?" He says it as if the answer is clear to them all, then lifts a small chrome trashcan from beside his chair. Flip pitches the sodden mass at the can, misses by a foot, and stares at it where it lies on the throw rug. "So close," he says.

The doctor stands gracefully and snatches a Kleenex from the box in Flip's lap. He uses it to pick up the damp tissue, deposits it all in the can with a hollow thump, and returns to his chair completely composed, legs crossed gracefully at the knee, slacks still creased. The can disappears beside his chair, and the pad and pen appear in his lap.

"Where were we, Lynn?" he says, turning to meet her gaze.

"You just asked if you could call me 'Lynn'," she reminds him warmly. "And I said 'of course you can.'"

"Oh yes. That's right. Thank you. I remember now. So, when I ask you how Mr. Mellis is feeling, I'm interested in your impression, Lynn. Clearly you care for him. You know him well. Your observations and opinions could be valuable to me. Plus, Mr. Mellis," he says to Flip. "Lynn needs the opportunity to be heard. You need to listen to how she feels about you trying to take your own life. In some ways the details are less important than how she feels about them. And besides. This incident didn't take place in a vacuum. There were circumstances that contributed to your decision to end your life. I would like to hear your wife's perspective. That way we can make the most informed decision possible about a course of treatment."

"It was just an accident," Flip says. If he felt he could be honest with Lynn, if he thought it was any of the Doc's goddamn business, he might tell them he felt too embarrassed about the shape his life was in to continue being alive. Or that the world's indifference to his constant emotional pain had overwhelmed him. But, looking at Lynn's cold disposition and the doctor's professional façade he couldn't muster the motivation required to be wholly honest. Instead he continued in the same vein.

"And I know how she feels, as we are married with two children. Also you may call me Flip if you would like."

Lynn snorts. Flip gives her a look. Dr. Hawkins scratches on the pad with his pen. Lynn watches him write to avoid looking at Flip. Flip picks at the cellophane around the mouth of the Kleenex box. Lynn nervously turns one of her earrings as she waits. Flip rubs his red wrist, making it look angrier. There is a clock ticking somewhere on one of the bookcases and Flip tries to locate it. He can't find it among the tasteful ceramic bowls, vaguely ethnic statuettes, and mismatched bookends. Finally Dr. Hawkins puts down his pen.

"The point, Mr. Mellis, is for Lynn to talk to you about her feelings and concerns in a safe environment in which she feels supported and respected. Lynn, I know from our conversation at the hospital what happened. I wonder if you've told Mr. Mellis how you felt when you found him?"

Lynn crosses her legs at the knee, in a mirror of the doctor's pose, crosses her arms under her breast and exhales heavily. "I was scared," she says to Dr. Hawkins.

Flip wonders why she wore such a low-cut top? He thinks it's a new top. He knows he's never seen her wear it. *She is dressed-up. She got dressed up.*

"Good, Lynn. Of course you were. But you need to tell Mr. Mellis. Not me. Turn and face him. Tell him how you feel."

She turns to Flip. Moisture wells in the corners of her eyes.

"When I found you there, I was scared. Frantic." The tears are coming now, but her face and voice are steady. "I saw the mess all over the kitchen. I knew something was wrong. I was getting angry, trying to keep the kids out of the paint and set down the bags and keep Mom from barging in, because I was afraid of what she might find. And then when I turned the corner . . ." Her voice breaks, then gets higher and louder as she continues. "I saw you there. With that belt around your neck. Twisting." She has trouble catching her breath, her face slick with tears. She sobs silently, shudders and holds her hands over her face.

"Are you hearing this Mr. Mellis?"

"Yes."

"Why don't you offer your wife a Kleenex, Mr. Mellis?"

Flip is offended that the doctor presumes to tell him what to do, knows he is right and feels guilty he didn't think of it himself. He twitches and drops the Kleenex again, then starts to extract himself from the chair, but the doctor is out of his chair and beside Lynn offering the tissues, a comforting hand on her back, and speaking to her reassuringly before Flip has a chance to react.

"Okay, Lynn. I know it's been hard. I understand your concern for your children and your husband and your mother. All the emotions of thinking your husband might be dead. Finding out he tried to kill himself. You've had so much to deal with. You've been so strong. It's okay to let it out now." The doctor continues to rub Lynn's back and speak soothingly as her breathing slows and her tears subside.

"Yes," Flip says. He moves to her other side and pats Lynn's back too. "It's okay," he says. His hand touches the doctor's, and they both jerk away.

Lynn sits up a little and gives Flip a cold look through red, wet eyes. The doctor returns to his chair and writes some more. Flip stretches his hand toward Lynn, wiggles his fingers so she will take his hand. She looks away and straightens her clothes, fluffs her hair and gently dabs the corners of her eyes, runs the tips of her fingers under her eyes to check for mascara.

"Lynn," the doctor says. "Do you have anything you'd like to say to Flip?"

"I would like to say something," Flip says. He shoves back into his chair with a loud squelching sound. "It was the chair," he explains.

"Let's let Lynn finish, Mr. Mellis. You'll have your chance in a moment. But your wife is making good progress here."

Flip nods. He looks back at Lynn, she's so beautiful. This is the woman he married. He loves her so much. He wants to make things right for her, wants to get things back on track, to tell her right now. But he waits. He defers to the doctor's professional opinion that she needs to talk.

"Flip," she says. She blots her eyes again and carefully wipes the tip of her nose. "I can't deal with seeing you like this anymore. I can't handle it. I can't handle it and keep our family rolling. I just can't handle it."

"I know, baby," Flip says very supportively.

"Shush," she says. "Let me finish." He nods again. She takes a deep breath. "I think you need to move out until you get your life together. I can't take care of you, the house, and the kids. It's too much. I think you need to move out."

"But," Flip says. There's a pressure in his chest like he swallowed a boiled egg without chewing. He feels panic rise, he can't catch his breath, the top of his scalp is hot and tingly and his face feels hot and flushed.

"I've been thinking about this a lot. I talked it over with the kids. They understand." Lynn begins to cry again.

"What? Can't we talk about this? You already told the kids? I really think things are going to be better now. I really do." He tries to stand but the chair still has him and he tumbles sideways onto the floor. His hips pop loose and he knee-walks toward her. "Don't do this. Please. Not now. Please. Things are going to be better. I promise."

"I am not doing this by choice, Flip," she cries. "It's the only thing I can do. It's all I know how to do. I don't know what else I can do. Don't put this on me. I'm out of choices. You left me no choice."

The doctor sets Flip's chair back up. "Mr. Mellis. Please. Return to your chair. Let her finish. It's her turn. You will have your say in a moment." He tries to steer Flip by his shoulders. Flip ignores the doctor, shrugs him off, pushes his head into Lynn's lap and starts to cry. Lynn cradles his head for a moment, as if she were holding an infant, reconsiders and shoves him away, his whiskered jowls catching on the soft material of her skirt. He sits back on his ass, and they sob separately.

"No. No. No. No. No," he says, his face ticks back and forth.

The doctor looks at his watch. "Maybe we should continue this later, Mr. Mellis."

FORCED EXODUS

"No way man," Kev says. He shakes his head with a genuine sense of deeply-felt disbelief, his hair swaying around his lean, smooth face.

Flip still looks like he's dressed for a luau. His back yard is stifling with late summer heat. He kicks off his shoes to cool down. His feet sink into the grass, but it's brittle and gives him no comfort. Looking over the fence at Kev, Flip has to admit Lynn is right; Kev really does look stoned.

Flip is having trouble catching his breath: *hay fever*. He takes a deep, wheezing breath, coughs up something salty and spits it in the grass. Kev is standing on the other side of the fence next to a lawn mower in a black T-shirt with the sleeves hacked off. BONEARAMA is printed across his chest. Flip knows it's Kev's favourite band.

"So Mr. Mellis. What're you going to do? Are you guys getting a divorce? Or what? I mean, I'm sorry. Don't feel like you have to answer that." Kev rakes his fingers back through his dirty-blond, shoulder-length hair and pulls his left foot in and out of his flip-flop. His tan skin gives him a healthy, fit look.

"I mean, if me and Aubrey broke up, I mean, I know it isn't exactly the same, but it would kill me. You know?"

"I know. I do. I know what you mean, Kev. It wasn't all that long ago that Lynn and I were young and dating. And crazy in love." Flip scratches at his still-tender wrist.

"Right on," Kev says earnestly. Flip hadn't expected Kev to understand. And honestly, how could he really? But Kev looks sincere enough, not skeptical at all. That's one thing Flip really likes about the kid. He doesn't seem to have a malicious bone in his body. He's uncomplicated, even if his eyes are bloodshot and he smells like he's been dipped in patchouli oil.

"So listen Kev, I know I haven't paid you for mowing in a long time." A rivulet of sweat runs down the small of Flip's back. When he moves he can feel his shirt sticking to his shoulder blades and love handles, his thick chest, his swollen gut and the backs of his fat arms. His body feels more bloated than usual. His skin itches and tingles, especially along the puckering scrape on his side. He winces, embarrassed at the memory.

He isn't used to sweating, and it has irritated his pores. Or maybe he has that disease where the epidermis peels off like a snake shedding its skin. That would make sense. Considering how much bigger his body has got. Human skin can only take so much before it splits wide open. He imagines himself crawling out of an old, dried husk of skin, standing there naked and slick and red, like a newborn baby.

"It's cool man," Kev says. "I mean I have to mow my yard anyway. Gotta pitch in or the 'rents get edgy. I'll just keep going. It's no big deal. You know what I mean?" Kev walks a little closer, leans his hands against the top of the fence and squeezes his face against the sun.

Kev is in his mid-twenties and not at all apologetic about living in his parent's basement. Flip has never spoken to the adult neighbours. All he knows is: they wear dark suits, carry briefcases, and drive matching BMWs. They carry themselves like attorneys.

"Yes, Kev. I know what you mean. But I made you a promise. And I don't want to just bail out. I want you to know, even though I'm going to be leaving for a while, and even though the house is for sale, I'm going to try and get a job right away, make things right, get the mortgage caught up. You know? Get everything back in order for my family. That's my top priority."

"Right on, Mr. Mellis," Kev says, "RIGHT . . . ," he makes a fist and Flip returns the gesture. They knock their knuckles together. ". . . ON, MISTER MELLIS. You can do it."

"Thanks. To be honest, I'm not sure. But I have to try." Flip's skin is drawing tight across the back of his neck. He should have worn a hat. Or sunscreen. Or both.

Unbidden, a visceral memory flashes through his mind: the medicinal slurry of half-digested sleeping pills, Pepto, stomach acid, ice cream, and booze; plus whatever they forced into his gullet to make him regurgitate. He almost yaks again and his anus puckers.

"Right on," Kev says empathetically.

"Hey Kev," Flip is looking at Kev's feet over the fence.

"Yeah, Mr. M?"

"You really should wear shoes with closed toes if you're going to mow. I had a co-worker once who cut off one of his toes mowing in sandals. After that he couldn't run anymore. He would lose his balance. You really should wear shoes. This guy used to be a marathoner. Ran every day for years. Real good shape. Had to give it up. Got real fat and miserable. I hate to be parental. But it's hardwired in my brain. Some things are like that. I'm just looking out for you."

Kev and Flip squint into one another's faces for a moment. Then Kev nods affirmatively. "Right the fuck on, Mr. M. Right the fuck on." They bump fists again. "Oh. Sorry about the language."

"I've heard it before. Don't worry," Flip says. "So I want to give you something to hang on to for me," Flip takes an object from his khaki shorts. "This belonged to my father. When I was little, my dad packed a few things and left us. I mean left the family forever. My mom says all he said before he left was 'raising a family is not for me.' I guess that was true. Anyway, after he left, this was one of the things still in his dresser drawer. He also left a coffee can full of wheat pennies and an all-metal Craftsman drill. Anyway, I've had it ever since. I don't know if it's worth much. But it means a lot to me. And I promise I'll come buy it from you. For whatever I owe you for mowing, plus a little extra for your trouble. You just keep track. Okay?" He passes an old wristwatch to Kev over the fence. It makes a gentle, mechanical, wrenching noise when he puts it in Kev's hand.

"Right on," Kev says, clearly moved. "That's cool. It looks expensive. It's kind of got a rattle. Is it busted-up inside?" He rocks the watch back and forth. It makes the wrenching sound every time he tips it.

"No," Flip takes the watch back. "That's an early self-winder. See?" He tips the watch. It makes the sound. "It's kinetic. When you swing your arm or move your wrist, counterweights inside spin around and wind the watch. When I was a kid I pretended it made me bionic." He hands the watch back.

"Right on," Kev says seriously. He doesn't talk for a while; just holds the watch and dips it up and down in the sun, the bulbous crystal face winking at him. Then he says, "So I'm like a pawn shop. I mow your yard for the watch. You come pay

me to get the watch back. Or not. Right? And I just keep it?"
Kev grins a little at Flip.

"You got it exactly."

"But, I mean, don't worry about it. I'll take care of it. Keep
track of it and everything. I know it must be sentimental and
everything. You know what I mean? I mean you can count on
me because I'm trustworthy."

"I do. I know what you mean Kev. And I trust you. If
there's one thing I am, it's a good judge of character. It's a personal point of pride." Flip leans his hip against the fence, feels
the whole thing tilt toward Kev. "The truth is though, Kev, the
watch is important to me; but not because I give a shit about my
dad. I did for a long time. But I just don't have the energy for it.
I haven't spoken to him at all in twelve years. He has never sent
me a birthday card. He didn't come to my high school graduation, college graduation, or my wedding. He has never shown
any interest in seeing Dylan. He only saw Sara because we ran
into him at a gas station."

They stand silently after that, cooking in the heat. Flip's
ankles feel like they're broiling. There's the sensation of something crawling down his calf. Maybe it's just perspiration, maybe
a wasp or an ant. It could definitely be a tick. He could easily
get Lyme disease. He slaps the back of his calf and scratches at
the spot. *You can never be too safe.* Behind Kev the air shimmers
above an asphalt driveway.

"Well," Flip says. "If you're cool with the arrangement, and
you can keep the grass mowed for my family, then I think we're
done here. I'll let you get back to it." Flip nods his head at the
lawn mower. He reaches over and shakes Kev's hand.

"Yeah, Mr. Mellis. It's cool. I'll keep the yard mowed."

"You going to get to it today?" Flip flicks his head, indicating
the lawn mower again.

"That's the plan. Soon as I change my shoes."

"Great." Flip turns in his bare feet, clumsily scoops up his shoes and starts to walk away. It's still hard to breathe. His whole body is damp, as if he's been standing in a sauna. He could literally wring his clothes out.

"I was thinking," Kev says, still looking the watch over.

"Yes?" Flip turns halfway around. It makes his lower back hurt.

"I was thinking that I'm a lucky guy to have a pretty good dad. And I was thinking so are your kids." He looks up, cocks his arm over his brow to shade his eyes, stares directly at Flip. "I know you didn't say. I mean, I noticed you didn't say about a divorce. And that's cool. But I wanted you to know, a lot of guys have lost their jobs. It doesn't mean you aren't good. You're still good. I think you're a good man." Flip walks back to the fence. Hearing someone, anyone, say anything the least bit kind threatens to overwhelm him. In that moment he wants to hug Kev, or adopt him.

"I didn't say anything specific, Kev. Because I don't know what's happening. I would tell you straight if I knew."

"Right on," Kev says soberly. "When do you think you will sort it out?"

"That's what I'm supposed to be doing right now. But instead of sitting in an air-conditioned kitchen with my wife, I'm standing in the heat, about to have a stroke, sweating my balls off and chatting with you. Know why? 'Cause that little woman scares the shit out of me." He laughs a humourless laugh. Then he says, "I'm scared to go in there. But here I go anyway." He turns, inhales a lungful of hot air and walks away.

To demonstrate his solidarity Kev says, "Right on Mr. M. Right the fuck on," just loud enough for Flip to hear.

Flip stands in the mudroom with his body in the shape of an X so as to better air himself out. The AC is luxurious. He needs water and feels he might faint if he doesn't hydrate. Though the pose is giving him a neckache, he just stands there, letting the cool air bathe his armpits and crotch. He feels the moisture drying on his face and forearms, tiny hairs all over his body pop up like daisies.

"Flip. What the hell are you doing back there?" Lynn asks loudly from the kitchen. "You know I'm waiting for you."

Flip lets his arms drop. "Sorry," he says. He walks into the kitchen, rubbing the back of his neck. The kitchen is spotless, with fresh flowers in a vase on the table, a cinnamon candle burning on the window over the sink, and something chocolatey baking in the oven. The evidence of his misadventure has been scrubbed and purged. There's a new tablecloth with matching cushions for the chairs. Lynn sits on the far side of the table, her laptop open, the cordless phone within arm's reach, and a sheaf of papers spread out around her. She taps the lidded end of a Bic pen against a scrap of paper scrawled with blue notes.

Sara sits at the head of the table, eating cereal. She glances at Flip as he enters the room, lets the spoon clatter in her bowl and shoves back from the table. There they are: the two most important women in his life. The nine months Lynn had spent pregnant with Sara had been some of the happiest of his life. He couldn't wait to meet his new baby daughter, to hold her in his arms.

"It's okay. You don't need to get up," he says.

"No no," Sara replies. She dumps the remaining cereal down the disposal but doesn't run it, rinses the bowl and deposits it and the spoon in the dishwasher. "You and mom have things to discuss." Then she leaves the kitchen without looking at him.

He watches her move down the hall and turn up the steps. She's angry with him. That short, defensive verbal reply was the first thing she'd said to him in a while. Though, to be fair, she did hug him when he got back from Dr. Hawkins'. When she was little, they used to be close. She spent most of her third year sitting on his foot and riding around the house, cackling like a fiend. But she had turned surly over the past year and downright hateful over the past month or so. Maybe there was something wrong, perhaps he was to blame or maybe that was just how teenage girls are. He just doesn't know.

Flip walks over and runs water down the disposal. He switches on the motor and lets it run for a dozen seconds. He turns it off and says, "She never runs the disposal." Then he sits in the chair Sara vacated.

"So," he says.

Lynn stops tapping her pen and looks at him. In the office someone turns on a vacuum cleaner. Flip doesn't know when or how Lynn has managed to get so much done. But the house looks transformed. She must not have slept a wink while he was in the hospital.

"It certainly seems like you have things in order here. The house looks great," he says. "It will be ready right on time. And one week until the open house, right? Plenty of time. Some-one will put in an offer right away I bet." He considers smiling his most encouraging smile and continuing his stream of com-pliments. But he reads the set of her jaw and knows it wouldn't be well received. So he keeps his mouth shut. Part of his brain notes his small exertion of self-control and feels a feeble pride for himself.

"Sort of," she says. "It will be as good as possible. And next week is a realtor open house. Not for the public."

Upstairs he can hear activity, several people walking around, furniture being dragged, doors being closed. "We got us a regular hub of activity here," he says looking up at the ceiling as if he can see through solid objects.

"Well, I had to call in the troops and spend money we don't have so we could get the house ready in time. It was the only way after . . ." she pauses for a few beats as if searching for the right phrase, ". . . everything that happened in the office and the kitchen. Have you packed yet?"

"No. No I haven't packed yet. I thought maybe we could talk about this a little more."

"So talk." She gathers her pages, straightens them in stacks. She closes her computer, places the phone on her pile of pages, sets her pen down and smooths the tablecloth. Finally she settles back with her arms folded. That's his signal to speak. He notices, not for the first time, how much Lynn has grown to resemble her mother, especially when she's sad. Though he knows enough not to share his observation.

"I would like you to please reconsider the idea of me moving out. I know you need the space. By 'space' I mean you need the time apart. I know . . ." He doesn't know what to say next.

She holds up her hand. "Let me stop you there, please," she says.

"Let me finish, please."

She refolds her arms and waits.

He gathers his thoughts and plunges ahead, "I have been a burden, not a help. We used to be a great team. We used to get shit done, pull together, we were on the same page. And I . . . I just quit. I gave up on us. I gave up on me. I know that now." He reaches a hand across the table towards her. She doesn't take his hand and says, "You're mussing the tablecloth."

"Sorry." He pulls his hand back and tries to fix the wrinkles. When he's satisfied he stops and looks to Lynn for approval. She frowns a little deeper and tugs on the cloth. He wants to weep. But she is clearly tired of Needy Flip. He must be Strong Flip.

"I hate seeing you so sad," he says. Her frown softens slightly. "It was horrible to see you in so much pain, like today at the doctor's office. But it was good to hold you. Even for a moment. I felt like I was doing something for you. And it felt right. I miss that." He watches her eyes. They are glazed and staring in the middle distance. "Did you feel it? When I was holding you? Did you feel that we were close? Like we used to be? Did you feel that I was caring for you?"

Her eyes meet his for a moment. "No," she says very sad. Then she looks away again.

"I see," he says. "Well, I felt it. At least, in that moment I remembered how it should be between us. How it used to be. How *I* used to be. And I want to get back to that." He picks up the cordless phone and turns it over and over in his hands. "Do you think it would be good to get back to that?"

"No," she says.

"I see." He puts the phone back down. He can feel the blood leave his face.

"I mean," she says very quietly. "I don't know if I want that. I don't know if it's possible. Honestly, if you asked me right now, I don't think it's possible. I love what we once had. I know that. But I don't think I love you anymore. Sometimes things get broken so bad they can't be fixed."

Flip picks the phone up again. He squeezes his hand around it until his knuckles crack. He squeezes harder, watches his hands choking the chunk of plastic. They're the only part of him that look nearly the same as a year ago. The same, except his fingers are puffy like sausages. He tries to tighten down on the phone, twist it like an ice tray, crack it. He wants to throw it against the wall. Watch it bust and send shrapnel around the kitchen. Or even hurl it right at Lynn. *Why is she hurting me like this? Can't she see I'm trying? I'm doing my best. She's supposed to love me for better and for worse. She isn't always a picnic, but I still love her.*

He looks up at her, wonders if she can feel his pain and rage through proximity and osmosis, sees her staring at something not there and the rage ebbs as if washed out to sea. He sets the phone down carefully, and breathes deeply to calm himself. There's a faint rattling when he exhales. *Most likely late onset asthma.*

"Okay," he says as calmly as possible. "Well. Let's get down to business then. I was going to ask if you would consider waiting for me to move out until I meet with Dr. Hawkins this afternoon." He turns and checks the time on the microwave. "But I guess if there's no point then there is just no fucking point. I will go and pack now. If that's okay with you."

He stands and shoves the chair back too far. It tips and smacks against the kitchen floor. "Thought maybe it would save us some money if we could work it out. But if your mind is made up, there's no point in having a conversation." He turns to pick up the chair, trips over the wooden legs, and stumbles into the refrigerator. A decorative cookie jar, a smiling pig in overalls, tumbles off the top of the appliance. Flip grabs for it and knocks it onto the counter where it busts against a glass canister of all-purpose flour. A cloud of white dust and jagged ceramics fill the corner of the kitchen.

Lynn is on her feet. "Leave it," she says. "I'll take care of it. You don't even have shoes on. You should go pack."

Flip looks down at his hairy toes. She's right. He could easily cut his foot and that would hurt; pain is not his favourite thing, he doesn't do pain well, never has. So he capitulates, taking cautious steps out of the kitchen, his shoes dangling from one hand.

"That was your grandmother's cookie jar," he says before he leaves. "Right?"

"It doesn't matter. I'll take care of it. Go pack."

Flip goes to pack.

In the office, two Mexican men are working. One is on a ladder in the middle of the room putting new wooden blades on the ceiling fan. The ceiling has been patched and painted where the fan gouged a hole in the plaster. The carpet has been replaced and much of the clutter has been packed in boxes. The walls are painted, the trim cleaned up, and a giant desk pad calendar with a tasteful floral border is convincingly covering the paint stain on the desktop.

He keeps moving down the hall toward the front of the house. Through the front storm door he watches a rent-a-truck back into the driveway. Lynn's mother, Coleen, and Dylan are giving contradictory hand signals to the driver to indicate in which direction he should veer.

He passes two men on his way up the stairs. One carries a bucket of dirty water, the other a carton marked *Master B-room*. He says, "Hey," and bobs his chin at them. They brush against his gut as he presses himself into the corner.

On the upstairs landing, he pauses. Sara's door is open, the bright afternoon sun reflecting off the walls. He hears her moving around and raps his knuckles against her doorframe.

"Knock knock knock," he says.

"What?"

"It's me," he says.

"I know. What do you want?"

He peeks his head into her room. The walls are yellow with a Holly Hobbie border around the top. The curtains, pillows and bedspread are white and lacy. But the yellow walls are covered in posters of pop/punk bands, hard-core rappers and gender-bending club acts. The room has half-filled cardboard boxes scattered across the floor. Sara is kneeling in the mouth of her closet, her back to him, shoving stuff from one corner into another.

"I wanted to talk to you for a minute. That's all. Can I come in?" he asks.

"I guess you're already in," she says without turning to see.

He watches her leaning deeper into her closet, rummaging, pitching things around and cussing.

"Are you upset?" he asks lamely.

"No shit I'm upset," she replies. "What gave it away?"

He assumes her question was rhetorical in nature, and he has found it best not to respond directly when she gets like this, so he says, "Looks like I'm moving out today. I wanted to say I'm sorry that you had to deal with this. I'm sorry I let you down. I'm sorry about all the upheaval. And most of all, I want you to know I love you. I have always loved . . ."

"Shut the hell up, Dad," she stands and gets in his face as best she can. "You don't have any idea what's going on around here. You don't love me. You know how I know? 'Cause if you loved me, if you loved your family, you wouldn't make us move. You wouldn't lose your job. You wouldn't be so fucking pathetic and self-centred." She shoves him on the shoulders. Then she hugs him, pressing her cheek against his chest and trying to hook her fingers together at the small of his back. He touches her newly-purple hair. He wants to lift her to his chest and hold her, but he knows she hates that.

One weekend when she was little, Sara fell off some monkey bars at the neighbourhood park. It knocked the air out of her.

Flip ran over, scooped her up in his arms and looked down into her four-year-old face. He told her it would be all right, to be calm. He told her he would take care of her, not to worry. He told her to just breathe, just relax. And she had looked up with wet eyes and nodded because she believed him. Moments later, as if by magic, she was ready to play some more.

He wants to tell her the same things now, to see her nod back at him, trusting what he says. But, "I will do my best for you," is all he can muster. "Please know that I will miss you and I will do my best for you. I really will." She breaks away and turns back to the closet, she snorts loudly and wipes her face on a T-shirt from her floor. Then she kneels down and goes back to work. He pauses before leaving her room.

"Sara, what do you mean by 'you don't have any idea what's going on around here'?"

Sara stops moving. "I was just upset," she says. He knows she's hiding something. He thinks it must be something Lynn has said, something about him.

"Maybe you could tell me what you meant? Maybe it would be all right to tell me, it would help you to tell someone," he says. "Has your mom said something to you?"

"Dad. You are a fucking idiot. You and mom have had your whole lives to grow up and get your shit straight. This is my time to be a wreck and make stupid mistakes. You're supposed to be stable and reliable and dependable and supportive so I can survive growing up. You're supposed to be wise and consistent. Helpful. You know, mature. Parents. But instead you two are in as bad a shape as I am." She is back on her feet and shaking a stuffed rabbit at him.

"I need help sometimes. I need advice. I need a car that fucking runs. But, instead I'm packing my closet and getting ready to move. Probably out of the school district. Classes have only been in a couple of weeks, and I don't know if I will be here or in some other school; with my luck, somewhere else. With no friends, no car and no boyfriend. No parents worth a shit and a needy little brother that I will be expected to babysit, but not get paid for. You are fucking my whole life up." She throws the bunny down hard for emphasis. She's trembling and red. The house is quiet. Flip imagines the house cleaners listening and looking through the floor at the bottoms of their feet.

He clears his throat and says, "Has your boyfriend been pressuring you? Did you two finally break-up? He was no good for you anyway."

She screeches in primal frustration and screams, "Go to hell, Dad!" She shoves him back out of her room and slams the door in his face, his shoes are knocked out of his hand. It might have been more dramatic if the doors weren't so light and cheap. Instead of crashing and rattling the whole house like a good solid wood door, this one just makes a kind of whoosh and thump. *They really don't make things like they used to.*

He considers knocking again. He wonders if her tummy is feeling better. But he decides now's not the time. He bends to catch his shoes on hooked fingers before leaving Sara to her own feelings.

At the far end of the hall, in the master bedroom, much of the debris he accumulated over the past several months has been removed. The bed has been stripped and on the bare mattress lies an open suitcase and his empty toiletry bag. He pitches his shoes at the suitcase.

After momentarily considering having a breakdown, he disregards it and goes to work in the bathroom, finding the familiar rhythm of packing surprisingly comforting. When he had a job, he travelled almost every month. He moves through his process ritualistically, and tries not to think too much. *Thinking never helped anything.*

He fills his toiletry bag, and is relieved not to need to refill the tiny bottles and shove them in the clear quart zipper bag he uses for liquids when he flies. As he finishes, he's winded and wheezing so he closes the toilet and sits on the lid. Over the past year he's lost his job, his body, his dignity, his wife, his kids, his sanity, his self, and now his home. *If I had just managed to kill myself, I'd feel so much happier now.*

He doesn't want to move, but also knows if he doesn't stand now he may never get moving. He stands up, knees crackling, stretches his back and rocks his neck. From the medicine cabinet he grabs a prescription bottle of pills with the label torn off. He shoves the bottle in his shorts pocket.

In front of his closet he stares at his power suits, dress ties, leather shoes, and pressed white shirts. None of the suits fit. The waists are too small, the legs too narrow. His chest is too massive, he can't move his arms if he shoves into the jackets. The belts are far too short to meet around his circumference. *Lynn didn't bother laying out my garment bag.*

Insulted, he finds the garment bag crushed in the back of the closet. He chooses his largest, best suit with its matching ensemble, including shoes, cufflinks and a watch. While he's at it, he grabs all of his watches and stows them. Then he fills the suitcase with socks, boxers and running suits. He piles in T-shirts, giant khaki shorts he has never worn, three more new shirts, and a pair of running shoes which have never been used for running. He looks for his robe, but it's missing. Lastly, he un-wedges the snapshots from the edges of his dresser mirror and puts them in his pocket with his driver's licence and debit card.

He sits on the end of the bed and works at putting on socks and his Asics. It's hard to keep his foot cocked onto his opposite knee and he can't quite bend far enough. Finally, panting and half-proud of his accomplishment, he tightens one lace into a perfect bow.

He hoists the garment bag, suitcase and workbag then lugs them downstairs. As his feet hit the first floor, Dylan blasts by him, nearly causing him to trip. "Where's the fire?" he asks.

"I gotta poop," Dylan says as he races down the hall. Flip watches him disappear into the bathroom and fail to close the door. He feels a malicious presence behind him and recognizes the sensation: his mother-in-law. He turns awkwardly in the tight space and sees her standing there. She's waiting for him to move.

"I'm all packed," he says. He lifts his suitcase a bit as evidence.

"I see," Coleen replies coldly.

He thinks she might say more, waits a few moments.

"I'll just go around," she says, and turns her back on him and heads out the front door.

"Bitch," he says quietly. The suitcase beats against the wall, leaving a mark. He tries to rub it off, but it doesn't help. He sets his stuff in the hall next to the bathroom.

Dylan is sitting sideways on the toilet, his cheeks red with effort, knees wide apart, his junk pointing right at the doorway.

"Dyl," Flip says. "Please remember to close the door when you poop. Pooping is private."

"Okay Dad," Dylan grunts. "Sorry. I was in a hurry."

"It's okay Dyl. Just try and remember."

"Ooooh Kaaaay," Dylan says as he finishes his business. Then he reaches for the toilet paper, makes a dubious effort to clean himself, and starts to pull up his underwear and shorts in one twisted mass.

"Wait," Flip says as he moves into the bathroom, kicking the door closed behind him. "You need to do a good job wiping." He hands Dylan more toilet paper. Dylan takes a few moments to be more thorough, jerks his pants back on and shoves past Flip on the way out the door.

"Wait," Flip says again. "You need to flush the toilet. Then wash your hands."

"Oh, right," Dylan says. "I forgot." He flushes the toilet and makes for the door.

"Wait. What about your hands?"

"It's okay, Dad. I didn't get any poop on them." Dylan holds up his hands to prove it.

"That is not really the point Dyl. You always have to wash your hands. You know that. You can't see germs and pooping is germy business." Flip turns the water on in the sink. There is pink paint dried in the bowl. He digs at it a bit with his fingernail and most of it comes right off. "Wash," he says.

Dylan sticks his hand under the tap and then turns it off. He drips water on the floor as he turns to go.

"Wash with soap," Flip says. Dylan washes with soap. When he reaches for the tap again Flip says, "Let your hands drip over the sink buddy. That way you don't get the floor wet." Dylan lets his hands drip over the sink. Flip gives him a hand towel. Dylan dries his hands, balls the hand towel up tight and leaves it on the side of the sink.

"Wait," Flip says. He considers explaining and demonstrating how to hang up a hand towel, but he's already tired of listening to himself. Instead he says, "Dyl, I'm going to be leaving for a while. I will miss you. You are a good little guy."

"Mom already told me," Dylan says.

"What exactly did she tell you?"

"I don't know," Dyl says. There's no point in probing further.

Flip notices Dylan is wearing a T-shirt with the Lakeside Amusement Park octopus mascot on it. "Nice shirt Dylan," he says. "I wish I had gone with you guys. Was it fun?"

Dylan looks confused. Flip taps the picture on Dylan's shirt. Dylan stretches his shirt out and looks down at it. He processes the image and text. Then he says, "Oh. Yeah. Yeah it was real fun. I drove the bumpy cars and Grandma bought me a big bag of cotton candy." *Figures.*

His mother-in-law was always trying to buy his children's affection. He couldn't decide if he was more offended by her actions or her success. He says, "Good to hear. Well, I will see you in a few days, I guess."

"Okay," Dylan replies as he heads out the door. Flip hears the storm door bang open and slam shut. He dries the sink and drops the hand towel on the bathroom tile, shoves it around with his foot to mop up the water. Then he folds and re-hangs the towel over the rail. He picks up his bags and walks to the kitchen.

Lynn and his mother-in-law are whispering by the kitchen sink. His mother-in-law stops talking when he enters, turns and goes out through the mudroom. A faint cloud of flour dust still hangs in the air, but the evidence of his accident with the cookie jar has been disposed of.

"I'm packed," he says to Lynn.

"I see." She fills a glass of ice with tap water and drinks it down. Then she upends the ice in the sink, and leaves the glass standing on its head.

"So, maybe you should have a seat," she says. He sits at the table like before. She takes her place and looks at her notes. "I found a place you can stay. We could only afford to pay for two weeks. It's an efficiency apartment. It's part of the Lakeside Motor Court." She doesn't look at him.

"I thought that place was closed down," he says.

"You remember where it is?" she asks.

"Sure I remember," he says.

When they were in high school he'd rented a room and taken her there. It wasn't the first time they'd sex, but it was the first time they had sex in a bed without fear of interruption. They had parked on the side away from the road and stayed for two hours, about the same amount of time as the movie they were supposed to be seeing.

He wonders if she remembers and if this choice is a coded message, some kind of subtle encouragement or sentimental nod. He wants to ask her about it, to let her know he remembers too. But he doesn't say anything.

"Well, they have converted half the rooms into suites with kitchenettes," she explains.

"Sounds perfect," he says. He honestly doesn't care.

"Well, I've had to empty most of the bank account. So be careful with the bankcard. There is basically no money left."

"Got it."

"You better get going, I guess."

"Okay," he says. He stands and picks up his bags.

She stands too. She pats him on the shoulder.

"That's it then," he says. "Do you have the number? To my room?"

"You are in Suite 3. Just pick up your key at the desk."

"I will," he says. "Thanks for making the arrangements. But, I meant the phone number. In case you or the kids want to get in touch with me."

She looks at him as if he is a chronically slow-witted cousin who should know that she is perfectly capable of finding the number to his room if she needs it, and he has a cellphone that the family knows by heart.

"Oh," he adds, hoping to say something she deems useful. "When the unemployment comes, let me know. I will come sign it. You can put it in the bank."

"It came already," she says. "I signed it for you and will deposit it later today." The news deflates him. Signing over his unemployment was the only useful contribution he knew how to make to his family.

"I guess this is bye for now," he says. The emotions hit him and his voice breaks as he says it. Tears roll down his round cheeks and catch at the corners of his mouth. He can taste the salt of them when he tries smiling apologetically. *So much for Strong Flip.*

He takes a shuddering breath. "I'm sorry about all this. Call me if you want to know how it goes with Dr. Hawkins. Or if you need to drop the kids by for a while, you know, while the house is showing, or something." He swipes his car keys from the counter and slips them in his pocket as he stomps toward the mudroom.

"Flip. I don't love you," Lynn says before he can leave.

"Clearly," he spits back.

"But, the truth is," she continues. "I don't love me, or the kids or life right now. I'm too stressed. Too angry. But mostly too exhausted to feel anything. I get up. I do what has to be done. Then I pass out. Maybe if you ask me in a few months I will have a more definitive answer." She is not crying. Not at all.

"That's fair," he says. But he doesn't mean it.

ACCUSED OF PERVERSION

Flip arrives ten minutes late for his re-scheduled appointment with Dr. Hawkins. He pulls into the lot and drags himself out of the car. His eyes burn from crying, his nose is raw from wiping and his head aches. He fishes in his pocket and finds the bottle of pills. He thinks they might be high dose Tylenol, but maybe they're muscle relaxants. He's not sure.

He knows it's not good to take medication on an empty stomach so he leans against the front fender of the car, unpacks a bag of fast food, and shoves two burgers and a large order of fries into his face as quick as he can. He's proud that he planned ahead. The line at the drive-thru slowed him up a bit. *But I needed some sustenance.* He drips mustard on his shirt. The stain is mostly lost in the busy pattern. He sucks down a coffee-flavoured shake along with several pills, then heads up the creaking stairs to see Dr. Scruffy Face.

When Flip reaches the landing, Dr. Hawkins is backing out of his office and locking up for the night.

"I'm not that late am I?" Flip says, looking at his wrist as if it had a watch on it.

"Oh," says Dr. Hawkins. "There you are, Mr. Mellis. I thought you were skipping out. I was already anticipating the need to contact the authorities." He chuckles and scruffs his miracle never-grow beard. "And yes. You are late. There are not degrees of late when it comes to an appointment with me. Either you are present when the appointment is scheduled to begin or you are late. You were not there at the appointed time, and so, officially late." The doctor slings a bike messenger bag across his torso. Flip can't believe he's hearing this shit. "I can't believe I'm hearing this shit," he says.

"Well Mr. Mellis, believe it." Dr. Hawkins brushes by Flip and bounds down the stairs. Flip follows less jauntily.

"Come on Dick. I mean Doc," Flip pants. His knees ache. His brow and cheeks are producing a damp, oily sheen. "This has been one of the worst days of my life. You can't just bail out on me."

Dr. Hawkins slows in the parking lot. "Well I admit that, relatively speaking, you are not *that* late, Mr. Mellis. But you did technically miss your appointment." He uses his handsome face like a prop, stroking his beard thoughtfully, pursing his full lips and tapping his chin. "I haven't eaten yet. You hungry?"

Although Flip has just eaten, he is never not hungry and always ready to eat. So he says, "Famished."

"I'm headed across the street to grab a beer and a burger. I guess it would be fine to meet in an informal setting. If you want to talk, I'm willing to listen. You are still my patient. I am still your doctor and all the normal rules apply. But, I'm going to make a note that you missed your appointment. Fair?"

"Fair," Flip replies and starts to gauge the traffic pattern so he can cross the small boulevard.

"Oh," Dr. Hawkins says, stopping at the kerb, "And Mr. Mellis, don't call me a Dick again. I might take it personally," then he darts across the street.

Shooter's is a sprawling cave of a sports bar: low ceilings, brown wood panelling, brown wooden chairs, tables, stools, booths and bar. It's packed with a mix of drunken idiots playing in the local darts league, college kids eating spicy buffalo wings and guzzling pitchers of beer, and neighbourhood guys lined up along the bar watching sports and nibbling salty bar snacks.

The pair take a booth as far away from the commotion as possible and order food and beers from the safety of a back corner. Dr. Hawkins flirts with the waitress and orders a Royal Grolsch. Flip has to work to get the girl's attention before she leaves and orders a Guinness. Flip and the doctor make small talk and play with their beer coasters. The waitress, Kelli, comes over with a tray full of drinks on her shoulder. She shifts the tray onto the table and produces more coasters from her apron pocket. She tosses them on the table and then, inexplicably, sets the damp glasses directly on the tabletop.

"There you are," she says. She cocks her hip, turns in the doctor's direction and smiles at him. She pushes some hair out of her face. "Can I get you anything else?" she asks. Flip takes note: she does not say, "Can I get you two anything else." She just says, "you" and she says it in a way that excludes Flip altogether. It also seems to exclude the kind of "anything" that might be on the menu.

"I'm just fine for now," Dr. Hawkins says.

"Well, y'all let me know," Kelli drawls with a slight southern twang that hadn't been there previously. Then she hoists the tray of remaining drinks and wiggles away.

"I'm fine for now too," Flip calls. He makes an exasperated little breath, shakes his head and looks to the doctor for some understanding. The doctor gives him a blank look and slurps the foam off his beer.

Flip's burgers and fries from the drive-through were pretty salty and the shake just didn't help his thirst at all. So he's happy to take a long pull on his dark beer. It's nice and cold.

"Ahhh. Good stuff," he says. He wipes his mouth with the back of his hand.

"Yes," says the doctor.

"If I knew I was going to knock back a few beers during our session I would have tried harder to make it on time," Flip jokes.

"Yes. About that Mr. Mellis. I feel suddenly uncomfortable about this arrangement. I fear this is horribly inappropriate. I have the impression from Lynn that you are self-medicating in order to avoid facing your situation. Maybe we should just call this off."

"No. No. It's okay. I don't think a beer is self-medicating. It's just a civil way for two adult men to end a hard day. That's all. It's fine. I'll take it easy. Promise. And you have to admit I had a hard day."

"And we *are* already here," Dr. Hawkins capitulates.

"Plus, I know I have a busy week ahead. I'm sure your week is busy. You are a busy guy. You can't just keep re-scheduling me. Right? Like you said we are already here. Might as well. Besides, beer might be the key to some good progress. Right?"

"Perhaps," the doctor says, doubtfully. Flip realizes he's not helping his case, so he shuts his yap.

They sit quietly looking at the table and sipping beer. The doctor is waiting for Flip to start the conversation, some kind of Psych 101 power play. Flip wants to wait, force the doctor to speak first, just to be spiteful, so he stubbornly keeps mum; but so does the doctor. To fill the silence, Flip watches the action at the dartboards.

There are about six teams of four players each congregated around two electronic dart machines. It looks like they're having a tournament.

A couple of the teams wear matching shirts. One set of orange bowling-style shirts reads *Lucky Strike* in black across the back. Another team's black pocket tees read *The F.U.s* with the subtitle *This means you Lucky Strike*. Flip decides he's rooting for the F.U.s.

Kelli comes back around and sets plates of food down. She leaves ketchup and a second round of beer. She tosses more coasters, then sets a plate of nachos with cheese and jalapenos on the table.

"Oh," Flip says. "I don't think these are ours."

She looks at Dr. Hawkins when she says, "Those are on me." That's all she says. Then she tucks the tray under her arm and leaves again.

Dr. Hawkins looks smug as he helps himself to a nacho with a jalapeno stuck to it.

"Stuff like that never happens to me," Flip says.

"Well," the doctor replies. "You have to be open to the things the world presents to you. You might be surprised how many opportunities are right there in front of you." He licks the salt and grease from his fingers and goes to work on his burger.

"I call bullshit," Flip says, and doesn't feel compelled to explain further. The doctor lets the comment go. Flip drinks down his second Guinness, belches and pops his neck. He's feeling pretty full but he decides there's always room for a bacon and 'shroom quarter pounder and a heaping pile of fresh cut cheese fries, so he eats.

After a while he sees Kelli looking over and lifts his empty glass. She doesn't seem to notice. He waves the glass in the air to gain her attention and the damp pint glass squirts from his greasy grip, plummets through the air and shatters across the floor. Kelli gives him a tired look.

"Now it's a party," Flip says.

Dr. Hawkins looks unimpressed and goes back to his burger. Some kid comes around with a broom and mop and hunkers down next to the booth to start picking up chunks of glass.

"Sorry about that," Flip says. "It just slipped."

"Happens all the time," the kid says. Flip considers asking him to hurry it up because his bladder is about to burst but he just keeps quiet. Instead, he covertly undoes the button of his shorts to relieve the pressure.

The doctor pushes his plate back with most of his fries and a portion of his burger untouched. The kid finishes cleaning and leaves. Kelli comes over before Flip can slide out of the booth. She tosses coasters like Frisbees and sets down another round, again avoiding the multitude of coasters.

"Can I get you anything else?"

"I'm sorry," says the doctor. "I think I've had enough." He pats his flat belly. "I need to watch my girlish figure."

"If I'm any judge," Kelli says, "Your figure could take another round with no problem."

"You think?" he asks in mock surprise.

Ass. Flip starts drinking his beer with sloppy swigs as fast as he can.

"Yes I do," she replies.

Flip finishes off his pint and slides to the edge of the seat, clears his throat loudly, but no one takes note. He bumps Kelli a bit with his hip to get her to move; again, she ignores him.

"It's on me," she adds.

"If you insist," the doctor says.

"I sure 'nuff do," she replies, all Southern again.

"Will you excuse me?" Flip asks. She ignores him some more, so he shoves out of the booth forcing Kelli aside. He leaves the doctor and the waitress to continue adoring one anothers coyness. On the way to the bathroom Flip hears a triumphant roar from the dart league. The F.U.s look dejected. Flip sees a big bald bastard give him a disapproving glance from behind the bar as he stumbles by.

"What?" he asks. The guy wipes at the bar with a towel and keeps staring.

Flip's gaze returns to the dart league. The Lucky Strikes are hugging and gloating. Flip stumbles a bit and nearly knocks some dude off his bar stool. The guy says, "Fat drunken douche." But Flip has to piss so bad he keeps moving.

He unzips his shorts as he turns down the hall to the men's room. A busty blonde co-ed in a baby doll tee comes out of the women's room and looks down at the front of Flip's shorts. She sees his zipper is down and his shorts are open. She gives him a disgusted look and backs into the women's room.

Flip wants to explain but the women's room door closes as he starts to speak. He pushes the men's room door open and barely makes it to the urinal in time. He pisses a long time. The bathroom smells like an ashtray, among other things, and smoke hangs in the air. He sneezes, coughs and pisses on his foot a little.

He's washing his hands when he notices that the bald bartender and the kid who cleaned up the glass are standing just inside the bathroom door, glaring at him.

"I should have known it was you. You think it's cool to waggle your old dick at young girls," the bartender says. He doesn't ask it, he states it. Flip tries making a raspberry sound with his lips but it comes out wet and he gets slobber on his chin. His lips feel numb. He shakes his hands over the sink, just as he showed Dyl earlier in the day. He doesn't see any paper towels so he dries his hands on the front of his shirt and turns to face his accuser.

"I just had to pee very bad," he says. He waves at the bartender for emphasis with a gesture that looks like swatting flies. Also, he realizes the word "very" has come out mushy like the word "fairy." The bartender sports a tight white T-shirt and a set of silver hoop earrings. Flip can't stop himself from blurting, "You have a very shiny head like Mr. Clean. Do you wax it?" He punches the V in "very" this time, just to be clear.

"Yeah, yeah, yeah," says the bartender. "I heard all the shit before, tough guy."

"I'm not a tough guy," Flip says. He tries to sound very laid back, like Kev. "Right on," he says. Then he makes to bump fists with Mr. Clean, but Mr. Clean leaves him hanging. *Not cool.*

Flip takes a pace back, his ass presses against the sink, and tries to explain himself. "It's all just a silly accident. I had to pee. Then I broke a glass. I couldn't get out of the booth until this one was done with his cleaning." He points at the kid. His movements are too loose. "Then the waitress whose name is Kelli was in my way too." He points in the direction he thinks Kelli should be standing. "Then I finally got here and that girl saw me." He waves his finger in a "eureka" gesture. "My dick wasn't even out of my pants," he says triumphantly. "I was trying to undid my zipper is all I was trying to do. But I was just trying to pee, not show some girl my pecker. I just needed to go pee and so I was trying to undo my pants." Flip lurches forward and hugs the bartender for support. The bartender shrugs him off and pushes him back on his feet. While Flip focuses on standing steady, the boy and the bartender have a conference.

Flip's legs are wavy and he thinks hard about that. He pats his shorts and digs out the bottle of pills. He holds it up. "Right the fuck on," he says in his best Kev impersonation. "This is why things are so wuzzely in my body. Man. I took some of my pills for my back. And I forgot about not drinking is what I did. You know what I mean?"

The two watch him. The busboy is doing the whispering right now.

"Don't listen to him," says Flip. "What does he know? Nothin' is what he knows." Someone tries to push into the bathroom.

"Occupied," says the bartender, wedging his foot against the door. Then to Flip he says, "Toby was backing your story about the glass and Kelli." He says it pretty sarcastic. "You really think I shouldn't listen to him?"

"No no," says Flip. "Listen to Toby. Toby is good people. He knows what he's saying and is a fine citizen. Proceed. I always did like Toby. Toby was my mother's name."

He tries to put his hands in his pockets, but can only find one. He keeps slipping his hand across his left hip trying to locate the missing pocket. He looks down to see and turns in a circle like a dog after his own tail. The bartender and Toby stop talking and watch him. He gives up on the pocket. Now he really feels dizzy. *Don't throw-up don't throw-up don't throw-up.*

"I was about to call the cops," says the bartender. "But I think you're telling the truth. You're totally messed-up. And a world class asshole. But, you're here with Dr. Dan and *he* is cool as shit. So if you go back to the table, and don't make any more trouble, we'll let this go. But I'm cutting you off. No more to drink. I'm telling Kelli you're cut off. And you best take a taxi home. Got it?"

"Right on," Flip says, a little defeated at being chastised by a walking, talking ad campaign for cleaning products.

Someone slaps on the bathroom door. The bartender and Toby leave. Two guys in Lucky Strike shirts come in, laughing it up big time.

Flip puts his hand on the door to leave, pauses and clears his throat to get the Lucky Strikers' attention. "You are not so wonderful at darts," Flip says very seriously. Then he walks as cautiously as he can back to the table.

Dr. Hawkins has his phone out and is scrolling through his email. "Where did you go for so long?" he asks. Flip shoves the table too much as he tries to get his ass over the wooden arm of the pew-like bench. The doctor grabs his fresh Grolsch before it can spill.

"Very shmooth," Flip says. Then he feels his numb lips with his fat tongue. He touches his mouth with his fingertips. "Very smooth," he articulates slowly. "That move getting in the booth was very smooth. Not." Then he explains, "I was just in the bathroom. That is all. There was a line."

"Okay," says Dr. Hawkins. He shakes his fancy watch on his wrist and checks the time. "We need to wrap this up. I have a date." Flip knows the date is Kelli. The doctor is clearly proud of himself. *Asshole.*

"Yes indeed," says Flip. "The metaphorical ball is in your metaphorical court."

"Well I'm sorry Lynn was so upset at our meeting earlier. I had hoped to have more time to speak with you. To be honest, you have some legitimate issues. You've had a hard year. And now with Lynn asking you for a separation . . . Well, anyone would feel a bit overwhelmed. You just need to exercise good coping strategies." The doctor sips a bit more beer. "Because right now I don't think you have the skills to deal with this amount of stress. That's why you're depressed. Your lack of coping skills is exacerbating the situation."

"I think you're right, Doctor Dan," Flip says. He's flooded with emotion, his eyes begin to water and his face feels warm. *This guy really knows his shit.* He has the urge to lean across the table and hug the doctor. But he thinks better of it.

"Earlier today, in my office, I handled that whole situation badly. It went sideways on me," Dr. Hawkins says. Then he drinks more beer, leans his forearms heavily on the tabletop and picks up one of the paper coasters and gives it a flick toward the back corner opposite the booth. *The Doc is pretty blitzed.*

Dr. Hawkins drinks more beer. "I like you, Mr. Mellis. You are honest. There's no bullshit with you."

"Thanks, Doc," he says a little weepily, and blows his nose loudly on a cloth napkin.

"But, as your doctor, I have to know what the hell you were thinking when you put your head in a noose, and I have to know you won't do it again. If you can explain it to me, and make me believe you aren't going to try it again, then I can feel I did my job. Understand?"

Flip looks hard at Dr. Hawkins. His head feels heavy, his chin wants to tip toward his chest and his mouth wants to hang open. But he keeps his head up, his eyes forward and he sees in the doctor a man who wants it straight.

So he says, "I felt so pathetic I wanted to die." He's pleased to see his words aren't slurred. Though he does have to concentrate and speak slowly.

"Good," says the doctor. "Go on."

Flip goes on, "I felt pathetic because my body is out of control, because I can't help my family, I lost my job, don't make a living, can't support my kids; and that is the only thing

I was ever any good for. Now what the fuck am I good for? I'm good for nothing."

"Good, Mr. Mellis." The doctor's eyes are wide. He drinks more beer and a little dribbles down his whiskers. He wipes his chin with a napkin. "Please, go on."

"All I know is, a man should provide for his family and be there. Just be there. Always. And now I'm not there and I am not providing." He leans back hard and the bench barks loudly.

"You feel very strongly about your role as a husband and father," Dr. Hawkins says.

"Yes. Of course."

"What was your own father's role in your life, growing up?" Dr. Hawkins asks.

"There was no role. He left when I was six," Flip says quietly. He doesn't look at the doctor.

"Nailed it," the doctor says triumphantly. "Let's continue with that, Mr. Mellis. Tell me about why your father left."

"No. Let's not," says Flip. "One thing has nothing to do with the other. I'm done talking about that old bastard. He doesn't have anything to do with this. End of story. And I mean it. I'm done." Flip crosses his arms petulantly.

"Okay, Mr. Mellis," the doctor says.

Kelli sashays over with a pint of beer. She whips out a single coaster and tosses it among the others. She places the beer in front of Dr. Hawkins while glaring disapprovingly at Flip.

"I'm good," Flip says. "I have to drive in a while. I think I'll stop now. Just the check."

Kelli lays a padded, faux-leather folder on the table. It has the remnants of a gold-embossed logo, but it's too worn to read. Flip opens it and notices all his beer and food printed on the bill. None of Dr. Hawkins' charges are listed. He slaps it closed and nudges it onto the doctor's half of the table.

Kelli leans in, like she's going to share a secret with the doctor, "The dart league is leaving, so I'm not needed any more," she says in a breathy whisper. She touches his arm and lets her nails trail along his sleeve as she goes.

The doctor checks his watch and drinks more beer. He looks over toward the bar where Kelli is sharing tips with the bald bartender. The bartender nods real cool to Dr. Hawkins, who nods cool back, then turns to Flip.

"Mr. Mellis, I think your feelings for your father could be at the heart of this," the doctor says. Flip starts to protest. The doctor continues quickly. "But we can get into that later. Right now I need to know you're not going to hurt yourself again."

"I won't. Not tonight."

"I need a little more assurance than that."

"I am a man of my word Doc. I am. If I say I won't do something, you can believe it."

"Let me ask you something, Mr. Mellis. Earlier today, at my office, you said you thought things were really turning around. I wonder if you were just saying that to appease your wife and me? Or did you mean it?"

"I meant it," Flip lies. He doesn't even remember saying it, but Flip senses the doctor is about to use his own words against him and he doesn't want that. He intends to outflank him.

"So what specifically did you mean? What *things* are turning around and in what ways are they turning?"

Flip stares at the doctor's nearly empty pint glass, at the striations coating the inside of the clear walls, like sea foam. He doesn't speak for a long time. Dr. Hawkins picks up the glass and puts away the last swallow of beer.

Flip says, "I got nothing. I don't know what I was saying. I forget what I meant." He looks up at the doctor's serious face.

"You realize that killing yourself is not the answer. Don't you, Mr. Mellis? Although you don't see a way forward, you know death is no answer."

"How do you feel about assisted suicide, Doc? Euthanasia? Right? How do you feel about it?" Flip waits and watches the doctor process the question. Flip feels he's gained the upper hand. Dr. Hawkins is anxious to get out of here and hook up with Kelli, plus he's getting drunk and probably needs to piss. So Flip just waits. After a long moment the doctor clears his throat.

"I think there are times when someone is in so much pain and has no chance of recovery and is likely to die slowly and painfully. And on those rare occasions, perhaps, there is a moral argument to be made that euthanasia is more humane than allowing the person to continue to suffer." The doctor looks defeated. He props his scruffy cheek against one fist like a stubborn kid. Flip wonders how old he is. He thinks he might have been in high school or even in college by the time the doctor was born. *I wish Kelli hadn't cleared the nachos.*

"Well, I think some lives are so emotionally painful for the people living them, that that person has a logical reason to end his own life," Flip says.

"That's not the answer I need to hear," the doctor says.

"I'm not going to take it back. It makes all kinds of sense to me. But, I give you my word I won't try to kill myself for a few days, not until we meet again," Flip swears solemnly.

"One week from today. I have you written down for a week from today. Morning appointment, same as today. Okay? You promise me you won't try to end your life for one week. Then we will talk again. We will go from there."

"Deal," says Flip. They shake a good firm shake on it. "But I promise you, if you hear me out, I'll be able to convince you my life is so pathetic I would be better off dead. It's hard for you to understand, Doc. You're young, handsome, with a good job and lucky to boot. But some people, their lives are different from that."

"I know that, Mr. Mellis. But I doubt your life is so dire we can't find a way to make it better. I understand it feels that way to you. And I can help you, Mr. Mellis. It's what I'm trained for. And, I might add, I'm pretty successful at it. I have your word? No suicide for a week?"

"I already told you, Doc. And we shook on it didn't we? My word is my bond."

"And Mr. Mellis," the doctor says. "My life has its challenges too. Trust me."

Flip doesn't believe him, but he nods anyway, as if Dyl just told Flip, "I have stress."

"Mr. Mellis," the doctor says. "I've got to go." He glances back to Kelli at the bar. She's rolling silverware in black cloth napkins and stacking them into a pyramid. "But I have a couple more quick points to make."

Flip was starting to unpack himself from the booth. He stops mid-motion and settles heavily. He suddenly wants to sleep.

"Mr. Mellis. What things would you like to turn around? No: one thing. Name one thing you would like to turn around." The doctor holds up one finger in a "number one" gesture.

"I need a job."

"A job is the result of a process. Do you have your resumé out? You could start with that. Is your resumé ready to go out?"

"Yes. It's out. It's out everywhere. It is re-written, re-organized. It's a magnificent document. I should have a job by now. But I don't."

"Okay. Let's find something you can do, starting in the morning. What is a way you can exercise some control over your life, starting tomorrow?"

"Get a job."

"No. Something small. Start small: a simple, achievable goal. How about stop drinking. I think you should take a break. I don't think you're an alcoholic, but you're using alcohol as a way of avoiding your problems. Does that sound right to you?"

"You're the Doc."

"Great. No more drinking. Don't drink until I see you next week. Deal?"

Flip shrugs his shoulders noncommittally and scoots out of the booth. As he brushes his arms over the table several paper coasters fall to the floor and into the seat he has vacated. For no reason he gathers a few from the bench and sticks them in his pocket. The ones on the floor are a long way down, so he lets them lie. He stands over the doctor and tries not to sway.

"But still. What is one of the things you would like to turn around, that you could start on right now?" Dr. Hawkins persists.

"I don't know Doc. I have to piss again though. Thanks for your help. I'll give it some thought," he says.

"Give it some thought."

"I will. I'll do that." He raps his knuckles on the table in farewell and marches off in as straight a line as he can manage.

"Mr. Mellis," the doctor says. He's standing and handing something to Flip. "This is my card," he says. "It has all my numbers. Call me if you need to, if you need someone to talk to."

"Thanks," Flip says, looking at the card, unable to make his eyes focus.

"Two more things," the doctor says. "One: you need to reach out to someone and ask for help. Promise you will call someone. Call a friend and talk. Someone who will be supportive; someone who doesn't know you tried to kill yourself. You have to admit what you did to someone who will care; someone besides Lynn."

Flip nods tightly.

"Two: you have a place to go tonight, right? Someplace safe?"

"Yes," Flip says. "It's all sorted out. My bags are in the car."

"Call me tomorrow on the office number and leave contact information. That way I can check in. Deal?"

"Deal," Flip says.

"And you are fine to drive?"

"I am as sober as a judge," he replies without waiting for approval. He walks out the door, crosses the street and stomps into the dark lot where his car is parked. He wishes he had thought to order flowers from the shop when it was still open. He could have written a nice note to Lynn and sent a bouquet. He just wasn't thinking. He finds a spot at the side of the building and pees.

He can't find his keys. Then he sees them dangling in the ignition, starts looking around for something to shatter the window with, finds a chunk of asphalt the size of a softball and throws it at his driver's side window. It bounces off. *That's a quality window.* He tugs the door handle. It's unlocked. He gets in and drives two blocks before remembering his headlights. He snaps them on and aims his car toward his new home.

PETTY CRIME COMMITTED

Flip rolls the windows down and lets the cold night air blast his hot, fat face. The beer and pills are still working on him and he has to focus hard to keep the car in the road. Every couple of minutes he sticks his head out the window and lets the wind inflate his cheeks and dry his teeth and eyes. He turns up the radio and blasts some tunes. *All I need is to wreck this car or get arrested for DUI.*

The car's headlights illuminate dark looming shapes that surge forward and recede at the edges of the road. He considers veering into a telephone pole or a tree. Maybe with enough speed he could just be done with it. *That would be a relief.* But he swore an oath to Doctor-Dan-the-head-shrinkin'-man. And if Flip Mellis is nothing else, he's still a man of his word. As a matter of fact, he is one of the most dependable people he knows of. At McCorkle-Smithe, when there was a problem that needed solving, he was the go-to guy. No drama, just results. That was his modus operandi. Maybe it was his downfall too. Not enough butt-kissing, not enough scrambling for credit. Too willing to stick his neck out and give his real opinion instead of hanging back. He feels his eyes getting heavy, so he smacks himself in the face a few times. It hurts, a lot. He decides not to do that again.

He's been driving too long. He looks at the clock, it reads 8:30 but he can't remember what time he left Shooters. Also, he knows the clock is off by an hour; but he doesn't know if it's fast or slow. His car makes an obnoxious dinging sound and the cab fills with a rhythmic orange flashing; the little gas-pump-shaped idiot light is blinking on his instrument cluster.

"Shit," he says.

Since Flip isn't sure where he is or exactly how long he's been driving, he determines it would be prudent to get some gas, ask for directions, and hopefully make it to the motel in time to call the kids and tell them good night. As his car tops the next hill he sees a building glowing in the night. When he gets close, he turns into the Quickie Mart.

He cruises past the pumps, because he can see they're pad-locked, and drives up to the building. There's a dark Crown Victoria parked crossways in the middle two of four parking spaces. Flip parks to the right of the sedan, rolls up his window and starts to slide out. He can't get his door open all the way because of the stupid parking job of the other car. His paunch presses hard against his car door as he sucks in his gut. One of his shirt buttons pops off, just as he makes it out.

"Fucking hell," he says. This was the best of the Hawaiian-style shirts Lynn bought him. He sticks his finger through the gap and prods his exposed belly. This button incident strikes him as a profound loss. He slams his car door and it crunches into the seatbelt buckle that failed to retract. The door rattles and stands ajar. He reaches in, tosses the buckle across the seat and grabs the door with both hands. Instead of slamming it shut, he opens it hard against the body of the Ford, repeatedly and with emotion.

"It. Is. Rude. To. Park. Like. A. Selfish. Asshole," he says, punctuating each word with another whack against the side of the sedan.

After the fact, he thinks to look up and see if anyone is watching. A greasy teen clerk is on a stool behind the counter of the convenience store, but doesn't stop browsing through his magazine. There doesn't seem to be anyone else in the store. Flip closes his car door gently, with a muffled click.

He runs his hand across the mark he left on the Crown Victoria; his fingers probe the line of a sizable dent and some minor paint damage. He can see chips of pale primer in the light cast through the store's plate glass windows. His finger nails dig and scrub the indentation a bit more to scour off any silver paint that might have transferred from the edge of his door.

He moves toward the Quickie Mart, winded and wiping at his moist brow. A blast of cool air hits him as he passes through the big glass doors. He feels his pupils squeeze shut from the sudden brightness; it gives him a headache.

The kid at the counter lifts his face and his lank hair parts like an unwashed curtain to reveal a pale, pointy weasel-face. He looks Flip up and down.

"Your car break down?" he asks. He has a high nasal voice.

"No," Flip says. "Just dropped by for some gas."

"Pumps are closed," the kid says.

"Can you open 'em up? Sell me some gas? I'm almost on empty?" Flip crosses to the counter.

"Why are you all sweaty man? You sure your car isn't broke down? 'Cause my uncle has a tow truck and he can be here in like fifteen or twenty minutes."

"It's still hot out," Flip says. "I just need some gas, not a tow."

"Gottcha," the kid says. "Sorry. I can't help you out. Pumps are locked until the morning." The kid tucks his dirty blond hair behind his ears. "Maybe Officer Steve has some gas on him. They usually carry a can to help people who run out and stuff." He flicks his nose toward the washroom in the back.

Flip looks toward the washroom. Then he looks out the plate glass window to the dark Crown Victoria. Through the glare and the reflected store interior, he can make out the county plates and the giant chrome spotlight mounted next to the driver's side door. He looks back toward the washroom and thinks he hears a hand blower snap on. Flip is suddenly sober. He turns back around, the kid is eyeballing him closely. Behind the kid is a shelf of booze, cigarettes and skin mags.

"I'll take a pint bottle of the Captain Morgan rum," Flip says. *What Doctor Dan doesn't know won't hurt him.* "And can you tell me how to get to the Lakeside Motor Court?" He brings out his debit card. Snapshots of his family tumble and litter the floor around his feet. He snatches them up and can't avoid noticing the one from two summers ago: Sara is tan, her hair is short, slick with water from the hose and light brown from the sun. Her long legs are covered in bits of grass and she's belly down on the Slip and Slide, body arced slightly up like a seal, with Dylan sitting on her back preparing to ride her down the tiny hill in the back yard. Flip stacks the snapshot with the other photos and stuffs it away.

"Sure," the kid is saying. "You want the pint, right?"

"Yes," Flip agrees.

"You want the traditional, the Tattoo, or the Lime Bite?" His back is to Flip and he indicates each of the choices as he speaks. A door opens behind Flip and he catches movement in a convex security mirror off to his right, the reflection of a uniformed man at the back of the store.

"Traditional," he says fast and over-loud.

"Sure thing." The kid pulls down the bottle, drops it in a paper bag and slides it across the counter. "Anything else?"

"No. That's it."

The kid tells him what he owes and takes Flip's card to swipe it. Flip watches the cop come down the candy aisle, check to make sure his fly is up and try to decide which variety of sweets to purchase. Flip grabs his card and rum and turns to leave.

"Oh. Hold on man," says the kid. "I gotta card you. It's the law," he adds.

The cop's distorted reflection looks toward the front and waves a yellow bag of peanut M&Ms.

"For Christ's sake," Flip says. "Are you kidding me?" he whispers. But he's pulling his driver's licence from his pocket, careful not to dislodge the photos again.

The kid takes the card, tips it toward the light and holds it close to his needle nose. He looks at the picture, looks at Flip's face, looks back at the card, then back at Flip.

"I guess this is you," he says. "Looks like you've put on some poundage."

"Thanks for noticing," Flip says.

He grabs up his stuff and makes for the door.

"Hey Steve," the kid calls to the cop. "This guy wants directions to the Motor Court."

Flip freezes with one hand on the door. The cop saunters up, drops his candy on the counter and hooks his thumbs behind the broad buckle of his utility belt. He looks like a High School Athlete who hasn't seen the inside of a gym in twenty years.

"No no," Flip says. "I got it. I remember now. I just got turned around. But I remember now. I got it. Thanks. I'm fine." He gives a farewell wave toward the officer and keeps moving.

"You sure?" says the officer.

"Mmmhmm. Yes. I'm sure. I got it." Flip turns halfway to Officer Steve as he speaks.

"Because I'm about to drive right past it, if you want to follow me. It's no problem."

"No no. No need. I know right where I'm going. Thanks though. Have a good night."

Flip's throat is starting to close up. His heart is swelling in his chest, he can't catch his breath and his face feels flush. His oily perspiration smells like Guinness. He could be having a series of small heart attacks. He's heard of it happening. He thinks perhaps pain is radiating up his arm and into the base of his skull. He absently juggles his hooch so he can scratch at his wrist and side.

"Okay," says Officer Steve. "If you're sure. But it's no problem."

"Oh, I'm sure. I got it. Have a good evening," Flip says, turning to the exit.

"Steve," the clerk chirps up. "Do you carry a can of gas in your cruiser? 'Cause this guy is almost out of gas and Brad locks the pumps at night."

"Yeah. I can spare a little gas to get you where you're going," says Steve. "Just sit tight while I pay for my bad habit." He pats the bag of M&Ms where they lay on the counter and smiles affably. The clerk rings him up.

Flip has his hands on the door pull. He cracks open the door and peers out toward the Crown Victoria. Moths and gnats beat against the glass door and warm, humid air seeps in. He has the urge to run for it, start his car and peel out. But he just rests his damp forehead against the glass, closes his eyes and tries to breathe. Each breath fills his head with the sweet, clean smell of processed sugar, which makes Flip hungry.

He hears the clerk shove the cash register drawer closed, hears Steve and the clerk exchange goodbyes, and the sound of the officer's shoes click across the worn linoleum floor, then deaden as they cross onto the rug Flip is standing on.

"All set," says Officer Steve from right behind Flip. He claps his hand on Flip's shoulder. Flip starts. His eyes snap open.

"Let's head out," the cop says. Flip pushes out into the night and holds the door for the cop.

"You know," says the officer, walking ahead. "If you just go out on this road, it turns right into Lakeside Drive."

"Yes," Flip lies. "I remember."

"So when you hit the T-junction, hang a right."

"Yep. Got it. Thanks. I got it."

The cop doesn't reply and that makes Flip nervous, so he explains, "I don't usually make this drive at night. I'm a family man. Kids and a wife at home. School age kids at home. So, usually I'm at home at this time of night. Not out. Wrapped in the bosom of my family. Home and hearth. That's me. I guess you could call me a homebody these days. A real family man. Kind of boring, I know."

"So you're from around here?"

"Yes. That's right. From right around the way."

"If you have a family around here, why are you looking for the Lakeside?" He asks it lightly. But when he steps off the kerb next to his cruiser, he stops, waiting for Flip's answer. Flip senses this is a tipping point; he has to make this lie count.

"My wife took the kids to her Mom's house for a few days. A last hoorah before school starts in earnest. And I spent the day re-glazing our bathtubs. The whole house reeks. Epoxy fumes are the worst. And I can't bathe for forty-eight hours because the epoxy has to set. So I decided to get a room out at the

Lakeside." He forces a smile he hopes appears casual instead of anguished. "The tubs used to be hideous; aqua in one bathroom and pink in another. Very dated. Very ugly."

"I know how it is," says Officer Steve. He walks to the back of the Crown Victoria and pops the trunk. From where Flip stands he can see the radio and laptop in the front seat, and he can see a shotgun in the trunk. He notices Officer Steve has a safety-yellow Taser in a holster at the back of his belt.

He wonders if the officer will lose his temper when he sees the side of his cruiser, and if that could lead to violence. *What does it feels like to get shot with a Taser?* He worries he will piss his pants. *Would that make the electric current more painful? Or will the abrupt shock give me a heart attack? What if it kills me, then revives me in the same moment? Stupid. It will just kill me.*

That would be a solution, though. He would be dead. Lynn and the kids would get some life insurance money, and maybe they could even sue the county. But Flip knows that's just a pipe dream.

"Okay," says Officer Steve. "Point me at your gas tank."

Flip points to the far side of his car. He follows the officer, who is now carrying a big red metal gas can with a long rubber spout screwed on its top. They move right past Flip's driver's side, past the damage he's done to the cruiser.

Officer Steve hinges open the little door and uncaps the gas tank. He hoists the heavy can easily and tips some gas in. "I run a full service establishment," says Steve, with another smile. He seems genuinely happy to help. Flip tries to imagine what that would feel like, to be content with one's life, to like one's job, to have a calling. But he can't quite get there.

Flip casually tries to glance around by pretending he is stretching his neck. The dent in the cruiser isn't visible from where Flip stands.

Steve finishes with the gas, screws in the cap and closes the little door. He turns to shake Flip's hand. "I didn't catch your name," he says.

"I am named Doctor Dan," he replies very stiff. "I am Dr. Daniel Hawkins and I am a psychologist. But you can call me Doc."

"Okay. I'm Officer Hartman," he says. Then he amends, "Steven Hartman. Nice to meet you."

"You too. I better get going," Flip says, and takes the keys out of his shorts. He heads to his driver's side, opens the door slowly, the edge of his door meets the crease in the cruiser's fender perfectly.

"You sure you're okay. You seem a little off, Doc." The officer picks up his can of gas and walks it back to his trunk.

"Fumes," Flip says. "Fumes from the re-glazing. Has me a little light-headed." He is so proud of himself. He's really an accomplished liar. Also, he is going to get away with jacking up a cop's ride. He feels cool, Steve McQueen-cool.

The officer sets the gas can in his trunk. Flip slides into his seat and slips the key into the ignition. He makes sure to buckle in. He snaps on his lights, adjusts his mirrors and starts his engine. The radio blasts out a roaring top forty, guitar-driven neo-punk anthem and he fumbles the knobs until it stops. He puts the car in reverse, checks his mirrors and backs out slowly. His headlights glide across the scar on the police cruiser. Officer Steve slams his trunk closed, steps over and knuckle wraps on Flip's window. Flip punches his brakes too hard.

When Flip looks over, he can't see Steve's head, just his body from the chest to his belt full of weapons and cuffs. Steve makes a generic cranking motion that means Flip needs to roll down his window. Flip dry heaves. Two times. Then he toggles the lever that lowers the window. Officer Steve puts one hand on Flip's roof and leans over to face level.

"Sorry," he says. "I parked kinda crazy there. I really had to get to the bathroom."

"Oh," says Flip. "I didn't even notice." His voice shakes a bit. His armpits are damp. He tightens his grip on the steering wheel.

Steve stands and pats the roof of Flip's car before stepping back. "You have a good night now," he says.

"Will do," says Flip. And he concentrates on not speeding.

A HOME AWAY FROM HOME

Flip's silver Passat rolls into the lot of the Lakeside Motor Court and comes to rest near the office. He snaps off the engine; the silence is shocking. He can hear the blood surging in his head. He looks in his rearview mirror for Officer Steve, but all he sees is the weathered sign for the motel, lit up by only two of the five visible lamps. He opens the paper bag, unscrews the Captain Morgan and takes a long pull. It burns sharp and sudden in his sinuses. He hacks and loses half a mouthful of rum all over the dash and down the front of his shirt. He screws the cap back on, pitches the booze in the passenger's seat, and shuffles into the motel office.

Inside, exposed fluorescent tubes strobe cool light across Flip's cheekbones and shoulders. It may not be the source of his sudden need for Dramamine, but it isn't helping either. On the counter sits an ancient, metal oscillating fan, its wire grill caked in fuzzy grey dust. He puts his face in front of it, lets the air rough his hair and dry the booze from his shirt; he thinks it might help to clear his head. He breathes a deep, calming breath: inhales slowly for a count of four, holds it for a count of four and finally exhales slowly for a count of six. It's a trick he used to use before giving a presentation at work, when he had a job.

On the exhale he sneezes loudly, three times, with such force he has to check to be sure he didn't rip a nostril. He moves away from the fan. There's a silver plated tap bell next to a houseplant that desperately needs to be watered. He smacks the bell in a shave-and-a-haircut rhythm. The bell doesn't ring so much as thump. Peeking beneath the bell, he sees someone has twisted a Band-Aid around the clapper.

A dusty curtain behind the counter splits and a grandma lady in a housedress comes out.

"You'll be needing a room then," she says. Her voice is deep and rich like a blues singer.

"Yes, ma'am," he says. "I mean no ma'am. I am Flip Mellis. I have an efficiency reserved. My wife called for me." Under the gaze of the woman's milky eyes, he feels a little self-conscious. He can smell himself, a sharp blend of body odour, fried food and rum, with a little second-hand smoke thrown in. He wonders if the old lady's sense of smell has improved to compensate for her cataracts or if her senses have simply diminished with age, along with her posture.

The woman stares as if she didn't hear what he said. He draws a breath to repeat himself more loudly. She jumps a bit as if her brain has popped into gear and says, "Oh yes. Mr. Mellis. Mmmhmm. You are in room three, over on the other side of the motel there, paid in advance fourteen nights."

She slips him a brass-coloured key on a big brown diamond-shaped key fob. It has a worn gold 3 on it. "Vanessa got it set for you today, so it should be all ready to go." She turns a registry book toward him and taps at it with a finger like a pale, gnarled tuber. He jots his name in a loose scrawl.

"Thanks," he says.

"Now, the price of the room includes laundry service for towels and bedding only. Towels and bedding only. Vanessa will come by and let herself in to change things out a couple times a week. Just use the hamper in the closet for the towels. Towels only. Okay? Also, there is a clock radio for an alarm. I know the phone has instructions for a wake up call, but that hasn't worked for years. Just use the clock. If the red light on the phone is blinking, that means you have a message. Have a good night, Mr. Mellis," the grandma lady says real flat, like she's asleep on her feet, or like she finds Flip incredibly uninteresting. Or both.

"Good night," he says. "Sorry I'm here so late."

"You get here when you get here. Makes no difference to me," she says. She turns and waves a hand before passing back through the curtain. He doesn't know if she was waving bye or dismissing him. Either way, he takes his key and goes.

He drives the car around the back of the motel without turning on the headlights and parks in a spot hidden from the street; just as he'd done decades earlier with Lynn sitting as close as the bucket seats of his ramshackle '66 Mustang had allowed.

He shucks the pint from its bag, wedges the flat rum bottle in his front shirt pocket and hauls his belongings out of the trunk. He steps up on to the cement walk that runs in front of the units. Each one exhibits an identical rattling window air conditioner poking out the front. To the left, Number Two has the curtains open, lights on, music playing, and two wire patio chairs and a matching metal table arranged in front, complete with a small tiki-style candle and a tall cocktail glass with ice slowly melting. To the right, Number Four is unadorned, with the curtains drawn. A periodic blue flicker around the edges of the window tells him that someone is watching TV in the dark.

Flip manoeuvres the key into the lock and nudges the door open with his foot. He flaps the switch by the door with his elbow, which turns on the lamp beside the bed. Number Three is freezing cold, but smells pretty good. Better than he does. It's so tidy and fresh he instantly wants to shower. He pitches his bags on the bed, retrieves his key from the door, locks it behind him, walks out of his shoes, shorts, socks and underwear and stands in the bathroom scratching his naked ass. He's developed an aversion to being completely nude, so he leaves on his tent-size, crazy-pattern shirt.

The bathroom is basic, but clean, with new taps and shower curtain. He gets the water going, jerks the plunger to start the shower, and closes the curtain. The curtain's hooks screech against the rod and make the skin on the back of his neck go bumpy.

He takes the rum out of his shirt pocket and sets it on the sink next to a complimentary bottle of blue mouthwash. He stands and watches as steam billows slowly through the tiny room to fog the mirror. *Just as well*. Flip hates his own reflection.

The place is too quiet. He moves back into the main room, glances briefly at the kitchenette, and punches the power on the TV remote. A loud, gregarious hipster is stuffing food in his face and talking with his mouth full, his jowls smeared with a creamy, pale sauce. The guy seems pleased with himself and Flip is disgusted. But it also makes him hungry. He scrolls through the channels and ends up back where he started. He turns the set off, walks over to the control panel on the air conditioner and twists the dial to low.

He sits his bare butt on the bedcover and opens the drawer under the phone. He finds a typed page that lists all the restaurants that deliver to the motel. He picks one he knows and orders.

"Okay Mr. Mellis. That will be an order of beef lo-mein and two orders of crab Rangoon," the Korean kid on the other end says. Flip has not told him his name, the kid just recognizes his voice. "That should be there in twenty minutes." The kid hangs up. Flip calls back.

"Hello. Thank you for calling Good China. Please hold."

"Wait, I . . ." Flip is on hold. There's no Muzak, only dead air. Flip spends a couple of minutes fiddling the tuner of the analog flip-clock on the bedside table. Each time he thinks he's found a station it slips into crackling static. When he gets tired of that, he switches the phone to his other ear and claws absently at his balls while staring at the floor.

"This is Good China. Thank you for waiting. May I take your order?"

"This is Mr. Mellis. I just placed a delivery order," he begins to explain.

"Yes Mr. Mellis. Did you forget something? You want an order of eggroll. No problem."

"No. No. I just need to change the delivery location. I'm not at my house right now." Saying it out loud makes Flip feel horrible.

"Very good. Shoot. Give me an address where you would like food delivered," the kid says.

Flip thinks *shoot* is a good idea. If he'd owned a handgun, or a shotgun even, then he'd be dead right now. A shotgun would be cumbersome and messy, but still, it seems preferable to this.

"I'm at the Lakeside Motor Court. Number Three. Okay?"

"Yes. Got it. Very good."

"Also, go ahead and add those eggrolls."

"Okay. Probably thirty minutes on that Mr. Mellis." The kid hangs up again.

Flip looks over at the clock: it reads seven fifty-six. The minute flap ratchets over with a crisp snap: Seven fifty-seven. He wonders if it's accurate. *It feels later than that.* He considers checking one of the watches he packed, but that seems like a lot of work. Assuming the clock is right, Dyl will be getting ready for bed. He thinks about calling his family. If he calls and Lynn is putting Dyl to bed, his mother-in-law might answer the phone.

No good. He takes note that the phone isn't flashing. *No one could be bothered to call me.* Instead of calling home, he walks to the bathroom.

On the way he spots his snapshots on the floor next to his shorts, rifles through them and lingers over one from the day they spent at the nature trail last Thanksgiving. It's four smiling faces poking out of scarves and caps. Sara's cheeks are red, Dyl is wearing that silly fuzzy coat with bear ears sewn into the hood, and Lynn looks genuinely content. Flip sees his own goofy face as he holds the camera out at arm's length to snap the picture. He looks young, healthy and happy; as if he was doing just what he was made for.

He lays the photos on the counter and unbuttons his floral shirt. He takes the rum with him into the shower. The water is alarmingly hot, almost enough to scald him. He tips his face up and lets the sharp, forceful drops scour his cheeks, scalp and his throat. He turns his back to the water to shield his booze, unscrews the bottle and swigs a bit. He fumbles the cap; it drops through the rising cloud and rolls down next to the drain. He covers the bottle's mouth with his left hand and douses his face in the water again. The cut on his hand tingles when it passes over the mouth of the bottle.

A year ago he ran in a half-marathon. He was sucking air when he finished, but he finished. Now, he feels too taxed to remain standing. He lowers himself into the tub and lets the shower beat against his fat knees and enormous belly. He hasn't looked at his middle from this angle in months. He jabs at it with two fingers; it's like a Hefty bag full of oatmeal. He drinks more rum.

Flip had been fired from McCorkle-Smithe on his birthday. His whole life he'd had the dubious distinction of having a birthday that was very close to Christmas; his birthday was often the day vacation ended, so people usually forgot to acknowledge his birth altogether.

As a boy, he had mused about it, imagining if no one knew he was born, he might simply evaporate like fog in a breeze, a harmless spectre or a half-recalled memory. That way of thinking had been natural as a child. But he had grown out of it.

When Hank called him up to the office, he'd thought it might be a ruse to allow his co-workers to finally throw him one of those pathetic office parties he was so jealous of. During the elevator ride he visualized how his co-workers would yell, "SURPRISE!" and clap while singing some variation of the birthday song. He would act surprised and shake everyone's hands or hug them, depending on a combination of personal associations and rank within the corporate hierarchy. They might make him wear a bright, pointy hat with an elastic chin string, or blindfold him and spin him and make him whack a Spongebob piñata with a dangerously long handle unscrewed from the push broom in the utility closet. There would be stale cake, or stale cupcakes decorated with black icing and white letters that read "Over the Hill." He might be asked to give a speech. Or, if he was really popular, and maybe he was, he wasn't a good judge of such things, they would buy an ice cream cake and have a karaoke machine. He wished the machine would have a Leo Sayer selection; that would be a crowd pleaser. "Loving You" by Minnie Riperton would be hilarious and he could totally nail it. That would make up for all the years of being overlooked.

As he neared the top floor he'd checked his reflection in the polished interior of the elevator's door. He looked youngish and fit-ish. He could see in himself someone who was well liked by his co-workers, loved by his wife and adored by his children. He was in a comfortable groove in his life's journey. Christmas vacation had been such a nice break. He had re-connected with his family and was ready to get back to work. He was certain all this was observable in his easy stance, his casual confidence, and his ready, boyish smile. He wore dark slacks, freshly shined shoes, and a crisp white dress shirt and blue tie. The elevator stopped, the doors split open and he strode out.

As he moved down the long hall toward the executive administrator's desk he decided to roll up his sleeves. Since he'd taken off his jacket and forgotten to grab it on the way out of his office, he might as well embrace this informal look. Perhaps he'd give the impression of having been hard at work. He considered loosening his tie, undoing the top button, but dismissed it.

Flip presses his feet flat against the end of the tub. His toenails are too long. Maybe he should trim them. He knows he has clippers in his travel bag, but he's not willing to commit to the effort at the moment. The water doesn't feel as hot now. He wonders if it's running out, thinks perhaps he should hurry and get clean. His Chinese food will arrive before too long. He should have brought a watch to the bathroom, or his cellphone. The rum's cap has plugged the drain and the water level is beginning to rise. He should get a move on, but he can't work up the energy to move. He drinks more rum and pushes the shower curtain aside a bit, stretches his arm and dangles the bottle over the floor.

On that day, Hank's assistant had shown him right in. She was even friendly about it, which was unusual because everyone agreed she was a bitch on wheels. He should have known something was up. Before entering the room Flip paused and took a calming breath, then gave a cursory rap on the door and pushed into the enormous corner office.

"Flip," Hank said, not without enthusiasm.

"Hank. Good to see you. How was the holiday?"

"It was trying," Hank gestured to one of the leather chairs in front of his desk. "Alexis invited her newest boyfriend to come open gifts with us. I don't know how easy it is to find a broke, inarticulate, tattooed and pierced starving artist at Yale. But she has a real gift for it. This is the third one in a row. A painter. Which somehow I find even less acceptable than the sculptor or the print maker." He was leaning back in his high backed chair. Not really talking to Flip so much as performing. But that was his way. He was a little man with thin blond hair which he wore slick to his skull. It was unclear if he was balding or if he simply had hair that was nearly the same colour as his scalp.

"I'm sorry to hear it," Flip said.

"Why do they call it print *making* anyway? They all make art. They don't call painters *painting makers* or sculptors *sculpture makers*. Shouldn't they be called printers? I think they should. I find the whole field confusing. The whole event was a misery."

"Daughters have a way of doing that to a father. Trust me. I know," Flip said knowingly. He judged it was always a smart move to intimate that he shared common ground with Hank.

"I just wish she would come home with someone who understands the rules of football. Or who plays golf. Or even someone who can actually do something useful with their hands, like fix a car, network a computer, do the books. An accountant would thrill me to no end. I would write a check for the wedding immediately. Someone who does something honest. Artists are mostly charlatans in my estimation. But what do I know?"

Flip didn't know what to say. So he said "You're right." Which always seemed like a safe bet when talking to Hank. There was a long silence. Hank looked at his manicured fingers, which he had folded on his desktop. Flip looked at Hank's fingers too. After a long pause, Hank unfolded his hands.

Flip's back is starting to hurt and the water is definitely cooling down. He rolls his torso forward into a splay-kneed sitting position. He looks like an un-pigmented cave frog, if a cave frog could sit on his ass, grow fur and nurture a gigantic Buddha-belly. He lets his chin fall forward to his chest. The folds of meat around his throat might cause him to suffocate if he presses hard enough, but when he tries it, he finds he can breathe about as well as usual. Though his sinuses are a bit stuffy.

He uses his right forearm to cradle his gut like a giant baby. He can't believe the size of the thing. He takes his left forearm and presses down on the misshapen mass of his mid-section from the top, trapping it in a scissor move and squeezing it like a massive zit. It's truly disgusting. *This is what it feels like to be old.*

He pulls his legs up and pushes with ample force to un-wedge his ass cheeks from the walls of the porcelain tub. Tepid water sloshes around his ankles. He works himself into a standing position, taking his time with straightening his lower back. He finishes his rum, leans out and tosses the bottle toward the little plastic trashcan next to the toilet. It doesn't land in the can, but it doesn't break when it hits the vinyl floor either. *Could have been worse.* The water spraying from the low-flow shower head is turning cold now. He grabs a tiny bar of soap and goes to work on his pits.

"You want a drink, Flip?" Hank had shoved back his rolling chair, crossed to an antique barrister's bookcase and raised its frosted glass front.

Flip had looked at his newest watch. It read eleven ten. He had never seen the bookcase opened before. He had always assumed it had books in it, not crystal decanters filled with amber liquids. Hank had never offered him a drink. Maybe he was stalling, perhaps his surprise birthday party was supposed to start at eleven thirty. Flip wasn't much of a drinker, but what the hell. If the boss offers you a drink, you should probably accept it.

"Sure," he said. "Whatever you're having."

Hank turned his back to Flip. There were tiny silver tongs used and the sound of ice clinking on glass. He saw Hank reach for a decanter, and then a silver pitcher. A long silver swizzle appeared. More clinking. Then Hank turned with a glass in each hand.

"How long have you worked for me, Flip?" he asked. Flip stood and took the tumbler.

"Going on eighteen years now," he said. He touched his glass against Hank's.

"Here's mud in your eye," Hank said. Then he pitched back an entire tumbler of scotch and water. *So much for stalling.* Maybe the party was at eleven fifteen. Flip sipped at his drink. It was pretty smooth, but too strong for him.

"Nice," he said.

"Flip," Hank said very matter-of-fact. This is it, Flip thought. A rush of people busting in Hank's office and yelling 'Surprise!' at the top of their lungs.

"I'm so sorry. We're going to have to let you go. We are doing some belt-tightening around here. And you just have too much experience for us to keep you."

Flip looked down at Hank's flesh-coloured hair. Hank wouldn't look back; his head looked absurdly tiny between his suit jacket's enormous shoulder pads. Flip drank his scotch and tried to absorb what was happening, what Hank had said to him. He walked over, poured himself another scotch with no water, and slammed it. He couldn't make sense of the internal logic of Hank's statement. It didn't make any kind of sense. He poured a third tumbler of scotch, this one all the way to the rim, and stood sipping it until it was gone.

"It's my birthday today," he explained to Hank, thinking perhaps this was all an elaborate birthday prank. And if not, somehow it would be too unseemly to fire a man on his birthday.

Hank joined him and put his hand on Flip's shoulder. "Happy Birthday," he said. "Now go home and spend it with your family." Hank guided Flip to the door. "I will have security escort you from the building." It was the last thing Hank had said before closing his door behind Flip.

Flip lathers his whole body; the bar of soap makes wet squelching noises as he scrubs. The water is getting very cold now. He uses fruity-smelling shampoo from a tiny bottle and scours his scalp. The water is so cold now he's getting a headache. He makes another turn in the deepening water; his ass catches on the shower curtain and pulls it open. He shuts off the water and steps out. He leans back in and fishes the rum cap from the drain.

There's a knock on the door to Number Three.

"One second," Flip calls. He briskly dries himself. His dirty clothes drag against his moist body when he pulls them back on. More knocking.

"One second," he calls again. He buttons his shirt, feeling mildly frustrated by the missing button, and walks to the door. He pulls the door open. "Come on in," he says without looking. "Let me get my money."

"Thank you." A trim little man with white hair enters the room and stands just inside the door watching Flip scrounge through his empty pockets.

"Um . . . I think . . . there might be a misunderstanding," the older gentleman says.

Flip looks at him. He's not carrying a bag of Chinese food. He's carrying a bottle of red wine. He holds it out to Flip. Flip thinks the man looks like a butler. He has always wanted a butler.

"Welcome to the Lakeside. I'm Dean." He indicates himself by patting his own chest. "I live next door." He gestures with his thumb to the wall on his left.

"The candle," Flip says.

"That's me," Dean says, with a warm smile and an affirmative nod. "The tiki candle."

"Oh. I'm Flip," Flip says. "I was expecting someone else." He takes the wine and appraises the label as if he knows something about wine. "Nice," he says. "Thoughtful. Thank you." He shakes Dean's hand. "I don't have anything to offer you."

"I wouldn't expect you to. I just like to make people feel welcome. Are you gay or divorced?" he says as he takes in the room.

"What?" Flip responds, confused.

"Gay," Dean indicates himself again, "or divorced?" He gestures to the right wall of Number Three. "You see, the men who move into the Lakeside are either gay or divorced. I am gay," again patting his chest. "I moved in over two years ago. Larry," indicates the right wall, "lives next door. He is divorced. He's been there for a few weeks. He's looking for a townhouse. He is depressed about the divorce and doesn't know what to do with himself. I keep hoping he will snap out of it a bit. But, so far, no such luck. But I shall not relent." Dean walks back toward the door. "Well?" he asks. "Which is it?" He puts his hands on his hips and waits. The silence is easy, not confrontational or challenging.

Flip processes the question.

"Neither." Flip says. "I am neither gay nor divorced."

"Wow. I would have guessed divorced," Dean says. He sounds genuinely surprised. "But I thought gay might be a possibility. Either way, I like for people to feel welcome. I, just so you know, am not offended by your sexual preferences. I am very open-minded that way. If you want some company, I'll be out on the 'veranda' smoking and avoiding mosquitoes." He makes very precise air quotes as he says *veranda*. "I bet you have a story to tell. I would love to hear it. We could break open that wine." He points at the bottle, then he turns and closes the door behind him. Almost immediately Flip hears a car drive up, sees headlights against his closed curtains.

Flip sets the wine on the counter in the kitchenette, finds his debit card, a couple of paper coasters and a wad of crumpled cash on the floor near the bathroom. Another knock at the door, more insistent than Dean had been. He opens it and pays the deliveryman. It's a new guy. He's about Flip's age, balding and dressed in black running shorts with a red Good China T-shirt. Behind him the delivery car sits, the door standing open, head-lights on and engine idling.

"Here's your change," the man says, passing over a dollar and thirty-five cents.

"You can keep it," Flip says.

"All for me?" The man replies with mild mockery. He doesn't wait for a response or a larger tip. He just leaves.

"See you around. I'll catch you up next time," Flip calls.

"That's fine," the man says. He slips into the red vinyl seat of the Good China Chevy Citation and crunches gravel on his way out of the lot.

Flip hefts the bag of Chinese food he's clutching in his hand. It's heavy, a lot of food for a third dinner. *I have to make some changes.*

He leans out of his door and sees Dean sitting at his table, legs crossed left knee over right, looking into the night as if he has an ocean view, and smoking a skinny brown cigarette. Flip looks out into the parking lot too, convinced by Dean there might be something out there. But there isn't.

"You still up for a visitor?" Flip asks.

Dean turns his head in a lazy way, smiles and nods. "I'd be happy for some company. Join me on Veranda de Dean," he says.

"You want an eggroll?"

"I doubt my wine choice will complement the Asian flavours particularly well. But, I'm really not that hard to please."

"Give me a minute," Flip says.

"I'll be here," Dean replies, while lifting his cigarette in a silent salute; swirls of smoky tendrils mimic his gesture.

Flip kicks the door closed behind him.

Sara was right. He does need to start acting like a grown-up. He needs to take responsibility for his actions. No one has forced him to eat junk food every night. No one has made him start drinking and popping pills. He has enough time on his hands to work out, to make healthier choices.

He unpacks the take-out cartons from the bag and wedges everything except the eggrolls into the mini fridge. When he takes the eggrolls out, they're cold, so he sets them on the rack of the countertop-oven and twists the knob to *toast*. Then he searches the cabinets for cups and a plate.

Lynn was right too. He might not have an income, but he could have helped more with housework, with the kids, with homework. He'd always known it took cash to run a family and that had been his primary contribution. Because he had no cash to contribute recently, he'd let himself believe he had nothing to contribute. But now he sees it differently, for the first time really. Family takes another commodity: time. Cash and time. He is short on cash but long on time. He should have helped more. *I'm pathetic.* Lynn had been right about that too.

He finds a stack of hard plastic plates and clear plastic tumblers. He rummages through the drawers and finds a corkscrew. He carefully uses a paring knife to cut the foil from the top of the wine bottle and goes to work on the cork.

Truth is, he'd never been good with the kids when they were babies. He was afraid he would break Sara. She was so tiny. He couldn't change a nappy to save his life. Maybe if she would have stayed still. But she never stopped peddling her fat little legs. It had irked Lynn and delighted Flip that Sara's first word had, inexplicably, been *Dada*.

He had come home and nearly knocked her over as he entered through the mudroom door. She was crawling after the cat, trying to eat its tail. He had scooped her up carefully. It had been a hard day at work, it felt good to see her silly toothless grin: all wet, pink gums. She had pulled on his ears and slobbered on his nose. Then she had said "Dada." She had looked at him, and patted him as if to say *I realize that you are my Dada*. At least that's how he had related it to Lynn.

Lynn had been such a natural with the kids. He'd tried at first, but slowly bowed out of the parenting responsibilities with baby Sara.

Dylan was another story. He had been born premature, had finally come home after weeks in the hospital and had been sickly. Lynn was really protective of him, pushed everyone else away. It was all about Dyl as far as Lynn was concerned, for a long time. Years. In those years Sara was on her own. She went from an only child with two doting parents to a first child with absentee parents. Flip had seen it clearly. The kids were born nearly ten years apart, and Sara was becoming more interested in socializing with her friends than hanging around her baby brother anyway. But Flip had stayed out of it. He saw that she needed some attention and he didn't do anything, didn't know where to start. He worked longer hours, made more money, and became a stranger in his own home. And now it's too late. At least that's how it feels.

The bell dings on the toaster oven. Flip pulls the eggrolls out and cuts them on an angle as he's seen in restaurants. He finds a shot glass in one of the drawers and fills it with packets of duck sauce, then nestles it among the lengths of eggroll. He pours wine into the tumblers, balances everything the best he can, and walks to the door. He can't open it, so he kicks it a few times. A moment later Dean lets him out.

"This is nice," Dean says, a few minutes later. "The wine is not as offensive as I would have imagined."

"It's nice," Flip agrees.

"You are a handsome man, if you don't mind me saying so, Flip."

"I don't mind," Flip says, feeling uncomfortable. "But I think you're full of it."

Dean laughs and sips his wine. "No. I mean it. I have spent a lifetime observing the relative attributes of men and I can say, with the eye of a professional, that you are lovely. You could use a haircut and a shave. But you are lovely."

Flip feels his face with his hand. His whiskers are getting long. They feel like they're nearing beard length. He can't remember the last time he shaved; maybe a week earlier. Probably not that long, but a while. Flip sips more wine and picks at a few crumbs from the eggroll plate.

"Well, thanks," Flip says. "You are very put-together."

"Kind of you to say. I do my best."

"So. I'm not gay," Flip says. "I mean, what you said earlier about being gay or divorced. I am not gay. I'm not divorced. But, I guess I could be, unless things turn around soon. Divorced I mean. Not gay. We are separated, my wife and I. Lynn and I. Well not, legally. But we're not living together for a little while; to try and work some things out. I wanted you to know. I didn't want to mislead you about my situation."

"Oh. I figured it was something like that," Dean says. "I hope things work out. In my experience they always do." Dean finishes his wine and looks back over the parking lot. The tiki candle begins guttering and the flame winks warm light over the left side of Dean's face.

"I hope you're right about that, Dean. I need things to work out. I need a break. I've had a rough time of it lately." Flip stares out into the night too. He can't see the Lakeside's sign from where he sits, but he can see the way it illuminates the night for yards in every direction. They sit together in the comfortable silence and let the time pass. Dean takes a last swallow of wine.

"Do you want more wine? I can go in and get the bottle if you want more," Flip offers.

"No. I think I will retire for the evening. This was nice, though, Flip. It's good to meet you. And if you want a haircut or a shave, just drop by. I will take care of you, no charge. Consider it part of my welcome wagon service." He stands and pats Flip on the arm. Then he blows out the tiki.

"That's a kind offer Dean. Maybe I will take you up on it sometime." Flip stands too and gathers his things to go in.

The phone has an oversized plastic bulb growing out of its face like a tumour and it is flashing red when Flip enters the room. He drops the dishes in the sink. The clock next to the phone reads nine twenty-three. It has to be a message from Lynn. He worries the kids are hurt, there's been an accident. He should have called to say good night. He may have promised to do that, but he isn't sure. He reads the instructions for retrieving a message off the plastic sticker on the front of the phone, running his finger under the words as he goes. He pushes the appropriate buttons and waits with the phone to his ear.

"Flip," the recording says in Lynn's voice. "Just a few minutes after you left today you got a call from a company called DynaTech Solutions. They wanted you to confirm a time for Monday or Tuesday of next week for an interview." She gives the contact information and other particulars. "I left two messages on your cellphone. But you didn't pick up. I expected you to call to say goodnight to the kids. Dyl asked about you. Maybe you could give a call tomorrow. Don't call tonight. I'm beat. I'm going to bed early. Congratulations on the interview Flip, give them a call. Okay? And let me know how it goes." The recording ends.

Flip searches his workbag until he finds a legal pad and pen. He replays the message and copies down the contact information. Then he plays the message once more. He loves the sound of Lynn's voice. He should be with her right now. He can hear the tiniest hint of hope in her voice and also, perhaps a kind of resolution that a job interview is not the same as a job, and a job doesn't solve all their problems. He doesn't erase the message. He might listen to it again in the morning. He considers texting Lynn. But if her phone wakes her, she'll be angry.

Wow. Things can change so fast. If he were honest with himself, he'd have to admit that he didn't really like his previous job, his career choice. He'd been comfortable with his role, with the pay and benefits. But the work was drudgery. He'd been exceptionally good at it, and that was rewarding in its own way. But how he feels or what he wants doesn't figure into the situation much anymore. Thinking about DynaTech, he doesn't remember exactly what he applied for, but he doesn't care.

He can't sit still; he paces back and forth. He gets down in the floor and does five push-ups. He's breathing heavily, sweat gathers on his brow. He turns and flops back on the matted carpet.

He had told Dr. Hawkins he would prove how hopeless his life was. He could still do that. He has a week. In one week he will either get permission from the doctor to kill himself or he will get his act together and turn things around. He just has to push for one more week. Then things will change. Permanently.

He puts his hands behind his head and attempts fifteen sit-ups. He finishes nine. *That's enough for now. Don't want to overdo it. Might pull a muscle.* He's excited.

He goes to the mini-fridge and digs out a crab Rangoon. Just one. He pushes his suitcase and bags onto the floor, sprawls out on the bed and flips channels in the dark. He cracks the crab Rangoon open and sucks the cream cheese and speck of fake crab out of the first half. He isn't hungry but he eats anyway. He wants to stop, but it's just one crab Rangoon, so he finishes it. He falls asleep after watching Stephen Segal pitch someone through a plate glass window.

POKED VICIOUSLY BY CRAZY PERSON

Saturday morning starts harshly, with the radio blasting "Walking On Sunshine" at six forty-five. Flip hadn't set the alarm the night before, but neither had he turned it off. These facts do not enter his groggy mind immediately though, as the sound of the chorus slipping into static has him distracted.

He'd slept facedown and with his body crosswise; he opens the eye that isn't pressed into the polyester quilt. Turning his head, he stares at an unfamiliar headboard. He's sore, hung-over, and disoriented. *Katrina and the Waves*, he decides, *is the worst possible band to be listening to when one feels this way.* He's embarrassed he knows the name of the band, yet can't name more than three of the presiding Supreme Court Justices. He peels his cheek off the quilt and rubs the drool from the corner of his mouth. His whiskers are long, his face feels raw and he can smell his own foul breath. *Wine, rum, and egg rolls are a poor combination.*

He hauls his body across the bed, lunges at the side table and slaps buttons and twists knobs until the clock radio is silent. It's too bright in the room; the TV is muted, but still on. He rubs his eyes and watches a breakfast commercial: browned and glistening sausage patties somersault and tumble gracefully through the air to land gingerly on a toasted English muffin. *Damn*. Flip isn't a breakfast eater, but it looks good. He checks around on the bed and finds only crumbs from his crab Rangoon the previous night. He crunches the largest morsel between his front teeth while considering his day.

He has an interview. He won't know when exactly until he can call the HR contact for DynaTech Solutions on Monday morning, but there are things he can do to prepare. He hangs his feet over the edge of the bed and shoves himself up. His knees throb and he pauses to take inventory of his aching joints and various internal ailments. He wants to scratch at his irritated wrist and side, but he is turning over a new leaf. Today he stops being a victim and stops playing the fool. Today he will be all grown-up and do man-sized work. He leans his girth forward and gets busy.

After his early morning bathroom needs are met, he flops to the floor and does twenty awkward sit-ups, then pants as if he had lost a Fight-Club-style clandestine brawl. He's scared and he blames his dad.

He never had a role model for how to be a father, or a grown man. He only knows what not to do: don't leave your kids and abandon your wife. Based on those criteria he's been doing admirably. But it isn't enough, not anymore. This feels like uncharted territory. He had taken a job after college, married, fathered children and never really thought more about it.

He rolls onto his gut in preparation for some push-ups. The thought alone makes him exhausted. He decides to postpone until the afternoon, and starts getting ready.

Forty minutes later, he throws his workbag over his shoulder, locks the door behind him and drops the room key in his pocket. He's dressed in a dark, monochrome, Cuban-style Guayabera shirt and khaki shorts. Though he's been assured dark colours are slimming, he doubts it applies to his XXXL box-shaped man-blouse. It's another purchase Lynn made and he doesn't feel like himself in it. Though to be fair, he doesn't feel like himself in his own body. He imagines he will remind people of a drug kingpin as seen on every episode of Miami Vice. *God, I'm old.*

"Well, good morning Starshine," Dean says from his chair as he refills his coffee from a pot with a plunger on top. The mug sits on one of the paper coasters Flip left out the night before. "You're up and at 'em, aren't you? Very industrious for a Saturday morning."

"No rest for the wicked," Flip says.

"You want some coffee?" Dean offers, indicating the pot with a television presenter's hand gesture.

"No no. I'm good right now. What do you have there? A French Press?"

Dean turns and shows Flip his profile, he taps his lip thoughtfully. "Do you know what the Chinese call Chinese food?" he asks, a slight curl to his lip.

"They call it food," Flip replies.

"And what do the French call French doors?"

"Doors?"

"Correct. And so what do you suppose the French call a French press?"

"A coffee press."

"Ha," Dean says and claps his hands gleefully. "No. They call it a *cafetière*." He touches the plunger on the top of the coffee press. "Excuse my little joke. You sure I can't tempt you?"

"I'm sure. Maybe later."

"Or perhaps a ride somewhere? I'm free for chauffeuring services as soon as I finish my second cigarette and my second cup of coffee."

"No thanks. That's my car," Flip says while pointing into the lot. "I need to find somewhere with free internet though," he explains. "I have some work to do." He pats his workbag.

"Ah," Dean says, then puffs at his skinny brown cigarette, an air of exquisite rapture on his face. Flip is mesmerized by the ritualistic quality of Dean's movements; like tai-chi, but with more nicotine. After a moment, thick tendrils of white smoke seep from between Dean's lips. He inhales deeply and the billowy mass seems to crawl into his nostrils. It's a cool trick and it makes Flip wish he were a smoker. *Never too late to start.* When Dean releases the smoke, luxuriating in the moment, the spell is broken.

"I was thinking of hoofing it up to the strip mall where that coffee joint is. You think they have internet?"

"Ah," Dean says again. "I really could drive you; unless you'd prefer to walk. It isn't a very pretty walk."

"No, thanks. I need the exercise. I have a job interview early next week."

"Congratulations. You have to let me cut your hair and shave you. It would take years off." Flip considers the offer. He discovers he's more frugal than he is uncomfortable about letting a stranger give him a free haircut. For reasons beyond Dean's easy manner and generous spirit, Flip is growing fond of the old man.

"Okay," Flip says. "Thank you."

"I have time tonight."

"Great. I'll see you then," Flip says. "Internet? Do you know?"

"I don't know about internet. Sorry. I still write letters by hand, on actual paper. I find it so much more human than digitized bits flying about. But then again, I am of a slightly older generation." Flip opens his mouth to point out that Dean is actually more than 'slightly older' but Dean gives him a warning look. Flip closes his mouth with an audible clop.

"I think," Dean goes on thoughtfully. "I would miss the haptic experience of unfolding the page with my own hands if I switched to digital correspondence. I love the soft feel of good paper with high rag content. It feels civilized, if you see what I mean. Turning a page or unfolding a letter is like opening a new present. It's a surprise. Also, I even file personal correspondence in shoeboxes, sorted by date. I suppose I'm getting sentimental in my old age."

"Yes. Not to the old part. To the sentimental part," he says, though he has no idea what Dean is going on about. "I agree completely. See you tonight." Then he heads across the parking lot toward the road, kicking up deteriorated asphalt with his trainers as he goes.

The Drum Roaster is farther than he remembered and by the time Flip walks in, he's feeling spent and has a tension headache in his neck. He steps inside, lets the door suck closed behind him, and is relieved by the low, cool, cave-like café. If he weren't so exhausted, he might feel embarrassed about standing at the entrance panting with his hands on his knees. But he's too fat and tired to care.

It takes his eyes a moment to adjust after leaving the morning glare behind. He un-slings his workbag and sets it in the nearest wooden chair. A guy with salt and pepper hair, thin on top and curly at his neck, nods to him over the morning paper. Flip nods back and walks toward the counter near the back.

The kid at the counter partakes of the nebulous fresh-out-of-High-School-look; complete with Justin Bieber hair brushed around his face, tattooed forearms and a soul patch that grows a little too long and scraggly down onto his chin. He's tugging at the tuft of whiskers, twisting it like a neo-Snidely Whiplash as Flip walks up.

"Water," Flip rasps as if he'd been crossing a desert.

Henry High School turns and scoops ice into a glass. Then he runs water and slides it to Flip. Flip stands there and drinks until it's gone. He slides the glass back.

"Thanks," he says.

"Sure thing," Henry says. "Can I get you anything else?" He seems unconcerned, not pushy or insulted. Just doing his job. Flip likes the kid. He's only a few years older than Sara. He considers asking if Henry knows her, if they are in school together, if they've been in the same classes. *You know Sara Mellis of the ever-changing hair colour? She's my daughter.* But he hesitates. He's afraid of where it might lead.

"Huh?" he says, stalling while he rewinds his brain to replay Henry's last words. "Yes. I want coffee. What's good?" he asks after a pause.

"The Nutty Professor is our most popular espresso drink. It's a hazelnut-mocha with an extra shot of espresso. Very good."

Flip is mildly bewildered by the explanation, but too spent to inquire further. He slept reasonably well last night. But woke badly and it's been ages since he's done so much this early on a Saturday.

"Okay. Sounds perfect. I'll have that."

"What size?"

"Normal size."

Henry punches buttons on a cheap cash register; the kind you can buy at an office supply store.

"Anything else?" Henry asks.

"Something to eat. Do you have fruit? I need some fruit."

"We don't sell fruit, just biscotti and muffins." Henry points at a countertop plastic display case.

Flip looks over the choices. He doesn't like biscotti or muffins. The choices are arranged in labelled rows that read: Chocolate Chip, Cinnamon Apple, Coffee Cake, Pumpkin Spice with Cream Cheese filling.

"Are they moist?" Flip asks.

"Usually," Henry says.

Old Flip would have ordered something, just because he was bored. But today he is Fresh-Start-Flip. "I'll skip it," he decides.

"Listen, I keep a bag of apples in the back. I'll give you one if you want," Henry offers.

"Very nice. Thanks. That's it then. Just the Nutty Professor, I feel silly saying that."

"You're telling me," Henry says. Flip pays and the drawer on the register pops open. Flip pitches his change in an oversized mug on the counter. Henry moves over to a giant bank of knobs, spigots and shiny metal wands, starts grinding beans, pounding things against the counter, wiping various surfaces with a damp tea towel and pouring milk into a metal pitcher. Flip walks down to the far end of the espresso machine to wait.

Other than himself and the paper reader, there's a middle-aged couple with a baby in a stroller. The baby is very young; maybe six weeks old, and sleeping. The couple sit very close to each other, holding hands, knees touching, staring at their child lovingly and whispering to one another.

"Do you have internet?" Flip asks Henry across the counter.

"What?"

"Internet?" Flip asks louder, over a painful squealing noise emanating from the pitcher of milk.

"Yes," Henry says. The squealing stops, the milk is poured, espresso is added, canisters are expressed and shakers are shaken. In short order, a drink is on the counter. "There you go," Henry says. "Let me know how you like it."

Henry slides the mug and saucer to him. It smells earthy and rich and looks like a liquid frosted cupcake barely contained in the oversized mug. He blows the foam, whipped cream and chocolate curls aside and takes a sip. It's strong, bitter and hot, with a silky texture and a sweet finish.

"It's just like heaven in a cup," Flip says, rubbing a bit of whipped cream from the tip of his nose. Henry smiles and starts wiping the machine again.

Flip carefully walks his drink to a café table and settles in. He's wearing one of his watches and he checks it. Still early, not even nine o'clock yet. He decides he can afford to enjoy his coffee before getting to work.

The couple with the baby are still canoodling in the corner across from him. He surreptitiously watches them between sips of his caffeinated hot chocolate. The woman is beautiful: statuesque, smartly dressed, lean and athletic looking. Too fit really to have just delivered a baby so young. He glances again at the baby, maybe as young as a month. He looks at the woman again, looks at her body, which is easy enough because her clothes are close fitting. Her breasts do look swollen, full and overlarge for her frame, so maybe she's nursing. She is lovely in the same way that Lynn is lovely. He feels warmly toward the couple, remembers how it was when Sara was first born, the combination of complete exhaustion mixed with a sense of absolute contentment. He has the urge to reach in his pocket and bring out his photos, to share them with the couple, to reminisce. He slurps his sweet coffee.

The woman whispers to her husband, kisses his cheek, nibbles at his earlobe and nuzzles her forehead against his. Flip decides not to interrupt.

The husband is Flip's age with two-tone hair: black on top, grey on the sides. He seems preoccupied with staring at his baby, not really responding to his wife. Abruptly, the husband looks in Flip's direction, perhaps sensing Flip's scrutiny. Flip concentrates on his coffee.

The months of Lynn's first pregnancy were the best of Flip's life. He was an attentive and genuinely interested father-to-be, and for a long time it was a secret that only he and Lynn shared. She'd had a miscarriage the year before, and they were reluctant to tell anyone about the new pregnancy, for fear of having to explain another loss. So for five months, they'd kept it to themselves, except for Lynn's mother, whom they told at the end of the first trimester.

They had been sitting across from one another at the tiny kitchen table in their tiny apartment with the phone, set to speaker, between them.

"That's great honey," her mother's curt voice projected from the phone. "Just remember, you have to take care of your body, so you don't lose your looks. Because no man wants an ugly woman."

"I don't think she has to worry about that," Flip said.

"Oh, Flip," Coleen responded icily. "I didn't realize you were there. I wish someone had told me."

"I'm already married, mom," Lynn said, holding Flip's hand. "I snagged a good man already," she joked. "And now, with a baby on the way, he's trapped."

"Well, things change, dear," Lynn's mom said, sagely. "Trust me Lynn. I know from experience. Things change when you least expect it."

Lynn had mouthed the words "I'm sorry," and Flip had leaned across the table and kissed her cheek.

The paper reader at the next table stands and carries his empty mug to a grey plastic tub near the front door, tucks the folded paper under his arm, and heads into the daylight. Flip watches him go, then stealthily glances at the couple again. The husband stares back at him. Flip makes a show of looking admiringly at a display of stoneware coffee mugs near the couple.

During Lynn's second trimester with Sara, Flip had called every day during his lunch break to check on her.

"How are you feeling today? How is the peanut? I love you. Rub your belly for me. And your butt, too."

"Watch your language in front of your child," she said. "I will rub my belly now. You can rub my butt later."

"It's a date."

"But, could you rub my back for a while first? It's killing me."

"Sounds less like a date, but still, count me in."

At night he would lie on his side in their bed and watch as Lynn undressed. Over the months he witnessed the slow round growth of her abdomen, the softening of her features, the swelling of her breasts; subtle, secret changes that they shared. She would catalogue them aloud as they revealed themselves. She lifted her breasts and aimed the tips toward Flip.

"The skin around my nipples is getting so much darker," she said moving her body toward him so he could see.

"Yes. It does seem darker," he agreed. "I guess your body is getting ready to put those babies to work."

"And look. Can you see this?" She raised her arm and ran her fingertips along her side just at the edge of her armpit.

"No," he said. "I don't see anything."

"Feel," she said. She took his hand and pulled him to a sitting position on the bed. She guided his blunt fingers, brushed them along her hot, smooth skin. He could just barely detect tiny raised bumps.

"Yes. I feel it. What is it?"

"Skin tags, I think they call it," she said. "My body has a mind of its own. More than usual I mean. It's so crazy to think there's a little person living in here." She caressed her belly, and he did too. Then she had straddled him with her long legs and pressed his face between her boobs, so hard it crushed his nose against her breastbone.

The baby in the stroller starts peeping like a yellow chick, punching little fists in the air and pumping his legs inside his blanket. Flip finishes his coffee, considers taking his bag with him to the john, but decides it's safe to leave. He heads down a hall at the back and finds a unisex restroom.

When he returns, the woman is crossing the café to get something from the condiment bar near Flip's table. He stops well back, checks to make certain his computer bag is still there, then glances at the baby in the stroller. He assumes the infant is a little boy, but it's hard to judge because they've dressed him in a pale green onesie with a matching green cotton cap, a yellow duck embroidered across the forehead. Flip wants to smell his head and feel his warm, fine hair against his lips. He wants to ask the baby's name, say how adorable he is, relate stories about his own children. But the husband is lost in adoration for his child and doesn't seem approachable. And besides, considering the shape of things now, he might not be the best person to distribute unsolicited parenting advice.

When Flip turns toward his table he's confronted by an unexpected sight. The woman is bent over slightly, with her butt sticking out and pointed right at him. She smacks her rump playfully and shakes her ass. She slowly looks over her shoulder, smiling at first, until she sees him there. Clearly the display wasn't intended for him, but instead for her oblivious husband. She's upset, straightens up and hustles past him. Flip glances at the husband who is still lost in thought.

At his table, Flip unsheathes his laptop from its protective sleeve within his workbag and turns it on. He uncurls the computer's cord and looks for an outlet. He hears the couple's hissing whispers. Peripherally, he can see the husband cradling his baby, can see him glaring, can see the woman pointing and the man's handover of the infant as he stands and pushes the stroller aside.

Flip turns his back on the couple and leans down, reaches around the legs of the café table and plugs in the computer's cord. When he stands, the husband is there beside him.

"What's the big idea, fat man?" the husband asks.

Flip extends his hand to shake and introduce himself. The husband slaps it away. It stings. He is a little shorter than Flip, but fit and full of self-righteous, berserker rage. Flip can read it in his face: he wants Flip to make a move so he has an excuse to punch him. Flip looks over at the wife for help. She is re-swaddling the baby and packing the baby bag.

"This is a misunderstanding," Flip starts to say.

"You just can't take your eyes off my wife, can you?" The husband is so close now, he's pressing against Flip's belly, his face tipped up, his breath blowing on Flip's chin.

"I was just . . . I'm a father. I have a baby. Two. And a wife. I was just happy for you. Seeing you and your wife, it made me happy."

"Listen, fat man," the husband says again.

"You really don't need to keep calling me that. My name is . . ." Flip tries to shake hands again. The guy slaps his hand and pokes Flip in his pudgy chest.

"I don't give a DAMN if gawking at my wife gets you off. You keep your DAMN eyes in your DAMN head. Or I might just take your DAMN head clean off." Each time he says *DAMN* he pokes Flip again. It really hurts. The mean man leans his flat face forward even farther, stares at Flip hard, twists his lips into a sour expression and shakes his head like he's deeply disappointed. Then he steps aside, shoves the door and holds it open for his wife.

"Come on," he says roughly.

"I'm coming," the woman says, with evident irritation. She pushes the stroller out of the door without a glance in Flip's direction. The door closes and Flip lets out a breath he didn't realize he'd been holding. He rubs his chest. *I'm going to have a bruise.*

Flip watches the woman strap her androgynous baby in a rear-facing car seat in the back of their Subaru. The husband is using both hands to force the easy-collapse baby stroller to fold in on itself, but is having trouble. He picks up the stroller and tries to wedge it into the hatchback unfolded. It won't fit and falls to the ground. The man leaves it and stomps away. The wife retrieves the stroller in one hand, leans into it and it shrinks and flattens to a third of its original size in a graceful, practiced motion. She lifts it easily and sets it in the storage compartment, then closes the hatch.

The Drum Roaster's windows are tinted and Flip trusts that no one can see in. But that doesn't make him feel any less vulnerable when the husband gives a final menacing glare before driving away.

"Sorry about that," a voice says at Flip's shoulder. His whole body, recently pumped full of adrenaline, involuntarily twitches when Henry speaks. He puts his hand to his chest, to protect his heart or his pulsing bruise, he doesn't really know. There's no logic to the reaction. He registers Henry's presence, and then his words. He exhales another huge, slow breath that had caught high in his ribcage.

"I've been bringing out the worst in people lately. But not usually when I'm sober," Flip says.

"Yeah," Henry laughs supportively.

"Those people are crazy," Henry offers after a moment. "They come in here all the time. They never tip. They argue and make the customers uncomfortable. And they leave a mess. Plus, I think the guy is the one who pisses all over the bathroom. Makes me think his equipment is jacked-up. Then, they broke up for a little while. She would come in here by herself. She was a little friendlier on her own. She would always be like *'Are you sure this is decaf? Did you remember to add one Splenda? This feels too heavy, could you make it drier?* You know: just high-maintenance. But I don't really mind that. Some people just need the attention. Then, she got pregnant and they decided to get married. I would say, there is a one in three chance they'll still be married three years from now. Statistically speaking. I just can't see that situation lasting long. Those people are just crazy. So don't feel bad."

"Oh." After another pause Henry adds, "I brought your apple."

"Oh. Right. I forgot. Thanks." Flip takes the apple and sits. He's angry about what happened, even to the point of being spitefully joyful about the notion of the guy's marriage ending badly. But he hates to think about anyone with a child going through divorce. He misses Lynn. He misses Sara and Dyl. If he can't get things together, it's over for them. Divorce is right around the corner; and his kids will have to live through some of the same pain he lived through as a child. If that happens, he will fail at the only thing that truly matters to him.

The table was bumped during the altercation. His saucer is full of Nutty Professor and some has splashed around the table-top. He nearly puts his elbow in it. He's emotionally drained and more clumsy than usual. He thinks a bag of salty, greasy potato chips might make him feel better. *Or a pie.*

"Want me to make you another one?" Henry asks, indicating the cup and saucer.

"No. I'm fine."

Henry lifts the saucer from the table and drains it into the nearest trashcan. He produces a tea towel and wipes down Flip's table and the bottom of Flip's mug.

"I'm going to tell my dad about this. Last time I closed, I had to mop the men's room, and I told my dad we have to tell that guy to take his business elsewhere. But he says *'you can't run a business if you chase off everyone you think is annoying.'*" He says it with a youthful arrogance that makes it clear Henry thinks he could run things better than his father.

"You need anything else?" Henry asks.

"No. I just need to get to work here," Flip says. Though he wants to ask if Henry can produce a fried bologna sandwich on white bread with chips crushed on top, like his mother used to make when he was feeling down.

"This is one of those times when it would be handy to carry a gun," Henry muses.

Flip watches Henry. He has moved off to tidy the tables and chairs that the paper reader and the couple have deserted. He wears oversized, black Dickies work pants and has a biker-style wallet leashed to his belt with an absurdly long silver chain. The chain sways and knocks against the table's edge as Henry works.

"You know," Flip says, "if I had had a gun, I would have shot that man. Knowing my luck, I would have killed him. And if he had a gun, I would be dead. No doubt in my mind. I think it worked out about as good as it could have."

"Well. It might have been better if you beat his ass," Henry says.

Flip has never punched anyone in the face, never really been in a fight. He couldn't even imagine what it would be like, but he could see it: the angry man with that sour look on his red face, drawing back his finger to give Flip another poke. Flip, reaching out with his left hand, snatching and bending the finger back until it snaps, his right fist coming over hard and battering the man's nose even flatter, like he'd been whacked with a ham.

"That might have been okay too," Flip admits to Henry. He logs onto the internet and calls up his email account.

Henry sidles back over to Flip. "If you ever need to get your hands on a handgun," he says. "I have a friend who's selling one."

Flip looks up from the screen. "I will keep that in mind," he says seriously, because he means it.

Flip wastes an hour or so nursing his remaining espresso beverage and scrolling through vapid email traffic. He's preoccupied with the chest poking and what Henry said about beating the guy's ass. He imagines a dozen ways it might have gone differently. He thinks about pulling a gun out from under his Cuban shirt and watching the husband apologize. Eventually, he has exorcized the incident from the front of his mind and feels he can concentrate. He pulls out a legal pad and a pen. *Time to get serious.*

He finds the cover letter and resumé he'd sent to DynaTech Solutions. It's the version that tips toward management and communication skills. The cover letter reads *I am applying for the post of Director of Internal Communications*. He scratches blue notes on yellow paper and surfs over to the DynaTech Solutions website. It's very clean and minimal and corporate.

DynaTech is a company that specializes in computer networking systems and supplying customized programming for specific industries. Their emphasis is in supporting large insurance providers. Kristin Cole, a former colleague who had left for greener pastures, had sent him the lead nearly three months ago. She does something with patient services, ombudsman maybe, at a local hospital which contracts with DynaTech. When she sent him the job posting to him, he considered it a long shot. But he was desperate and willing to take anything that would pay the bills. It would be smart to contact Kristin, maybe get some more information.

He checks his watch, eats his apple, makes a list and takes another trip to the can. The Drum Roaster is pretty quiet. A few people stroll in to grab coffee to go. A heavy-set woman in her late twenties orders a giant blender drink that reminds Flip of a wedding dress, white and pastel with a decadent flourish. She sits straddle-legged at the table across from Flip, tucks her bobbed hair behind her ears and drinks the twenty-ounce drink in three long pulls on the oversized straw. She licks her lips like a cat that has just finished a tongue bath and leaves. Flip no longer feels hungry.

He imagines that people must feel sickened by him when they see him eat. And when he takes a pizza order through the crack in his door, dressed only in a bathrobe, the driver must take the tip and make an oath to never, ever, turn disgusting like *that guy*. It's a sobering thought and it makes him feel hungry again. *I'm not that heavy though, am I?* He tries not to give himself an honest answer.

Outside, the sun has crept high overhead. It's getting hot out. He's not looking forward to the return trek back to the Lakeside, so he stalls by meandering up to Henry and returning his cup and saucer. The kid is leaning on the counter, reading an old Gibson cyberpunk novel with a horribly creased spine. Flip read it his senior year of high school.

"Ready for another drink?" Henry asks, setting the book aside.

"No. No thanks. I'm Flip," he says, extending his hand.

"Mathias," the kid says. "But you can call me Thi." He pronounces it *thigh*.

"Okay Thi. I better get a move on. I have work to do." But he doesn't leave. He presses a fist into an eye socket, in the international sign for a migraine headache, and tries to remember a question he wanted to ask.

"You okay?"

"Yeah. Just had a question." He sees the book on the counter and asks, "You like *Neuromancer*?"

"Yeah. Pretty sick. My dad turned me on to it." Flip remembers his question.

"This is your dad's business then?"

"Yeah. He owns it and does the books. But it doesn't pay enough, so he paints houses too. He wants to move the place to a better location. But rents are still pretty high everywhere. Maybe commercial properties will be cheaper soon, if the local businesses keep closing their doors. But, who knows. There's this cigar shop that might go under. Good location. So we're keeping our fingers crossed on that one. Although the stink may never come out of the place. Anyway he's saving up, my dad. You know. I work here most the time. Just until I go to college. I took a couple of years off."

"I see. Well, do you have a card I could have?"

"You mean a coffee card?" Thi produces a card with little coffee bean images printed in a grid. He stamps over one of the beans with a red X. "There. Every thirteenth drink is on us," he explains. Flip takes the card.

"Thanks. I just meant a business card. You know. In case I want to call. In case I need to get in touch with you for some reason."

"Oh. No. Not really. But I can write the number on there." He takes the coffee card and writes on the back in red pen.

"Thanks."

Flip gathers his computer, cord and other materials. Thi joins him so he can wipe the table.

"Thanks again," Flip says, and pushes on the door.

"See you around."

"Hey Thi. Did your dad grow up around here?"

"Yeah, sure did."

"What's his name? If you don't mind me asking."

"Christopher Hafner."

Flip nods, then he walks out into the glare and the heat. He hates feeling so visible, so exposed.

His hunch had been right. He and Chris Hafner had been friends in high school. Graduated the same year. Flip had gone off to college and Chris had stayed to work for his dad's contracting business. Thi might have been reading the same copy of *Neuromancer* that Flip loaned Chris twenty-five years earlier. *Small world*, he thinks. Then he starts walking.

HEAVY BREATHING

Back at the Lakeside, when he tramps tiredly into the back lot, Flip can see his door is standing open. He looks over at Dean's table and chairs to double check his bearings. *Yes. My door is standing open.*

He tries to hustle it up, but he's too beat. He's panting, his shirt is sticking to him, his shorts are plastered to his thighs and he has a pebble in his shoe; it's a sharp pebble.

He approaches his room cautiously, spies someone smallish through a gap in the curtains. His body blocks the sunlight and casts a shadow as he steps into his doorway. He draws breath in order to ask what the hell is going on. But hesitates when he finds a woman leaning over his bed. For a frightening moment his mind flashes to the crazy mom from that morning and then to Lynn. Perhaps she has come to him. Perhaps she has missed him. But then the figure turns and smiles.

She is young, completely unadorned with jewellery or make-up, and has her long dark hair pulled back into a practical pony-tail. Despite his body blocking most of the daylight, her teeth and eyes sparkle next to her caramel-coloured skin. She tugs down the tail of her fitted shirt and tucks her hands into the front pockets of her jeans, like a bashful kid.

"Hello, Mr. Mellis. I'll be out of your way in a moment. Just straightening up a bit." She sounds slightly nervous.

Then she's all motion. She snags a wadded pile of towels and sheets from the floor and strides toward him; he doesn't move out of her way.

"I'm sorry. Who are you?"

"I'm Vanessa," she says, looking up at him. "I do the bedding and towels. Didn't Mrs. Wallace tell you? Sometimes she forgets." She stands very close as she speaks, her body giving off a pleasant, fresh smell, like something tasty baking in an oven. His mouth starts to water.

"Yes. I think she told me. She said something. I remember that she said something," he says uselessly.

"Could you excuse me, Mr. Mellis?"

"Oh sure. Sorry." He moves to let her squeeze by, then leans out his doorway to watch her go. She drops the bedding in a push cart sitting past Dean's door.

"I'll be back again on Tuesday." She twists a bit at the hips and looks over her shoulder as if she could feel him watching her, expected to have his attention. Her neck is graceful, like that bust of Nefertiti. "Remember to use the hamper for towels, please." She gives a quick, warm wave and disappears around the corner with her supply cart.

He completely forgets his exhaustion and hunger, the fact he has a rock in his shoe and that his bag's strap is wearing a groove in his shoulder. *Dazed* is the word for how he feels as he sets his bag on the freshly made bed. *Maybe I'm having a blood sugar issue.*

He sees that he left dirty clothes, including boxer shorts the size of a child's sleeping bag, randomly littered across the floor.

Figures. He flops back on the bed and wallows in the smell of the clean bedcover and his own loneliness. He drifts into sleep.

A few hours later, the kitchen tap spits a few times like an angry kitten when he tries to run the water, and when it starts to flow it's warm and tinted orange. He lets it run across his fingers until it's cool and clear. He fills a plastic tumbler and guzzles it down. He repeats the process a number of times then showers and changes clothes. Refreshed, hydrated and no longer sticky, he sits on the side of the bed near the telephone and takes out his to-do list. His clean outfit is nearly identical to the one he changed out of.

He calls information and jots down Kristin's number. When he dials it, it chirps a few times before going to the answering machine. He leaves a message. Then he retrieves a card from his pocket and calls Dr. Hawkins.

"This is Dr. Hawkins," a rich voice says, very professionally.

"Doc. This is Flip Mellis."

"Mr. Mellis. Is everything okay?"

"Yes. I just wanted to leave the contact information like I promised." He leaves the information. "I guess that's it. See you Thursday bright and early."

"Hold on just a second Mr. Mellis. Do you have a minute to talk?"

"I'm kinda in the middle of something here," Flip says.

"Really, it will only take a moment. I have something pressing to get to also."

Flip can hear a woman's voice in the background. He imagines it's the waitress. What's her name? Kelli. He thinks of her lounging naked on the Doc's bed, a sheet strategically covering parts of her body, but leaving long stretches of smooth skin exposed. In this scenario the Doc is sitting at the side of the bed, much as Flip is now. Flip looks back at the bed behind him. He tries to imagine Lynn, nude and playful, but he can't quite get there. An image of Vanessa pops into his head instead. He banishes it as quickly as possible.

"Do you have a minute?" the doctor asks again.

"All right. Yes. What is it?"

"How are things going? Did you contact someone to speak to?"

"Like I said, things are okay. I got a call from a company that wants to interview me sometime next week."

"That's great news. You said that was the most important thing. You must feel happy. How do you feel about it? Do you feel happy?"

"I'm relieved. But mostly I am focused on getting prepared. Not really thinking beyond that right now. I have to get focused, get my game face on. One step at a time." Flip finds he's doodling on his legal pad, making an expanding labyrinth pattern.

"And what about contacting someone to talk to? A friend or family member who might be supportive?"

"It's on my list." Flip thinks he hears the woman's voice again. It could just be a TV.

"Try to get to it today. Okay?"

"Yes." Flip continues to make marks on his note pad.

"And no alcohol at all. Right? No pills, no chemicals."

"Perish the thought," Flip replies.

They say their goodbyes and disconnect. He finishes his maze and sets the pen down, then stews over the idea of calling a "friend." He's a grown man. He doesn't really have friends any more. He has responsibilities; responsibilities which he has failed to take care of. He has never been the kind of person to hang out over beers or sports and complain about how much of a nag his wife is to a bunch of middle-aged men who happen to have kids in the same school as his own.

Lynn is his best friend, his only true, adult friend. But she can't stand him and is kicking him to the kerb, which may disqualify her as 'supportive.' *At least for the moment.* Besides, the Doc meant someone outside the current state of bedlam that constitutes his life.

Maybe he could call up Christopher Hafner. Ask if he wanted to get together and play a round of Car Wars. *Dumb.* He knows who he'll end up calling. But he isn't up to it yet.

It would be marginally easier to call home. Though that scares him too. He punches the buttons on his phone.

"Hello," Sara answers.

"It's me. Just wanted to check in."

"Oh," she says, unenthusiastically. "It's Dad," she says to someone. The phone knocks against a hard surface. Moments pass, and Flip wonders if the connection has been lost. That phrase strikes him as apt. *The connection has been lost.*

"Hello?" he says. "HELLO! HELL-O!" Nothing. Then he hears quick feet and the phone knocked around.

"Hi, Dad," Dyl's voice is sweet, but he pants heavily into the receiver, like some grade-school pervert.

"Heya buddy, how you doing? Did you watch cartoons this morning?"

"What?" Heavy breathing.

"Did you watch cartoons?"

"What?" Heavy breathing.

"Dylan, put the phone on your ear. Dylan?" A dial tone blares. Flip returns the phone to its perch.

He thinks about calling back. He wants to be with his family; he should be in his own home. If he can't get back there, he'll kill himself. That's all. He will do it right: with a gun. He will call Thi and buy a gun from Thi's buddy, then he'll drive somewhere, or walk, and just put the cold barrel against his temple, right there on the side of the bed in a cheap motel; maybe in the same room where he and Lynn made love all those years ago. Just sit right down, put the gun on his temple and pull the trigger. *Easy-peasy-ham-and-cheesey.*

But he made the Doc a promise. He'll have to wait. Death isn't what he wants, not really. He wants the stress and pain to stop. He can't see any reason to persevere if there's no hope that things will get better. What he truly wants is to be home, with his family. To be in a bed he shares with his wife, not at the other end of the house. And definitely not all the way across town. He'll give things time to develop, buck up and push through for a while longer. But one way or another, it will all be over soon.

Truth is, he was already offered a good job. The day he was fired from McCorkle-Smithe he called up a headhunter who had been courting him for a while. Within a week he had a solid offer for a position down in Houston. But with the crash of the real estate market, all the equity they had built in their home was dried up. They couldn't put a down payment on a new mortgage, his kids would be miserable if they had to move, and Lynn wouldn't want to leave her mother. The only option had been for him to move on his own, live out of an apartment and send his paychecks back. But that didn't feel like family. He wouldn't do it. He turned it down and told Lynn it had fallen through. Looking at the shape of his life now, he realizes what a stupid decision it had been.

He looks down at the legal pad, takes up his pen again and begins at the opening of the maze. His pen races through the design until he comes to a dead end. He moves the pen tip back to an intersection and tries a different direction, again a dead end. After several more attempts he realizes he's left himself no way out.

He feels suddenly tense and short of breath. The only thing he's really ever felt proud of is his relationship and his children. Maybe he took them for granted for too long.

He touches his palm to his chest. His breath catches in his lungs; his eyes burn and his heart aches. There is a pressure building and he thinks, *this is me having a heart attack.*

He takes a deep breath. He counts in his head. He exhales. The tension passes, though he is damp with sweat again.

It's nothing he tells himself. *Just emotions.* The older he gets, the less capable he feels of processing deep emotion. *It hurts to feel so much, or maybe it's only my bruised chest.*

INITIATES CLANDESTINE PURCHASE

He has other calls to make, but feels too shitty. He tries eating cold leftover Chinese food. The sauce has congealed. He scoops it with a plastic spork and spreads it on one of the remaining crab Rangoons. After a few bites he feels horrid and puts the rest away.

He does a few push-ups, and checks it off his list. Then he goes next door and knocks on Dean's door.

"Uno momento, por favor," Dean calls.

Flip takes a seat on the veranda as a red convertible rips around the corner and into the parking lot. It's an early '70's Cutlass Supreme with matching red-painted mag wheels. The top is down and the driver shoves on the horn as he whips into a parking spot. The driver leaves the car running and the driver's side door open. He stands beside the car with his hands on his skinny hips.

"VANESSA," he yells toward the far end of the motel. "VANESSA," he yells again in Flip's direction. He waits a few seconds, then storms toward the motel office.

The door to Number Four creaks opens. The back of a grey head leans out. The head watches the loud-mouth driver;

then tucks back in and lets the door slam. Flip hears Grey Head employ the security chain.

"Ah," Dean says as he steps outside. "The boyfriend is pissed again."

"It looks that way."

"He is pissed every other day. She could really do better than him. Though he is a tall drink of water."

"You think so? He looks like a snot to me. But first impressions can be deceiving."

"No. I think you nailed it."

They both look fixedly toward the office for a while. Then Dean says, "Let me just finish something inside and I'll join you in a moment. Oh. Tell me what happens." He goes back in.

Flip picks at the hardened wax-flow on the side of the tiki candle and snaps off delicate little sections, pitching the crumbles on the ground between his feet. After a minute the boyfriend's voice precedes Vanessa out of the office.

". . . think I give a shit if the dryer is getting old. You want me to pick you up, you be fucking ready. I drive all the way out here and you ain't even ready." He has Vanessa by the elbow and is quickly marching her toward his car. He opens the passenger side door and deposits her. He slams the door and strides around to the other side. He doesn't look around, but Vanessa looks over at Flip, makes a face he takes to be an unspoken apology. He nods and waves to let her know it's fine, but he can't imagine what she thinks she has to apologize for. The Cutlass backs in a huge arc, skids to a stop, slams into gear, and peels out of the lot, kicking out asphalt pieces as it goes.

Flip feels bitter emotions rise up in him, a white, hot ember of rage pinches between his eyebrows, his whole face gathers into a painful scowl. He slaps his hand against the café table so hard the candle clatters over, extinguishing the flame and spilling liquid wax. He sets the tiki up and goes in his room.

He paces and punches the mattress a few times. He doesn't like to see people bullied, especially not Vanessa. Which is strange and stupid, but true. Maybe he feels a kind of warm and gentle promise implied in her large dark eyes and her generous curves. Maybe she's just a beautiful, blank slate for all his wants and dreams for a woman in his life. Or maybe he's feeling parental toward her. If he stopped to analyze closely, he might say it's a combination, which upon further analysis, seems sick and wrong, but he is too unreasonably angry to pause and think. The higher functioning part of his brain has taken a back seat to something deeper and more basic. When he replays the moment when Vanessa looked over to him, he thinks maybe she was asking for help. *And I want to help.*

He looks around his room and finds the bottle of pain pills sitting next to the clock radio. *Not where I left them.* He tips two into his palm and pops them. The bottle is over half gone. *I must be going through them faster than I thought.* He shuffles business cards and snapshots from his pocket until he finds the one with coffee beans, turns it over and reads the handwritten number. He gets on the phone and calls Thi.

"Drum Roaster," Thi answers.

"This is Flip. From a little earlier. Remember?"

"Yeah. Hey. What's up?"

"I would be interested in purchasing that specialty item from your friend. You know the one we talked about? As soon as possible."

"I don't know what you mean. Sorry. What were we talking about?"

Flip doesn't want to say it over the phone. He wants to speak in code. But *specialty item* didn't do the trick. Kev must use a special language for making subversive transactions, something cool and easy. "You know. I want to buy that *ticket* to that show your *friend* is selling," Flip tries.

"I'm really confused. Are you sure you called the right number?"

After a brief hesitation he goes, "A handgun. I want to buy a gun. Can you see if your friend still wants to sell a gun?"

"Right," Thi says. "Now I get it. That's what you meant? I remember. Yeah. Is that what you were talking about? Oh. I get it," Thi laughs a small good-natured laugh. "I don't think the Feds have the phone tapped, man. I can text him now. When you want to do it?"

"Tomorrow." Flip says. "And please don't say Feds." Then he realizes he said it too. He immediately becomes aware the whole situation is a bad idea. His anger begins to ebb, and he feels tired, old, fat and foolish. The tension leaves his face, seeps from his shoulders until he slumps down on the side of the bed.

"No can do. Chad's dad is a preacher. He's got church stuff all day tomorrow. How about Monday after school? Four o'clock maybe. Unless you want to meet him at the church?"

Shit. He's on the phone trying to make an illegal handgun purchase from a high school kid. *Maybe he's at the community college.* He should call it off, but instead he says, "Monday is good. Just let me know the particulars after you check with Chad."

"You want to buy some weed or anything while you're at it? 'Cause Chad is the guy who can make it happen."

"No. Just the gun." He leaves his number and hangs up. *Weed might not be the worst idea.*

Back on the veranda he's bothered that the gun dealer's name is Chad. He hates the name, considers it a bad omen. All the bad guys in eighties movies featuring evil yuppies and spoiled trust fund kids were named Chad; they dressed in blazers with the sleeves pushed up on their forearms, travelled in roving herds of sneering sycophants, like a malicious Ralph Lauren ad.

Dean sets a bottle of white wine on the table and fills the plastic margarita glasses.

"Well?" he asks. "Did you get a show? I heard the evidence of a dramatic exit, all the way in the kitchen."

"No. Not much of a show," Flip says. "He just treated her like shit."

"Well, I will tell you one thing," Dean says. "No kind of sugar daddy is worth that kind of treatment. I know from experience. From what I've seen, he spends most of his money on his car anyway. But she's young. She has time to figure it out." Dean settles into his chair and touches plastic glasses with Flip. Dean says, "Clink."

"Do you think he's violent with her?"

Dean takes a minute to consider the question. "You really are straight, aren't you?" he says, between sips of wine.

"Yes. I'm straight. We've been over all that. What does that have to do with this?"

"Well, plenty of married men with children claim to be straight. But they end up down at the Southern Bell trolling for boy tail. You never know."

"I'm pretty sure I know," Flip replies.

"Well, you have a case of the white knight syndrome. I have seen many a man throw his life away because he thinks he needs to save someone who doesn't need saving."

"Is that so?"

Dean crosses his legs at the knees, smooths his shirtfront, wipes the corners of his mouth delicately with a paper napkin and folds his hands in his lap. He gazes at his imaginary view. Then he says, "I have never seen the boyfriend hurt Vanessa. I have never seen a mark on her. I have only heard him yell and storm around." He lets that sink in. "And that tells me he is not hitting her. He is all emotion with no control. If he were hitting her, he would leave marks, and I would have seen it by now, because I've been looking. That is what I think."

Flip isn't convinced.

Dean takes a long sip of wine, refills both glasses, and returns the bottle to its spot. "So you don't need to save her. If you ask me, she likes pulling his chain. I've seen her do it. You know, I have this theory that people generally deserve the relationships they end up in. And I suspect she's getting something we don't understand out of the relationship. Perhaps she has daddy issues, or is trying to irritate her mother. Who knows? Human behaviour is complex," he adds. "Now, let's deal with that mop of yours. We need to get you a job." Dean stands and heads into his apartment.

EVIL TWIN

Dean returns moments later with an electric trimmer, a plastic cape thrown over his arm, a spray bottle worn in a special holster and a lime-green tote. The tote reminds Flip of a tackle box, but is clearly made for other paraphernalia. Dean unclasps it, tips back the lid and removes a comb and two expensive-looking pairs of scissors.

Dean moves the chair he'd been sitting on into an empty parking space between two cars, and pats the seat. "Your throne awaits," he says. He bows low.

Flip feels dizzy as he stands: wine and painkillers. He tops off his drink before moving to his assigned seat. In a deliberate attempt to be cautious, he makes exaggerated, cartoon-style strides off the small kerb and over the parking stop.

Next to the table, and leaning with its back to the wall, the tiny patio chair had seemed perfectly adequate. But as he stands over Dean's chair now, Flip worries it will crumple like an aluminium can under his weight. He slowly lowers his rump onto the seat; his ass hangs off both sides. The chair creaks and its feet bite deeper into the still warm asphalt. After a short, trepidatious pause, it seems to be holding, so Flip exhales.

"We better get moving while the light is good," Dean says. He twirls the plastic cape like a showy matador and fastens it behind Flip's pudgy neck. Flip giggles. He puts one hand over the mouth of his wine glass and balances it on his knee under the cape, and uses the other hand to cover his grin.

"And what, pray tell, is so humorous?" Dean asks, while he works.

"Nothing really. Just feel like laughing. It just came over me all of a sudden. I think my moods are swingin' like a loose gate in a storm. Not eating much in combination with sleep-deprivation and self-medicating can do that to a guy. Even a big fat guy."

"Oh stop. You are handsome. Now let's make some magic," Dean says, and works his scissors like castanets for emphasis. He quick-draws his atomizer and spritzes Flip's hair and forehead with cold mist. He rakes his fingers across Flip's head and a shock of sensation runs around Flip's scalp and tingles down his spine. His grin evaporates as quickly as it appeared; he's overwhelmed with a wave of melancholy weepiness. *It has been too long since someone touched me.*

"Now. Let's get started," Dean says. "What did you have in mind?"

"This is all about getting a job. The interview is for a corporate gig. So I guess something acceptably professional and conservative."

"And what about the beard?" Dean asks, accessing Flip's facial hair while pensively tapping the flat of a comb against the side of his leg.

"Just haven't shaved. You can just take it off," Flip says. Dean moves behind Flip and doesn't respond. Flip worries he's offended Dean. "You're the expert. Do whatever you feel is best.

I thought you said 'shave and a haircut.' So if you want to shave me, go ahead. But, if you'd rather not, I can do it myself."

"No. No," Dean says pleasantly. "I have had a vision of what you could look like. And it involves keeping some of the whiskers. Are you okay with that?" Dean lays a hand on Flip's shoulder. "I think it's a look that will be taken seriously. It will let people know you mean business."

Flip has never trusted men with facial hair. He has always assumed they're hiding something and he worries it might appear he doesn't care enough to shave for the interview. But he nods once. "I am in your hands," he says.

"Very good. So how was your day?" Flip tells Dean about the crazy parents with the tiny baby, the subsequent ass-shaking and chest poking. When Flip finishes the story, Dean clicks on the clippers. A fervent, mechanical humming fills Flip's senses, like being swarmed by wind-up bees.

"That," Dean says loudly, "is why I try to stay away from breeders. In my experience they tend toward emotional instability. No offence."

"None taken."

"Now don't move." He runs the clippers up Flip's left sideburn, bends his ear down and works around the back until he makes it to the other ear. Flip watches clumps of hair tumble down the cape, across his chest and gut and come to rest in a valley created between his hidden Chablis and his belly. Dean changes the guard on the clippers and starts on the sides of Flip's head.

"And you? How was your day?" Flip asks.

"I had an uneventful day. I am essentially retired. So I walked to the park, I smoked my two midday cigarettes. I had a pleasant lunch with an old lover who is married and has adopted a baby from Honduras. Smoked again and returned home."

More hair slides down Flip's torso. The clippers shut off, and scissors come out.

"How do you feel about that? About the ex's new family, I mean. I assume he married another man. I mean, you didn't drive him to heterosexuality did you?"

"Good God no. He's still quite queer. I feel fine about it. Just fine. Gary always wanted to adopt. I never did. It was one of many reasons things didn't work out. He will make a good father though. I'm certain of it." Dean stands in front of Flip and turns Flip's jaw to the left, tugs his chin down a bit. "Now, don't move," Dean instructs.

"Kind of old, for starting a family. Could be tough on your friend. I would hate to start having kids at your age. No offence."

"Ah. I see how you would think that. But no: Gary is twenty-years my junior. And now, his husband Bruce, Gary calls him Brucie with a saccharine level of affection," he says the pet name with evident distaste, "is actually a year or two younger still."

"I see."

Dean snips, combs and periodically spritzes. He roughs Flip's hair with his fingers.

"Your hair is thick," he says. Then he changes scissors, and combs and snips some more. He uses the clippers again on the back of Flip's neck, on his eyebrows, and on his earlobes, where hair shouldn't be growing, but apparently is.

"Stage one is complete. And you already look like a new man." He stands back and crosses his arms, grooming implements sticking out of his hands at odd angles, like that character from the Tim Burton movie. "You may drink now. I need to get my beard trimmer."

Flip moves his wineglass from under the cape and downs all the remaining room temperature liquid. He leans to set the glass down. The chair creaks. His butt has scooted forward on the seat, so he rearranges himself, tries to sit up tall and pulls back his shoulders, like he'll need to in the interview. It doesn't feel right, so he just slumps forward again, like a great lump. In his mind's eye Flip sees himself as a pink mountain gorilla; massive, hunched and endangered.

"Okay," Dean calls as he approaches. "Here we go. I wish we were at my old shop. Raise this chair and this would be easier." Dean has a smaller pair of clippers in one hand and tilts Flip's face around with the other. "Would you mind standing?" Dean asks.

Flip stands, hair falls onto his shins and the tops of his shoes. Dean steers him to the appropriate spot and turns his face toward the waning light. Dean steps up on a parking stop, checks his footing and moves in with the clippers; a swarm of smaller mechanical insects has arrived.

"So you had your own shop?"

Dean makes a shushing sound and lightly smacks Flip on the top of the head. "Don't talk until the process is complete. Artist at work. I need to concentrate. And you need to be still." He grabs Flip's chin, turns his face and neck again, and goes back to work. The clipper scrapes as it mows strips of whiskers from under his neck.

"I shall do the talking," Dean says, his cadence slow and distracted. "I had a salon. I owned it with my husband."

"You were married?" Another shush and smack. Dean twists the clippers this way and that. He concentrates. His brows bunch and relax. The tip of his tongue pokes out from time to time. Flip's foot hurts from the spot rubbed by the rock, his legs ache from the walk, and his back hurts on general principle. He tries hard not to sway. He wants desperately to sit for a few minutes, and he wants more wine and pills.

"Yes. Happily married," Dean speaks as if the conversation never lulled. "We opened the place together. Shear Design. That was what we named it. Walter and I. Walter was older than me and we were very much in love. I was in charge of the beauty salon, the spa, the staffing, and client services. Et cetera. We had a tanning bed. He was in charge of the books. We owned the building. Condo above. Work below. It was an ideal situation for a couple of queens-in-love. It sounds a bit stereotypical to say it aloud. But it made us very happy for over a decade." He stops scraping the clippers along Flip's skin, steps off the parking stop, takes several paces back to scrutinize his work. He seems to come to a decision about Flip's face, makes a little clicking-tisk-sound with his tongue. "Then Walter got very sick and died. I sold the shop. Gary was my rebound." Dean is very matter-of-fact about it.

He approaches and uses his fingers to check the length of Flip's sideburns. He closes one eye, nods and opens it again. He shortens the right sideburn a fraction. He steps back again.

Flip looks down, as he if he might catch a glimpse of his own face.

"Don't move," Dean says. Then he steps behind Flip and rattles around in his tote.

"I'm sorry about Walter. Your husband," Flip calls in Dean's direction.

"Oh. Well. Thank you. But, no need to be sorry really. Of course I miss him. But we did have a good life together. He was my husband. Not legally like Gary and his Brucie. But, for all intents and purposes." He returns with two large hand mirrors.

"You must have been torn up when he passed."

"Oh yes. It was a terrible loss. But I've learned that often the things we judge to be curses in life, actually turn out to be great blessings. And vice versa." He hands Flip one mirror and walks around behind with the other. "This is the big reveal," he says. "When you are ready, hold up the mirror and behold the new you."

Flip raises the mirror and is horrified. Being confronted with the broad expanse his face has become is immediately shocking; especially after avoiding his reflection for so long. To see himself in a magnifying hand mirror is brutal, cruel even. He stops himself from wincing out of concern for Dean's feelings, but he wants to fling the mirror away and hide somewhere dark. He longs to hop up and order takeout, something fried and salty followed by something sticky and sweet. But he continues to stare, stricken and appalled by the image before him.

His haircut is high and tight, just enough to part and brush down on top and so close at the sides that he's almost hairless. It does look darker with the grey sheared off and his eyebrows do look better, his eyes larger. He squints and touches his fingers to his temples. His crow's feet are nearly non-existent. One good thing about a fatter face: less wrinkles.

He's most disturbed, not by his jowly face, but by a collection of faint, angular strips of whiskers. Two vaguely triangular shapes spread out beneath his sideburns and stretch around his soft jaw line to point at one another, not quite touching, over the fleshy knob of his chin; like a geometric abstraction of Man reaching out for God on the ceiling of the Sistine Chapel, but in facial hair.

Two darts wrap from under his nose and bracket the corners of his mouth, again leading the eye to a meaty, pale negative space on his chin. Finally, a tiny triangular soul patch aims at the same fatty, negative space. He doesn't look much like himself, more like his own gay, evil twin.

"What do you think?" Dean asks.

"I am truly blessed," is all Flip can think of to say.

Flip says, "Thanks," repeatedly, and in several different ways while Dean tidies up. He doesn't want to be ungrateful. The haircut will do very nicely.

"I may need to shave the facial hair," he says. "It looks great. But I'm not sure it will work for an interview." Flip says it friendly and Dean responds in kind.

"I understand. Corporate America can be a bit on the conservative side."

"Exactly," Flip says. "But it's the most creative beard I have ever witnessed. I am honoured. Clearly you have talent." Flip returns Dean's chair to its spot on the veranda and settles into his own seat.

The sun is setting. Dean takes a disposable lighter from his pocket and lights the tiki; a flame flickers within its grotesque visage.

The chain on Number Four slides free, the deadbolt snaps sharply and the door comes open. Grey Head is tall and slender, wearing a stiff black uniform. He fixes a matching eight-point cap in place before closing and locking the door behind him. The brim of the cap is glossy black and matches his shiny belt and patent leather work shoes. He swings a cheap black briefcase with a brass combination lock in his left hand.

"Flip. This is Larry. Larry, this is the Lakeside's newest addition, Flip." Dean peppers in his usual flourish of hand gestures as he speaks.

Larry comes over and shakes Flip's hand firmly. "Pleasure," he says. He speaks in a high tenor and has the yellow teeth of a heavy smoker.

"Same here," Flip says.

"Did you hear all that ruckus earlier? Woke me up before my alarm went off," Larry says.

"Yes. The boyfriend was in fine form today. Flip heard him yelling at Vanessa," Dean says.

"She deserves it far as I'm concerned," Larry replies. He keeps talking as he moves to a compact car backed into a nearby space. He walks to the driver's side of the two-door Dodge Neon and unlocks it. The car matches his uniform; Larry's demeanour is like an undertaker commanding the world's tiniest hearse, commandant of a funeral home for the diminutive.

"She's been stealing from me," Larry continues flatly. Then he lays his briefcase and hat in the back seat, slides into his car, snaps the headlights on, and drives away. Halfway across the lot he reaches out his window and snaps a magnet mount siren on the roof of his car.

"He works nights and hates women, at least since his divorce," Dean explains. "Also I suspect he's not so fond of homosexuals or non-whites. Not very pleasant company. He reminds me of my second boyfriend."

"He's a security guard?"

"Yes, something like that. Building security out at a business park, I believe."

Flip watches, expecting the siren light to start flashing blue. But Larry is a professional and leaves it turned off.

"Would you like to join me for dinner in about an hour? Nothing is so depressing as eating alone." Dean asks. He offers as if he feels obliged to ask, because Flip is still sitting on his veranda.

"No. I'm sorry. I have to make a few calls and get to bed early. Are you sure I can't pay you for your fine work?"

"No. No. Not necessary," Dean uses his hands to ward off the offer. "Once you get your first paycheck you can take me out to dinner. Maybe sushi."

"You bet," Flip says, although he hates sushi.

They watch as a cloud of gnats bob around one of the working streetlights in the parking lot.

"Well, thanks again," Flip says.

AN INCREASINGLY CROWDED ORGY

Inside, Flip sees the red light flashing on the room phone. He punches some buttons and listens to his message.

"Hi Flip," Lynn's voice sounds close and intimate. His breath catches. "Sara said you called and spoke to her and Dyl. She was not very forthcoming with details. I just finished homework with Dyl. It's so hard to get him to sit still and focus. I asked Sara if she'd finished her science report for Monday. Apparently I insulted her horribly, because she yelled and stormed upstairs. Dyl and I left a message on your cell. You should check it. Let me know what you find out about the job interview. I'm beat. Mom is driving me nuts. I'm going to turn in early. Maybe we can speak soon." There was a pause in which Flip thought she was preparing to say *I Love You. Come Home. Let's have dangerous sex.* She only says, "Good night."

Flip doesn't get time to think much about Lynn's message because another woman begins to speak.

"Why Flip Mellis. Long time no see." Flip can't place the voice. "I got your message. I would be happy to talk with you about DynaTech." *It's Kristin.* "Just give me a call. Or we could meet over lunch. I'm free to grab something most days. Or dinner would be good too. You still running? I'm training for a marathon, my first. Just a few weeks away now. I could use some pointers. Talk to you soon."

A pre-recorded voice gives him options and he deletes the messages, including the ones from the previous night. Immediately he wishes he'd listened to Lynn once more. He misses her. His eyes are heavy. He wants to sleep. He looks at his watch. It isn't even eight. Why is he so tired?

Right: he woke up early and accomplished more today than he'd done during the previous month. Also, he had taken a nap and that always makes him feel sleepy. He heaves himself to a standing position.

He strips down to his boxers and scratches the back of his meaty shaved neck. He feels his sinister facial hair. *If DynaTech is looking to hire a tyrant from the future, I've got it in the bag.* He shakes his head and hustles his balls while he walks into the bathroom to get ready for bed.

In the bathroom he uses his palms to rub brisk circles on the sides of his prickly head. His hands come away coated with bits of hair. He should shower again, but he doesn't. He feels a painful zit forming in the centre of his forehead. He examines it without glancing too hard at the rest of his reflection. A unicorn horn is about to burst from his angry flesh. He wonders if that means he gets to make a wish. *I wish for a good job.*

While he's thinking about it, he pulls open the folding door on the closet and unzips his suit bag. He takes out the largest suit, the only one that might still fit. He slips into the pants. They are voluminous, but as he pulls them up, they become snug. He leaves the pants open at the front and slips into a white dress shirt. He concentrates on gingerly working the tiny plastic buttons. He stretches his arms, the shirt pulls taught across his massive back. It's definitely tight, but passable.

He attempts to suck in his gut, tucking in his shirttail and buttoning the pants; the button barely meets the buttonhole. But the pants hold. He zips his fly and fixes his front pockets. He finds the belt and guides it around the belt loops until the buckle meets the tail. Try as he might, it doesn't quite reach. He whips the belt loose and lets it drop to the floor, defeated.

Lastly, he slips into the suit jacket to test the fit. He buttons it across his front: small, but not embarrassingly so. He braves a quick glance in the mirror, decides the suit will have to do, and shucks the uncomfortable get-up off, returning it to the closet.

The whole episode makes him depressed; depression makes him hungry. He thinks of the jellied sweet and sour sauce in the mini-fridge. He musters his will and decides to skip it.

He sits back on the side of the bed and looks over his Saturday list, one last time. He had a productive day. He starts a list for Sunday, and makes a note to listen to his cellphone. Then crosses it out and listens to his cellphone.

"Hi Dad," Dyl says. "I miss you." Heavy breathing. "Grandma bought me a new bike with Transformers on it and those parts that stick out for doing tricks." Flip is not pleased. Dylan's old bike is still big enough, and he hasn't had much success without the training wheels. Coleen is buying Dylan's love, again.

In the background Lynn supplies the words "Foot pegs."

Dylan says, "Feet pigs, for doing tricks like when you stand on the seat and jump over a ramp." More heavy breathing.

"But you are not going to do that," Lynn's faraway voice says.

"Right," Dyl says. "I am not going to do that, until I practice."

Then Lynn is on the phone. "Just wanted to check in." Dyl's voice, some distance away, continues describing, in great detail, his strategy for building a stunt ramp off which he clearly plans to jump his bike. It involves pieces of cardboard. Lynn doesn't seem to hear him at all. "Couldn't make any forward progress today because I spent every free minute cleaning up after the kids. Mom went to a tea with some ladies from church. Which was a mixed blessing. I will try the room phone. Bye." When the message ends he plays it again and is careful not to delete it.

Next he pulls the phonebook from the side table and looks up a number.

"Hello," a gruff, suspicious voice answers.

"Hi Dad," Flip says.

"Who the hell is this?"

"It's Flip. Your son."

"What the hell are you doing calling me? It's late. I'm about to get in bed."

"I want to buy you dinner. You have time to get together sometime soon?"

"You said *you* are buying. Right?"

"Yes."

"Great. Tomorrow night will be fine. I like the food over at the Country Sizzle Buffet. Five o'clock on the dot. Try to be punctual. You were never very punctual. If I don't eat by five-thirty I get grumpy."

The words, "Unlike now," slips out before Flip can stop it. He regrets the comment immediately. Not because his father doesn't deserve it. But instead because he knows there's no point. Byron is as Byron has always been and is far too old to change now. Flip will either have to deal with him as he is or not at all. He would prefer not at all. There is, however, a comforting familiarity to his father's consistency.

"What did you say?" Byron asks, a threatening tone rising to the surface.

"I said five will be fine, Dad. That's fine. See you then. Thanks for meeting with me."

"We'll see," Byron says and hangs up on Flip.

Flip puts the phone in its cradle and lets his fat back and freshly trimmed head flop across the bed. His eyes want to close and he lets them.

A moment later he's joined by several women. Lynn is there, but not Lynn now. Lynn that he lived-in-sin-with, before-marriage-Lynn; before-children, young and happy Lynn who laughs at his jokes and spends long stretches of time wearing no clothes at all. His travel companion and conspirator. Her face fills his field of vision.

"I hate that we have to work," she is saying. "I just want to stay in bed with you all day." She lounges lazily with her naked upper body pressed against his. She's absently tracing circles on his young, hairless chest with sparkly blue nails. "When I'm at work, I think about you all day. Do you think about me?" The truth is he thinks about work when he's at work. But he's always happy to get home. Planning the upcoming wedding is the most stressful thing they've had to contend with as a couple. He's sick of wedding magazines, but looking into her face makes every inconvenience worth it.

"I think about you always," he says.

Vanessa is there too; half-covered in a white sheet beside him. Her hair is out of its sensible ponytail and spread across the pillow behind her. The sheet contrasts her rich skin tone. His head fills with the warm smell of her and again, his mouth waters.

"I will be back to see you on Tuesday," she says with feeling. But when he looks at her face, he sees Aubrey's pale, freckled, sun-kissed cheekbones. He's surprised to see Kev's girlfriend here. But she smiles at him, and giggles a high girly giggle, her tiny tummy fluttering under the sheet, one thin hand reaches to cover her grin as if embarrassed. He doesn't know why, but she seems happy to be there. One of Vanessa's long legs sticks from under the sheet and rubs against the side of his. Her toes flex against his ankle as if she is trying to pinch him playfully with her toes.

Lynn presses her weight down onto his hip girdle and grinds against him. He catches a movement behind her, leans his head around Lynn's face and peeks through her sea-scented hair. He can see another woman sitting with her naked ass between his feet at the foot of the bed. Her back is shapely, her skin creamy and as she turns her profile to him, her silky hair sweeps across her shoulders. Her breasts are engorged with milk to the point of looking hard and painful, and she cradles a nude child to her chest, its mouth latched and suckling at her left tit. The woman from the coffee shop smiles sweetly and invitingly to him. She holds his gaze for a long moment, then gets angry and storms away, switching her round rump, and swaying curvaceous hips as she disappears into the deeper shadows of the room. He wonders how a woman can change from flirtation to vindictive outrage in the blink of an eye.

He seeks comfort by touching Lynn's hair. She still strokes his chest and smiles that familiar smile for him while gently and rhythmically pounding him deeper into the mattress. It's not young Lynn though. It's Lynn from Thanksgiving, from the day of their nature walk. But she looks distant, as if viewed through the lens of a camera. She poses and puts on her best smile, gestures at the spread of food on the dining room table, illuminated in an island of light to his right. He wonders what he's done to deserve the kind of love in her eyes? He fears it's all an act for the camera, for the sake of performance, for history and familial fiction that their progeny can cling to a generation from now. Once the moment's documented, she'll scowl and turn away.

Someone is touching his scalp. He looks through the tops of his eyes and finds his head is resting in Dean's lap. Dean is shirtless, has an upper body like an adolescent. He wears pressed khaki slacks. Chills run down Flip's back and he can hear Dean's carefully enunciated whispers of support.

"Stop it," he says. "Hush now. You are a handsome man. Gay, divorced or both?" he asks. He stops stroking Flip's hair and waits for an answer.

"I don't know," Flip says. "Not gay. I'm sorry. But not divorced either. Not yet."

"Oh just shush," Dean says, smacking Flip lightly on the forehead. "Sometimes what one perceives as a curse might actually be a great blessing."

Flip nods his head in agreement. Dean's voice fades as another sound rises. He finds himself listening to his dead mother. She hums a tune while standing at the sink doing dishes, her yellow gloves dripping with white suds. In the dark of the room, he hums along. He can smell baked macaroni and cheese and the lemony scent of Mr. Clean. He can hear the sizzle of chicken frying in a cast iron skillet. The creamy-smooth chocolate taste of Jell-O brand stove top pudding rolls around inside his mouth.

He rocks his head on his stiff neck and lets his eyes come open again. Sara and Kristin are there side by side, their bodies in an identical pose, knees tucked-up under them and so close they are locking arms. They're both dressed in flannel pajamas like it's a junior high sleepover.

"Your father is very sweet. He was always helpful to me at work. Especially when I first started, I was in over my head. He helped me through and stuck up for me." Kristin says, looking at Sara. They don't acknowledge Flip. Their hair is done up in big curlers that bob as they talk.

"That's nice," Sara says. "Good for you. But where is he when I need him? I am going through some shit." She abruptly crosses her arms petulantly and turns her head away, curlers flailing.

"I got drunk at a conference and hit on Mr. Mellis, your father," Kristin confides. Flip shakes his head in the negative. He doesn't want her to tell that story, but the words don't form in his mouth, the breath doesn't gather in his lungs. Lynn is still pounding him against the mattress, and it's making it hard for him to take a breath.

Kristin nods her head in the affirmative, curlers drop from her hair leaving long twists of luxurious, satin waves. "I hit on him hard. I threw myself at him and hung all over him. I touched him too much and was very obvious. I talked about my sex life. I may have told him I was lonely. I know I told him I was very good at keeping secrets and that I was on birth control. I played with my throat and fingered my blouse, when I was sure his eyes were on me, I unbuttoned another button, claiming it was getting hot at the bar. I asked him to my room, and he was such a gentleman. He helped me to my room, made sure I was safe, took my shoes off and set a trash can next to my bed in case I got sick. He said he was in love with one woman and that that was more than enough. But, he didn't leave. He sat on the edge of the bed for long, tense minutes. Silent. I held my breath so long it hurt. Then, he let himself out." Her amber-flecked brown eyes lock with Flip's.

Young Lynn is back and smiling on his chest. "You *are* sweet," she agrees with Kristin.

"Good for you and Flip," Sara says. She doesn't say, "Dad." She knows this bothers him. Then she slides off the bed. When her feet hit the floor she's tiny, pre-school age with bouncy pigtails. She marches her footy-pajamas over to the bathroom and slams the door. It doesn't shake the room as a good door should.

Flip can see Kristin, Dean and Vanessa all shaking their heads in a combination of empathy and mild disapproval, as if to say, *That one is going to be trouble.* Kristin is now in a too-small baby doll tee. Flip is embarrassed by this and looks to Lynn. She has pulled away from his bloated and furry torso. She is dressed in a series of shapeless layers that keep her body secreted away from his gaze. She's shaking her head too, but there is no empathy in her expression, just the hard line of a mouth and cold, distant eyes. It feels like they bore a hole right through his face and out the back of his head.

He misses the other Lynn. Not the teen Lynn he fell in love with, happy to waste hours simply passing time and feeling in love. He doesn't have the patience for her. But the Lynn from months ago, the Lynn he built a life with, attended his mother's funeral with, friends' weddings, and parent-teacher conferences. He misses that Lynn so much he aches in the centre of his chest. His fat hand comes to rest over his heart to ward off further abuse, and everyone in the room slowly deserts him.

BREAKFAST AND SHOPLIFTING

Though Flip had frantically manipulated the alarm clock the previous morning, he had failed to turn it off or change the time. So on Sunday he wakes to a barely perceptible chirping that has slowly wormed its way into his mind. The chirping is preferable to a happy wake-up serenade, but not by much.

He feels full. He thinks back over how little food he consumed yesterday and marvels that he isn't famished. He has an urge, however, for cheese grits. He hasn't had grits since he was a boy, hasn't even thought of them.

He shifts to a sitting position and listens to his body's interior architecture pop into place. Then he stands on his feet and gets moving. In the bathroom he's shocked when he catches his reflection. The facial hair is just crazy. But it might actually make his face look a little leaner. He considers shaving it, but doesn't want to insult Dean. He'll leave it for the day. The zit in the centre of his forehead is truly gruesome. He squeezes the goo out for half a minute. *That's attractive.*

He steps into the tub and starts the shower. Tiny dark hair bits stick to the white porcelain sides. He catches water in his cupped hands and splashes it around to rinse the hair down the drain.

He does three sets of push-ups to exhaustion, with sets of sit-ups between. He lies on the floor until his body cools. He gets dressed in the same khakis from the previous night and a too-bright-yellow, pineapple-themed Hawaiian shirt.

He slept plenty but needs coffee. He wonders if the Drum Roaster is open. He dismisses the idea. He knows a place he can go to take care of all of his errands at once.

He tears his to-do list from his legal pad, makes certain he's gathered all his dirty boxers in a pile and placed wet towels in the closet hamper, and throws his suit bag over his shoulder. He locks the door behind him.

Outside, the tiki candle has caved in and melted into a dark puddle of hard wax across the tabletop. Larry's tiny hearse is backed into its spot. Flip gets in his car, deposits his suit bag and as he turns the ignition, a dinging bell sounds and an amber light flashes. He's almost out of gas again. He drives toward Bull's Eye: the most perfect one-stop, big-box department store known to man.

He can see the iconic blue building with its over-sized con-centric white circle logo from several blocks away; and though it's early on a Sunday, when Flip pulls in, he finds the lot full. He parks pretty far back and walks it. He's lightly winded when he arrives. Thank goodness the door automatically opens for him.

He hangs a right and grabs a tray at the café. They don't sell cheese grits. He orders coffee and oatmeal and grabs a cup of melon cubes. He doesn't like melon much, but he feels that he's on a healthy roll and doesn't want to jinx it.

The girl at the counter is named Tyrone, according to the name-tag on her apron. She has no eyebrows and wears a cheap wig.

"Will there be anything else," she asks. He wants to figure out the eyebrow/wig issue. His first guess is that she is going through chemotherapy. But, she has a pleasant smile, high-energy and doesn't look or sound ill.

"No. I think that's it. Tyrone."

She touches her nametag, tucks her chin to look at it and laughs. "Forgot to wash my apron again," she explains.

Flip smiles and hands over his card.

"Debit or credit?"

"Debit."

"Would you like cashback?"

"No," he says. "Can you check my balance?"

"Only if you get cashback."

"Make it so," he says, in his best Jean-Luc Picard. No reaction. "Make it twenty please."

She punches some buttons and he enters his PIN. She hands him a receipt and a twenty.

"Thank you, Tyrone. I like your hair," he says in parting.

"Oh. Thank you." She smooths her wig with an exaggerated caress. "I like your beard," she says and points toward his face.

"Really?" He feels his bizarre, high concept stubble, shakes his head and carries his tray to a built-in table.

He pockets his cash and scans his receipt for an account balance. Only a hundred and sixty bucks remain in the account, and he needs to buy supplies to get ready for the interview, buy dinner for him and his dad, gas-up the car and get his suit pressed; among other things.

The oatmeal is bland, the coffee is weak, and the melon reminds him why he doesn't eat melon. But he wolfs it, places his trash and tray in the trash-and-tray-area, and waits his turn for a blue plastic shopping cart.

He unfolds and smooths his list, sets it in the child seat where he can read it and works his way into the stream of angry cart traffic. In Health and Beauty Aids he finds the aisle of hair products. It's crowded with three women, their carts jammed in a knot in the centre of the row. They're animated in their noisy discussion about which brand of hair dryer is quietest.

He snags a tiny tub of goop for his hair and waits patiently for the women's debate to end. They are unconcerned that they block his way and ignore him almost completely. Except for one thirty-something woman in black yoga pants, bright white running shoes and a fitted peach fleece zipper-top. She glances in his direction, evaluates him and turns back to her conversation. All the women gesture with manicured fingers encased in flashy wedding rings.

He reverses direction and heads the long way around to the elastic hair bands. In the next aisle he picks up a box set of teeth-whitening strips, toothpaste and mouthwash. *Expensive but necessary.*

He rounds the corner and has to stop to avoid a tiny blonde girl gawking at the Axe shampoo endcap display.

"Hi there," he says.

"Hi." She doesn't look over at him. She's obviously enthralled by the image of a very athletic-looking woman in tight clothes lathering a young, shirtless man's hair into something that resembles a large dollop of whipped cream. The little blonde girl is dressed in a pastel tracksuit.

"Do you think that his head looks like a dessert?" he asks.

Blondie scrutinizes the image. Then she smiles. "Uh-hum," she says.

"If we put a strawberry on top we would have a nice treat." He places a pretend oversized strawberry on top of the Axe man. He makes a strawberry placing sound effect and says "Yum yum."

Blondie giggles and looks at him. "Your shirt is funny," she says.

"Yes. I agree. It is funny; very yellow. My name is Flip," he says. He pushes the cart a little to the side and reaches over to give her tiny hand a shake. She only stares at him, seemingly confused by the social ritual. He turns his palm up and says, "Give me five." Still nothing.

"You have a funny name. You're funny," she says.

"You don't know the half of it," he says, dryly.

Yoga Pants comes around the corner. "Come here, Caroline. Where did you go? I told you to stay with me." She doesn't look at Caroline. She snaps the sculpted fingernails of her right hand and her jewellery flashes and clicks together. She extends her hand and Caroline moves over to take it. Yoga Pants gives Flip a warning glare, scoops her daughter into her arms and marches away.

"Bye bye, Caroline. Nice to meet ya," he says to the empty space little Caroline had just occupied. He stands up and practices his breathing. A few measured exhalations later he claims his package of extra-thick black hair bands. The aisle is empty, but he can hear the gaggle of women making disapproving clucking sounds from nearby.

In the grocery area he buys fruit.

"Flip?" a woman's voice asks behind him. He turns. She is forty with rounded features and wearing a conservative dress; probably on her way to church. She has her head cocked and is looking closely at him while moving in his direction; the long skirt and stiff upper body gives Flip the impression she's gliding across the store like a ghost. "Flip Mellis? Is that you? Connie. Darnel's wife," she says indicating herself. The clop clop of her heels becomes audible as she approaches, then stops. She stands a couple of feet away, just inside his personal space. She has an uncertain look. He remembers her from various company dinners over the years. She'd hit it off with Lynn one holiday party. Darnel worked in accounting at McCorkle-Smithe. Correction: works in accounting. He's a dud, the kind of guy who wouldn't merit a hug at a surprise birthday party, only a cursory handshake. Flip sees she's trying to decide if the fat man in front of her could possibly be the man she knew. Her expression asks, could this round man with the radical beard be the former marathoner?

"Darnel is around here somewhere," she says, while making a vague gesture toward the front of the store.

"I am sorry," Flip says with a robotic rhythm and a slightly lowered voice. "You must have me confused with someone else. I do not know anyone named Flip."

"Oh. I'm so sorry. You look a bit like someone who used to work with my husband. So sorry." She still isn't convinced.

"It is not a problem," Flip says. "I have one of those faces. People often mistake me for others." *Worst lie ever.* He turns his cart and points it toward the back of the store before Darnel arrives.

"Sorry again," she says as he strides briskly away.

In the Men's Department Flip searches the hanging dress belts for one that claims to be long enough to circumnavigate his own personal equator. He finds a fifty-inch belt in brown. But he needs black, plus when he tries it on his shorts, it's a little snug. That, predictably, makes him feel like eating.

He looks a while longer, because he's nothing if not persistent, and eventually finds a reversible black and blue belt with a giant decorative buckle. He unhinges the buckle and swaps it with something less offensive. It's also listed as fifty inches, but seems to work better. He starts to unbuckle the belt and stops.

He looks around for the dark tinted domes that periodically hang from the ceiling to indicate a security camera. He sees several, but none is in a position where they could easily observe his actions. He impetuously leaves the belt on, rips the tag off, and tugs his shirttail over it.

The theft will save him some money. He feels anxious and excited as he drops a pair of dark dress socks in his cart. He looks at hats he would never buy and T-shirts that are too small, in order to give the impression that everything is normal. He calms himself and decides to check his list before leaving the scene of the crime. He moves back to the dress clothes end of the department and finds a rack of black waistcoats.

He reasons that a black waistcoat will hide many of the problems his ill-fitting suit might cause. He scours the rack to find one large enough. He throws it on and buttons it. It feels good. He considers removing the tag and wearing it out the front door, but knows it would be asking for trouble. Besides, it looks clownish over his tropical muumuu. He drops it in the cart and walks away, making a concerted effort to project innocence.

In Home Décor, he searches the candles until he finds a giant tiki. It's pina colada scented and expensive. He agonizes over the price, but eventually sets it in the child seat.

He's reminded, once when Sara was tiny, he failed to use the seatbelt in a cart, he turned away and she stood, tumbled out and landed headfirst. The top of her skull hit the floor with a hollow crack, followed by a prolonged silence. And when she screamed, it was like the screech of a wild animal, a mix of shock, pain and primal panic. He'd abandoned the cart and rushed his baby girl straight to the ER.

To be careful, he buckles the tiki candle into the child seat, tightening the strap as much as it will allow, before moving toward the front of the store.

Tiny blonde Caroline exits a row of backpacks to Flip's left, crosses in front of his cart and enters the Greeting Cards to his right. Her mother is nowhere in sight. Clearly, the girl has made a break for it again and is wandering unattended. He wants to help her find her mother, but immediately worries it's a poor strategy.

"I bet her mom would freak out again," he says to the tiki candle. The tiki candle pulls a horrible face.

"Well, I can't just leave her alone in the store. What you say we peruse the cards. Maybe we will grab a thank you card for Dean. That'll take the edge off when he sees I have shaved his masterpiece. What say you Tiki Face?" He takes the candle's stoic expression as tacit agreement.

Flip spies Caroline standing transfixed in front of a display. He noses his cart into the next row and hangs out among cards about love, friendship and life's various accomplishments. He can see the top of Caroline's head between sections of cards. It looks as if she's pulling down handfuls of wrapped stickers. He grabs a card from eye level and reads.

Several minutes pass. Flip makes his way through the sympathy cards. *These are the kinds of hollow sentiments Lynn will get if I go through with my plan to kill myself.* He takes down one of the cards, but it seems too morbid to read. It does however, make him imagine the kinds of things people would say about him at his funeral.

"Flip was the kind of man who, like his own father, found a way to abandon his responsibilities when family became too challenging." Or, "He lacked the emotional wherewithal to cope with common human challenges." Or more likely, "He was a once fit man who became too obese to fit in a normal casket. The increased charge for the extra wide casket was significant, but a testament to Flip's capacity to be as much a financial burden on his family in death as he had been in life."

Flip is saved from further speculation when Yoga Pants passes the end of his row.

"Caroline," she calls. "Oh there you are. Where did you go?" There is finger snapping and jewellery rattling.

"Can I buy these?" a tiny voice asks.

"No. Now let's put these back." A horrible shrieking, like a car alarm or a tornado siren starts. "Caroline. Stop it. This is not going to work." More shrieking. "Okay. You can pick one." Abrupt calm.

"Can I have two," Caroline squeaks.

"One." Yoga Pants says, firmly.

More shrill shrieking.

"Two. But that's all. Just pick two and leave the rest on the ground. Someone will clean it up. That's what they're here for."

A moment later Yoga Pants storms past carrying Caroline. Yoga Pants' eyes widen slightly in recognition when she sees Flip. Caroline flaps her sticker packs in farewell and grins broadly over her mother's back. Before she's out of sight she wipes her nose along her mother's peach fleece shoulder. Caroline has a lovely smile with perfectly-spaced miniature teeth and the eyes of a serial poisoner.

"They deserve one another," Flip says to Tiki, who seems content to remain silent. He selects a card with a Van Gogh self-portrait on the front and a blank interior, then leaves.

Flip finds the shortest line, which turns out to also be the slowest. He has forgotten about the belt at his waist, until he reaches into his pants to get his debit card. His rubs the unfamiliar leather strap, and he is instantly nervous. He flings his card across the tiny counter at Kurt, the checkout man.

"Sorry," he says. "It got away from me."

"I got it," Kurt says. He bends and retrieves the card. He passes it back to Flip and touches the keypad in front of Flip. "Just swipe it, enter your PIN and follow the prompts."

"I knew that," Flip says.

Kurt hands him a small receipt and a large fist full of coupons. He bags Flip's purchase and sets the bags in Flip's blue cart. Flip pushes on toward the door where he entered.

"Excuse me," a young male voice says. "Excuse me, sir. May I speak to you a moment?"

Flip turns to see two boys in dark blue store security uniforms.

"Would you come with us," the bulkier of the boys asks, taking Flip by the arm with one hand and grabbing Flip's bags of merchandise in the other. Flip can feel the soft meat on the back of his arm squish under the kid's grip and he feebly pulls away because he doesn't like being touched. The boy doesn't let go. They leave the cart where it is.

On the way, Tyrone watches and makes her eyes big at Flip, her meaty hairless brow arches on her forehead. Flip shrugs.

Darnel and his wife are leaving the checkout with an overflowing cart. Darnel's wife points toward Flip and says something to her husband behind her hand. Darnel looks at Flip closely as they pass. Flip turns his face away.

"That's not him, honey," Darnel says, with absolute certitude.

UNWANTED CONFESSION

The bigger kid steers Flip down a side hall and opens a door marked SECURITY. The room is lit only by a series of monitors set in a console along one wall. A counter that runs the length of the console has three swivel chairs tucked under and a keyboard with a joystick attachment. In the centre of the room is a square folding card table scattered with skateboarding magazines and two open soda cans. The kid releases him.

The thinner one rolls a chair over from the console and offers it to Flip.

"There you go, Mr. Mellis," he says. He smiles and nods like someone might at the end of a joke; as if to say *You get it? Huh? You get it? Pretty funny huh?*

Flip does not get it. He suspects some neo-youth-culture-form of good cop/bad cop.

"This shouldn't take too long, Mr. Mellis." Smiley says. "We will have you on your way in a few minutes." He smacks Flip between the shoulders in an awkward attempt at a supportive gesture.

Realization dawns on Flip, something is amiss. Smiley keeps using his name though he hasn't given it to anyone. His eyes explore the room, trying to find an explanation.

The black and white monitors show bird's-eye views of different departments around the store. On the various screens he recognizes Health and Beauty, Pharmacy, Jewellery, Grocery, Women's Apparel and Sporting Goods. Then the monitors cycle to different cameras and Sporting Goods snaps to Greeting Cards. The light in the room shifts slightly as the monitors change. Flip fears they've used facial recognition software on footage of him stealing the belt in order to ascertain his identity.

Bulky digs around in a drawer under the console and brings out some photocopied forms. Smiley rolls another chair and tucks it across from Flip. He's still grinning like his life depends on it, as he gathers the magazines into a neat stack and places them out of the way. He tosses the soda cans while Bulky brings over the forms and a blue ballpoint pen with a missing lid, claps them down on the table dramatically.

"You know this guy?" he asks Smiley.

"Yes. This is Sara's dad. Mr. Mellis." Then it hits: Smiley is What's-His-Face, Sara's boyfriend. For a split second he starts to relax, the tightness in his chest eases. That explains the smiling; the kid wants to endear himself to Flip. *I can use this*. He suddenly feels back in control.

But relief gives way to utter terror as he realizes his daughter's boyfriend has just busted him for shoplifting. That means Sara will find out, which in turn will play perfectly into the narrative she's created, with little effort, of Flip being a totally inept father; and if Sara hears about it, then Lynn will know, and his mother-in-law. That will be the final nail in the coffin of his marriage; and by extension, his own life. But, at least that would decide things for him. *One less decision to make*.

"Well," Bulky says, thumbs in belt, pelvis forward. "We still need to handle this fair and square."

"Mr. Mellis, this is my supervisor. Jeffery Hartman. Jeffery, this is Mr. Mellis."

"Okay, thanks D. Now pay attention," Jeffery Hartman says. Smiley pays attention.

Jeffery clicks his fingernails on the tabletop and bends a little forward to be closer as he speaks. "Mr. Mellis. A woman came to the front of the store with your description. She explained that you tried to touch her daughter in Health and Beauty. And later she found you watching her daughter in Greeting Cards." *This is great news*, Flip thinks. *They don't know about the belt.* "To be specific," Jeffery continues in a mildly menacing tone. "The woman claims . . ." Serious Jeffery starts reading from an official complaint form: "'The fat man tried to tell my daughter a shirtless man looked yummy to eat. Which clearly has inappropriate and sexual undertones. Then he touched my daughter.'"

"Big misunderstanding," Flip explains. He tries to laugh, but it sounds forced and artificial, as if he were channelling a robot with hiccups.

"It very well may be," Jeffery says, without any commitment and puts his hand up to warn against further interruption. "We have not reviewed the tapes. But we will make a note of the general time, date, and camera numbers. In that way we can assure the digital file will not be deleted. It will be transferred to our archive. In cases like this we have to make a record of the complaint. And if it's founded, we have to hold you for the police, review the tapes and turn over copies of any pertinent visual documentation to the authorities." Though Jeffery is probably fresh out of high school, he carries himself with a self-important authority and grave conviction that Flip is forced to take seriously.

Flip nods soberly. "I understand. May I explain?"

"Sure," D says.

Jeffery frowns and puts a hand on D's shoulder. The two boys look into one another's faces and an understanding passes between them. The shadows in the room shift as the monitors cycle again.

"Sorry," D says.

"Take down what he says," Jeffery instructs.

While D digs in the drawer for the proper form, Jeffery tells Flip, "You need to fill this out with your personal information. I need a photo ID to copy."

Flip hands over his driver's licence and takes up the Bic. He fills out the form with his particulars. He writes down the address of his home, and wonders if he can still call it his home address. D takes a seat, a clipboard and pen in his hand. Jeffery leaves the room with Flip's ID.

When Flip finishes the paperwork he pushes it away. He looks at D who immediately smiles. Flip feels sorry for the kid. He seems so nervous. *He must really like Sara.* And that makes Flip like D, a little bit. The monitors cycle, the shadows jump.

"All done?" D asks.

"Yep. All done."

"Now, in your own words, explain exactly what happened with the little girl in question. Do you recall the incident of touching the girl in Health and Beauty?"

"This is all a misunderstanding, D. May I call you D?" Flip is proud of this dodge, because he really doesn't know the kid's name, never bothered to learn it.

"Yes. Of course Mr. Mellis."

"You may call me Flip if you'd like. Since we know one another. Unless that would be unprofessional?"

"No. No. Flip," he tests out Flip's name. Then he takes it for a test drive. "Flip, between you and me," he says in a hush. "Jeffery wants to be a cop. His dad's a cop. So he takes all this very seriously, Flip. He is very by the book. I think he wishes you were a real perverted creep, so he could turn you over to the police, Flip. But Flip, if your story sounds legit, then we will just let you go. No big deal. Flip."

"That's a relief. D."

"To tell the truth, we know this lady already. She has lost her daughter twice in the store. So Flip, if you work that kind of thing into your statement, I'm sure Jeffery will just file it and that will be that. Flip." D smiles.

Jeffery comes back in the room and returns Flip's ID. He hooks his thumbs into his belt in a stance that looks familiar, but Flip can't quite place it.

"Did you take his statement yet?"

"Just getting going," D answers.

"Let's get it rolling. Remember you just need to paraphrase the important information."

"I remember," D says.

"Mr. Mellis, please explain your interaction with the little girl in question," Jeffery says. The shadows change again.

"Caroline," Flip says.

"I'm sorry?"

"The little girl. Her mother called her Caroline."

"Okay," D says. "I'll make a note.

Flip tells what he remembers. He punches up the parts about the mother not seeming very attentive. He emphasizes that he did not actually touch the girl, but only tried to shake her hand and give her five. He explains that he found her wandering alone in the card aisle and hung around until her mother found her. When he's done he says, "I'm a father who used to have a little girl like that. I just wanted to look out for her, because I miss having a little girl, but not in a creepy way." D's pen continues tapping on the form, he turns the form over and scratches another paragraph.

"Sorry," Flip says. "Did I go too fast?"

"You're fine," Jeffery says on D's behalf.

When D is done Jeffery grabs the form, puts it with some others and draws a stapler from somewhere. He loudly cracks the stapler and drops the paperwork in a slot marked *outbox*.

"I'm going to get back out there," Jeffery says, like a shift commander on a cop drama. "Mr. Mellis, you are free to go. But don't leave town." He sounds so threatening when he says it, Flip nods agreement.

"Can I take my break?" D asks.

"Yes. Take your fifteen." Jeffery looks at his watch, then pulls open the door and exits with purpose, clearly intent on making another big bust.

"Come on, Flip," D says. "I'll walk you out." He picks up Flip's plastic bags but doesn't hand them over.

Outside, Flip points toward the back of the parking lot. "I'm over there," he says and shakes D's hand. The boy looks suddenly ill, his hand is clammy and cold; his face has gone blotchy and slick. Flip sees D isn't smiling anymore. When Flip tries to take his bag, D pulls it away.

"Flip, I'd like to walk you to your car. Make sure you get there okay."

Flip tries for the bag again. Again, D pulls back.

"I really can make it to the car by myself. I'm not that old," Flip says. D laughs without humour and smiles a nauseous smile. "Well, okay. Why don't you just walk me to the car," he says. "And carry my bag." He angles toward his Passat, D follows.

It's a long walk, and D isn't talking, so Flip says, "Oh. Thanks for your help getting the room ready to paint. I hope Lynn paid you for all your hard work."

"Yes. She insisted. No problem. I mean, I was really glad to help. Made me feel like part of the family. Flip, I told Mrs. Mellis she didn't need to pay me, but she insisted."

"Okay." Flip says. They stop as a car backs out, apparently oblivious to the pedestrians they nearly hit. D looks at his shoes while Flip looks at D.

"This is me," Flip says when they reach his car. He takes his keys out and again reaches for his bag. Again, D pulls the bag back. "What the hell, D?"

"Sorry Flip. Mr. Mellis. I mean Flip Mellis. Of course this is your bag. You can have the bag. It's yours." He passes the bag over. "I just had something I wanted to say, something to tell you. That's all. In private." D looks up at the sky and squints. He looks around the lot. He looks back at his feet.

Flip makes a show of checking the time on his watch.

"Okay Flip. I really like Sara, Flip. As you know, Flip, your daughter and I have been dating a little while now. Nearly a year. And we are serious. I really care for her. I love her." He looks Flip in the face now. "Nice beard, by the way, Flip."

"Thank you. What are you getting at?"

D takes in a lot of air and lets it out in a rush of words. "I love Sara and I think she loves me. I want to ask your permission to marry your daughter. I think it would be the right thing to do."

Flip doesn't respond to D directly. He says, "This is a serious issue," and he says, "I appreciate that you came to me. Very mature. I respect that." And he says, "I need to give this my full consideration and get back to you." Then he climbs in the car, his idiot light mocks him, the bell sounds and he drives away.

REGRETTABLE ATTEMPT AT SECOND BREAKFAST

As Flip rips out of the Bull's Eye parking lot, a familiar vertigo surges through him, a sense of balancing precariously on the edge of chaos, his toes just gripping the edge, his body swaying over a bottomless precipice.

Buying a gun from a preacher's kid seems like such a very good idea right now. The emotional see-saw is more than he can handle. One moment he's up, the next he's down. One moment he's excited about being a petty criminal; the next, he thinks he's going to jail. He's getting away scot-free; he's pulled into a disturbing vortex of parental concern that he simply isn't equipped to handle. *What does D mean anyway?* '. . . *it would be the right thing to do.*'

He passes a fast food joint with a giant banner declaring *Home of the Breakfast Burger* next to a giant glistening, full-colour, human-sized image of a burger topped with bacon and a fried egg. He impulsively makes an illegal U-turn in the sparse morning traffic. This earns him a honk and red-faced cursing from a family of four. From the back seat a ten-old-boy with spiky red hair and yellow sweater-vest uses a bible to hide a covert middle-finger salute. For a split second this enrages

Flip beyond all reason and he considers following the car and ramming it or performing the PIT manoeuver, as seen on Cops. Instead he pokes into the Maximum Burger drive-thru lane and waits his turn.

There are several cars ahead of him in line. His face is hot, his eyes water and there is a pressure behind them. He massages his sinuses and wonders what glaucoma feels like. He pulls his car up one spot.

His heart is racing. He rubs his chest with his fingertips. His muscles are sore from the combination of push-ups and physical assault. *Or I need a pacemaker.* He takes a deep breath, holds it, counts in his head, and releases it. He pulls up another spot.

He thinks about seeing his father for dinner. He doesn't want to. Cancelling wouldn't be so bad. Or maybe just not go, stand his dad up, as his dad had done to him his whole damn life. That would be poetic. But he can't. He likes to keep his word and he said he'd be there. He told Dr. Hawkins he'd meet with someone too. Though the criterion was someone who would be supportive and God knows, no matter how much Flip might want it, his father would never offer any kind of support. The car behind him honks its horn.

Flip sees he can pull ahead, but the honking was unnecessary, so he takes his time. He adjusts the Passat's rearview to glare at the car behind him; it's a guy in a super duty work truck. Flip starts to pull up, but his car hesitates, eliciting another long blast from the truck's horn. Flip gives the car more gas and it lurches ahead.

The work truck pulls close. Its giant grill takes up the entirety of his rear-view mirror. The truck's diesel engine revs impatiently.

Good, Flip thinks. "Get pissed off. I don't care. You have to wait your turn. I was here first," he says into the interior of his car. The mini-van in front of Flip eases around the corner. The truck revs. Flip gooses his car's accelerator and he lurches up to the order board.

"Welcome to Maximum Burger. Home of the Breakfast Burger," a very loud and peppy woman says. "Would you like to try our Breakfast Burger Special?"

"Yes."

"Would you like soda, coffee, juice or milk?"

"Coffee."

"Today only, we are offering our special Glazed Donut Breakfast Shake for only a dollar more." The shake sounds simultaneously like a horrible monstrosity and the very best idea he has ever heard. *Why didn't I think of that?*

"Sir? If you would like me to add the Breakfast Shake for only a dollar I would be more than happy."

"I think not. But it was a tough decision."

"That will be five oh two with tax. Please pull around."

Flip stomps the pedal. The car hesitates and stalls. He shifts into park and turns the key. The starter clicks, the engine turns slowly. Behind him the truck's engine races and its horn blasts. Flip twists the ignition so hard he thinks the key is bending. The starter keeps clicking but the engine won't catch. He pumps the accelerator over and over. The idiot light seems to be flashing brighter than normal. The trucker is now leaning on his horn without cease. Flip throws up his hands in exasperation.

In his driver's side mirror Flip can see the truck's door swing open and slam closed. The trucker walks back along the muddy bed of his truck and reaches in, his hand comes out with a claw hammer. The hammer starts moving in Flip's direction. Flip shoves the button to roll his window up. He rocks his bulk to get it moving and tries to climb over his console into the passenger seat. His seatbelt is still buckled, so he's stopped short.

The trucker edges between Flip's car and the Maximum Burger order board. A number of car horns blare from behind the truck. Flip thinks they are honks of support for the threatening trucker. He catches a glance of the hammer being drawn back and leans away from the blow. Though he knew it was coming, the sudden sound of impact makes him yelp like a startled puppy. His driver's side window holds its shape, but is covered in a network of cracks.

"Wise ass," is all the trucker says. He tromps toward his truck, then comes back to punch Flip's trunk lid and smack a brake light with the hammer. "Wise ass," he yells again.

Work boots step in the truck cab and crush the pedal to the dirty floorboard. Flip braces for impact, but the truck manages to miss his rear bumper. When the truck is gone, Flip thinks about trying to record the truck's plate number. All he can recall is the truck sported a my-child-is-an-honor-student bumper sticker.

The next car in line pulls up behind Flip and parks. A silver-haired man gets out and walks to Flip's passenger side window. Flip doesn't see a bludgeon, so he straightens himself and rolls down the window. The Grandpa Man leans his face down and tells Flip to put his car in neutral. Flip does. The old man hunkers down behind Flip's car and slowly shoves Flip into the nearest empty parking spot. Flip gets out and shakes the man's hand.

"Thanks. Sorry about that. I'm grateful for the assist."

"It was no problem. People have lost all sense of civility these days, like wild animals. When there's plenty to go around, everyone gets along. When resources get tight, conflict arises. That's all it is. This economy. It has people on edge. You need me to pull up and run some jumper cables?"

"No. No thank you. I think I ran out of gas."

This earns a mildly disapproving shake of the head. But all the man says is, "I guess you're gonna be okay then." They stand there a few beats. He looks over his shoulder where he has left his car.

"I guess you better get back," Flip says. "I'm Flip by the way."

"Windle."

A teen, whose every fibre exudes misery and dejection, slouches his way out of Maximum Burger in a maroon button-down and a burger-logo apron. He hands Flip his order in a greasy waxed bag and a Styrofoam cup. "Manager says you can have this. But please get your car out of our lot." The kid jabs his hand in his baggy pants and grumps away.

Cars have started bypassing Windle's car in the drive-thru. Flip hands the bag and coffee over to the old man.

"Why don't you take this? Thanks for the help."

"All right then," Windle says.

The walk to the gas station is short but unpleasant. There is no sidewalk and the ground is uneven. Flip's ankles ache. He buys a gallon container and fills it with gas. He regrets the expense and is painfully ashamed that his shortsighted decision-making has led to yet another financially costly mistake. He considers, not for the first time, going back to McCorkle-Smithe and begging for his job back, offering to take a substantial pay cut. *I'd rather be dead.*

On the return trip, his shoulders and hands ache from the sloshing and shifting liquid weight of the gas can. The sun is high and the day humid, as if rain is coming. Fortunately, once the car has gas it starts right up.

Flip isn't hungry for a second breakfast anymore. He takes a moment to look at his list and carefully backs out and hits the road.

Although he's blasting the air conditioning, he rolls down the fractured side-window so he can better pretend he wasn't assaulted by a psychotic redneck. A few miles away he parks and takes his suit to be pressed at the X Press One Hour Dry Cleaner.

"Ready tomorrow morning by 10:00," the woman tells him.

"I thought I could get it in an hour."

"Sunday is only drop off, pick up. Will there be anything else?"

"No. Wait. Yes. Hold on a second."

He steps outside, removes the waistcoat from the Bull's Eye bag and snaps the tags off. Inside, the woman takes the waistcoat and tosses it into the pile.

"Just need this pressed please. No need to clean it."

She gives him half of a perforated ticket. In the car he slips the ticket in his visor and heads home.

At the Lakeside, Larry's car is still backed into its spot and his curtains are drawn. Dean's curtains are wide open, but the space with his car is empty; the puddle of tiki wax has been removed from the veranda table.

Flip works the key to Number Three. He fills out the greeting card: *Thanks for your kindness Dean. It is rare to make new friends at my age.* Then he sets the card on Dean's table and uses the new tiki candle as a paperweight. Flip is wistful at the thought of leaving Dean at the end of the week. But he doesn't intend to be around much longer, one way or another.

He wonders if the motor lodge will refund the second week's rent to Lynn once he's dead? He decides they won't.

Standing in the mouth of the closet, he removes his stolen belt and hooks it over an empty wire hanger. He sees his dress shoes and remembers he intended to buy shoe polish. *Shit*. It was on his list, which he left in the blue seat of his shopping cart. *Again, I say shit.*

In the bathroom he unpacks his shaving supplies and lets the water run. He lathers and plays at shaving his facial hair in different configurations. Eventually his wide face is clean-shaven except for a bit he leaves under his mouth, a nearly unnoticeable tuft hidden in the cast shadow from his lower lip.

He dries his face and applies lotion. He uses his teeth whitening toothpaste and mouthwash. He tries to dry his teeth and apply the teeth whitening strips.

He finds his back pills and pours his palm full. He gets a rough count and swallows two without water. He sets the alarm for 3:00 and tries to sleep.

It takes some time to calm his nerves, slow his brain and drift off. When he's completely asleep the phone starts to ring. He sits up.

"Hello," he says very groggy.

"Mr. Mellis? This is Chad. Thi gave me your number."

"Yes," Flip says. The names make sense, sound familiar, but his brain hasn't woken yet. Then he remembers. "Oh, Yes. Hello." As he talks the slimy strip of whitening film slips slowly off his top teeth and he spits it out on the carpet.

"Do you still want to meet?"

"Yes," Flip says. Though he isn't as committed to the idea as he had been earlier. "I thought Thi said you couldn't meet on Sundays."

"That's right. I have nursery duty today during the service. Wanted to see if 4:30 tomorrow would be okay? I have marching band after school, have to show up, but I can cut out early."

Not at the community college. "Yes. 4:30 is fine."

"Cool. Do you know where the Food Time Diner is?"

"Sure."

"I'll have on a Gamecocks baseball cap. Bring a hundred and fifty dollars cash. 4:30."

"Wait. I can't afford that."

"What can you afford?" Chad asks, clearly annoyed.

"Seventy-five?"

After a long pause during which Flip thinks he might be off the hook, Chad says, "Fine." His tone of voice says it's not really fine.

Chad hangs up. Flip falls back into the bed, rolls onto his side and bunches his pillow. He knows he won't sleep.

The phone rings. Flip starts awake again. The corner of his mouth is wet. When he wipes it away he finds the remaining whitening strip has washed from his mouth in a stream of drool. More ringing. He slowly rolls toward the sound, is closer to the edge than he realized, and tumbles painfully onto the hard floor. More ringing. If he had to make an educated guess, he would say the Lakeside did not splurge on carpet padding during the last remodel. The ringing stops.

Flip rotates his mass onto all fours and looks down at his drooping gut. His hip is going to bruise and his knees are achy. He gets one foot under him and puts a hand on his raised knee, gathering his energy before pushing into a standing position. His lower back doesn't straighten. He forces a fist into the tight knot of muscles close to his spine and unfolds slowly until his back is erect. The light on his phone begins to flash.

He paces around to warm up his back, finds the prescription bottle and pops two more pills. He pushes the code on the phone and Kristin speaks into his ear.

"Just wanted to let you know I have time for dinner tonight if you want to get together and chat about DynaTech." She leaves her number again.

Intuitively, the undercurrent of neediness in her tone scares him, and although the dinner with his father is early and likely to be short, there is no way in hell he will meet with her. *No good could come of it.* Besides, Flip knows she would be appalled by the way he'd let himself go, and he isn't strong enough to cope with the look on her face.

Carefully he lowers his haunches onto the bed, rotates gingerly and lays out flat. He pulls a pillow over his eyes and tries to find a few more moments of peace.

THE LEAST FLATTERING REFLECTION

At the Country Sizzle Buffet, Flip's father is already seated at a booth in front of a plate heaped with food when Flip finds him. It is only five fifteen; the drive had taken longer than Flip expected and apparently Byron couldn't wait.

"Philip?" his dad says. "Is that you? Wow. You got fat."

"Byron," Flip nods as he scuffs his butt across the cracked, padded bench seat. He chooses not to respond to his father's observation.

He scrutinizes his father while the old man salts and peppers his gravy-laden pile of meat and starch: chicken fried steak, a fried chicken leg, a pork chop and a T-bone, mashed potatoes, macaroni and cheese, and hash browns, also a little side of tapioca pudding.

Byron is lean, but not in a healthy way. His flesh is grey, his stubble white, head bald and peppered with liver spots. His cheeks are slack, hollow and seem to be hanging off his jawbone. His eyes have dark bags and the whites are falling into their sockets. His nose is long and drips from his face like a skin stalactite. He has a crust at the corners of his mouth, a silver tooth in the front of his head and his neck is crinkled with criss-crossed folds and wrinkles like a paper bag that's been bunched up and smoothed back out. The sight of his father makes Flip sick and he wants to leave immediately.

"You know who started calling you Flip?"

"Yes," Flip wants to cut the old anecdote off at the knees.

"When you were just big enough to walk, you would run up to me and say 'flip flip flip.' You would hold your little arms up and wiggle your wet fingers 'til I held your hands so you could walk your feet right up my body. Then you'd flip over and land right back on your feet. You would do it for an hour if I would stand there."

"Then you started calling me Flip," Flip finished. "So even though Mom named me 'Philip' after her father, you called me Flip and it stuck. Which always pissed her off a little, which I suspect is why you like to mention it so often."

"I guess you heard it before. You gonna get yourself some food? You're paying. Might as well eat." Byron shakes out a bunch of sugar packs, rips the tops off and dumps a fist full into his glass of tea. The granules collect on the ice cubes until he goes at it with a butter knife, then they burst into an angry cloud and mostly settle to the bottom. Byron takes a swig.

"Ah," he says. "Sweet tea." He stirs it a bit more. "I said are you gonna get food or not?" He points at Flip with the damp butter knife when he says *you*.

"I ate," Flip lies. He'd slept through the alarm; the volume was too low in relation to how exhausted he was. So he'd rushed out without a shower or a watch, much less any kind of food in his gut.

"Suit yourself Mr. Moneybags." Having reminded Flip several times who is responsible for the bill, Byron is ready to get down to business. He tucks a paper napkin in the neck of his pocket-T and picks up a utensil in each fist. He saws off a piece of breaded meat, swipes it through some gravy and mashed potatoes and chews with his mouth open. The sound is wet and violent and he grunts and breathes through his mouth as he goes. After a while he reaches deep into his maw and pulls out some gruesome, mangled bit.

"Gristle," he explains. Then he picks up the chicken leg and crunches through the glistening skin.

"Dad," Flip says.

"Go ahead."

"I need to talk to you."

"Go the hell ahead I said."

Flip shoves the table away from his middle a little. Byron's tea sloshes a bit and Byron glares at Flip. "God damn it if you haven't changed a bit since you were a whiny little baby." Flip knows generally what's coming. He'd heard it before.

"When you were born you was a little runt. You needed your mommy all the time. No one else would do. You were jaundiced and had the colic. You didn't sleep at night, and you wouldn't wake up during the day. Plus, you had a weak stomach, so you shit yourself about every ten minutes and when your momma went to change ya, you'd shit and piss all over her if she didn't move out the way.

"When you weren't crappin' you were spittin' up curdled milk and strained vegetables. You ate so many carrots you turned orange, like one of them little singing midgets from that candy movie. The point I'm making is you were a mess. And looks like you haven't changed so much after all." Byron takes a big pull of tea and some runs down his chin. "Except you got fat."

"I was a baby. That is how babies are. My two kids had some of the same issues. Did you know I have two children? They both had the same kinds of issues. They grew out of it. I grew out of it too. Oh wait. You wouldn't know that would you, because you weren't around the house much. Were you?"

"No. I suppose not," he admits. "Is that why you brought me here? Try and make me feel like a bad father? Mission accomplished. I was a shitty father. Better than my old man. But only because I paid my child support and didn't hit anyone." Flip lets the comment pass. But he knows the child support had started out spotty, and eventually stopped all together.

Byron gnaws the residual scraps of flesh from the chicken's leg bone and lets the remains of his carnage fall on the table. Then he goes back in for more breaded meat and gravy.

"Well. That isn't what I want to talk about. I wanted you to know that I moved out of the house for a little while."

"Ho ho," Byron says triumphantly, gravy-tinted spittle spraying across the table.

"I lost my job at the beginning of the year, money is tight and Lynn and I are fighting so we're taking some time. That's all."

Byron grins like a shit-eating opossum. "Not as easy as you thought huh? Being married? You remember any of the bullshit you said to me over the years about how you would be a real man, not like me? How you weren't like me? You wouldn't make the same mistakes? You remember that? Well the chickens have come home to roost is what I would say," he said.

"Dad. I know I said some harsh things. I was young and pissed about not having you around, angry how you treated Mom and me. I was trying to let you know I was hurt, standing up to you out of loyalty to Mom. Besides, this isn't the same."

"You said you were better off without me and that leaving was the best thing I ever did for you. That's what you said." He takes the last bite of chicken fried steak on his fork and smears it with the last of the potatoes before stuffing the oversized bite right in his face. He works his jaws in an exaggerated way, like a horse chomping a whole apple. But he continues to glare right at Flip.

"Yes. I said those things. And I'm not sure they were wrong to say. I still feel that way about it. Mostly."

Byron swallows hard and follows it with sweet tea. "Well. You are still full of shit and think you're better than me. But at least you're man enough to stick by what you think. Right to my face even. So that's something. Maybe your balls finally dropped." He picks up the pork chop with both hands and starts chewing the meat away from the bone.

"I asked you here though to tell you something else, Byron."

"Why you always call me 'Byron'? Why don't you call me Dad? You never called your mother Belinda. Did ya? No. You didn't. You called her Mom."

"Byron. She raised me. You are practically a stranger to me, more bad memory than reality."

"Well at least you have a good reason. Not just to be an asshole to me then?"

"Not today, Byron. Maybe in the past," Flip admitted. "But not today."

"Go ahead then. What did you bring me here for? What do you have to tell me? 'Cause if you want money, I don't got any." He drops the half-eaten pork chop back on the plate, grabs another paper napkin from a chrome dispenser and scrubs it on his face, leaving bits of napkin crumbs stuck to his cheeks and chin whiskers.

"To be perfectly clear, I've never needed money worse in my life than I need it right now. But, I would never ask you for help. Never." Flip's voice is getting loud and shaky. Several tables of elderly diners look his way. One man twiddles with a hearing aid; if it's to turn it up to eavesdrop or to turn it down, Flip doesn't know. "Shit. This is pointless. I don't know what I was thinking." He starts to slip out of the booth, but the tops of his thighs press against the underside of the table, impeding an abrupt exit.

"Cool your jets," Byron says. He puts out his hands in a slow down gesture. "You gotta pay for this. Besides. Least I can do is trade you a little of my attention for some free grub. So you have my attention. At least until I finish my tapioca puddin'."

Flip settles. After a few moments he says, "My court-appointed counselor thinks some of my recent actions might be related to how I feel about you. I am supposed to talk to someone. Tell them what I did."

Byron takes all this in. By the look of his face it's clear he wants to say something, take another verbal jab, but he stops himself and only nods before shovelling some macaroni and cheese onto his fork. Flip appreciates his restraint. It's very unlike the Byron Flip remembers. *Maybe people do change. Even mean old bastards.*

"So," Flip continues. "I tried to kill myself. That is how I ended up being forced to see a counselor."

Byron's mouth stops mid-chew.

"I tried to hang myself and Lynn found me." Flip can't look at his father.

Byron doesn't speak. Instead he finishes his pork chop. Then he goes at the T-bone the same way, kind of like he's eating ribs. When he's done he knocks out the last of the mac and cheese. He uses the hash browns to sop up the remaining gravy.

In the long silence, Flip watches his father and remembers this from his childhood: Byron always wiped his plate completely clean with something. When Byron's plate looks as if it hasn't been used, he pushes it aside.

He takes the napkin from his throat, snorts, clears his throat and hacks something into his mouth. He rolls it around on his tongue, then spits it into the napkin. He balls all his soiled napkins on the plate.

"Let me tell you about what changed my perspective on marriage," he says to his son. "Just hear me out. I know it's wrong to speak ill of the dead. But what I'm about to say needs to be said." He pauses to give Flip time to object. Flip doesn't.

"When your momma was pregnant she told me flat out that she was not at all interested in me. What she was interested in was making a baby boy and since I'd played my part she was done with me, I could just go. I thought it was the hormones talking 'cause women can get a little crazy during a pregnancy. And I would be damned if I was going to leave my wife while she was carrying my baby, so I stuck around. But after you were born, she still didn't want me. And neither did you really. You were a miserable momma's boy. I loved you like I never loved nobody else my whole life. But I felt like I was an intruder in the relationship you and your momma had. So, eventually I went."

He peels the plastic wrap off his tapioca and starts eating it. As he scrapes the glass dish clean he says, "I got the skin cancer real bad. I'm not going to be around much longer. All my money will be eaten up by the bills. If I had some extra, I would help you out."

Flip doesn't know how to respond. Thinks Byron is just jerking his chain. So he just stares.

"You remember that time I taught you to swim?" Byron asks.

"I remember you threw me off the end of a dock and watched me struggle."

"It's true. But, once you quit fighting it so hard, once you relaxed, you just floated right to the top and splashed right back to the dock. I bet you still know how to swim, don't you?"

"Yeah, Byron," Flip admits. "I guess I do."

"That's good."

Byron pushes out of the booth. "Thanks for dinner," he says it as if he means it and then adds, "Wish we'd done it years ago. You know how to get a hold of me if you want." Then he turns and leaves Flip.

In the moment, it's easiest for Flip to simply dismiss everything his father has said as bullshit, because if what he said about Flip's mother was true it changes the emotional calculus his whole life is built on. And if his father really does have skin cancer, well it means Flip will have no family left except Lynn and the kids. Which shouldn't matter, but it does.

Flip takes the bill and scoots himself out. He reaches in his pocket, comes out with three crumpled dollars, realizes he left the house without his debit card or the twenty bucks he'd got at Bull's Eye. He takes the three ones, smooths them and leaves them for the busboy, then he heads to the bathroom.

In the mirror he sees his father: years younger, much heavier, with plenty of hair and lighter eyes. But still, the same face. He tried so hard over the years to be more, better than Byron. But he's not really so different after all. Despite everything, he's still his father's son.

Flip walks out the front door and drives away.

Again, the orange glow from the idiot light radiates the message that his car is low on gas and the bell repeats the reminder. Flip knows he should swing by a gas station on the way home, just to be safe. But he willfully ignores good sense. *I already bought the gas can*, he reasons. *So all it'll cost me is time if I run out of gas again. So fuck it.*

He swings by Ed's Drive Thru Liquors.

At the window he says, "I want Captain and a six pack of Coke."

"Do you want Traditional Spiced, Silver, or Private Stock?" the woman asks. Her voice is rough from smoking and drinking.

Her face is leathery and desiccated from too much sun, her age impossible to guess.

"Spiced. A big one."

"Sorry sir," the woman tells him. "Sunday sales are limited to beer, wine, cigarettes and other non-alcoholic beverage choices." She reaches her hand out the window and points to a sign that has the same information printed on it. Her skin is slack and brown on her bony hands, but her nails are glossy, two-tone, white over hot pink with tiny plastic jewels.

"Are you shittin' me?" he asks.

"No sir. I shit you not," she replies.

"Why did you ask the kind of booze I want then?"

"Force of habit," she rasps.

"Forget it," he says with real disgust and tries to peel out of the lot.

He parks back at the Lakeside and turns off the engine. In the dark of the car he sits with the heat leaching out of the engine block; it ticks like a time bomb as it cools.

He sits alone a long time, waiting for something. His breathing slowly settles into an easier rhythm and he can't find a good reason not to go to his room. He intentionally leaves the shattered driver's side window down when he exits the car.

He wants to see if Dean has any liquor he can have to drink alone. But Dean's car is gone. He notices that the card he left under the new candle is missing. He drops his keys twice before managing to unlock his door. He turns off all the lights and spreads himself across the bed.

He's hungry. He thinks about the Chinese food in the mini-fridge. He tries to recall how many days it's been sitting. Two? Three? He guesses it's still good, but he doesn't get out of bed.

BULLSHIT FOR BREAKFAST

He sleeps until eight forty-five and wakes according to his own internal rhythms, without the startling jolt of the alarm clock. He actually feels rested. Maybe for the first time in months he got enough sleep and doesn't wake irritated by his life.

His joints are stiff, so he takes some time to stretch. He does push-ups and sit-ups. He cleans his body, puts his dirty clothes back on and goes out for a walk.

"Thanks for the card," Dean says from over a cup of press-pot coffee.

"Thank you again for the haircut and shave," he replies. He rubs his smooth face guiltily.

"It looks good like that," Dean says. "You want to sit and have a cup of coffee?" Dean delicately touches the plunger on his cafetière.

"No thanks. I'm going to get a little air. Then I've got a call to make. Can I take a rain check?"

"Suit yourself," Dean says. He shakes a skinny brown cigarette from a pack and rests it in the corner of his mouth. "Thanks for the candle too," he says, the cigarette bobbing. He picks up the tiki candle and holds the flame to his cigarette. "I am happy to have you as a neighbour," he adds. "For your sake though, I hope your stay is short."

"It will be," he replies, giving Dean a friendly wave as he goes.

Flip expels the sharp smell of smoke from his nose as he strides out toward the road. His feet dodge puddles that have pooled in potholes and low spots during the apparent storm the night before.

He doesn't have a destination, but ends up at the Drum Roaster. The toes of his shoes have soaked through and his feet are cold and damp. He walks in the door and stands in line behind two men in business suits, a woman in Dora the Explorer nurse's scrubs, and a guy dressed in white painter's pants and a check flannel shirt.

When he makes it to the counter, a pleasant thirty-year-old woman he doesn't know takes his order.

"Small coffee. Black."

"Will that be all?"

"Yes please."

He pays and sits, sips his scalding coffee for a while, watches people with places to go rush in and out and envies their apparent industriousness.

He only drinks half the mug and places what's left in a black bin near the door. He takes a long way back to the Lakeside. Dean is not in his chair, but a lone cigarette stands on the tabletop on its filter end, slowly burning down.

Once in the room he realizes he forgot to eat.

He thinks of showering again and putting on fresh clothes.

He notes that he needs to go to the laundromat.

He thinks of walking again to get breakfast.

He weighs the pros and cons of walking for breakfast versus driving for breakfast.

Then he realizes he's stalling.

He takes out his yellow pad and sits on the side of his bed near the phone. He dials the number for DynaTech Solutions and a woman answers.

"This is Myrna Mays. How may I help you?" She sounds like a young go-getter.

"Myrna. Ms. Mays. Hello. This is Flip Mellis. I received a message that DynaTech Solutions would be interested in setting-up a time for an interview . . ."

"Oh, Mr. Mellis, so good to hear from you. I was expecting your call. I have your file on my desk somewhere. Here it is. Are you available for an interview this week?" She sounds genuinely excited.

"Yes." He loudly turns the pages of his legal pad to give the impression he's looking over his calendar. "I think I can find time in my schedule." His throat constricts and squeaks slightly with involuntary feelings of enthusiasm and anxiety. He holds the phone away and clears his throat. "I'm just getting over a cold," he explains. "Excuse me if my voice is a little tired. What day is good for you?" he enunciates with exaggerated calm.

"Well. Let me see." She seems to change her mind. "Actually, Mr. Mellis, let me give you a little background. We have already interviewed two other candidates for this position. And including you, we will interview three more this week. The response to the Director of Internal Communications posting has been amazing. We received over eighty highly qualified applications for the position. And well over a hundred and twenty total. That's triple the normal volume of response we've had for similar job openings over the past few years. Of course, with unemployment so high, we expected a substantial response. But this was far beyond our expectations."

"How many candidates do you intend to interview?" Flip is busily scratching out notes on his legal pad, trying to glean as much information as possible.

"We invited six people to interview. One of those applicants has accepted another position and just moved to the east coast. Given that, the total will be five, including you."

"Yes. Great. I'm very excited about the position. I feel like my skill set would be a good match for DynaTech's needs. From what I know about your corporate culture, I would feel very much at home there," he says. It's a complete fabrication, but sounds pretty convincing as it comes out of his mouth. He thinks again about Kristin, wonders if he should call her after all. It would be the smart thing to do. But as needy as he feels right now, as emotionally spent, he might not be able to resist her advances if she chose to make them. Although honestly, given the shape he's in, not even a desperate, lonely woman with unresolved daddy issues would be interested. *Unless she were blind too.*

"Oh really? What have you heard?" Myrna asks.

"Excuse me?"

"What have you heard about DynaTech's corporate culture?"

Shit. He drops his pen on the floor. He was sidetracked and hadn't anticipated a follow-up question to his bullshit.

"The usual," he says to buy some time. "I'm sure you are aware of DynaTech's reputation," also a bluff.

"Well yes. We are a growing company in the U.S. market. I've been here for four years. In that time this office has tripled in size. My perspective is as an insider. I'm really curious about your impressions," Myrna prods him politely.

"Okay." He tosses the pad of paper beside him, stands and starts to pace. He once read, in a book on public speaking, that if you stood and moved around it would make you sound lighter and more assertive. "I understand the environment is professional; but not cold. While DynaTech employees are qualified and skilled experts, it is not a competitive culture. Instead there is a sense of support among peers and a healthy striving for excellence that helps lift all boats." When he's done, he isn't sure what he said or if it even made sense. He wants to ask Myrna if it formed a complete thought, if it was just gibberish. But he holds his breath and waits. The pause is excruciatingly long.

"Thank you for that Mr. Mellis. That's good to hear. I would like to think that's an accurate assessment," Myrna says. She sounds distracted as if she's taking notes of their conversation. He imagines she's holding a file with his name on it. The file has his application and resumé, and now some version of the story he just generated.

"Have you already heard from the references I provided?" he asks.

"Yes. Yes. I have them right here. All very good."

"That's great to hear." He is careful not to sound surprised. *Why should I be surprised? I was good at my job, worked hard and was well liked. I think.*

"So what day works for you Mr. Mellis?" He sits back on the bed and snatches up his pad, scoops his pen from the floor. "I will make time in my schedule. Whatever is most convenient for you is fine with me. I will make it work. I'm a problem solver who gets things done. So, I will make it work. This opportunity is my top priority."

"Great to hear. How about tomorrow at 10:30?"

Oh my God. Too soon. I'm not ready for this. He wants to say *no*, but he says, "Yes. Fine. That should be just fine. I have a few things to rearrange. But, I'm happy to do it. I look forward to it. The sooner the better."

"They will have your name at the security desk. Just let them know you have an appointment with me: Myrna Mays in HR. They will call me when you arrive. You can expect the interview to take a couple of hours. First, we will take care of some paperwork, you'll get a tour, at least of the Communications Department, and we'll get you in with some of the senior executives. I know Mr.

Krueger will want to meet with you. He's the one who makes the final decision, very hands on. Any questions?"

"Yes. Actually, I am curious about the other two candidates yet to be interviewed. Have they contacted you already?"

"Yes. They will be coming in this afternoon."

Flip is happy about that. He would rather be first or last. Either set the bar or have the last impression. Interviewing in the middle of a pack is just a recipe for getting lost in the shuffle. As he thinks this, he realizes he really doesn't know that to be true. It's just something else he read in a self-help book once; probably something Lynn bought for him, likely it's now lying in a landfill reeking of Samuel Adams. But the notion sounded right to him, so he adopted it as fact.

His nerves get the best of him and he adds, "Saving the best for last?" *Stupid.*

"Yes. Well. See you then Mr. Mellis. Please bring a picture ID." Myrna Mays hangs up.

Flip holds the pen tip over the legal pad and attempts to recall everything from the exchange. His mind keeps turning to Lynn.

There's a scenario playing in his mind: He's back in their house, in the kitchen. The remains of a family meal are scattered across the table between them. He sips the last of his wine. The house smells like baking cookies. Dyl is on the floor rolling Matchbox cars over the linoleum and making engine sounds with his lips. Sara cleans plates and loads the dishwasher. Flip clears his throat and proclaims: "I've been offered a job." Lynn looks at him with pride. Dyl jumps around with five-year-old-enthusiasm, but with no real concept of the implications. Sara leaves the water running at the sink to hug him around the neck from behind, her cheek pressed to his. It's all he can think of for many long minutes.

HATEFUL PEOPLE
ARE HATEFUL

Flip kicks off his shoes and peels off his rain-wet socks. He strips an oversized pillowcase from the bed and stuffs it full of dirty clothes. His dry-sock-feet go back in wet shoes that he leaves unlaced. He throws the sack over his shoulder like Santa Claus and lugs it out the door.

The Passat's shattered driver's side window is still down, the driver's seat and door panel are soaked. Flip is on a mission, so he is unperturbed. He pitches the dirty clothes in the trunk and heads back inside.

He throws a couple of dry towels over his shoulder, grabs all his dress watches and locates his cellphone. He dries off the car's interior the best he can, folds a towel as a cushion to keep his rump dry, and sits sideways in the seat, his feet still on the asphalt. He hears the car's suspension squeak as it shifts under his weight.

When he reaches around the steering wheel to turn the ignition, the orange light shines on the side of his face and the bell chimes. He opens his phone and dials home.

"Hello," his mother-in-law says.

"It's Flip."

"I know that."

"Is Lynn in?"

"Of course she isn't. She's at work. She works for a living. To keep bread on the table and a roof over her children's head." Flip can hear the TV in the background. He knows his mother-in-law is sitting in the den, watching her soaps and drinking hot tea as she lectures him.

"Can you leave a message for her?" No response. "Please?"

"Yes. I suppose I will do that. What is it?"

"I have a job interview. I was able to schedule it for tomorrow. Can you tell her that, and ask her to call me when she can? I will have my phone with me."

"Well, bully for you."

"Can you just leave the message?"

"I said I would."

"Fine."

"Fine," then before he can hang-up she adds "Oh, don't expect a call today though. She's going straight from work to an appointment of sorts. Kind of like a date. Seems to me she is getting on with her life. Maybe you should just do the same."

"What do you mean *a date*," he asks. His mother-in-law hangs up. He calls back, but it goes to the machine. *Mean old bitch*. He hangs up without leaving a message.

Of course, he knows she's just making trouble. *Probably.*

He dials Lynn's work number. *Ring.* He isn't supposed to ever call her at work. *Ring.* She worries about it. *Ring.* Her boss gets irate when people take personal calls on the clock. *Ring.* But he needs to hear her. Just for a moment. *Ring.* An automated voice service answers.

"It's me. I wanted to let you know I have a job interview set for tomorrow. If you could call me sometime, I can give you the details." He wants to say more, to ask about her evening plans. He doesn't though. He says, "Bye," and disconnects the call.

He pulls his legs in the car and closes the door a little too hard. He worries he's made the window worse. It wouldn't take much for it to come completely apart.

It takes him long minutes to decide what to do next. His fingers clench and release the cold steering wheel. The conversation with the ancient-she-devil, Coleen, bothers him. First, he doesn't know why she's such a venomous, deceitful wench and second, he's afraid she's telling the truth. He thinks of Lynn in her new, low-cut blouse, shapely skirt and heels for the appointment with Dr. Hawkins. The doctor certainly seemed to notice. An image of Lynn wrapped in a sheet on the doctor's bed jumps unbidden to mind. The doctor sits naked and damp from sex on the edge of the bed, a phone to his ear. On the other end of the phone, Flip obliviously yammers on about his insipid life.

Flip smashes his fist into his car horn repeatedly. *Fuck. That. Can't. Be. True.*

His hand smarts. He shakes it out and counts his breaths. Larry opens his door and pokes his head out. He sees Flip in his car and gives a hard look. Flip shrugs and makes a show of looking around for whoever was honking a horn. Larry looks around the lot too. Then he pulls his head in and closes his door. Flip realizes his car is just eating gas, so he puts it in drive and goes.

The Quickie Mart's pumps are open and Flip stops to fill up. While the car's tank fills, he tries to calculate how much money he has in his account, but he doesn't have a head for numbers and he can't seem to focus. He's sure it's not much. Inside, a dark, round young woman takes his card.

"Will it jus be da gas for you today din?" She asks with a Pacific island accent. She smiles and her whole face shows it.

"I haven't had any breakfast yet."

"Oh. Well you have ta have someting for breakfast. Let's get you off ta a good start today." She turns a little to her left and points to a basket of fruit and individually wrapped muffins. She has a head full of long dreadlocks pulled into a high ponytail. It makes her head look like an exclamation mark. He likes that, it makes everything she says seem exciting.

He hustles over and grabs a mushy Red Delicious and a nearly green banana. While she rings up the fruit, he looks at her chest to find her nametag. She catches his gaze.

"Fix your eyes on my tits, why don't cha?" she says. "You git yourself a good look?" She lifts her bosom with both hands and shakes it. "Is dat what you are aftah?"

He shakes his head, eyes wide, and takes a step back from the fleshy spectacle. She finishes the transaction and flicks the debit card at Flip's head. He bats it away reflexively, then retrieves it from the floor.

"No," he says. He grabs his fruit.

"Go on, you dog. Git out ah here," she makes a shooing gesture.

"I was looking for your name. I was just looking . . ." He tries to explain as he backs toward the door, his fruit cradled in his arms.

"Yeah. You were lookin' all right. I saw ya sure enough," she reaches her hand into the nearest display. "Have a good look at dis now," she says, and hurls a stick of beef jerky at him.

He dodges away from the dried meat projectile and stumbles out of the door, dropping his fruit and stepping on his banana.

He can see her still, behind the counter, her mouth moving and arms waving in an animated rant; with herself or with him he doesn't know. But she keeps talking and gesturing as he peels the banana from the cement and drops it in a can by the door. She makes more shooing signs as he examines his horribly misshapen apple, soft white meat bursting from its split red skin, all around the point of impact.

He moves to dispose of it too, but the volatile islander is rounding the counter and reaching into another display, still talking. He clutches the apple and runs to his car, looking back over his shoulder. He trips on his untied shoes, falls hard and skins his hands and knees, his nose stops inches from the front bumper of his car.

"Serves ya right you mangy dog," the woman yells. Something small and hard hits the back of his arm as he gets to his feet. He keeps hunched over in case she throws something else, and gets his keys from his pocket. He looks back at the Quickie Mart and sees the woman go back behind the counter and put a phone to her ear. She points at him, still talking.

Before getting in the car he brushes the grit from his palms. He sees a brand new, purple, disposable lighter on the ground between his feet. He rubs the back of his arm, takes the free lighter and his damaged apple and goes.

The X Press One Hour Dry Cleaner is attached to the X Press Laundromat. Flip parks, grabs his mashed apple, gets out, and hoists his pillowcase full of clothes. The Laundromat is bright, clean and nearly empty. The sterile interior and strong scent of detergent remind him of the hospital. His fingernails find his wrist, but he stops himself from clawing. His roughed palms itch from the gravel, and they look chewed-up, but not bloody.

A man with a fifty-year-old face and shaved head is at the back table folding towels. He wears a black leather biker jacket over a white T-shirt and cutoff jean shorts. When he sees Flip he makes the tiniest nod of acknowledgment, then pulls more hot towels from his wire basket.

Flip dumps his clothes at a table near the door and sorts them into three piles. He remembered to bring the twenty he got from the cashier at Bull's Eye and uses the change machine mounted to the wall to get quarters. He loads three washers, buys detergent from a pay-dispenser, sprinkles it over his clothes and drops the lids. He places seven quarters in the appropriate slots of each machine. He checks the load-size-knobs and the temperature setting knobs, then shoves the coins home. All three machines start to fill with water. He does his best to find some eatable portions of his apple, while he waits for the clothes to begin their wash cycle. One at a time, the washers stop making water-running sounds and start making clothes-oscillating sounds. He discards what's left of his apple in the trash outside, grabs his ticket stub from the car's visor before going next door to the dry cleaner.

There's a woman, with a blond-headed boy pulling on her skirt, already in line.

"Momma? Momma? Momma? Mommm Mahhh!" the little boy is saying.

"I'm sorry," the mom says to the woman at the counter. She places her hand on her son's head and strokes him. It isn't a loving gesture exactly, but it is intimate and it seems to soothe the child. "He wants to know if he can have a lollipop," she explains.

"Oh yes. Sure. What kind does he like?" The counter woman, the same one who took his suit the previous day, pulls a plastic screw-top container with a wide mouth from under the counter. It's filled to the top with colourful, individually-wrapped lollipops. Flip thinks they look pretty good. He might ask for one himself.

"We have green apple. We have red cherry. We have blue flavour. What kind you like?" She comes around the counter and kneels down next to the child as she speaks. She tips the container in his direction.

The boy looks up to his mother for reassurance. The mother smiles and nods and makes a 'go ahead' gesture. He looks at the counter lady. She smiles and nods too, holds the container a little closer to the boy. His face is wet with tears and the space between his nose and upper lip is slick with green-tinged snot.

He uses the back of his hand to smear it around, and then plunges the same hand into the lollipops, starts feeling around as if the ones on the bottom might be superior to the ones right on top. Flip decides against asking for a lollipop.

"Just one, Donny," his mother says. She holds up one finger, but Donny isn't looking. She leans down to assist.

He continues to paw among the bright sugar spheres, eventually squeezes as many as he can into his small hand and pulls them out.

"Just one," she says again, and holds one finger in front of his face. She starts to pull lollipops out of his grasp and drop them back where they came from.

"Mommm Mahhh," the boy wails. Clearly he believes he is being wronged.

"Donny," she warns. "You keep this up and you won't get any lollipops. Understand? No lollipops."

"It's fine. It's fine," the counter woman says. She stands and moves back around the counter. Donny still clutches four lollipops in his hand, paper sticks poking out in every direction.

The mother, obviously embarrassed by her son's behaviour, looks diminished by the defeat. She takes a hanger full of men's suits from a hook and turns to leave.

She notices Flip for the first time. "He usually isn't like this," she says. "He just got back from Grandma's house."

"I've been there," Flip says. "It can take days to de-program." She gives a weak smile.

"Come on, Donny," she says.

Flip moves to the door and holds it for them to exit. Donny walks past, chewing the clear plastic cellophane from the top of a green lollipop and spitting the wrapper on the ground as he walks. He tries to stick the lollipop in his mouth, but the stick from another lollipop pokes him in the eye. He wails and drops the whole handful. Flip lets the door close on the cacophony as Donny loses all control.

He lays his ticket stub on the counter.

"Very good," the woman says. She takes the ticket, turns and presses a big red button on a control box that hangs down from the ceiling on a thick cable. There's a clacking sound reminiscent of a very large toy train set, and three levels of hanging clothes start to spiral up, around and down again in a whirling helix of attire. Abruptly she lets off the button and the contraption stops; several hundred grouped outfits sway in unison. She pulls down Flip's clothes covered in thin plastic sheeting and deposits them on a hook next to the register.

"Just press," she confirms. "No dry clean."

"Right." He pays with his card and leaves, stepping around crushed lollipops on the pavement on his way to the car, where he lays his interview suit flat in his trunk.

The man in the biker jacket is gone when Flip returns. The washers are quiet. He lifts the lids of his three machines and finds his clothes are clean, wet and plastered to the sides of the perforated tubs.

He steers over a wheeled wire basket and pries slabs of damp clothes from the first washer. He wheels over to a giant front load drier and pitches the clothes in. He drops a quarter in and twists the knob. The drier churns to life and he watches his clothes tumble and knock into each other.

Tomorrow is on his mind. He tries to form a picture of Myrna Mays in his head, what her office might look like. She had a tight little voice, so he sees her as little, buttoned-up in a professional grey pants suit. Her office is tidy and small. In his mind he chooses one of the two seats made available for guests.

"I see here you have been out of work for the better part of a year," she chirps. She reads from a pile of papers stacked square on her desk. Her fingers mark the place where she stops and she looks to him for a response. Her eyes are like Lynn's: green and clear and direct. He leans forward to hear her more clearly, before speaking in a casual, friendly voice.

"Yes. I have been between jobs." He tries to soften the situation with a euphemism.

"Sometimes we find employees who have been out of work for so long have a difficult time returning to work. Have you been doing anything during your down time to stay prepared for work?"

"That's a great question," he says. But he can't imagine a response. *I'm in trouble.*

He starts working on the dark load of clothes. A sudden metallic keening startles him, he twists his neck to look quickly, and it kinks painfully. His hand comes up to rub the injury, and he watches a van barrelling too fast toward the laundromat's front entrance. The strained grinding of worn brake pads trying to grip worn rotors intensifies. The van's front wheels hit the kerb with enough force to bounce up and onto the walkway, a mere three feet from the front door. Flip, trying to back away from the potential collision, presses himself so hard against the bank of washing machines, he shoves the interlocked mass across the tiles; just a bit.

As quickly as it started, the danger passes; the van stops, the engine isn't turned off so much as dies with a hard cough and a series of sputters.

Flip turns back to his work, his hands shaky as they continue to pull at his clothes. He keeps an eye on the van. Through the windshield he sees a couple, probably eighty years old. They're packed into the front of a van whose cargo area is crammed with stacks of old newspapers and magazines, and pile upon pile of plastic grocery bags, filled with unseen contents, their handles tied closed with coloured shoelaces. He's reminded of a bag lady's shopping cart, only enclosed and motorized.

The van was once white, but the paint has worn down until the dusty grey primer shows through. The passenger side door creaks open loudly and the woman gets out. Her door is smashed-in and rusted along the peaks and corners of the damaged area. The dent is evidence of a violent wound.

She's bent with age, wearing a faded, snap-front housedress, and she struggles to force the door shut. The housedress is not unlike other such garments Flip's seen old women wear, but has never seen for sale anywhere. In fact, she and old Mrs. Wallace from the Lakeside might shop at the same store. He watches her shuffle her slipper-feet to the back of the van, the hot smell of oil and metal seeping in through the door.

He takes his dark load of clothes over to another drier, adds a quarter and turns the knob. He checks the heat setting, adjusts it and goes back for his last load.

The old man is out of the van and walking with a hooked walking stick when he approaches the door. He's short and paunchy with thick, rounded shoulders and brown arms sticking out of a tight-fitting T-shirt with yellowed armpits. The hair on his arms and coming out of his V-shaped collar is silver, but he sports a slick, black, and full head of hair. It's as if it's been coloured with a black Magic Marker. His forearms are marked by dark splotches of black and blue, which were once tattoos but now read as massive bruising under his deeply tanned skin. He hangs the stick over his wrist and reaches for the door handle.

Flip strides over to hold the door.

"I got it, I got it," the old man says. He's missing most of his top teeth and it makes his upper lip pucker in when he speaks.

Flip can see the old man's fat, grub-like tongue wriggling as he wrangles the door and starts moving on his stick again. Flip backs away.

He gathers the last load of damp clothes while watching the old man find a place to sit among the rows of white machines. The man supports his left leg under the knee and props it in the next chair.

Flip rolls the wire basket over and empties it into another drier. He snaps the knob and watches the clothes tumble. Then he adds quarters to the other loads.

The woman in the housedress comes up the side of the van with a cardboard box overflowing with clothes. Flip holds the door for her and leans back to give her good clearance around his middle.

"Thank you," she says, smiling a sweet smile. She sets the box down fast on top of the closest machine.

"You need some help with that?" Flip asks.

"No," the old man says from his seat. "She don't need no help."

"I can get it," she replies to Flip, without ever looking in his direction. She slides the box back into her arms, the weight makes her hunch over even more, and she finds a table next to her husband.

Flip lifts a free newspaper from a rack near the door and reads an article about a local farmer's market that's being held in the high school parking lot every weekend over the summer. It says the event will continue through Halloween weekend. There's a colour photo of a wicker basket full of fruits and vegetables, jars of honey and jams, wedges of cheese and loaves of artisan bread. He realizes he's hungry. He checks the clothes, drops more quarters in his machines and walks out the front of the store.

The van gives off a hot stink. He looks all around to spot a likely place to get some grub. Across the street there's a service station with a tiny office and a drive-thru car wash. He knows it will have a cooler with sodas and maybe some candy and crackers. But he worries that the old man will steal his clothes if he leaves, and the old woman wouldn't try to stop him.

Instead he slides into his front seat. He sees his cellphone and opens it. He has a message.

"Flip," Lynn says. "I got your message. I'm glad the interview is moving ahead. I'm calling from the bathroom, so Ron won't get upset. I have a work event tonight. I won't be home 'til late. If I don't get another chance, good luck tomorrow. I'd better go."

Work event. He tries to decode the phrase. But there simply isn't much to go on. Bottom line is, he needs to trust Lynn until she gives him a reason not to. There's nothing he can do about it anyway.

He rests an elbow on the open window frame and taps the phone on his forehead. He considers trying to get a hold of Chad to cancel their illegal transaction. But, he reconsiders. *If.* If he finds out his monster-in-law was right, if he finds out Lynn is already dating, then his meeting with Chad will make things easier, come Thursday.

He takes the purple lighter from his shorts and sparks the scratch wheel with his thumb, presses the button. The flame is set on high and he feels the heat it gives on his cheeks. Through his dirty windshield he can see his clothes have stopped tumbling. He didn't bring hangers, or a clothes basket, so it seems pointless to go back in and fold his clothes. He's got the urge to simply drive away, leave his possessions for anyone who needs them. He doesn't care.

Instead, he digs around between the owner's manual, maps and ketchup packets in his glove box and finds a car charger for his phone. He plugs it into the cigarette lighter and pushes the tethered cellphone out of view under the passenger's seat.

He heaves himself out of the car and accidentally drags the towel out with his ass. He pitches it back in the car and walks inside. When he checks the clothes, they're still damp. He drops more quarters into the machines.

The old man talks at his wife. "I told you not to spend all our quarters on those damn honey buns. We had a box of dry cereal. Why are you so damn stupid? Why don't you listen to good sense? You need me to smack the crap out of your ears to get you to listen? 'Cause you know I can. I'll box 'em good." The old man shifts around and puts both feet on the floor.

"I said I was sorry," the woman replies. "If that isn't good enough for you, then that's too bad. That's the best I can do. It's all I'm willing to do." She has her back to Flip, her hands on the lid of a washing machine that's spinning loudly, the motion vibrating through her small, bent frame.

"Sorry? I'll get up and show you sorry," the man says. He gathers his strength and uses his stick to push up to his feet. He falls back into the chair, starts the process again. He catches Flip staring at him, and winks conspiratorially. Flip shakes his head. He doesn't want to be involved. He wants to get out. But he especially doesn't want the old man to take his presence as support or encouragement.

"When I get up I'm going to beat your ass like the old days," he says. "We have enough money to get the clothes wet, but not enough to get them dry. Are you a fucking retard, Dottie? I think you are. I married a retard. I been fucking a retard all these years. I suspected as much, but I didn't know for sure. But now I know. You're a one-hundred-percent, dirt-eating retard." He pushes up to his feet, teeters, catches his balance and starts to move forward.

Flip moves towards the old man, not sure why he's doing it.

"Buck, you were always a hateful man," Dottie says. The machine she's been leaning on quits spinning and the room is much quieter.

"What? What did you say to me?"

She turns to face Buck. "You were a mean little man when I met you. I felt sorry for you 'cause you were a loud mouth and a bully, but you seemed sad and lonely too; like an angry little mutt that'd been kicked too much. I got knocked up and that was that. I've tried to make the best of it. Thought you might change your spots. But if you try and hit me again, it'll be the last time you get the chance." She moves away from the machine, steps towards Buck. His jaw hangs open.

Buck's slack face bunches up and looks hot, as if he might cry or vomit. He takes a long stride toward Dottie and draws back his free hand to take a swipe at the side of her head. Flip walks closer still, holds up his hand, trying to stop Buck through force of will; he forms a thought but he doesn't say a thing, the words stay trapped in his chest. Dottie pulls back one fuzzy-slippered foot and kicks Buck's walking stick out from under him. He goes down hard, his forehead striking the floor. He starts to writhe around in his outrage and pain. A wet yowling emanates from his downturned face.

Flip doesn't feel compelled to help Buck, to turn him over or check on him. He's content to leave him where he lies.

Dottie stares down at her husband. "I wasn't always like this," she says without looking over to where Flip stands, but he knows she speaking to him. "He was. He was always just like this. But not me. I was different." She straightens herself a bit, fusses with her hair and adjusts her housedress. She holds her hand over her neckline near her throat and says, "Is there something I can I help you with?"

"I just heard that you needed some quarters to dry your clothes."

"I don't need your charity."

"Actually, I was going to see if you would sell me a cardboard box. I need something to carry my clothes in."

Dottie looks up. "Yes. I will sell you a few boxes. I think I need about four dollars to get these clothes dried. You okay with that?"

"Yes."

"Right then," she says. She leaves, comes back from the van with two boxes. Flip hands over a pile of coins.

Flip unloads his clothes and folds them. At first Buck continues to howl. But there isn't much spirit in it. He begins to mumble and weep. He makes quiet excuses to Dottie. He makes breathy apologies, Dottie steps around him to transfer clothes from one place to the next, ignoring her husband.

Flip loads his boxes and packs them in his back seat. He walks back in.

"I'm going now," he says.

"Okay," Dottie waves to him placidly.

On impulse, Flip carefully rolls his driver's side window up and steers his car through the car wash across the street. Blue and pink foam suds crisscross on his windshield, a curtain of long cloth strips sway as the car passes through, clean water cascades, and a blower chases the moisture away in jerky, backwards rivulets. Flip rubs his hand along the fractured glass, finds the window is holding strong, smooth and cool to the touch, but maybe a little damp. When he drives out of the carwash, he still feels unclean.

In front of the laundromat the van is gone. Buck stands out front alone, leaning heavily on his stick, his black hair standing-up, as if he'd been shocked.

THE WORLD'S DEADLIEST CRUMB CATCHER

Flip has hours to go before his meeting with Chad. He considers heading back to the Lakeside, but he knows he'll be more productive elsewhere. He's still hungry, can't think of what to eat. His watches are in the car, so he drives to Family Pawn.

He can't find parking in front, so he goes around the block and pulls in at a bar called Old Fellow's. He tugs all his watches onto his wrist and locks the car.

Family Pawn is booming. The window displays are packed with band instruments of every description: guitars, basses, amps, tubas, saxophones, violins, clarinets, cellos and two complete drum kits. Inside, half a dozen people mill around the rows of home appliances and power tools while several others stand over the glass cases of weapons, jewellery, watches and coins that line three sides of the space. *Good to know the economy has been good for someone.*

Flip browses a display of leather coats with security chains running through the sleeves, leashing them to their racks. One of the wall cases has ceramics and he sees a Smiley Pig cookie jar, like the one he shattered on his kitchen counter. After a while an employee approaches.

"What can I do you for," the woman asks. She is low and thick with man-sized shoulders and forearms, and a wispy moustache, as one might find on a pubescent boy.

"I brought in these watches," Flip presents his wrist.

"Uh huh. I see. You looking to sell or pawn?"

"Sell."

The woman makes a cluck cluck with her tongue. "Okay. Bring 'em on over to the counter." She walks around to meet him across the case. He takes three of the four watches off and sets them on a dark hand towel she produces from somewhere. She picks them up one at a time. She listens to them, tests the works by twisting the stem, examines the crystals.

When she's done she asks, "What were you hoping to get for them?"

"Three hundred."

"Wow. Slow down daydreamer. We aren't running a charity here."

"Too much?"

"I could do ninety dollars."

"Really? You mean ninety a piece?"

"Ninety for all. Thirty a piece. That's my best offer."

Flip looks hard at the watches. He knows they're worth a couple of hundred bucks a piece. He doesn't want to leave feeling screwed. But he needs the cash.

"How much for that pig cookie jar?" he asks.

She looks across the way. "That's seventy-five. It's a real collector's item. Very good condition."

"How about the cookie jar and fifty dollars cash?" Flip offers.

"I could do the pig and thirty cash," she sticks out her manly hand to shake. He hesitates. "Best offer," she says. He shakes on it. Her moustache bristles when she smiles.

Ten minutes later, he leaves Family Pawn with a cookie jar in a box and a little more cash in his pocket.

He spends a couple of hours sitting on a stool, down the bar from a couple of other non-communicative old fellows, eating bar snacks and sipping light beer. He thinks he has nothing in common with these sad old guys, staring into their half-finished beers. But then he realizes, they are all men without women. He keeps an eye on his remaining watch and pushes back from the bar long before it's time to go.

He takes the Passat through a bank and empties his checking account at the ATM.

Flip slides into a booth at the Food Time Diner almost an hour before the appointed time. The beer made him hungry, so he orders a cup of French onion soup and half a turkey club from a girl born in 1991 but who is dressed like a teeny bopper from the fifties.

He sips coffee before the food arrives and sips more after the empty dishes have been cleared away. He double-checks his cash on hand and separates enough dough for the contraband.

At four forty-five he decides Chad has bailed out. He's relieved and disappointed in equal parts.

Then the door opens and a kid with a maroon Gamecocks hat walks straight to Flip's table and slides in opposite.

"Mr. Mellis, right."

"Mmmhmm."

"I'm Chad," Chad says. He puts his elbows up and folds his arms on the tabletop. He looks around like he's nervous and tugs the brim of his cap down a bit, hunches his shoulders as if he's trying to pull his head in, turtle-style. "You bring the money?"

"Yes."

"Give it to me under the table."

Flip takes the cash from his pocket and passes it under the table. Chad takes it and holds it low, counts it, and sticks it in his jeans. He nods his cap brim. Then says in a whisper, "You go to the bathroom. When you come back I'll take a turn in the restroom. You take my seat. The merchandise will be in the crumb catcher."

"Okay," Flip says, and slides out. "What's a crumb catcher?" he whispers.

"The seat, the seat. The big gap in the corner of the seat," Chad says. It's clear Chad does not think Flip is taking this seriously enough, or being cool enough.

"Right," Flip says. He gives Chad a two thumbs-up/big smile combo and leaves.

Flip needs to pee anyway. He realizes Chad might just take off with the gun and the cash. If he does, that would be fine. If not, that would be good too. Flip is past the point of caring.

When he returns, Chad slips out of the booth and heads to the bathroom, according to plan. Flip scoots into the spot Chad vacated and looks around the restaurant. A thirty-year-old busboy is clearing a table across the room. The Teeny Bopper is seating some teenagers and chatting in the partitioned area that used to be a smoking section.

He casually slips his hand behind him and feels around the crack of the seat. He feels a package there, wrapped in paper. He pulls it on to the seat beside him and unwraps it, takes it out of the Admiral Chicken to-go bag it's been hidden in. He hefts it in his palm; it's heavy, different from what he expected, long and angular with a worn, ridged, plastic grip. He slips the weapon back in the bag, scrunches the paper around it, and tucks it under his leg. Chad joins him.

"We good?" Chad asks.

"What is this thing? It looks ancient. Does it work?"

"It's a Walther P38. My grandpa took it off a German officer during World War Two. Some famous battle. I forget. He's dead now."

"So it works?"

"It's German, man. They really make good stuff. It works. Watch out, it's loaded too." Flip feels the hard chunk of metal stuck under his thigh, lifts some of his weight off, just to be careful.

"It's so heavy."

"I know. It's a steel gun. All steel. Heavy stuff."

"That makes sense."

"So we're good," Chad states.

"Yes."

They shake on it. "Remember. That didn't come from me. My dad's a preacher, for Christ's sake. You get busted with that thing you don't want to try to implicate me. My dad will tear you a new asshole." With that parting comment he walks away.

Flip feels a little smug: his opinion of all Chads has been confirmed.

He leaves cash on the table and tucks the wrapped Walther in his waistband at the small of his back. He tugs his shirt over the lump and exits quickly.

At the car, he stuffs the gun in the side of one of his clothes cartons and drives straight to the Lakeside Motor Court.

As he pulls into the front lot, near the Lakeside's office, he notices a police cruiser following, its lights start flashing silently.

The Walther!

The Walther is just behind me.

In his mind's eye, he sees himself slipping the gun, still stuffed in a paper sack, between the side of the cardboard box and a stack of boxer shorts. *It should be fine.*

The officer sits in his squad car, talking on the radio; probably calling in his plate number. Flip checks his seat belt, adjusts his mirrors and turns off his engine. He slowly rolls his shattered window down. Then, he remembers his conversation with Officer Steve Hartman. A few days earlier Flip had belligerently bashed Officer Hartman's car and then given him a fake name. Maybe someone cool or lucky could get away with that. But not Flip. *What was I thinking?*

Flip tips his rearview to get a better look at the cop. He's sporting a severe looking blond flat top. Not Officer Hartman. That's good. But the cop could be on the radio with Officer Hartman. Or Hartman might have found the dent and put out an all points bulletin.

The officer steps from his cruiser and walks slowly toward Flip, one hand resting casually on his gun. When he draws near, he takes out a torch and shines it in the back seat of Flip's car for a long, deliberate moment. He flicks the cast beam around, a spotlight in a prison yard.

Perhaps Flip has been the unwitting victim of a police sting operation. His gun purchase was filmed. Chad was wearing a wire. *So Stupid. So Stupid.*

The officer leaves the giant torch on, tucks it under his arm and somehow manages to aim it right in Flip's face. "Do you know why I pulled you over?" The cop has a soft, ragged voice, a little too much like Dirty Harry.

"No sir. Officer," Flip says, holding his hand against the glare. "But I have my driver's licence and proof of insurance. I think this has all been a big misunderstanding."

"What has?" the officer asks.

"This. Getting pulled over," Flip explains.

"You seem nervous. Are you nervous about something?"

"No no. I am not at all nervous. Not a tiny bit. I am very not nervous. Even less nervous than usual." Flip knows he should stop talking. "Well actually, maybe a normal amount of nervous.

Or just the right amount of nervous for being pulled over by an Officer of the Law, such as yourself; maybe not nervous. Just concerned. Or curious." He drops his hand and tries to make a reassuringly honest smile at the officer. But, squinting as he is, it looks more like a scowl. "You know. Curious about why you would pull me over. That's it. Just curious." He nods to show he's completed his circuitous thought.

"I will take that licence and insurance," the officer says. He peeks into the cab of the Passat and looks around a bit more. Flip reaches into the glove box and takes out his insurance card. He passes it, along with his driver's licence, to the officer.

The officer steps back a few paces and pulls a microphone from where it's clipped to his shoulder. He keys the mike, twiddles a knob on the radio on his belt, then keys it again. He spends a couple of minutes reading numbers off the cards. He takes the torch from his armpit and shines it on Flip's licence. He finishes reciting numbers and re-clips his mike, takes a slow circuit around Flip's car, casting the light along the car's exterior and again illuminating the cartons in the back seat. His radio starts squawking. Flip can't make out the words. The officer keys his mike again.

"Thanks, Janie," he says.

He walks up to Flip's window again. "You've got a box full of clothes back there," he rasps.

"Yes," Flip acknowledges. The officer looks irritated by the response. Flip adds, "I was doing my laundry at the X Press laundry. Just heading back to my place in the back here."

"Okay," the officer says. He takes his time before speaking again. "Well, the reason I pulled you over is because you have a busted tail light. Were you aware of that, sir?" He uses the light to point out the shattered taillight. Flip leans out of his window and looks back down the side of his car.

"Oh. Yes. I was. It just happened. Yesterday. It happened in a parking lot." The officer nods and sticks the torch back under his arm.

"Well. You know you need to get that fixed, don't you? You can't drive around like that."

"Yes sir."

"Can I ask why you didn't get it taken care of today?" He holds Flip's ID into the light so he can read it. "Mr. Mellis?"

"Honestly, Officer. I just forgot. Well, I remembered this morning, but I forgot as the day went on. Time just gets away from me."

"Well, get it taken care of, okay?" The officer passes his cards back through the window.

"Yes, sir."

"You have a good night now." Officer Aryan walks back to sit in his car.

Flip doesn't want to move. But the cruiser doesn't budge from its position behind him. Flip rechecks his seatbelt and mirrors, then turns the ignition and pulls around the Lakeside.

"Can I give you a hand?" Dean asks without giving any indication that he intends to rise from his chair.

"No thanks." Flip carries the box with the hidden weapon.

On his next pass, Dean says, "You want me to pour you a drink?"

"Yes," Flip says. "Give me a few minutes. But I think today calls for a drink."

"Ooooo goody. I smell a story. I shall be waiting with bated breath."

Flip retrieves his cellphone from under his seat, makes a last trip for his suit, decides the piggy jar can stay put, locks the car and walks inside to the closet. He rips the plastic away and looks the suit over. It's pressed and presentable. He leaves the cartons on the bed and goes out to pass a little time with Dean.

They spend a while drinking wine, as Dean flicks ash from his cigarette. He tells Flip he met a new man.

"He is very lovely: my age, gentle, sweet and thoughtful. He's a retired professor of Romantic poetry. He throws a lot of quotes from Shelley into casual conversation. But it never feels forced. Well, almost never. For fun and profit he organizes tours of other retirement age Americans, takes them to poets' homes in England, the Lake District. Supposed to be lovely. Coleridge, Wordsworth, Byron et cetera."

The only Byron Flip has ever heard of is his father. Flip had been a business major, very practical. Unlike all those liberal arts students with their humanities and soft sciences, he had valued financial self-reliance over self-actualization. But he guesses these are the kinds of names educated people are supposed to know, so he says, "He sounds pretty great."

"Yes. I agree. He has invited me to travel with him on his next trip. As his guest."

"That seems fast. Exciting, but fast."

"Oh. I agree," Dean says. His legs are crossed at the knee and he leans down now to stub the butt of his cigarette on the bottom of his brown leather lace shoe. When he finishes, he pinches and twists the remaining tobacco and paper and scatters it in the evening breeze. He puts the spongy, used filter in his shirt front pocket. "But," he adds thoughtfully. "Neither of us is young anymore. We know what we like. We know what we need. And neither of us has time to waste. Only so many good years left to us."

"Good point," Flip says with complete conviction.

"Conversely, the whole situation feels like a practiced pick-up line. Don't get me wrong. I am flattered to be picked-up. Especially by someone I find very easy to be with. But I want it to be special. And I'm afraid I will simply be the most recent in a long list of similar companions."

"Also a good point," his previous position completely supplanted by Dean's own counter-argument.

Dean doesn't speak, just looks into the night. Flip wants to say something helpful. "What did you say, when he asked you to go with him?"

"I said I was interested, but undecided."

"That sounds right. When do you need to give him an answer?"

"Oh. There's no real rush. I suppose I have weeks before the trip."

"Well, you shouldn't get in a hurry. Take some time to get to know him better. Then decide." Flip recalls the kind things Dean has said to him and adds, "You are a handsome man with a lot to offer."

Dean reaches over and pats Flip on the hand. "Good suggestion," he says. "And thank you." He gives his head a slight shake, as if his train of thought is an Etch-a-Sketch that can be cleared, just so. "And you? What has been going on?"

"A lot." Flip turns across the table and tells Dean about being interviewed by security at Bull's Eye, about little Caroline and her mother. About D asking to marry his teenage daughter. He omits the stolen belt. Pointing to his car window, he mentions the redneck and his hammer. He tells Dean about the laundromat and what happened with Dottie and Buck.

"Oh my," Dean says, pressing his fingers to his chest as if he has a mild case of the vapours.

Flip mentions his mother-in-law's insinuations about Lynn, the crazy islander with the aggressive chest, and the stern, blond officer. Finally he recounts the dinner with his father and the fact that his father is ill and his mother may have died without ever having shared the truth about his parents' divorce.

"That is a lot," Dean agrees.

"Buck, at the coin laundry, was such a bitter, mean asshole. I was kind of proud of Dottie. But, I don't know. I hate to think she wasted her whole life being miserable. Still, I feel for the old man too. He was broken and down on his luck. Now he's those things, plus completely abandoned. Alone."

"Maybe so," Dean agrees. "But, I have lived with others and lived alone. I find both states of being have their drawbacks and advantages."

"I know you're right, Dean." Flip turns in his overtaxed metal chair and stares into the void of the surrounding darkness. "Buck and my dad," he says. "They're alone; alone at the end of their lives. And it just seems so – I don't know the right words – tragic, I guess. Tragic that they would spend their lives among people, yet have no one there for them. It just seems tragic."

Dean pours the rest of the wine and drinks. Flip drinks too.

"Maybe someone does care about your father enough to be there."

"Who?" Flip asks.

"You, his estranged son. He needs you and you know it. And it's working on you. I can see it. Do you know the reason it weighs on you? Because you are a decent person."

"I can't even hold my own life together, Dean. I don't have the time, means or know-how to help my father." Without intending it, Flip's voice rises and his tone becomes harsh. "Plus, I hate him. He's gross and unpleasant and selfish."

Dean nods his understanding. "My mother was an unpleasant woman who never really accepted me. But in the end, I was the only one able to take care of her. Well, not really. My sister Beth could have helped. But she basically refused and left it all to me. It didn't matter that I never felt she loved me in all the ways I wanted. That ship had sailed. I realized, I was a grown man. I had to forgive her shortcomings as a parent and just do what needed to be done.

"Listen, I know everyone's situation is different. I'm not telling you that you have to do anything. Not at all. But I will say, it was good *for me* to be there at the end with my mother. It gave me some closure and peace. I think, in the end, she appreciated it. And if I'd hesitated, it would have been too late. There are always excuses not to get involved when someone is ill. But, when it's a parent, in your case I imagine your children or spouse would count also, you have to be there if you're needed."

Flip turns his head to look at Dean. He can feel he's scowling. But he doesn't care.

"I will keep out of it if you'd prefer and I don't mean to sound condescending. But I have been where you are now. So I just want to help."

Flip continues to glare. But his expression softens slightly.

"If you don't want my opinion, you should keep your stories to yourself," Dean says flatly.

Flip drinks more wine. "You're right," he says. He thinks about how angry and uncivil the man at the Drum Roaster had been, how on edge the trucker had been, and even the little church boy with the bible. Every other person he's crossed paths with has been ready to explode.

Sitting here, across from Dean, he's tempted to stand up and walk into his apartment, slam the door. He's angry at Dean's intrusion. He sees the wisdom in his comments, but doesn't want to hear it. If he stormed away, that would get his point across.

That's what he wants, to give in to his simmering rage and just let it carry him where it wants. But, for the first time in a long while, he really considers his actions. He doesn't want to be like Buck, the trucker or his father. There are enough shitheads in the world already. Plus he likes Dean. Really likes him and meant what he wrote in the Van Gogh card.

So he says, "You're right about that, Dean. Thanks for being honest with me. I will think about it." He swallows the last gulp of wine. "Dean. I should go get ready for bed now. Tomorrow morning is the interview. It's my last shot at turning this ship around."

"Okay," Dean says. Flip can see Dean stop himself from commenting further, notes his restraint and commits to exercise some of his own.

Flip stands from the chair with a creak, excuses himself. Inside he exerts some energy on push-ups and sit-ups. He sets his box of clothes on the closet floor and pulls out under-wear, dress socks and a white T-shirt the size of a twin sheet. He spends some time rubbing his dress shoes with a flannel. He checks over the suit and dress shirt. He selects a tie.

In the bathroom he showers, just to calm his mind. He takes out his toiletries. He clips and files his fingernails and toenails. He trims some hair growing out of his ears and nose. He exam-ines his eyebrows, and looks at his hair. He thinks he can see his own cheekbones. If he tips his head in the light, he looks rather good. He uses the tooth-whitening trio again, careful to dry his teeth before pressing the film into place.

In the kitchen, he pulls the leftovers from the mini-fridge and dumps them in the trash. He takes his snapshots and sits on the edge of the bed. He sets the alarm on the radio clock. He checks the time against his remaining wristwatch. He makes certain the clock is set on PM and his alarm is set for AM. Then he finds his cellphone and sets its alarm too, just to be safe.

He looks at a picture of Dyl in his Pee Wee league baseball uniform. He is such a happy kid, so fearless, so enthusiastic. Flip feels bad he hasn't been more encouraging. Sara in her robot Halloween costume which she made herself from cardboard boxes, tin foil and dryer vent tubes. She still looked soft and round like a kid less than a year ago. But lately it was as if someone had flipped a switch. She's a teenager, long and leggy and showing a few curves. A lot like Lynn had looked when he first laid eyes on her. He can't bear to look at Lynn right now, so he puts the pictures down.

He turns off the lights, slides between the sheets and, surprisingly, feels sleepy immediately. The sensation of his legs against the cool sheets causes him to think about how clean and trimmed he is. And that makes him think of Lynn; in the past she always let him know how much she appreciated it when he took care of himself. What a shame to let all that grooming go to waste. *God I miss her.*

Her body: skin soft and warm and perfect; legs, long and shapely and moving along his. And her neck: graceful, smooth and arching to the side, gently tempting his mouth to taste its curves. Her scent, when his face presses against her, is enough for him live on. A steady diet of her limbs tangled with his could sustain him like nothing else ever could. *Good God in heaven, I'm lonely.*

For a moment he entertains the idea that she really is on a date. He imagines her, at that exact moment, laughing with some office mate, some young intern who plays water polo and is on a raw food diet. Someone employed.

In the dark of room Number Three at the Lakeside Motor Court, he can see her smile flash for his imaginary young rival. He can see the poor kid doesn't stand a chance. She lays a hand on his shoulder, leans her chest forward to speak over the din of the party. If she wants him, there is no way to resist her, and who would want to?

His cellphone is within arm's reach. He could stretch his arm through the dark room and call her now. Perhaps interrupt whatever it is she's doing. Maybe interject the notion of the time they've shared, of the life they've built, of the challenges they've met and the children they've made and raised. But he doesn't call. Either, he's aware his imagination is getting the best of him, or he feels it's too late to change things. He doesn't know which.

He notes his own thought processes. This tendency towards considering the outcomes of his actions is not a new habit, but it's been a while. He hopes it's a sign of progress. He rattles his head against the pillow to clear it. He shakes his head until his neck hurts and squeezes his eyes until he sees stars. He breathes and focuses on counting through his inhale, then holding and counting through his exhale. He has little control of his life, but for now, he can control the simple act of filling his lungs, of letting them empty. It relaxes him and weariness comes on fast.

The angry brown woman with the exclamatory hairdo is there with him. As he stood at the counter, trying to pay for his gas, he really hadn't noticed her breasts until she lifted them and shook them at him. He honestly hadn't been staring at her chest, had only been trying to read her name because he believes in calling people by their name and shaking their hand when appropriate; common courtesy, good manners. He doesn't believe one person is inherently more important than the next. He's no better than someone who works across a counter. He got that from his dad.

"You judge a man by his actions, not by his clothes or what he has to say," Byron tells him. Little Flip has rolled from his bed to pee in the twilight hours. He finds his daddy in the hall, one hand hoisting a suitcase, the other hand clutching his work boots. Byron hadn't said goodbye. But he'd stopped long enough to give some manly advice before leaving Flip to sort the rest out for himself.

"You git yourself a good look?" Again, she lifts her bosom with both hands and shakes. "Is dat what you are aftah?" This time, his eyes linger, he doesn't turn away or try to explain himself or make excuses. He leers openly. There is no need for a man to explain to a grown woman the expression he wears on his face.

Now, in the privacy of Number Three, as if he is seventeen and making love in a bed for the very first time, he openly gazes on her full breasts and he feels them in his hands, hefts them and squeezes them and feels his face against them. His lips kiss the soft skin, his tongue seeks out a firm tip and he takes the nipple in his mouth. His dick is hard and insistent under the sheet. He works it with his hand and continues to explore the strange woman's body.

Minutes later he wakes from the dream as he climaxes. He feels immediately miserable and messy and knows deep in his soul he will never be loved again.

He needs his rest, but knows he will never sleep. He thinks that thought for several minutes; he thinks it until he sleeps.

A PERSONAL RECKONING

A digital bleating from his cellphone wakes him at seven a.m. His sheet is stuck to his lower torso, it rips at his body hair when he pulls it away. He rolls over and punches buttons on his phone until there's silence and knocks the phone to the carpeted floor as he tries returning it to the side table.

Seven in the morning he thinks. *Three and a half hours before Magic Time.* He forces himself to his feet, leans down to swipe the phone from the floor, startles at the sound of his clock radio blaring low grade rock and roll. His back torques as he involuntarily jerks away from the sudden noise.

He leaves the cellphone where it is and gingerly straightens his back: *painful, yet functional.* He probes the sore area along his lower spine with the tips of his fingers. It's tender to the touch. *Pills,* he thinks, *I need my pills.* He turns off the music. Unbidden, the name Great White Snake comes to mind. He doesn't know if that's the name of the band, but he thinks it's close. He takes stiff, small, shuffling steps around the room until he finds his prescription bottle.

He pours all the pills into his beefy palm. Would twenty pills kill him? He used to have a weak stomach when it came to pills. As a kid, he could barely even swallow them, if he got one down he'd throw it right up. His mother would crush them into powder with the back of a spoon and fold them into apple sauce or mashed potatoes so he could keep them down.

His body has a visceral reaction to the idea of tossing back all those pale blue pills. His stomach churns and he burps sour air. The psychosomatic response, a reaction to his recent and unpleasant experience at the emergency room. He's careful to shield himself from acknowledging any personal responsibility for the series of events that led to that trip to the ER. He closes his fingers over the pills and rattles them like dice. *Not yet,* he tells himself and puts the pills back in the bottle.

He thinks about his choices over the past week. So many of the foolish things he'd done occurred when he was on either booze or pills, or both. He twists the cap back on the bottle. If he's going to have a chance of giving a good interview, he needs to avoid the pills. He needs to get ready, see if his back loosens up. If not, a pill or two might be needed.

The previous night, his intention was to wake early, get in a short walk, do some push-ups and sit-ups and then get cleaned up. Now, he decides to get straight in a hot shower and see if he can get his body working right.

After the shower he feels better. The towel won't wrap around his middle, so he stands with his naked body in the cold air, leaning towards the mirror as he shaves. He removes the tuft of whiskers under his lip, then dries his face. He drags the whitening strips from his mouth and flicks them in the trash.

On closer inspection, he sees his face is clean and smooth, his hair looks nice, his teeth may be marginally whiter, he has no offensive hair growth visible, his eyebrows are under control and clearly two separate and distinct strips of hair. *I may be a pudgy behemoth,* he thinks. *But at the very least I'm well groomed with reasonable facial proportions.*

His eyes are not too far apart and not too close, his ears are proportional to his head, and his nose is attractive; perhaps his very best feature. He's gratified it hasn't started to turn down and elongate like Byron's. Though Lynn used to say his ass was his best feature, he chooses not to take a peek in the mirror.

He nods to himself and practices his smile. He smacks the meat under his chin with the backs of his fingers. His eyes crease at the corners when he grins too big, so he takes the grin down a notch: less crinkling. *A fat face doesn't hide all signs of age.*

He uses his fingers to rake his damp hair into place. He sees the dry scab left from the magic pimple in the centre of his forehead. He gambles and picks at the crusty bit of skin. It flakes off to reveal healthy skin underneath.

"Yes," he says, genuinely enthused. He takes his victories where he can get them.

He moisturizes his face and neck, applies Sport Scent deodorant and licks his thumbs before smoothing his eyebrows. He opens the new puck of hair goop and is very careful to use the minimum amount needed. He rubs it vigorously on his fingers and applies it carefully to his salt and pepper hair. He gives his sideburns a final stroke to smooth their tendency toward curliness. Byron's momma, Granny Mellis, once told little Flip curly hair was a mark of a sinful soul, which he now realizes, may have been a subtly racist remark. Odd that she should employ such nuance when she was openly bigoted most other times.

One last look in the mirror as he steps back tells him that everything above his shoulders is fairly inoffensive. *If only I didn't have to transport it on the lumpy monstrosity it's attached to.*

In front of the closet he slips into silken, maroon boxer shorts, because everyone likes to feel pretty. He checks the time on the clock: too early to put his clothes on. He pulls a crisp white T-shirt over his head.

The cellphone is still on the floor next to the bed. He refuses to let it defeat him, not today. He walks towards it, paying attention to the way his back feels. He spreads his stance, bends a little at the knees, and scoops the phone right up.

"Yes," he says again. It's a forced enthusiasm, but he's trying to get his spirits up for the interview.

Slowly he lifts his feet through a clean pair of khaki shorts and slips his feet into his trainers without worrying about socks or laces. He finds his door key and marches out into the morning air for a brisk constitutional. By the time he makes it across the parking lot he knows he's making a mistake; his lower back throbs and his muscles clinch in a tight knot like a fist.

He makes a few slow circuits of the Lakeside, careful not to take long strides or step too high. When he approaches his door for the third time, he thinks the knot in his back may have relaxed a bit; but he wouldn't swear to it. He goes back inside.

He feels hungry. *Breakfast is the most important meal of the day*, he reasons. But there's no food to be had, except a packet of Saltine crackers he discovers in a drawer under a badly burnt potholder. As he eats all four crackers at once, he decides it's time to suit up.

He takes out his white dress shirt. It doesn't have a starched look, but it isn't wrinkled either, so he throws it on and buttons it, forgoing the ironing board. Next, he wanders into the bathroom and finds the black elastic hair bands he'd retrieved from the row where Yoga Pants had been holding court with her ilk.

He slips his slacks from their hanger and leans one hand against the wall as he slides into them. He tucks his capacious shirttail into the waist of his pants, carefully arranges and folds the excess material, then tugs up his zipper. The pants fit. Actually fit. He can latch them in front and they feel comfortable. Not boxer-shorts-comfortable or khaki-shorts-comfortable. But they are definitely suit-pants-comfortable.

"Right the fuck on!" He unintentionally mimics Kev.

He'd intended to use one of the elastic hair bands to make an extension for the waistband by looping and hooking it through the buttonhole. But now, it isn't needed. He triumphantly pitches the unopened package on the bed. He sits to test the pants. Snug yet acceptable.

Flip retrieves his watch from the counter next to the bath-room sink and secures it to his wrist. He runs the belt around his middle and is able to use the second hole. To his delight he finds it has enough of a tail to tuck properly away. On the corner of the bed he leans down and pulls his slick socks up to mid-calf, slips his feet in his clean shoes and ties the laces into neat bows. When he stands again, his back moves smoothly.

In the bathroom mirror he watches his hands work a tasteful blue tie into a perfect knot, first try. The tie was a birthday gift from Sara.

A longing for his family, for his home, wells unbidden and threatens to overwhelm him. His eyes fill with tears, his legs feel weak and he wants to sit on the toilet lid and cry. But he can't. *Not now.*

He rubs his face with his hands, they're very rough, still skinned from his fall at the gas station. He searches out moisturizer and applies it liberally, works his palms together until the greasiness seeps in. Now, his hands smell like Lynn. He holds them over his nose in the shape of a surgeon's mask and breathes deeply.

He pushes his family from his mind, before the profound sense of loss can take root. He must stay present and focused.

Being distracted by a pining desire for human intimacy will only make the interview harder. Longing to know the unknowable outcome of his personal drama will only distract from the one thing he can control, his odds of getting a job.

He focuses on his tie. It's a nice tie. He likes it. It brings out his eyes, is approachable and professional. He pulls the upturned collar down and pushes the knot all the way against his throat. The tie length is good, the tip just at his belt buckle.

He loosens the tie for now, leaves the top button undone. He digs one finger in his collar at the back of his neck and scratches. *Itchy*. He brings the finger out and inspects it. *Hair*. There are several tiny bits of hair stuck to the end of his finger. He remembers, with a sinking feeling, that he'd tried on the dress shirt after Dean cut his hair. Now the inside of his collar is peppered with irritating bits.

"Damn."

He takes a damp flannel and delicately swabs around the back of his neck. When he draws the cloth away, he can see he's removed some portion of the offending detritus. He turns the cloth and tries once more with similar results. He decides it will have to do.

Back at the closet, he puts on the waistcoat and buttons it, tucks the tie inside. He slips his arms into the substantial suit jacket and tries to assess himself honestly in the bathroom mirror. He is a well-dressed man, of middle years with salt and pepper hair and at least seventy extra pounds. Not hideous. Not attractive, but passable. Passable is the most he had dared to hope for. He forces himself to say, "Yes," with a weak fist pump.

He gathers some papers, his cellphone, and his notepad into his workbag. He takes an extra jacket hanger from the closet, double checks that he has everything and starts to leave. As he reaches for the door his back twinges a bit. He returns to the counter and grabs his pills. He takes two pills from the bottle and screws the lid back on. The pills go in his pants pocket, the bottle he throws onto the rumpled bedcover, and he closes the door behind him. Before locking up, he goes back in and taps his snapshots into a tight pile, inserts them in his front pocket and walks away. *For luck.*

At the car he hangs his suit jacket over the hanger and hooks it in the back seat. He removes the remaining towel from the seat and throws it into the back where it joins the cookie jar. The seat feels dry to the touch. He straightens himself the best he can, decides against the seat belt so as not to wrinkle his ensemble more than necessary. The morning is already warm, so he starts the car and turns on the air conditioning. A pale mist seeps from the vents and warm air blows at him.

By the time he parks at the Drum Roaster he's come to accept the harsh fact that the car's air conditioner needs coolant. *Shit.* Or the compressor is out again. *Double shit.*

As he slowly rolls down the shattered window he notices several cars pulling into spots near him. He rushes, and when the window slides into the door there is a definite sound of glass grinding against glass. He gets out and closes the car door very carefully behind him before hustling in the coffee shop ahead of the other customers.

A line forms behind him as he arrives at the counter.

"Hello Thi," Flip says.

Thi does an exaggerated double take and pretends to rub his eyes while making a 'squeak squeak' sound in his throat.

"Is that you Flip? Look at you. You look great, man. Downright respectable. I love the tie and waistcoat look. Makes you seem knowledgeable. For real, all you need is a pipe and a monocle, then I would believe anything you had to say."

"Oh," Flip says. "This old thing. It was all I had clean." He smiles big and genuine, remembers his crow's feet, and modulates his grin. He likes the attention.

"Okay," Thi says knowingly.

"Just kidding. Big job interview today." The man behind Flip clears his throat to announce his presence in the line.

"What can I get you, Flip?" Thi asks.

"I will have one of those drinks from last time. Nutty Professor right? I'll have that. To go please."

"What size?"

"Normal size."

Thi punches buttons on the cash register. "Anything else?"

"Can I bum some more fruit? Oh, let's make it no whipped cream please."

"Sure. No whip. I'm fresh out of fruit. Sorry. Want a muffin?"

Flip absently scratches the back of his neck under his collar while considering his baked goods options. After a long moment the customer behind him exhales loudly. Flip is tempted to draw the decision out, just to spite the self-important douche-bag behind him. But memories of a trucker with a hammer ricochet around his brain pan, so he tries a different approach.

"No. I'll skip it," Flip says. Then to the man behind him, "Sorry to take so long. My mind doesn't make decisions until my first cup of coffee."

The young man is tall, dressed in dark blue surgical scrubs, and has skin the colour of café au lait. "It's no problem," he says, not unkindly but not over-friendly either. A woman in a business suit, farther back in the line, gives Flip an understanding nod. *Beats a broken window and a busted taillight.*

Thi punches in a few more orders then starts his performance at the espresso machine. In no time at all he calls Flip's name and wishes him good luck.

"I'll need it," Flip says. Then he takes his coffee and leaves.

DynaTech is located in a business park. Apparently business park is code for several commercial office buildings arranged along a meandering strip of asphalt whose parking lots are separated by sparse landscaping and an occasional bench. Flip drives around until he finds the appropriate building and checks the time. He has almost an hour before he needs to meet Ms. Myrna Mays.

On the drive over he'd refrained from slurping his coffee for fear of spilling it on himself. Also, he feels it's essential to get the caffeine intake just right. Too much stimulus and he might have trouble being succinct, he could just blather on and on with no real point other than to expel his nervous energy. And too little caffeine might lead to a headache or a low-key demeanour. It was Flip's experience from interviews he'd conducted over the years that it must be difficult to know how strong to come on. But being too unassuming can leave people with the impression that you have no passion or you don't care at all. If given a choice, he'd rather be slightly too hyped, a little excitable and clearly anxious to get the position, rather than seeming too cool or meek.

One of the winning strategies he developed at McCorkle-Smithe was to try and match the energy level of the highest-ranking person in the room. That's what he would try today. But too much caffeine or too little could tip the scales.

He parks close to the glass and steel building. The shattered window, he rolls slowly up, conscious of the likelihood it could simply crumble. But it's still in one piece. He slips out as smoothly as he can, considering his size and his sore back. He sets his espresso drink on the roof of the car and claws at his neck. From the back seat he unhooks his jacket and slides it on. He picks up his workbag, closes and locks the car, takes his coffee and heads across the lot to take advantage of one of the benches.

The morning is humid. He feels sticky. The coffee makes him sweat; his forehead and underarms feel damp. His neck itches, so do his back and shoulders. He has an urge to strip down to his T-shirt and violently shake the hair out of his shirt. He wills himself to endure and ignore his irritation and discomfort the best he can. He remembers his breathing, counts his breaths. *That helps.*

He balances the paper cup on one of the tilted slats of the bench, careful to set it far from him, in case it tips over. He puts the workbag between his feet and pulls out his legal pad and resumé. He had every intention of doing this yesterday, but the time never seemed right.

He takes notes, writing long persuasive paragraphs regarding his unique qualities, work experience and skill set. He's careful to relate everything to how he might help DynaTech. After three pages he drinks some coffee while staring up at the dark glass building.

He can't see into the twelve-storey building, but he knows what it looks like. There are middle manager's offices all around the perimeter of each floor, with the corner offices reserved for the senior managers and VPs. In the middle there's a maze of high-walled, carpeted cubicles, a break room, restrooms, a bank of elevators and some storage closets for supplies and custodial products. Although DynaTech might boast an *open concept office*; which means lower walls on the cubicles or even no cubicles, the desks arranged in little clusters to encourage more socialization and foster a tighter work community. *God I hope not, I hate that.*

His back twinges as he shifts his girth on the bench. He remembers the pills in his pocket. He stands and fishes them out, knocks them back with a little coffee. As he swallows he wonders if he just made a mistake. *Did I have to take them both?*

He slurps a little more coffee, sets the cup away from him and rereads what he's written. It's solid. *I'm good at this stuff.* Even in high school he had a gift for the written word; especially persuasive rhetoric. *I still got it.* He checks his watch, half an hour to kill.

He lets his mind roam the possible avenues the conversation might take during the interview. Some of them he likes and takes a few notes, while others he rejects. He drinks more coffee, scratches his neck and uses a finger to squeegee the wet from his forehead. He flicks his perspiration onto the hot cement slab the bench is fastened to, watches the splatter pattern of dark spots until they evaporate.

Flip's as ready as he is going to get. Just to be safe, he takes a couple more minutes to write down questions he might like to ask. He is of the opinion that smartly worded and insightful questions are at least as effective in interviews as delivering really thorough answers.

He reads over the questions, tucks his pad and resumé in his bag and checks his watch. Almost time. He takes one more swig of barely warm coffee and begins to pour the last third into the grass, but reconsiders. Maybe someone from the building is watching and would find such an act rude. He carries the cup back to his car, just to be safe.

He unlocks the car and places the cup in one of the cup holders. He uses his nails on the back of his neck, one last time, before initiating the struggle with the stubborn top button of his shirt. As he pulls and tugs at the collar his head feels as if it might pop off, his face turns red and pressure builds in his skull. He might be having a heart attack. *Or a brain aneurysm.*

No matter how much he tugs, the infinitesimal, pearly button refuses to be coaxed into the microscopic slit of a buttonhole.

He draws a deep breath and holds it, tries one last time. He gives up, gasping for air. His neck is too big, his fingers too fat. He settles for pushing the triangular knot of his tie all the way up, largely hiding the shamefully unprofessional gap from view. *That will have to do.*

He has to piss. *Coffee goes right through me.* He looks himself over in an unfractured car window, decides everything is in order, and walks toward the lobby.

Flip avoids looking at his reflection in the doors as he strides forward to grip the handle. Cold air washes across his body when he pulls the door open, and he's immediately grateful for wasteful corporate energy usage.

Inside, he takes in the twenty-foot ceilings and the elaborate, large scale, dangling light fixture that glitters high overhead. The glossy black, reflective tile clicks against his hard-soled shoes as he moves forward purposefully, flanked by undulating, low-relief wall sculptures.

He approaches the amoeba-shaped security desk, rests his arms on the chest-high counter surface, and speaks with forced authority to the man in uniform seated in a rolling chair.

"My name is Mr. Mellis," he says, absently rapping a rhythm with his knuckles on the expensive-looking marble counter. "Ms. Mays is expecting me. I have a ten-thirty appointment. Job interview. Director of Internal Communications."

The tall, slender man stands in his stiff black uniform and fixes a matching eight-point cap with a glossy black brim on his head. "You don't have to give me your life story, Flip."

Flip looks at the man. Larry. The name comes to him. His new neighbour Larry.

"Larry," he says.

"Yes." The 'obviously' is implied.

"I didn't see you there, Larry. What a surprise."

"I need to see a photo ID and you need to sign here." He says it with no apparent warmth, even an undercurrent of contempt. He makes a quick stabbing gesture toward a Plexiglass clipboard near Flip's forearm.

Flip uses the pen and prints his name in one spot, signs it in another. He checks the time and jots it down along with Ms. Mays' name.

"We could have carpooled this morning," Flip tries to make small talk, one more time, as he pushes the form toward Larry.

Larry doesn't answer. "The ID," he reminds Flip impatiently.

Flip remembers Larry's claim that Vanessa has been stealing. Given Larry's generally sour disposition and pessimistic outlook, it's hard to take any of his claims seriously. He watches his driver's licence disappear behind the counter.

Being in Larry's presence makes Flip feel proud. He may very well be a depressed, suicidal, fat, miserable and unemployed waste of genetic code. But compared to Larry he's almost happy-go-lucky. *Next to this sad sack I'm a regular ray of fucking sunshine.* He's tempted to share this observation with Larry, but refrains. *Progress.* He also tries to take note: being a pessimistic shit-heel is no fun for the people around you. Flip recommits himself to be less of a mope; if he's still alive this time next week he will definitely try to stop being so gloomy.

Larry returns Flip's ID. "Look at me," he says while aiming a tiny camera at Flip's head. Flip looks. There is no sound or flash. Larry puts the camera down, jabs at some buttons and Flip can hear the sound of something printing. Larry slaps a fresh, sticky-backed nametag on the counter, complete with Flip's name and photo, as well as the word 'Visitor' emblazoned across the top. "Put this on. It must be visible at all times."

Flip follows orders by applying the sticker to his lapel. He hates it. His face fills the whole frame with no negative space left over.

Larry grabs a phone, checks a list of extension numbers, and taps on the keypad. "This is Larry at the security desk. Your ten-thirty is here." He hangs up. "Walk through the turnstile," Larry says.

Flip walks through the turnstile. Larry comes around and appears to buff Flip's aura with what he assumes is a security wand. *Little circles, little circles.* Apparently Flip passes the test.

"Ms. Mays will be with you in a moment. Wait there." Larry points at a low-slung, creamy leather couch with chrome legs in the shape of a squashed X.

"Larry. Question: is there a restroom I could use real quick?"

Larry's expression curdles to indicate how deeply annoying he finds Flip and his question. He starts to turn away and Flip is sure he's going to be ignored completely.

"Past the elevators, on the left," Larry says, while scooting his chair back in position and removing his cap.

"Thanks, Larry," Flip says. Then, just for the fun of it, he adds "Lare Bear, do me a solid: When Ms. Mays comes down, be sure to put in a good word for me. Okey dokey?" He makes an over-zealous double thumbs-up and walks away before Larry can give him another bitter look.

Standing at the most beautiful urinal he's ever had the opportunity to defile, Flip regrets harassing Larry. He knows from Dean that Larry's having a rough time. Maybe he should have been more empathetic, felt more compassion. But honestly, Flip is tired of eating shit. He figures Larry's upset that Flip woke him with his horn the previous morning. It had been rude and inconsiderate. Flip is a big enough man to admit it. He wonders why

Larry is even working during the day; maybe to pick up shifts so he can get into his townhouse.

He shakes his dick, tucks it away and fixes his shirttail and belt. He spends a few moments straightening and washing and primping. He removes the nametag from his lapel, folds his fat head over on itself and sticks it in a side pocket of his workbag. *That's better.* Satisfied that he looks as good as he can at present, he pats his front pocket where his family pictures are stashed for reassurance and motivation. *Here goes nothing.* He shoves out the door with a medium-sized smile fixed on his large-sized face.

A tiny young woman in a fitted grey suit and a splashy mint shirt calls to him from the reflective interior of one of the elevators.

"Mr. Mellis," she says while advancing with her hand extended. She cocks her hip against the open elevator door.

"Ms. Mays I assume," he replies. She looks remarkably like he'd imagined.

She pumps his hand with vigour, and engages him with her smile. She's sure to make eye contact and hold his gaze as she speaks. "I am so happy to meet you. Did you get signed in with security?" She exudes Peppy-Go-Getter and Regular-Juice-Fast with a dash of Tiny-Dog-In-A-Purse thrown in.

"I sure did. No problem at all. Larry took good care of me," he says, intentionally matching her general rhythm and tone, even raising his voice half an octave. When she glances toward Larry, the smile leaves her eyes without leaving her lips.

"Shall we?" she asks, and gestures him into the elevator, removes her hip from the door and pushes one of the buttons. He follows her in.

"So. How are you feeling Mr. Mellis?" Honestly, he's feeling wretched. The elevator is lined floor to ceiling with polished, reflective, metal panels and everywhere he looks he's accosted by his own image. He stares at the toes of his black shoes before answering.

"Me? I'm feeling good. You may call me Flip if you like. Everyone does. What about you? How are you feeling?" He really wants to ask inappropriate questions about his competition for the position. But it would make him sound as needy as he really is. So he leaves it.

"Just fine, Flip. Thanks for asking. The week is just starting and I'm ready for the weekend already. I hate to be inside while the weather is so nice out."

Nice? It's like a sauna out there. Despite his conviction that his core temperature won't drop to normal levels until November, he says, "Oh, I know what you mean. Not many more days like this one." Which he knows isn't true. The heat could continue unabated for another six weeks. But it's the type of thing one is expected to say in such situations.

"This is us," she says, as she exits. Her heels clickity-click along the tile corridor and Flip has to move fast to keep up. She pushes a glass door open and says, "Come in."

As Flip goes in he reads the black lettering printed across the door: Ms. Myrna Mays, Director of Human Resources.

The office is long and narrow, with the door at one end and a single window at the far end. Between is an elaborate organizational desk system of matching modular, wood-veneered shelves, drawers, file cabinets and work surfaces. Myrna scoots around to the far side of a horizontal peninsula and takes a seat. Flip squeezes his rump between the arms of the chair opposite, setting his workbag on the floor beside him. He finds his pad of paper and pen, holds them at the ready, trying to appear attentive.

His mind is racing from one thing to the next. He wonders if he overdid his caffeine intake. Or maybe the caffeine and the back pills are a bad combination. His back feels good though.

He had forgotten about it completely until just now. His neck however, feels as raw as a carpet burn and he longs to rake at it. He's jiggling his pen, making the cap knock out sixteenth notes against his legal pad, forces himself to quit. He counts his breaths and looks across the desk at Myrna.

She's swivelling and rolling from cabinet to cabinet, gathering various materials into her lap before scooting back into her place across from him. She puts a file folder, some forms and a couple of glossy packets on her desktop.

"So sorry for the delay. I had to rush straight from a meeting, didn't have everything ready before I left," she explains. "Now. Let's get down to business."

Flip has regained his focus enough to realize he's already ahead in this psychological chess match. She's being very deferential; it's likely due to his age. *Finally these greying sideburns are paying off.* Also, she has seen his resumé and apparently received good recommendations on his behalf. So what if she's employed, fit, peppy and has a Director in front of her alliterative name. He has more than twenty years of experience. She's probably only been out of college for six years, or less even. Four maybe. No wonder she's apologizing.

Now, to match her tone and be magnanimous: "Oh, no problem at all. I understand completely. There is always so much to juggle and not enough time." He considers adding something about his own winning time management strategies. This is an interview after all; if he doesn't toot his own horn, who will? But he concludes there will be plenty of time.

"My hope is to give you an understanding of the company structure, the retirement plan, stock options, company matching, performance bonuses, sick leave, and the health and dental coverage the company offers. After that, I will give you a tour of the departments and take you to a conference room to meet some of the folks you might be working with." She looks at a tiny, rectangular, designer watch on her slim wrist.

"Excellent," he replies. Though in truth, he finds this process a little backwards. Typically one might have to give some basic contact information at the most. Getting a big spiel about the details of the benefits package before being interviewed or offered a job is unusual. But he holds his tongue, for now.

"I'd hoped you could meet with the current Director of Internal Communications, Mr. McCloud, but he's out of town for the day," she explains. "Let's get started, shall we?"

Myrna Mays methodically and professionally covers the materials she has in front of her. She turns each relevant page toward Flip and uses the eraser end of a number two pencil to indicate the passage of text that relates to the policy she's articulating, all while reading long passages upside down. She is practiced and capable. He thinks it's too bad she comes across a bit like a tabloid socialite princess. It will make it hard for people to take her seriously. But maybe she'll grow out of it.

With one part of his mind Flip takes a few notes and asks a couple of penetrating questions that he believes will demonstrate he's aware of how the corporate structure works. He sits up straight and smiles when Myrna looks his way, nods encouragingly, and is careful not to fidget. But another part of his mind is thinking of Byron. Dean's words must have been working on him.

The summer before he abandoned his family, Byron had packed his beloved Scout International with camping supplies and forced Flip to go for a weekend of fishing. They drove along back highways for hours, had a lunch of chilidogs at a picnic table next to a roadside restaurant with a walk-up window. Yellow jackets buzzed around the mouth of Flip's bottle of Hires root beer and he left it on the table unfinished.

They took a red dirt utility road into the woods, the windshield brushing branches slowly aside, the front bumper bending down the tall grass that grew down the centre of the path. At the top of a hill, Byron stepped out and turned a dial on the front hubs and pulled a lever inside to engage the 4-wheel drive. He put the car in drive, but didn't step on the gas or put his hands on the wheel. He just sat, his hands resting on his legs, his feet tucked back from the pedals. The engine idled, the Scout edged forward, bouncing slowly down the hill toward the secluded lake, the wooden dock, and the fishing cabin below.

Byron grinned warmly as Flip's eyes got big, watching the car drive itself.

"This old car has been to this lake so many times, I don't even have to steer it," he'd said. "The car remembers the way."

Something about being back in a business suit was like that for Flip. He could just let go, and his mouth would find an easy way down the worn ruts of past conversations and tired, comforting jargon. He barely needed to be present at all.

Myrna stops her presentation and sets her packet of information down. "That about does it," she says. "Do you have any other questions?"

"I was curious about the bonus structure. You say 'performance based.' I imagine the bonus is given to the head of each department based on the department's contribution to meeting or surpassing sales goals. Is that accurate?"

"Yes."

"Ah," he nods his head meaningfully. He asks a series of follow up questions, just hoping to demonstrate his knowledge.

At one point she says, "I bet that's true. It makes sense."

He's not even sure what he had said. "While we're on the subject, Myrna, may I ask another quick question?" He decides to push his advantage.

"Yes. Of course you can. That's what this process is for." She sounds very earnest, but she still checks her watch to be certain they're on schedule.

He asks about the bonus structure and stock options, he asks about vacation days, flex time and sick days. Myrna answers all of his questions thoroughly and to his satisfaction. She finds the appropriate folders and fliers to point to as she speaks. But he barely registers her replies.

What else had Dean said? Something about a curse being a blessing, and the other way around. Is it really a blessing to be back here, back in the world I was forced from, to a career I don't care for and barely even have to consciously think of in order to perform in?

When she stops again he asks, "Speaking of stock options and stock matching I'm curious about one detail: is DynaTech a privately held company or is it publicly traded?"

"It's privately held."

"Oh. That's good. Thank you."

Myrna nods and continues to read and point and slide pages at Flip. When she's finished the entire stack, she asks, "If you don't have any more questions," she doesn't pause for an answer, "then we should get started on the tour."

"Actually," Flip says, gathering the materials she's provided into his workbag. "I do have one more question, and I think it would be better discussed in your office, rather than in the hall.

"Yes?" She turns her slight wrist and glances at her watch again. She moves around the end of her desk and continues past Flip, heading for the door.

"I don't know what the salary range is for this position."

"Oh. Well. The range wasn't posted intentionally." She holds the door open for Flip, but he stands facing her, giving no indication that he's ready to leave. After a moment she lets the door close again.

Flip says, "I know you can't, and shouldn't, divulge insider information, so to speak. And that isn't what I'm asking. I wouldn't ask that. I'm simply curious about a ballpark range. Just to get an idea. This is a big decision for my family and me. Did I mention I have children?" He reaches for his back pocket as if he's about to remove a wallet and intends to subject her to pictures, though he doesn't carry a wallet and doesn't intend to share his snapshots. They're only for him.

As he expects her to, she stops him. "Yes. And I can only imagine how this kind of decision will impact your family." She waves off his attempt to share by flapping her tiny pale hand. "As you say, I can't tell you a specific number. But I can tell you, the salary you listed for your last job is near the bottom of the range that DynaTech would consider to fill this position."

Flip's chest constricts. For the first time today he feels like this opportunity is real. The salary he listed for his last position was a generous exaggeration. If he could come in at that number, he would be happy. The notion of getting more than that makes his head swim. His eyes feel fat in his head, and his neck itches.

At his last job, he had reached the end of his potential advancement. Here, even starting with the inflated numbers he supplied, there's potential for more growth over time. He begins to hope.

But, as soon as he does, the preponderance of recent life experience warns him he's about to be disappointed. That brings him back to reality. He gains control over the distracted, loopy feeling from wishful expectations and back pills. *There is no way they will offer me this job.* He feels he's adequately impressed Myrna Mays with his knowledge of corporate nuance, artfully gleaned information from her and positioned himself for any potential negotiation that might take place. He gives a polite smile and a nod and follows her out the door.

Myrna hustles to the elevator while narrating: "The third floor is home to Human Resources, as you know, Book-keeping, Payroll Services, and other internal financial departments."

In the elevator she pushes the button marked with a four and says, "The second floor is all Mail Room, Print Services and the cafeteria. You can see that some time. For now though, I think we should push ahead.

The elevator doors open and Myrna strides out. A man and a woman in similar business suits step aside to let them pass. The man gives a friendly nod and the woman lifts her coffee mug in a pleasant acknowledgement. The mug reads: We Can Do It, over an image of a woman rolling up a sleeve over a muscular forearm.

"Oh, Hello Rob. Hi Tonya. See you at three thirty," Myrna says, waving over her head as she passes. Flip is impressed with Myrna. *She's a little dynamo.*

"That was Rob and Tonya," she tells Flip. "So, this is the fourth floor." She leads him in a circuit of the floor, amid a maze of cubicles. Only the colour scheme is different from the image he'd formed in his mind.

"So here we have the Marketing group. The Graphic Design team, and Video Production." She waves to a few people. At the end of the first hall she peeks into an open door and gives a cursory knock as she enters, leading Flip behind her. The fiftyish woman at the desk looks up, removes her reading glasses and pushes a laptop away.

"Flip Mellis, please meet Kris Harmon: VP in charge of Marketing," Myrna says.

Kris Harmon is a little on the heavy side, but very lovely. When she stands she's surprisingly tall. Flip approaches and she leans over her desk to shake his hand. She has warm, dry skin with rough places. Something about her wide, honest face says *gardener* to him.

"I'm interviewing for the Director of Internal Communications position," he says.

"Of course. Great," Kris replies. "Well good luck. If you get the job, we will be working together a lot. DynaTech is a good company. I've been here nine years now. Best job I've ever had. So, good luck and see you around."

"Aren't you meeting with Flip upstairs?" Myrna asks.

"I was supposed to, but I got pulled into a phone conference with the Columbus job. They need a lot of hand-holding right now."

"I didn't know," Myrna says.

"Just happened."

There's a clear current of tension in the exchange. Perhaps Myrna thinks Kris should have informed her of a change in plans. Perhaps Kris feels she is too high-level to be concerned with Myrna's feelings. But they both behave professionally, and not knowing them, he can only speculate. He backs toward the door and waits for Myrna to finish.

Myrna says her goodbyes and glances at her watch again. Flip looks at his watch too, but doesn't really register the time. He's bored. Bored by the whole familiar corporate song and dance.

"Nice to meet you," he calls to Kris.

"You too," she says, pulling her laptop close and bringing a phone to her ear.

Flip falls into pace with Myrna. They complete their circuit, Myrna gives an occasional greeting or points out the minuscule distinctions between one set of contiguous cubicles and the next. They return to the elevators and wait for the doors to open.

"She seemed nice, Kris Harmon," he comments leadingly.

Myrna smiles and nods, but her eyes stay narrowed; similar to how she looked at Larry. He feels proud of his finely-honed observational skills. No wonder he is such a talented manager. The elevator opens and Myrna's finger depresses the five button.

They make the same circuit of the fifth floor. "This floor is devoted to our computer engineering department," she explains. Flip nods and tries to care.

Back in the elevator, they ride to the top floor. "The sixth floor is where the Communications department, the Executive Offices and the Corporate Sales Office is located."

He takes it as a good sign that his future office would be near the top executives. Proximity leads to access, access leads to influence and job security. They step out, into a space that looks like a high-end law office. There's rich wood panelling, wide, open spaces and groups of dark leather chairs positioned between walled office suites.

"Wow," Flip says.

"I know. Nice, huh?" Myrna replies. "It's a different world up here compared to my shotgun office." She uses her head to indicate the direction they are headed and leads the way a few yards to the door of a glass box conference room. She opens the door for him. There's a long, high-polish wooden table that could seat sixteen, complete with rolling, black leather chairs.

"It was nice to meet you Mr. Mellis," Myrna says. She smiles sweetly at him, just as Kristin used to, when she started misdirecting her daddy issues onto him.

"Flip," he reminds her.

"Nice to meet you, Flip," she corrects herself. "And really, I hope the interview goes well. You will be fine. You're a natural."

"That's sweet of you Myrna. And regardless of how things go here, it was nice meeting you too. I'll be sure to mention how gracious and professional you were. You're a very good person to have representing this company to potential new employees." While it seems like the right sort of thing to say in order to further endear himself to her, he also kind of means it. He shakes her hand warmly, giving an extra little squeeze at the end.

She looks appreciative. "They should be in to see you in a moment. Make yourself comfortable. There's water and coffee across the hall there." She points through the glass back wall to a lounge area. "If you think you can handle it, you'll have to make your own introductions. I'm sorry." She taps her watch face and shrugs her slight shoulders.

"I can handle it. I'll be fine. No worries."

"Take care." She leaves.

Flip moves to the far side of the table and chooses a chair near the middle. For a moment, he considers sitting at the head of the table, but worries about seeming too presumptuous. He pulls his notepad and pen out and glances at the questions he fashioned before coming in. He refreshes his memory by reading the few notes he had scrawled in Myrna's office. They don't amount to much. He spends most of his time trying to decipher his chicken scratch and muse over what *Seemingly left dog* could possibly mean. He gives up, and writes the name 'Kris Harmon' and her title. He documents some of the departments he walked through. He absently doodles a blocky handgun in the margins of the page. Motion catches his eye.

Through the glass wall he sees three white men in dark suits demonstrating corporate-style, jovial camaraderie. They all carry similar workbags and manage to look casual and loose in their expensive suits while they joke and jostle each other. Flip has a sense they are happily retreading some old incident. As they near the door to the conference room they stop to finish their conversation, and one of them checks his Blackberry. The other two, caught in a corporate Pavlovian response, take out their matching Blackberries and scroll around the screens for a moment. There is a jocular exchange about some memo they are each reading separately yet simultaneously.

When they're done, they turn into the room and start introducing themselves. Flip stands and tries to look as relaxed as they are. He pretends they're all gathering to compete in a good-natured sporting event, like a company softball league.

"JonJon Baur," the first man says. He's middle-aged, of medium build, medium height, with a moderate amount of thinning, dusty brown hair. He dresses in layers of expensive-looking and lushly-textured earth tones. "I'm VP in charge of National Sales Strategies."

"JonJon," Flip says, as they grasp hands across the table. Many people repeat names upon introduction in order to commit a new person to memory. Flip simply believes self-important people like to hear their own names. He has no illusions that he will remember JonJon's name by the afternoon. "Flip Mellis. As I am sure you know, I'm here for the Director of Internal Communications position."

"Yes. Of course." JonJon turns to his companions and makes introductions. "This is our Director of Government Relations, Connor Craig."

The tallest and lankiest of the three stretches his long arm diagonally across the table, not really needing to get any closer.

"Connor," Flip says.

"I like how you said *I'm here for the job* not *I am interviewing for the job*. Like you're here to claim what's yours. Very cool," Connor says. Connor has thick, blond hair, cropped so short on the sides Flip can see his head has a reddish tan. His suit is dark and his tie brings out his scalp.

"And this," JonJon continues, "is the newest member of our team, the highly-esteemed Mr. Amos Zimmerman."

A short, stocky man in his forties with a shaved head and a full beard comes around the end of the table and takes Flip's hand.

"Amos," Flip says.

"Flip," says Amos. Amos looks a little scuzzy; his beard looks as if it was trimmed by gnawing rodents and his black suit looks as if it has been slept in. Flip can easily imagine him sitting on a flattened cardboard box and jangling a cup full of change in the mouth of some alley.

"What department are you with, Amos?"

"I'm the VP in charge of Computer Products and Networking Services."

"Good to meet you, Amos."

They all take seats and each of them hoists a computer bag into an adjacent chair. JonJon and Connor on one side, Flip and Amos on the other. They each turn to search through their bags and pull out copies of Flip's resumé and application. JonJon clears his throat as he looks at some notes, obviously preparing to lead the discussion. Flip readies himself to pay close attention to his tone, rhythm and energy level, in order to emulate it.

"So," JonJon says in a conversational tone. "Why don't you take a moment to tell me what you know about DynaTech."

"So," Flip says, in a conversational tone, arranging his arms and tenting his hands in a casual variation of JonJon's physicality. "I would love for you to fill in the gaps as I go. But as I understand it DynaTech is a national data management and technology consulting firm that employs computer engineers to create proprietary computer programs and networking packages to serve particular industries. Namely health insurance and medical care facilities." Flip impresses himself with his capacity to re-organize and regurgitate the stream of information Myrna has already shared with him.

"Yes. That is basically accurate," JonJon agrees. "But DynaTech is not just national. We have two offices in Europe and one in Canada. We are preparing the way to open an office in South America."

"And we don't sell just a few products to a few industries," Amos adds. "While it's true all of our largest clients are hospitals and insurance companies, each of those hospitals has different needs. So each program and network we design . . ."

"And maintain," Connor says.

"And maintain," Amos agrees, "is actually designed specifically for each client. It's a huge undertaking."

"Impressive," Flip says. "I was aware of your reputation, of course, but not the scope of your operation." Flip knows flattery is the coin of the realm with upper managers.

"Your resumé indicates an impressive amount of experience in writing and communications. But, tell me, is it safe to say you don't have a depth of knowledge in programming? Is that fair?" Amos asks.

"Yes. Absolutely," Flip says.

"How do you hope to write about what we do with limited background knowledge?"

"Good question, Amos." Complimenting the questioner is always a good place to start. "And I understand your concern. In fact, I share it with you. But I understand the Director of Internal Communications' role in the company is as an interface between your department, Amos, and that of Marketing and Corporate." He looks around the table to see heads nodding. "I don't have your knowledge about computer engineering. Clearly. But I am capable of capturing the most important elements of the work your department does and relating it to Sales and Marketing in a form that they can use to find more clients, and to communicate with existing clients." Again, more nodding. He directs this last comment to Connor, "And of course boil it down into a persuasive set of bullet points that can be communicated to state and local politicians, help them understand how increased efficiency can save money and improve service in a cost effective way. Which in turn smooths the way with regulators and utilities whose services support the good work DynaTech does." Flip stops talking and leans back in his chair. He wants to keep talking. He finds the silence scary. He wants to fill it up, keep selling. But he wills himself to breathe.

"Good," JonJon declares. "Connor, do you have any questions for Mr. Mellis?"

Connor gets a sly look on his face, his long neck pushing his face forward. "I was going to ask the same question," he says. "But Amos beat me to it." They all laugh, Flip too, though he doesn't get the joke. "But seriously," Connor says. "If knowledge of our products is not a requirement for doing this job well, then what qualifications do you bring? What do you offer that the next guy . . ."

"Or gal," Amos adds.

". . . Or gal, doesn't offer?"

"Again," Flip says, leaning forward to engage Connor better. "That is a good question. I could mention many things." The truth is, he can only think of one, so he decides to riff on it. "I will start by sharing an important one: experience. There were times in my last position when my work, if mishandled, could have cost McCorkle-Smithe tens of millions of dollars. Or if handled strategically and with subtlety, could have prevented a financial disaster. In those particular cases, I'm happy to say, I made all the right choices.

"I know how to work with people I like, and people that are more difficult. I know how to manage those who work for me, and whose quality of work I am responsible for, as well as understanding how to manage up, if the situation ever demands it. Because for me, it is all about what's best for the company, and that means always keeping the client happy." *Wow. I totally pulled that out of my ass.*

He looks at the faces around to check if they seem as dazzled by him as he is with himself. They are all nodding again. Amos is holding Flip's resumé and pretending to look at it. It's obvious he's already checked out of the meeting. Connor's still grinning like he wants to share another witticism. JonJon looks more thoughtful. He holds Flip's eyes with his.

"Flip," he says. "As you say, you were at McCorkle-Smithe for many years. And your references raved about you. They backed up the kinds of things you have been saying here. Team player, problem solver, works well under pressure, highly recommended and so on. I get all of that. Why did you leave? Why leave when you didn't have anything else lined up?"

"I'm sure you can all read between the lines. I was asked to leave as part of a broad corporate reshuffling. McCorkle-Smithe is an international construction consultant. When the economy went in the tank, here and abroad, tons of projects we'd already won simply dried up. There was stockholder pressure to cut overheads, to eliminate employees. I was well paid and non-essential. You understand Communications and Graphic design are two of the departments that a firm like McCorkle-Smithe considers extra, even fluffy and unnecessary. I would like to argue that it was a short-sighted decision, that the company will fail because they fired many good, experienced people. But I don't know that for sure. And honestly I don't wish them ill," he lies convincingly. "In my last few years at M-S, I had grown a little bored. I was looking for a new challenge." (This last part he manufactures on the fly, but he runs with it.) "Some people close to me knew I was shopping my resumé around. I think it made the decision to let me go much easier. It's one of the things that excites me about DynaTech. Here, I will be applying my experience in a new industry. My unfamiliarity with the product is the very thing that makes me feel enthusiastic about this company. I have the kind of nervous buzz I used to get before a football game." Again, complete fabrication. He never played football, or watched it. Frankly he despises team sports, only finds it valuable for the metaphors it offers. Though the idea of hot wings and beer on a Sunday does get him going. "You know what I mean?"

Everyone nods. Though mentioning sports may have alienated Amos a bit; he nods only very slightly and seems much less engaged. In fact, Flip sees him slip his Blackberry from his pocket and thumb the roller ball, careful to keep it below table level.

"Well, fellas," JonJon says to the room. "You guys get back to work while I deliver Flip to the decision maker."

They all shove back from the table, shake and exchange pleasantries. JonJon lets the other two leave ahead of him. Then he holds the door for Flip.

"Thank you," Flip says, and exits the conference cube.

"No problem. Let's walk and talk. I wanted to give you the chance to ask any unanswered questions. Connor and Amos are travelling to a conference in Las Vegas this afternoon. I needed to get them on their way."

"I understand." They walk at a slow pace, side by side.

After a few moments, JonJon looks over at Flip and stops walking. "So? Questions? Do you have any?"

"Oh, right. Sorry. I was just trying to take it all in." Flip nods his head to the large, artsy, black and white photos framed and hanging along the corridor. He assumes they are images of hospitals that are clients of DynaTech. JonJon acknowledges the comment by pushing his lower lip out and eyeing the images too.

"I'm mostly interested in the corporate culture. I have a generally good impression of DynaTech," Flip says. Though truly he has very little impression at all, except that they might supply him with work and a paycheck. "But I would like to feel I'm making a good decision for my family, and for myself."

"Well," JonJon says. "I have been with the company coming up on six years. I've been happy here. Largely. There are some challenges, but nothing unusual: personalities, egos and pissing contests. Typical stuff really. Nothing to complain about."

"I understand," Flip says. "Do you generally feel supported and challenged?"

"I do. I mean some days are monotonous. But the company has been growing the entire time I've been here. That means the ability to move within the company both vertically and laterally." JonJon's hip rattles and he pulls his square phone from a holster at his side, under his jacket.

"Excuse me," he says without looking up and starts typing with his thumbs.

"We should wrap it up. The boss is ready for you."

Flip faces back down the corridor toward what is clearly the most important office on the floor. He asks, "And do you think DynaTech makes a good product, provides good service? Do you feel like you make a difference?"

"What? I don't follow," JonJon says, holstering his phone.

"Never mind." *Now is not the time to get philosophical.* He can do that in the cafeteria a few months from now, after he gets the job. *Focus*, he warns himself. *Your head isn't in the game.* They pass an empty desk where Flip supposes an executive secretary must reside, and comes to a halt next to the decision maker's office.

"So here we are." JonJon shakes Flip's hand again. "Just knock on the door when you're ready. Mr. Krueger is expecting you." He flees like a rat leaving a flaming tenement. *That doesn't bode well*, Flip thinks. Then he knocks.

Clifton Krueger stands from behind his desk when Flip enters and gives a friendly wave. His shoulders are so wide, his chest so broad, he looks like a billboard wrapped in a dress shirt. His head is bald on top with a thin rim of dark hair growing long and over his ears. From across the room, he reminds Flip of Peter Boyle as the monster in Young Frankenstein, minus the squared off head and neck bolts.

"Hello," Flip calls and returns the wave.

Flip closes the door behind him and takes several long strides toward Mr. Krueger. The executive comes around his desk to meet Flip halfway. Despite his width, he carries himself well and moves fluidly. He delicately shakes Flip's hand. Flip is relieved Mr. Krueger is an imposing figure. It allows Flip to feel that he is of a normal size, not the biggest human in the room.

"Mr. Mellis. So glad you could make it," he says in a warm, gentle tone. "I hope you enjoyed your time with us so far." He's a little taller than Flip, but trim in spite of his expansive frame.

"Yes," Flip says. "You have an impressive company, lots of good people. By the way, Myrna in Human Resources seemed really on top of things down there."

"Oh yes. Myrna is great," he says, walking Flip toward a couch and a pair of overstuffed chairs. "Let's do this over here. And I can't take credit for the company really. I've only been with DynaTech a short time myself. Actually, Myrna took me through the paces when I was recruited. You need a drink of something? Coffee? My assistant is out with a sick child today. But I'd be happy to get you something." Mr. Krueger takes a seat in the centre of the couch, drapes his arms along the back and spreads his legs wide, clearly claiming the couch as his domain.

Flip picks the larger of the two soft leather club chairs and settles in. "No. No, thank you Mr. Krueger. I'm fine. I had coffee before I arrived."

"Good. May I call you Flip?" His voice is monotone, almost hypnotic.

"Of course." He doesn't ask to call Mr. Krueger by his first name.

"So, Flip. Let me cut to the chase. We are interviewing a number of people that are equally qualified for this position. You are the last we will see. Tomorrow morning I will meet with my people, listen to their impressions, then I will, hopefully, hire someone."

Flip nods.

"What matters most to me is how a potential employee will fit at DynaTech. Group dynamics are funny. The most qualified person on paper isn't always the one who will be most successful on the ground. There are indefinable qualities that affect this decision. To be honest, no matter how thorough the selection process, it's always a crapshoot. You never know how someone will work out. But, in order to attempt an educated decision, I try to take a few moments to get to know people. I want you to answer a few questions for me. Be honest. Be yourself. Can you do that?"

"Yes," Flip lies earnestly, with a confident smile. *This is clearly a trap.* There is no way he's going to let down his guard and say what he really thinks. That's not how the game is played. He'll be diplomatic, give the appearance of being unguarded and honest. A straight shooter; Mr. Krueger has a confident, direct and easy way about him. Flip tries to mirror it.

"From the little I've seen of your company so far, I'm pleasantly surprised how comfortable I feel here," Flip says conversationally. "But I agree with you. I know I can do the work. But, I don't know for sure that DynaTech is the right home for me.

Hopefully we can find that out together." *Restating and agreeing with Mr. Krueger's premise is a safe, conservative way to start.*

"We are speaking the same language," Mr. Krueger says. He sits forward and crosses his legs, lets his big hands hang loose on their wrists over the knob of his knee. "You've been out of work for a while now. Tell me about that."

Flip clears his throat to buy time. He has to turn his long-term unemployment into a positive. He needs to sell it. He gently coughs into his fist.

"You sure you don't need something to drink?"

"I'm fine," Flip says, fake-coughing again. "Just a tickle." He composes himself, takes a calming breath and starts. "When I lost my job, I tried to look at it as an opportunity. Luckily my wife and I had managed our money well over the years," he lies again. "We had enough money to allow me to take my time, find the *right* position. I was offered a job the first month. But, it was wrong for me; for my family. So my wife, Lynn, and I agreed it was best to pass on the offer."

"And how much longer will that money last?" Mr. Krueger asks, not unkindly.

"Well. Not much longer."

"Yes," Mr. Krueger says, as if he's familiar with the story. "And how has the job search been? How many places have you applied?"

"I applied for a couple of dozen positions. Positions where I was a very good fit and qualified, and that interested me. The truth is, I was just as concerned with not taking the wrong job as I was with finding the right job, if you see what I mean."

"I think I understand your point, Mr. Mellis. But would you explain a little more?"

"As I have searched for a new position, I've tried to ignore the mounting financial pressure. Instead, I've focused on finding the right job. Because this could very well be the company I retire from, the company where I share all the skill, experience and insight I've accumulated over my professional life."

Mr. Krueger nods at this encouragingly.

"Also, I have friends who lost white-collar jobs and took the first thing they found. Now they're underpaid and unable to leave. I don't want to make that mistake, not if I can help it."

"Yes: the perpetually under-employed. It's an ongoing problem. It was prudent of you to be selective," Mr. Krueger says supportively. Flip feels slightly buoyant. Mr. Krueger's apparent sincerity and empathy foster a spark of confidence deep within Flip. Something genuine he hasn't felt for ages. This makes Flip nervous.

His face feels flushed and he's winded by his monologue. His neck is beginning to itch again. His lower back is not happy with the chair; as nice as it looks, there's no lumbar support. But he nods to Mr. Krueger again, in acceptance of the compliment.

"The question that follows is," Mr. Krueger seems very relaxed and speaks in a kind of mesmerizing hum-speak, "Do you feel that DynaTech meets your personal requirements?"

Flip tries to pause, to give an impression of thoughtfulness, before saying, "Yes. Absolutely. I believe I could do good work here. Also, I'm happy to hear DynaTech is still a privately-held company."

Mr. Krueger uncrosses his legs, a puzzled look on his face. "I don't think I follow your line of logic. Did you jump to a new subject?" He no longer sounds relaxed.

Flip pulls at the knot of his tie, he can't breathe. He digs at the back of his neck. "No. No I didn't change subjects. Let me see how best to say it." Then he doesn't say anything. Mr. Krueger is either sitting patiently, unbothered by the lull or he's glaring witheringly at Flip. It's hard to tell.

"Mr. Krueger," Flip says carefully, aware he's about to articulate a business stance that could be controversial. It's an observation he's never spoken out loud. But he decides to risk it. The only way to leave the impression of shooting straight is to take a stand. So he says it bluntly, as he thinks Mr. Krueger might: "It would seem that making good business decisions should lead to profitability, which would lead to a higher valuation of a company's stock. But, in fact, sometimes, bad long-term decisions can make a company more profitable in the short-term and drive stock prices higher. Once a company is traded publicly, I think the pressure to show gains every quarter becomes more important than making good decisions, providing good service, or being a good employer."

Mr. Krueger is stone-faced, unreadable. Flip regrets heading down this path. But it's too late now. He has to bring it home. He scoots to the edge of his seat and begins to gesture more broadly, speak a little more loudly.

"You see Mr. Krueger, if a company shows significant growth from good decisions, inevitably that growth slows or reaches a plateau. It's a natural arc. But stockholders become spoiled by the high growth; they want more. They demand it. They turn the screws and apply pressure. The company looks for ways to save money. They make systemic tweaks; cut waste and find efficiencies. All good. Quarter after quarter the pressure continues. The upshot is, the workforce is often asked to work longer hours, under greater stress, while benefits are cut and bonuses are slashed or non-existent. Meanwhile, a few people at the top are taking large profits, based on stock prices which have continued to improve on paper. But at the expense of hollowing all of the talent out of the workforce."

Flip is getting wound up now, almost frantic. He thinks he's losing Mr. Krueger. He has an urge to leap to his feet. Though he has enough self-awareness to know that would be reckless; not to mention his back might not allow it. He scoots even further in his seat and the volume of his voice continues to rise.

"You see, business ethics is to corporate America as religion is to the people: an opiate that helps keep the workers in line. The executives and large investors aren't believers. They aren't subject to the same rules. The only rule for them is to do what's profitable for now, whatever they think they can legally get away with and screw all those people who have devoted their most productive years to helping make the company profitable." Flip realizes he's yelling. "The only concepts they understand are *more* and *right now*."

He slumps back in his seat, sure he just blew it; certain he said too much. But he straightens his tie, tugs his waistcoat down, pulls his shoulders back and holds himself as tall as he can.

Mr. Krueger stands. "Well, I appreciate your candour in these matters. I had a few other questions, but I think you've been very forthright in articulating your perspective." He walks toward his office door and opens it to let Flip out.

Flip hustles the best he can. He feels rumpled and spent. "You understand the things I just said apply to my concerns about publicly-traded companies. Not privately-held companies like DynaTech," Flip attempts to explain as he's ushered out the door.

"Yes. I think I understand your position," Mr. Krueger says. "You can expect Human Resources to contact you, one way or another. I trust you can show yourself out."

Flip starts to turn and shake hands, to say *thank you* and say *goodbye*. Mr. Krueger's office door closes before Flip gets a chance.

Fuck.

In the elevator Flip loosens his tie and unbuttons the second button of his shirt. On the first floor he strides straight through the turnstile without acknowledging Larry.

He shucks off his suit jacket as soon as he exits the front door. Walking out of the artificially cold interior into the raw, wet, heat of the day is brutal and sudden, and it steals Flip's breath for a moment. He storms to his parking spot at the side of the building and by the time he reaches the Passat, sweat is sheeting down his body. He drops his workbag and jacket on the hood just to get his hands free. He quickly removes his waistcoat, rips his tie off, and pulls his shirttail out. He unlatches his belt, placing one hand on the front fender for balance, and instantly pulls his hand away and blows on his palm. *Hot hot hot.*

The belt goes on the pile with everything else. He has to excavate in order to reach his car keys. He unlocks the door, slips into the driver's seat and jams the key in the ignition. He cranks on it hard, the engine comes on and the blower blasts him with hot air. He snaps off the blower and rolls all the windows down, willfully ignoring the degraded integrity of the damaged window.

As sure as he's sitting there, he knows he's just blown it. And for him, that means it's over. It's time to start preparing to put the Walther to use. This time he will leave a note. Something meaningful. What breaks his heart is the idea of telling Lynn about the interview; having to dash her hopes again. He'd been harbouring hope that his family would be proud of him. That he could save the day, be the hero, get his shit together. He punches the dashboard until his knuckles are scuffed and sore. Slowly, he undoes the buttons of his dress shirt.

A cross breeze pushes some of the stifling air from the car's interior, but not enough to make it pleasant. Beads of sweat crawl down the back of his scalp and over his irritated neck. He happily gives into the urge and scrapes at the chafed skin until he thinks it will bleed. He brings his other hand back and pries at the meat over his vertebrae as if searching for a seam, as if he will peel his disguise open and reveal the actual Flip hidden beneath. All he achieves is to inflame his skin further.

He's reminded of the parable of Job, scraping at boils with broken potshards after God has taken everything from him on a bet with Satan. He wonders if cosmic gambling is to blame for his situation. *Makes as much sense as anything.*

His mother would be proud, that in a time of personal crisis, he has considered anything biblical. She was always such a calming force in his life. If she were here she would know what to say to put things in perspective, to soothe him and lift his spirits. The conversation would probably take place over fried food. But given the revelation Byron had dropped on him, if she were here now, Flip might tell her to go straight to hell. *God I'm a mess.*

He stares a long time through his windshield at his suit and workbag piled on the hood of the car. He's tempted to drive off without moving them. But, after a while, he stands painfully and snatches them up, dumps them in his backseat.

He removes his dress shirt, wads it into a knot and pitches it in with the rest. He kicks off his painful, shiny shoes, flicking the first one expertly inside the open car door. The second one goes under the car. He just leaves it, doesn't even consider lying on the melting asphalt to fish it out.

While he's at it, he unhooks his pants and lets them drop around his ankles. He kicks them into the back as well. The snapshots of his family fall to the ground, and a hot breeze scatters them like dead leaves. He lets them go.

He has to laugh. Here he is. Standing in nothing but silky boxer shorts, dress socks and a sweat soaked white T-shirt. A whole building of tinted windows staring down on him, like a wall of cold soulless eyes. And he couldn't give a shit. He stands a long time looking at the building, trying to stare it down, see who will blink first, hands on his hips as if issuing a challenge;

David before Goliath, except with even God betting against him. He scratches his neck some more and then his ass. He hustles his balls too, for good measure. The asphalt begins to burn the soles of his feet through his socks.

He settles heavily into the driver's seat, shoves the car in drive, and pulls forward. The coffee is there in the cup holder, he pours it out the window and drops the cup in the lot. Then he builds speed and hops the kerb driving straight through the "park" that separates the parking lot from the main road. He extends his arm and waves his middle finger out the window in a final fare-thee-well.

I need a drink.

RED-HANDED

At Ed's Drive Thru Liquors, he goes right to the pick-up window and honks his horn.

"What do you need?" asks a man who looks like skid-row-Santa in a black Ozzfest tour T-shirt.

"Rum. The strongest I can buy for the lowest price." The guy looks down on Flip, takes in his boxer shorts and hairy thighs. He gives a tight nod and slides the window closed.

Flip snaps the car in park and turns around in the seat; his silky ass pressing on the steering wheel. He feels around for his slacks, grabs them, the horn honks once as he moves back into driving position. He turns the pants over and over, frantic that he has lost his debit card and cash. Eventually he finds them. He throws the pants in the floor of the empty passenger seat, and waits.

His boxers feel twisty, so he hitches them around a bit, realizes his dick has slipped out. He puts it back and tugs his boxers down his big thighs, making sure Santa isn't watching through the window. He wonders how long his stuff has been hanging out.

Santa comes back and says, "I got this big bottle called 'Drunken Seaman'." He shakes a giant plastic bottle so Flip can see it. "It's seven hunerd and fity em els and high alcohol content.

About forty-seven percent. That's high for rum. Eighteen twenty-six with tax."

"Forty-seven, forty-eight. Whatever it takes," Flip tries to joke. Santa is nonplussed. So Flip asks, "How's it taste?"

"You didn't say nothing about taste before," Santa answers.

"Touché," Flip replies and passes his money through the window. The man hands him change and a bottle in a paper bag.

"You have a nice day," Santa says. But he says it as if he can tell by looking that Flip's day will not be good.

"Ho ho ho Motha fuckah," Flip replies cavalierly. He twists the cap off the rum and takes a swig. It tastes like spicy aluminium, and not in a good way. The bottle goes between his legs, and he stomps the pedal to leave. The engine revs but doesn't move.

"Oops," he says through his open window. But Santa is already gone. He shifts the transmission into gear and drives away.

At the Lakeside, Flip sees several things at once. Dean is sitting on the veranda, Flip's door is standing open and a push-cart of cleaning supplies and linens is jammed sideways in his door. Intuitively he knows what he'll find if he can get in the room fast enough. He leaves the car door open, the engine still idling. He takes his bottle, hobbles in sock feet across the pebbly pavement and sets it on the table with Dean.

"Hello," Dean says. It's clear he's about to start asking questions about Flip's attire.

"Be right back," Flip says fast, walking away before Dean can get going.

He pulls the cart out of his door and shoves into the room. Vanessa says, "Oh. Mr. Mellis. I was just finishing up. " He's startled her and she looks guilty.

Flip thinks back to when he left that morning: he had pitched the pills onto his rumpled bed. Now, the bed is made with a fresh coverlet, and the pill bottle is on the kitchen counter. He can see her face turn toward the pill bottle, in unison with his own eyes.

"I'm going to be leaving now, Mr. Mellis. Have a good day," Vanessa says. She makes for the door.

Flip snatches the pill bottle from the counter and rattles it. He pops the lid and upends it into his hand. Two pills remain.

"What the fuck?" he says, half to himself and half to Vanessa. He holds his hand out so she can witness the evidence he has against her, but she's out of the door. He rushes after her.

"Hey. Vanessa. Wait." She doesn't wait. She keeps pushing her cart, almost at a run. "I can call the cops on you, Vanessa. Or you can stop and talk to me." She stops.

He walks after her, catches up as she turns to face him.

"What?" she asks defiantly. She leans around him to see if Dean is watching.

"You stole my pills. I know you did. Don't try and deny it."

"No I didn't," she denies.

"You know what a nanny cam is? It's a tiny camera that parents hide in their homes to keep an eye on their children and the people who are supposed to be taking care of them." He concocts the beginnings of the lie easily.

That gets her eyes back on him. "What do I care," she says. But there isn't much heat behind it.

"I'm a parent," he says. "And I have a nanny cam. It's set up to feed directly to my laptop. My laptop is in my car. And the camera is in my motel room." He pauses for Vanessa to process everything. Her eyes look past his left shoulder at his car, and past his right shoulder at his room. "I recorded everything that went on in there," he bluffs. "You are so busted. Now either you come clean, or I give the video to the cops when I turn you in."

"What the hell, man?" she says. "That isn't legal is it? You've violated my civil rights; my right to privacy and shit." But, she works her hand down into the pocket of her jeans and pulls out a Zip-Lock snack bag full of pills. "There. Take 'em. Happy?"

He doesn't take them, just leaves her holding the bag out in front of her. "What do you do with these?" he says, nudging the bag with one finger.

"What do you think? I sell 'em." She starts to gain her composure, starts to think of how to get out of this situation.

"How much?" he asks. She looks confused. "How much do you get for them?"

"I don't know. My boyfriend moves them. I think he gets five bucks a pill or something like that." She glances toward the road, as if her boyfriend might come ripping in any second. But he doesn't.

"Okay," Flip says. He tries to do the math and then reaches out for the baggy and takes two pills. He puts them on his tongue and swallows them dry. "You pay me fifty bucks or I turn you in and supply enough video evidence to convict you."

"Now, Mr. Mellis," she says breathily; slowly she moves a little closer to him, touching his shoulder. "You don't have to do that. I bet we could work something out."

"Listen to me closely," he whispers back, as if they were longtime lovers. "If you pay me, you and your gear-head boyfriend can still make a profit. Don't pay me, and you will end up in jail. And don't try to manipulate me or the price goes up." She takes her hand away.

"Are you stupid? My boyfriend won't pay you. He'll come in here and beat your ass if he hears about this. Let me make you a deal. Drop this whole thing and I won't tell him about it."

Flip thinks about his gun tucked into the cardboard box in his closet. He says, "You get me that money today or I go to the police and I implicate your idiot boyfriend. If he doesn't like it, tell him to come see me. But I am not five foot five and a hundred pounds. I'm not a girl. I'm big and feeling mean and I've got nothing left to lose. Nothing. You can bet I'll fight back. He might just get an ugly surprise if he fucks with me."

She looks him up and down and says, "You're mental."

"I'm giving you a chance. It's the only one I'll offer. You know where to find me."

She turns back to her cart and walks away.

"One other thing, while we're negotiating. If I hear you've been stealing from anyone else, the police get the video. Except Larry. Help yourself to his shit." He walks back toward Dean's veranda.

"What was all of that about?" Dean asks. "And why are you in your underwear?"

"The short answer to both questions is that I feel liberated by embracing the inevitability of my circumstances. If you pour the rum, I'll come and give you a longer answer in a minute."

He cleans out his car and rolls up his windows, carefully. He finds he still has a couple of pills in his hand and drops them in the empty prescription bottle, slips into some shorts, and changes his shirt. He tucks the loaded gun in his pants pocket, just in case he has to shoot somebody, and goes outside with every intention of getting royally shitfaced.

THE HARSHEST OF HANGOVER CURES

When his phone rings the next morning, Flip assumes it's the alarm clock and he knocks it, as well as the lamp, onto the floor trying to swat it with a pillow. The phone falls out of its cradle and he can hear a tiny, faraway voice calling his name.

He fumbles the phone and holds it to the side of his head, upside down, and speaks into the earpiece. "Hello? Hello?" He hears what he thinks is Lynn's voice, but can't understand it.

"Hello? Lynn? I can't hear you." He looks around the room, expecting to see her coming out of the bathroom.

"Flip," the voice says. "Flip." He knows that tone: she's scared. Something's wrong with one of the kids. Clarity comes immediately. He turns the phone over and says, "I'm here, Lynn. What's happened?"

"Flip. It's Dylan. He was hit by a car." Flip goes numb with fear. "We're at the emergency room at St. Elizabeth's. Please, come. I don't know how bad it is yet. We're waiting on the doctor now."

"I understand," he says. "I'll be there in fifteen minutes."

He speeds the whole way. Fortunately, after a late night that included loads of cheap rum and a clandestine, if otherwise uneventful, cash payoff from Vanessa, Flip had slept in his clothes.

When he rushes into the waiting room twelve minutes after hanging up the phone, he has foul breath and clothes that smell of acrid body odour, booze and smoke from skinny brown cigarettes.

"What happened," he asks.

Lynn, who is pacing the perimeter of the room, turns to see him, puts her hands over her face and tries not to cry.

"What do we know?" he asks.

Sara rises from her seat and puts her face in his chest; her breath is hot and ragged. She begins to sob. He presses her head against him.

"Somebody say something," he demands. His mother-in-law turns her face down, a crumpled tissue clutched in her hand. He knows by looking, she was supposed to be with Dylan when it happened. He knows it's her fault, and she knows it too. He starts to move toward her, tries moving Sara aside, to shake some kind of response from Coleen. But Lynn is there and pressing against him, draping her arms over his shoulders.

"What happened to my boy," he says quietly into Lynn's hair. "What happened to Dylan?"

Still no one speaks. He thinks the worst, thinks Dylan is dead. He wants the hell out of there, he can't take it, wasn't built for all this, isn't strong enough. He starts shoving at Lynn, and trying to pry Sara's arms from around him.

"Stop. Stop it," Sara says. "We don't know anything yet, Dad. We don't know. The doctor is still in with him. No one's spoken to us, yet."

That calms him down a bit. She called him Dad. He stands still. Lets the women in his life find what comfort they can in his expanse. He sees his mother-in-law twist around in the chair, putting her back to him. After a few moments he says, "I'm going to try and find out something from someone. But I need to know what's going on. Somebody talk to me. Now."

"Sara," Lynn says. "Keep your grandmother company." Sara doesn't argue. Lynn takes his hand and leads him to the hall.

She finds a spot between two empty trolleys shoved along the wall.

"Dylan wanted to ride around the block after breakfast. Mom said she would walk him. She swears she told him to wear his helmet, but he couldn't find it."

"Typical," Flip says.

"He took off down the sidewalk and left her in the dust. She saw the car backing out of a driveway and tried yelling for Dylan to slow down. He was busy trying to coast and stand on his pegs. He couldn't hear her, or ignored her. The car backed right into him as he shot across their driveway." She looks to him like a five-year-old who's fallen at the playground.

He wants to say, 'Didn't I say . . .' or 'What was she thinking . . .' or 'This would never have happened if I . . .' but he says none of that. Instead he takes her hand.

"This is the hospital where he was born," he says.

"I know." They stand quietly for a long moment, letting things go unsaid.

"I wish it had been handled differently, but honestly, it could have happened anytime," Flip says. "It isn't your mother's fault and we need to be careful not to blame her. He's a kamikaze every waking minute. God knows he's gotten away from me before."

"I know. But I'm so fucking mad about it."

"Me too," he says.

"Do you think you could tell her what you just said? About it not being her fault? She's all torn up right now."

"I can. And I will. But first I want to find out how Dyl is doing. Tell me what you know, where is he hurt?"

"Okay. There was a cut on his head. Lots of blood and the side of his face was swollen and starting to bruise. His left arm and right leg both seemed really tender, or the other way around. The good news is he landed in the grass and the bike seems fine. So I'm hopeful he's just banged-up. The neighbour, the old man that was driving, he tried to help. Offered to drive us, said he would pay. His wife said it wasn't their fault, asked why no one was watching him, why he wasn't wearing a helmet. I think she even called a lawyer while she was standing there."

"Ok. Fuck her. I'm going to the nurse's station now," he says. He turns to leave.

"Flip," she says. "Thanks for being here. We need you here."

"You're welcome." He starts to go again.

"Flip."

"Yes?"

"I don't know what this means for us. I mean, it doesn't change anything. You understand."

"I know it doesn't," he says. "And honestly, right now that is the last thing I give a shit about. Can I go now?"

"Sorry. Go."

At the nurse's station, three women in matching light blue scrubs are hunkered over their charts and try to ignore him.

"I need to know what's happening with my son. Dylan. Dylan Byron Mellis. He was hit by a car and no one is telling us anything," he says.

None of the nurses move; each hoping someone else will deal with Flip. Eventually the nurse farthest from him sets her chart down and comes around the counter.

She is low and plump with black hair, skin like a caramel apple and Polynesian features. Her nametag reads, Fulala Palaylay. She claps her hands together in front of her mouth, like she's about to pray for him.

"Mr?" He expects an accent, but she sounds like your average mid-westerner.

"Mellis," he answers. He's afraid to say more. Afraid to ask questions, scared they will be answered.

"Mr. Mellis. I was with your son when he first arrived. There was a lot of blood, and I know that can be scary. Your son . . ."

"Please," Flip says. "His name is Dylan. Is Dylan okay?"

". . . Dylan. He is stable and safe for now. He has both a broken arm and a broken leg. He also had a laceration on his scalp. Not too serious. That's where the blood was from. A scalp lac can really bleed, but he didn't lose a lot of blood. That isn't the concern. They were able to set his bones and stitch him up. All very routine. But the bruising on his face and head, that has the doctor worried. Your son, Dylan, passed out before we started working on him."

"But, he's stable and safe."

"Yes, for now, as I said. The doctor ordered a head CT. The reason the doctor hasn't been in to see you is he's waiting for the results. He's very busy and wants to wait until he can give you more information."

"What does that mean? Exactly what? Be as honest as you can please. I need to know, need to tell my family something. We need to be prepared. Need to do something to help Dylan. How can I help? Can I give blood? I could give blood. If it would help. We're the same type, Dylan and me." Flip looks behind him. Lynn is still there, her expression is expectant and her big eyes ask a question. He gives her a nod, by which he means she should wait a minute longer.

"No. No need for blood. As I said, he didn't lose much blood," Fulala says. "It's pretty likely he has a concussion, but his pupils are even and regular. He hasn't had a seizure-like event and his reflexes seem normal, he hasn't vomited. Those are all indications that the head trauma isn't too severe. He's been unconscious for almost half an hour."

"Why? Why is that significant? I don't understand the significance."

"It's a concern." She chooses her words deliberately, her round face drawing him in, willing him to be calm. "Because the length of the unconscious period can be an indication of severity of brain bleeding. Also, the doctor is going to check the CT to see if his cheekbone is broken." She uses two fingers on her own cheek to indicate the area of concern. "With the swelling and bruising, it's hard to tell."

"Then again, he's just a little guy. Maybe he's just emotionally exhausted. He had quite a fright," Flip says hopefully.

"Absolutely. That's true. That's why the doctor is waiting for the test results. So he can really let you know where things stand. You'll be able to go and see him soon. I'll be in when he's admitted to his room. As soon as he's admitted, I'll let you know." After a pause, she adds, "I will."

"So he's going to stay?" Flip asks.

"Yes. The doctor wants to keep an eye on him overnight."

"Okay," he says. He wants to attempt the nurse's name, but is afraid to mispronounce it. He says, "Okay," again and holds her comforting, pudgy hand. "He's my son and I need to be with him if he's hurt. He's my boy, my only son. You understand me? I need to be with him this minute. Let me know the second I can go up. Okay? Please. It's important. He will be scared."

She gives a weak smile, pulls away and goes back to her charting.

After relating what he learned to Lynn, they mutually relay the information to Sara and Coleen.

"Well, I'm going to stay the night," Coleen says right away.

"I'm staying too," Lynn says.

"That's right," Coleen says. "He will want his mommy when he wakes up."

Flip wishes he had choked his mother-in-law earlier. But he says, "I want to stay too."

"Flip," Lynn says, taking Flip by the hand and looking into his eyes, very serious. "Would you be willing to go and pack a bag for me and mom? Then, take Sara home. Stay with her at the house tonight. She doesn't need to miss any more school."

"Who gives a shit about school?" Sara protests.

Her parents ignore her reflexively. "I can do that," he says to Lynn. He wants to protest, he wants to be there with Dylan. But Coleen is right, he will want his mother most of all.

He drives to the Lakeside and parks. Inside he sees he left his gun lying out, as well as the wad of crumpled money that Vanessa reluctantly forked over. He stuffs it all in the carton he bought from Dottie at the X press laundromat. Then he takes the overflowing carton of clothes and carries it to his trunk.

Before he leaves, he gathers his toiletries and takes one last look to make sure he has everything. The bottle with its two remaining pills is still on the counter. A personal inventory tells him his back is feeling okay. He pockets the pills and leaves the bottle where he found it.

He knows he hasn't been invited back into his home. Lynn made it clear that Dylan's injuries didn't solve any of their problems, and he knows that's true. But, he needs to have clothes and he needs a shave. So, why not grab everything. *Just in case.*

The light on the phone is flashing; he punches in the code and listens to his messages.

"Hello Mr. Mellis," Dr. Hawkins' voice says. "I had hoped to hear from you by now. I understand you're preoccupied with the changes in your life, but I'd like to hear how your job interview went. Don't forget our appointment tomorrow. I look forward to seeing you. And remember to call if you need to." There's a clicking, some static, another hard click.

"Oh, hi Flip," a woman's voice says. "This is Kristin again. Sorry we couldn't get together. Curious about the job interview. Call me anytime."

He locks the door to Number Three, and pitches a last armful of belongings into the back seat. He looks around for something to write on. He wants to leave Dean a note, tell him what's happened. When he can't find a pen, he gets impatient. He backs his car in an arc and speeds all the way home.

Kev is in his driveway catching some rays in a pool chair when Flip drives past. Flip throws his arm out the window in greeting, but Kev's eyes are closed and he has ear buds in. Flip pushes the button on the garage door opener he keeps clipped to the car's sun visor and pulls into the spot where Lynn normally parks her minivan. His mother-in-law's Ford Escort is parked in his space.

Next to the door into the house, Flip finds Dyl's new bike dumped on its side. He wonders about the logistics of its arrival at that spot. He imagines Lynn must have dragged it in, or she had asked Sara to do it.

He sees the front wheel is twisted off-centre and the paint has a few fresh scratches, but it isn't too mangled. He takes that as good news. He holds the front wheel of the bike between his knees and twists the bars until they line up. He puts the kickstand down and parks it in its place next to Dylan's other, nearly new bike of the exact same frame size. Flip notices his missing paint pot on the shelf next to the bikes. *God damn it.*

The house looks clean and organized, except for a couple of half-full coffee mugs and breakfast plates left scattered around. He goes straight to the extension to grab Lynn some clothes, but the closet is full of Coleen's things. He finds a duffle bag and packs a few outfits, a robe, slippers and some pajamas. Also, he grabs a toothbrush and other necessities from the attached bathroom. He drops the duffle bag in the kitchen and heads upstairs.

In their old bedroom, Flip finds Lynn has moved back in and redecorated. It's tasteful but definitely feminine. He thinks about his mother-in-law's insistence that Lynn had moved on with her life. He tries to picture a man in this bed with Lynn. But, it just doesn't work. It looks like the bed of a woman who has no desire to share it with a man. *If there is such a thing.*

In the top of the closet he finds Lynn's favourite suitcase and packs her clothes. He wants to linger over the chore, try to hold the moment, it could be the last time he's allowed into Lynn's life like this.

He's devastated by a feeling of loss, has to keep telling himself Dyl is fine; just to be able to keep that avalanche of misery from crushing him, twisting his insides and suffocating him. The knowledge that he let his whole life slip away: Lynn, his children, his home, his career, everything he'd spent the last twenty years building; just let it go while he tried to mend his own fragile ego; it's too much. But his family needs him, for now, so he keeps moving.

The Walther in his car is whispering to him. Tomorrow he will meet with Dr. Hawkins. He will live up to his promise to give it a week. Then he will be free to do whatever he thinks is best.

First things first.

He knows Lynn must have rushed around like this, scared for her family, for her future, even for him, as she collected his clothes to take to the ER, a few short days ago; the day he tried to hang himself.

He walks into the bathroom and grabs Lynn's makeup bag, toothbrush and her favourite hairbrush. All of his clothes are missing from the closet. *Ignore it.* He finds a few outfits for Lynn and some sweats and a T-shirt to sleep in. He finds her a change of underwear and grabs some fluffy socks she likes to sleep in.

He takes the bag down the hall to Dylan's room. Though no one asked him to get Dyl a change of clothes, he wants to do what he can to make the poor little guy feel more comfortable, safe and loved. There's a new, non-Thomas-the-Tank-Engine spread on his bed. He finds Dylan a pair of his favourite pajamas, some little socks and some Ben 10 underwear. On the way out of the bedroom he grabs Dylan's echidna stuffed animal, Pokey, he sleeps with every night.

One long weekend while Lynn and Sara were travelling to a wedding, Flip had taken Dyl on a train ride down to St. Louis. They had spent the day at the zoo and Flip had bought Dyl the echidna in the gift shop. Dyl had used it as a pillow on the train ride home, and slept with it every night since.

He puts it in the same bag with Lynn's clothes and jogs down the stairs, picks up the duffle bag for Coleen and goes out the way he came in.

His mother-in-law is the only one in the waiting room when he walks in with the bags.

"Where is everyone? Did you hear anything?"

"Yes."

"Well?"

"The doctor came in just after you left. Lynn tried calling your cellphone and left a message at the house. You should keep your phone with you when there's an emergency," she says.

"And you should make sure a child wears a helmet," he snaps back. "You shouldn't volunteer to watch my son and then not keep him safe," he says more loudly. "And if you are going to buy him a bike he doesn't even need, you should fucking make sure he knows how to ride it before you let him rip off down the street," he yells.

He doesn't know what to expect in response, because he has never spoken to Coleen that way. When she starts to cry, he finds it completely unrewarding. Her face is hideous when she sobs, and he desperately wants her to stop.

"Stop," he says. He doesn't know where Lynn and Sara are, but if they walk in with him standing over Coleen, bawling her beady pink eyes out, it could put a dent in any possible reconciliation.

He sits next to his mother-in-law, sets his hand awkwardly on her shoulder. He remembers he promised Lynn he'd tell Coleen something.

"Coleen," he says. "I promised Lynn I would tell you something." Her tears slow and she catches her shuddering breath so she can listen. "I promised I would say," he stalls for time; trying to remember what the hell he was supposed to say. She turns her face to him. Her mascara has smudged and run, tracing paths through her crinkled, pale skin, staining all the deep creases. He tries hard not to make a face at her, but she looks like a raccoon with the mange. Then he remembers.

"Hell, Coleen. I'm just upset. Things have been hard. I'm stressed, to put it mildly, about all this. Truth is, Dylan gives me the slip about every other time I take him anywhere. It's what he does, it's what little boys do and it could have happened to anyone."

"You mean it?' she asks. She sounds almost civil.

"I do mean it," he says.

She digs more Kleenex from her handbag and honks her nose. She takes out a small mirror and fixes her face, applies powder and lipstick. The process takes a long while. When she's satisfied she turns to Flip and says, "Thank you, Flip." She's completely composed, but her voice is not as cold as usual.

"Coleen, can you tell me what the doctor said? Please?"

She nods crisply. "He said the CT showed no broken bones in his face or skull, there's moderate swelling, but it's consistent with a lot of sports-related concussions he sees in children. He's a little concerned that Dyl wants to sleep so much. But thinks things should be fine. He said some other things too. But I couldn't understand. He had a funny little voice." Then she adds, "Foreigner," in a whisper.

"That's a relief," he says, ignoring the soft racism common in her generation. He realizes his hands are stacked with Coleen's. "Where are Lynn and Sara?"

"They went down to the cafeteria to grab a sandwich. When they come back, we can head to the third floor and see Dylan."

"Okay," he says. They sit for several long minutes. Then he says, "Looks like you've moved into the extension."

"Yes."

"Well, that's really why we built it in the first place. So you could stay with us, once you needed a little more help."

"I don't need help," she says fiercely, drawing her hands away.

"I know. But my family does, your family. It's nice of you to help out."

She turns her face to him to see if he means it. When it appears that he does, she says, "Thanks, Flip."

They sit in a comfortable silence for nearly a quarter of an hour. But something starts to bother Flip. He tries to let it go, but he is simply incapable.

"Coleen. Why would you tell me Lynn was out on a date? Why would you tell me she had moved on? Huh? Why? Why try to put that idea in my head when you know it isn't the truth?"

"I don't know what you mean," she says curtly.

"You remember saying those things to me? On the phone?"

"I may have said something."

"Listen. Don't deny it. There's no one here but me. Just tell me the truth, for once in your life, just be honest about what you're up to." He gets to his feet.

"I admit I may have coloured the situation a bit," she admits.

"That's it? That's all I get? You lied and made me miserable and nuts and you can't even do the decent thing and explain yourself? That is rich. What a crock of shit. I can't believe I just welcomed you into our home and thanked you and . . ." he's pacing in full rant. "I tried to make you feel better about nearly killing my son."

"Okay," she says.

"What?" he replies, confused by her acquiescence.

"Okay, Flip. Sit down and I will try to explain." She touches her hand to the chair he exited. He takes his seat.

"It seems clear to me, you and Lynn make one another unhappy. Divorce is hard; hard for everyone. But hard on the kids most of all. I know. I went through it, put my children through it. And if I learned one thing about divorce, it's better not to drag it out. So, I was trying to speed things along a bit. I admit it was wrong. I was trying to help, in my way. I hope you see that."

Flip has severe issues with her meddling. But he believes her, so he nods. Before he can form a more coherent response Lynn and Sara come in. Flip stands and claps his hands together.

"Let's go see my boy," he says. They gather their things and move together toward the elevators.

Dylan looks so tiny, tucked into an adult-size bed. The crisp white sheets and the bright, harsh fluorescents make his blue, swollen face look shockingly painful. Lynn begins to weep quietly the moment she sees him. She goes to the foot of his bed and holds onto his foot through his blankets, afraid to get any closer to her slumbering son. She absently lets her other hand drop onto the hard cast on his other leg. With no prompting, Flip finds a box of tissues and passes it over to Lynn.

Sara stands back, staying close to the door, unwilling to confront directly the reality of her little brother's injuries. She regrets being so thoughtlessly hateful toward him over the past several weeks. He's a good kid, not a malicious bone in his frail little body.

Flip and Coleen each move to opposite sides of the bed, and touch Dyl's hair. Flip is on Dylan's left, the side with the arm in a cast. He carefully holds the tips of Dylan's fingers where they poke out.

"Hey, buddy," Flip says quietly. "You got pretty banged up. Gave us a good scare."

"I tried to yell," Coleen says. "I tried to warn you to look out for the car, Dylan. I really did."

"He knows that," Lynn says.

They spend several hours watching his breathing, talking to him quietly, and telling stories. Lynn tells about how difficult her labour was with him, recalls every detail. Sara talks about how silly he is, about how she found him in her room dressed only in layers of her underwear and bras. He had them on his head and face, his arms and legs, like so many brightly coloured pelts. She takes a phone from her pocket and passes it around so everyone can see the digital evidence. On the phone's screen Dyl looks like a medieval jester, proud of his ridiculous appearance, and happy for the attention his big sister is paying him. Coleen shares how much Dylan likes her cooking, about how he ate a bowl of pie filling before it made it into the crust.

After a time, Flip scoots a chair and sits near Dylan's face. He says, "I was not so excited when I heard your mommy was pregnant with a little boy. I just want to be honest with you here. Talk to you straight, you know, man to man. When I heard we were having a boy, I just felt confused. From the beginning, I had assumed we were having another baby girl. I didn't know what I would do with a little boy. I'd this picture in my mind of my two little girls playing together, all dresses, tea parties and pigtails."

"But when you came along," he says to his sleeping son. "You really taught me something. You had a different kind of energy, a different way from Sara at the same age. I guess it's a gender thing. Watching you grow taught me that boys are pretty cool. I always thought my dad was so wretched and my mom was so innocent. I felt like maybe all men were bad, even me. Deep down, I was destined to disappoint everyone who counted on me, hurt people, prey on women, objectify them and use them up. That's how I grew up thinking about it; it's how I thought about myself. Dylan, you made me kind of appreciate what I have to offer in a new way. That's a pretty good gift for an old dude like me." He leans over to kiss Dylan on the head, and whispers "Thanks buddy." Dylan doesn't open his eyes, but his eyeballs shift under their thin, closed lids.

A small Middle Eastern man with delicate hands walks in and takes a chart from the end of the bed. He doesn't wear a lab coat, but the stethoscope worn jauntily, like a rubber scarf, around his narrow neck is reassuringly medical.

"I," he says, then takes a dramatic pause. "Am Doctor Pradhan. I worked on Dylan earlier in the ER. Have you seen him wake yet?" He speaks with a slightly British accent.

Everyone shakes their heads in the negative.

"Not yet," Coleen says.

"Ah, well," the doctor says. "There's nothing to get too worried about. We do need to keep an eye on him." He moves to Dylan's side and uses the stethoscope. He opens Dylan's eyes and shines a pin light into each of them.

"He looks good. Everything still appears normal. The CT was good. No surprises. Will someone be staying the night?"

"I will," Lynn and Coleen speak in unison.

"Very good. If he wakes please alert the nursing staff." Dr. Pradhan takes up the chart again and makes a note before leaving the room.

NO PLACE LIKE HOME

Flip throws his crumpled suit trousers in the back seat to make room for Sara. "You want to grab some food on the way home?" he asks.

"What the hell happened to your window?"

"A rock," he improvises. "A truck threw a rock. A big red-neck truck."

"Guess you're lucky the window was up. Might have taken your head clean off," Sara observes.

He starts the car, rolls the window carefully down, and drives out of Emergency Parking. "What about food? You hungry?"

Sara picks at a pimple on her cheek. "Nah. I'm not hungry. I'm tired. Really really tired. But, the realtor people are coming tomorrow, so I guess if we were going to eat, it might make less of a mess to eat something out. You know?"

"I do know. I'm on the fence about it. I'm wiped out too. I'm looking forward to being back in the house, sitting at our table to eat. Like the old days. Maybe we could play cards if you want."

"Sounds fine," she says noncommittally. "But what are you going to do, cook? No offence, but cooking is not your thing."

"I could order out."

"True, that is your specialty," she says. "That actually sounds good. Pizza Pizza?"

"If you want pizza. I'll order pizza. Or Chinese."

"Yeah," Sara says. "Grandma doesn't like Chinese. Now would be a perfect time to get some."

"Chinese then," Flip declares.

"Poor Mom and Grandma. Eating cafeteria food, again," she says happily and Flip likes it. It's been a long while since he's heard her like this. He wants to blame himself, but wonders if there's more going on.

There's an electronic tweet tweet that indicates Flip has a voicemail on his phone. The sound comes from under Sara. She looks around, feels under the seat, and eventually finds the phone down between the seat and the door. She passes it over.

"Is it Mom?" she asks.

"I don't know," he says. He doesn't recognize the number and supposes it could be the hospital. He pushes buttons with his thumb and plays the message, puts the phone to his ear.

"Flip. It's Byron. Your father. About what I said the other night, what I said about your mother wanting me out and about my cancer. Well, it's not true. I mean the part about your mother. Wanted to make out like I was a good guy. But I'm not a good guy. I'm just what you always thought I was. Let's just leave it at that. But to be clear, I am dying. Okay. Bye. Take care." There's a sound of the phone being knocked around before the recording stops.

Flip holds the phone away from his ear and stares at it. Flip prides himself on knowing when he's being lied to, and he knows Byron just lied. Took all the blame back on his own head. Flip doesn't know why Byron would bother, but he isn't falling for that noble bullshit. He's offended that Byron would be so selfish, so vain as to make the situation all about him. *It's not about him, it's about me.* He drops his cellphone in a cup holder and watches the road.

"Was that the hospital?"

"No," Flip says. "Just an old friend. He's sick. Wanted me to know something in case he doesn't get better."

"Oh," is all Sara says.

While waiting for the Chinese food to arrive, Sara takes a long shower and Flip unloads his stuff from the car. He stashes the gun under the passenger seat, because he doesn't like the idea of a loaded gun in his home. *Accidents can happen.*

He's arranging his suit so it looks less abused when the doorbell rings. He stomps down the steps and opens the door. The deliveryman is the same one as last time: about Flip's age, bald, in running shorts and a Good China T-shirt.

"Hey," Flip says in greeting.

"Order for Mellis," the deliveryman says. He doesn't seem to remember Flip.

Flip pays the man and gives him a couple of extra bucks.

"Aren't you the one who said you'd catch me up next time?" the guy asks.

"Did I say that?"

"Yeah. I think you did," he stands still, holding his two dollar tip, waiting to see if he can add to it.

"Oh," Flip says. "I will have to catch you next time."

"I assumed as much."

"Just kidding." Flip digs in his pocket and takes out the rest of his pill payoff, hands it over.

"Cool. Thanks. A lot," the delivery guy says happily. "Thanks a lot," he says again.

At the table, Sara has her hair twisted in a turban of terry cloth. She eats fast and burns her mouth on an eggroll.

"Shit," she says. "Hot." But she keeps putting food in her mouth.

"Slow down lady. You act like you haven't eaten in days. I thought you weren't that hungry."

"I got hungry."

For a while it's like old times. Sara starts talking and doesn't stop. She talks about her friends from school. She talks about Gina who was short and dumpy last year but stretched out over the summer.

"She has curves like a Kardashian."

Flip thinks this is code for fat ass. Specifically, good fat ass, not bad fat ass. But he can't think of an appropriate way to ask.

She describes who is dating whom, whose braces have come off, whose braces have been put on and who should really get straight to an orthodontist. Flip doesn't care about any of it and is bewildered by the glut of names she throws at him. He's happy to watch her expressive face as she speaks. *So hard to believe how grown-up she is.*

"What have you been up to, Dad?" she asks. "Mom said you interviewed for a job. How'd that go?"

"I don't have high hopes. The boss asked me to be honest, I made the miscalculation of believing him, and I don't think he liked what I had to say."

"That's too bad."

"Yes," he agrees solemnly.

"Donald said he spoke to you at the store," she says.

Flip is confused, "Who?"

"Donald. D. My boyfriend," she reminds him. "He said you had a nice chat. Is that true?" She asks between mouthfuls of lo-mein.

"Mmmhmm. Yes. I did speak with D. I actually like him, I think. He seemed nice." Flip really means it. Clearly Sara is way too young to marry, and D is far too earnest for his own good. But, he does like D. "He seems like he's serious about you. He really likes you."

"Yeah," she says without enthusiasm.

"What's up, girl?"

Sara sets her plastic fork down and wipes her mouth on a paper napkin. She sits up straighter and places her hands in her lap, below the tabletop.

"Dad," she says. "I think I'm pregnant." Flip's mouth gapes, partially chewed food on display. He drops his fork, wipes his hands and finally remembers to finish chewing.

"You think?" he says. "So you might not be."

"No. I am. I really am. I am all the way pregnant." Her mouth curls down in a hard spasm, her lower lip trembles. Flip comes out of his chair and kneels beside her. He holds her and lets her cry. She sobs and wails and blasts him with Chinese food breath. He grabs a paper napkin for her to use.

Of course she's pregnant: The upset tummy, the mood swings, the appetite, and of course D talking about marriage. I should have seen it. I'm going to kill that kid.

He thinks hard about the right thing to say. *Congratulations* doesn't seem right because she's underage and unmarried and clearly upset. But things like, *How did this happen* and *Are you going to keep it, What are you going to do, Have you told your mother, What did she say* and, *How the hell could you be so careless,* all feel a little out of line. *This is Lynn's fault. She can't put this on me. Sex talk and birth control is her domain.*

Finally he says, "We will figure this out." Though his knees ache, he holds her until she's ready for him to let go.

He slowly lifts his weight into a standing position, his lower back protesting the entire time. He sits back down, slides his food aside and reaches across the table for Sara's hand. She takes it and they sit a good long while. He wants to let her talk, say what she needs to. He knows the odds are very high he'll blurt something that will upset her. So he holds his tongue and waits.

He thinks what a nice kid D really is, he could make a good dad. He has a job, seems ambitious enough. It'll be hard, but they could make it work. If he and Lynn pitched in and helped, they could get Sara through high school at least. He wonders if the high school has a day care. He saw an episode of *60 Minutes* about high schools with nurseries. The girls would go and nurse their babies between classes. *Or was it prisons?*

"I don't know who the father is," Sara says weakly.

"D is the father," Flip replies, as if he knows.

"Listen to me. I am not sure the father is Donald. I told D about the baby, or he kinda figured it out. Now he thinks we have to get married. But I don't think he's the father."

"Did you tell D that part?"

"Should I?"

"I don't know. Shit. What the hell, Sara? How did this happen? Fuck. Are you going to keep it or what? Have you told your mother? What the fuck were you thinking? How the hell could you be so goddamned careless?" The litany tumbles from him. She jerks her hand back, crosses her arms under her breasts and gives him a familiar hard glare. *Like mother, like daughter.*

"Sorry," he says. She relaxes her pose and her expression softens.

"Whatever, Dad. I understand. I've been asking myself the same shit."

He stands and pulls her to her feet. She lets herself be led out through the mudroom and across the back yard. They head down the driveway and start walking down the street. It's turned dark out, and the sky is clear. Flip points into the night sky.

"See those three stars. Remember what that's called?"

"Orion's belt."

"Good girl," he says. "You always were smart." They walk to the end of the block and hang a right. "Well? What happened?"

They stride through the evening air for a time. Then she answers, "D and I broke up a few months back. I didn't tell anyone. Mostly because I thought it might not stick. The fight was over some bald girl he works with. He was always talking about her. I got mad and broke up with him. It was stupid. I needed to get out of the house. I went out, sat on the porch swing and was texting some people. Just felt moody and trapped. That's all. This guy I know came along and started chatting me up. Next thing I know, we are on his couch." She stops her story there, and he's grateful she does.

He quits walking. "So, have you told this guy?"

"Yes. But he has a girlfriend. And honestly, I don't know whose it is for sure." She rubs her belly, but Flip can't see that she looks any different. He continues walking, she falls in and matches his pace.

"You haven't talked to anyone? You haven't been to the doctor?"

"I told *you,* Dad. That's all. I haven't done anything else about it."

They make it back around the block, pass by Kev's driveway. Sara looks at Kev's house real angry. And like a punch in the face, Flip knows: *that fucking stoner knocked up my daughter.* A rage builds in him, but he tamps it down. He needs a plan.

Inside, they clean the kitchen together, just like a normal family. He says she needs to tell Lynn about the pregnancy, that Lynn will get Sara in to see a doctor. She needs an exam and blood work and antenatal vitamins. She seems resigned, maybe even relieved, to let her parents make some decisions for her. He tells her she needs to come clean with D. See how he wants to handle it. She says she'll think about it. Then he tells her to go to bed.

"Because you need your rest."

"Okay Dad. Thanks. Thanks for listening. I know it's a shocker. I actually feel a little better." He leans down a bit so she can peck him on the cheek. "I missed you," she says. "Are you moving back in?"

"I don't have any answers just yet," he says.

He showers in his own bathroom and dries with his favourite towel. He puts on clean boxers and a clean T-shirt. He shaves and grooms and generally indulges himself in any excuse he can find to linger in his home. Aware the entire time, each thing he does may be the last time he ever does it; either in that house, or in his life.

He attempts to push his fears for his daughter out of his mind, but it's useless. He sneaks to the end of the dark hall to check on her. She's sound asleep and snoring softly.

Back in bed, he lies to the left, just as he used to when he and Lynn still shared the room. He considers what act of violence would be most appropriate to subject Kev to, and if he should kill himself directly after speaking to Dr. Hawkins, or not.

Eventually, all the worry and stress seep from him, as he sinks deeper down into the mattress.

Lynn slips her long naked body under the sheets and curls up at his side. He puts his arm around her casually, not surprised at all.

"Flip," she whispers with quiet insistence. "Flip. Wake up. It's about Dylan."

Flip wakes up, sits up a bit in the bed. It isn't a dream. Lynn is in bed with him, naked.

"Dylan woke up about midnight and started talking non-stop," She has her body pressed to his, her face above his. She speaks breathy and excited, she smells like coffee. "Dylan talked for nearly two hours. He's fine. The nurses checked on him.

They helped him to the bathroom. He asked if he would get his own wheelchair, or his own crutches. He seemed totally jazzed by the idea. He ate three cups of cherry Jello, they gave him some meds for the pain and he finally fell back to sleep."

She kisses him on the mouth. Initially, it startles him, for a split second he wants to push her away, then he returns the kiss.

She throws the blanket back and together they get his boxers down. She puts her leg over him and straddles his crotch. She grabs his cock and guides it where she wants it. He's afraid to touch her, scared she'll be offended or will simply disappear in a twist of vapour. She takes his hands and presses them to her tits, they grind at one another fast and hard. Near the climax he finds himself on top, her nails digging painfully into his shoulders. It doesn't last that long, but Lynn was so emotional and ready, she barely needed him there to get the job done anyway.

He flops back to his side of the bed and drags the covers over them both. She rolls on her side to face him. He can't see her in the dark of the room, but he knows she's there, knows exactly how she looks, could stretch his hand out through the dark and touch any part of her damp body.

"Thanks," she says. "I needed that."

"Welcome."

"I need you to pack up your stuff and go in the morning," she says. He doesn't speak. "This doesn't mean everything is okay. You know. And the open house is tomorrow. I need things to be perfect. You understand, right. We're grown-ups. We needed that. But it doesn't change things. Right?"

"Right."

"I told Mom I was going to shower and change clothes. Then give her a break. I need to get moving," she explains.

"By all means."

She rolls out of bed and feels her way to the bathroom. The light that comes under the door is enough for Flip to see the whole room. He finds his boxers, his pants and a shirt. He slips on socks and shoes and gathers the few things he had left scattered around.

He knocks on the bathroom door and cracks it open. "I need to grab a few things," he says. The shower snaps off as he brushes his teeth. The shower curtain slides back and Lynn dries her hair and body.

When he's gone, Flip will miss this most of all. Not the sex or the conversation. Not the birthdays or meals. But Lynn's presence; being adjacent to all kinds of mundane feminine activities. He's always found it comforting and soothing and he will miss it when he's gone.

"I was thinking, about the situation with the mortgage and house," Flip says, after he rinses his mouth. "Your mom. She wants to be helpful. Maybe if you asked her to pay a little rent and let her move in, permanently, take care of the kids after school, it would help out. I talked to her like you asked me to, about the accident. And that went all right."

Lynn has one foot on the side of the tub and is drying her leg, leaning way over and shuffling the towel along her ankle. She stops moving.

He adds, "As well as could be expected. Better than I would have thought." Satisfied, Lynn continues working the towel up her leg.

"But the conversation turned a little," he continues. "Turns out that, although she's a proud woman, doesn't want to feel like she needs to be here for herself; she actually might need to be here. Living where she is is expensive," he concocts a likely narrative. "And you know she would never admit it to you. But

I get the impression that she's happy to be here as long as she can tell herself, and her coffee buddies, that she's helping you, not the other way around. I think asking her to pay, letting her know it would help out financially, that would actually make her feel better. Would be a help for her too."

Lynn stands and dries her lean, hard arms and shoulders.

"Do you think you could live with it? Having your mom around the house? If it meant keeping the house?"

"Maybe," she says, but it sounds like a *no*. "I've thought about it. It would be hard for me, having her here. She makes me a little nuts. You know how she is. But when I tried to bring it up, she was absolute about needing her own place."

Flip nods. "Like I said, she's a proud, stubborn woman; like most of the women in your family. But if you ask the right way, I think she'll go for it." He watches as Lynn's reflection holds the towel at the ends and works it down her back. *God she's beautiful.* He looks away. "Also, you and Sara really need to talk. She has something to tell you. Something you need to hear. Be calm and patient with her. Okay?" Lynn stops drying and wraps the towel around her chest like a strapless dress.

"What is it? She's not pregnant is she?" She says it joking as she steps from the tub, her body next to him in the too bright, tiny bathroom.

He turns to face her. "Just talk to her. And be calm."

"I will. Why are you all dressed? It's like four-thirty in the morning. I didn't mean for you to leave now."

"I should go," he says. He snatches up his toiletry kit and tucks it under his arm like a football.

"Flip. You never said how the interview went?" He stops.

"I wouldn't get my hopes up if I were you," he says. "I'm not so sure I'm even cut out for that life anymore. The interview felt good and easy in some ways. I don't trust that kind of work

anymore. Not after the way McCorkle-Smithe dropped me."
He turns to go and adds, "I guess there are limits to the kind
of treatment I can suffer; some things I just can't get over, no
matter how much I want to."

"Flip. Thank you. It made it a lot easier that you were there
last night. At the hospital with Dyl. And all of us. It really helped.
I was losing it."

He moves slowly past the bed they used to share, "That's
what dads do. Right? And honestly, I needed to be there." Then,
before leaving the bedroom he adds, "Be sure and hug Dylan for
me. Let him know I was there with him, when he was hurt."

ALL PENT UP

If this is going to be his last meal, he might as well go out big. There used to be a truck stop out on Highway 55. He'd been once.

About the time Flip was in kindergarten, Byron had a job running loads of gasoline from the local refinery to various gas stations. One day he'd taken Flip out of school, against his mother's wishes, and let him ride along. Flip hadn't wanted to go, but it was part of Byron's ongoing efforts to make Flip into a man.

It was a big climb to reach the ramshackle cab of the tanker's cab and Byron had grabbed Flip by his tiny hips and pitched him into the passenger's seat. After that, Byron settled in the driver's seat, got the rig warming up and let it rattle them around until the heater started blowing warm air. He pulled a couple of glass Pepsi bottles out of a cooler wedged behind his seat and produced an opener, bent both metal caps back and pitched them in the cooler. He passed an ice-cold bottle to Flip. The bottle was still wet and it made a dark circle on the thigh of his tan, corduroy pants.

"Mom would want me to have breakfast first," Flip's little boy voice said. He'd wanted to chug the Pepsi down, but felt guilty enough to stop himself.

"This *is* breakfast," Byron answered. "And your momma's not here." He took a long pull of Pepsi and stuck the bottle between his legs. "Drink a little of that off," he told Flip. Flip tipped it back too hard and it fizzed in his mouth, foamed and burned in his nose.

"Good," Byron said. Then he demonstrated something Flip has never forgotten: he used his teeth to rip the top off a cellophane tube of salted peanuts, used one hand like a funnel over his Pepsi bottle and poured in half the peanuts. Byron checked to see Flip got a good look at the process. "You watchin' this, boy?"

"Yes sir." Flip gawked at the pale nuts floating and bobbing like a horrible, junk food lava lamp. Byron shook his bottle to mix it, filthy suds frothed up and belched out the mouth of the bottle. Byron reached over and repeated the procedure with Flip's Pepsi, emptying the rest of the peanuts and an extra helping of dusty, salty debris.

"Put your thumb on the top and swirl it around, get it good and stirred up." He demonstrated the technique. When Flip tried, his thumb was too small to cover the bottle and sticky soda splashed his shirt.

"Don't worry about it," Byron said. Little Flip watched his dad take a swig and chew the peanuts that came out. "You see, that way you can eat and drink with one hand. An old trucker showed me, now I'm showing you."

Byron got the rig moving, working the long-armed shifter and turning the giant wheel as if he was steering a ship. He took another swig, and Flip copied him. They both chewed on their sweet, salty breakfast and listened to trucker songs on the eight-track. They didn't talk much, just watched the traffic. Once some teenagers pumped their arms out the window and Byron told Flip to unbuckle and yank on the pull cord for the air horn.

Flip pulled it and didn't let go, making a long sustained blast.

"Enough," Byron fussed. When Flip sat back, he must have looked scared, so Byron added, "Good job. Now you're a trucker. You need a handle, a trucker name."

"I don't know," Flip said.

"Well, I'm the Red Rider. Like the airgun."

Flip thought a long time.

"You can be whoever you want, Flip. That's the fun of it. You get to make it up."

Flip thought some more then said, "Little Red Rider?"

"Sure boy. That's fine. You can be Little Red Rider if you want. Now buckle yourself in."

On the way back through, after they filled the in-ground tanks at three different Sinclair stations, they had stopped at the Fifth Wheel Truck Stop and Flip had made an early dinner of a ham and cheese omelette. It was the first time he'd eaten an omelette, but Byron had assured him he'd like it. He hadn't eaten anything else the whole day, except the trucker breakfast, so he was ravenous. It came to the table, buttery eggs overflowing the edges of a large plate. Flip ate every bite. Byron had said, "You did a man-sized job today and it gave you a man-sized appetite." Flip still remembers it as the best meal he had in his whole damn life.

When he takes the exit off the highway and drops down to the parking lot, he's pleased to see the Fifth Wheel looks the same as at it did forty years earlier. He follows the signs to the four-wheeler parking area.

Inside a woman with an old face and a young body hustles him to a booth next to a window with a phone mounted to the wall at one end. She leaves him a pot of coffee and a plastic menu with every item illustrated with a full colour picture, so no reading is required.

He pours himself coffee, fixes it like he likes, clacks the spoon around inside the cup and watches the cream swirl.

When the woman returns she says, "So what can I get you, honey?" He likes being called 'honey'. He points to a picture on the menu and gives it a tap. She holds the pad close to her face when she writes, like she should be wearing glasses. "You want some juice or anything else, honey?" she asks.

"No thank you, ma'am."

On the day Byron pulled Flip out of school, he'd been wearing that watch, the one he left behind. A few years later, after Byron cut out, Flip found it in a dresser drawer and he stole it, hid it. He'd always pretended Byron had left it for him, a parting gift. But that was a lie he told himself, and he still chose to believe it.

Flip thinks about Kev and hates that he gave that shithead his watch. For no good reason, it suddenly means a lot to him. If he lets himself, he feels a kind of affection or even love for his father. Maybe the reality of possibly losing his father is colouring his perspective. His father's warped sense of honour too, he finds endearing. Maybe his own impending death, or seeing Dylan's tiny body bruised and helpless. Whatever the reason, he wants the watch back. If he's going to kill himself, he wants to be wearing his father's watch when he does it.

"Okay, honey," the woman says. She slides a plate with steak and two fried eggs in front him, a side of wheat toast and a two-egg, ham and cheese omelette on a second plate. "Can I get you anything else?" she asks.

"I think that will do it."

He only eats about half his food, which is still more than enough to make him feel ill. The omelette tasted better in his memory.

When he takes up the bill and fishes around in his pants for some cash, he realizes he's out. He had tipped the Good China driver all of his cash. He leaves his last dress watch on the table. It ticks to 6:08 as he walks away.

At the Drum Roaster Flip orders a Nutty Professor from Thi, just because he has time to kill.

"Make it to go," he says.

"Your wish is my command."

Flip pays with a card and hopes for the best. He's surprised it goes through. Maybe Lynn put more money in the account for him, taking care of him. He watches Thi do his stuff at the espresso machine, mildly impressed. Two men in silver suits come in talking loudly about their latest cheap real-estate acquisition, about how great the glut of foreclosures has been for them.

"Be right with you," Thi says. He slides Flip his drink. "Did you ever get a chance to . . ." he drops his voice very low and Flip leans over the counter a bit ". . . take your new purchase out for a test?"

Flip leans back and says, "Today's the day."

"Cool. Let me know how it goes," Thi says.

"If I get the chance," Flip replies, "but I doubt I'll be around for a while, Thi."

"Okay. Whenever you get a chance. Oh hey. You want an apple? I bought a fresh bag yesterday."

"No thanks, Thi. I'm set." He smacks the side of his belly like a bass drum.

Flip finds himself parking in his own driveway. He turns off the car and takes his time sipping coffee. His back is sore again and he needs to pee. He takes the last two pain pills in his mouth, lets them rest on his tongue until the taste becomes bitter, then swallows them back with a little coffee. He's proud that he timed it just right: he had just enough pills to get him through his last day. He thinks this demonstrates his inherently superior capacity for time and resource management. *Those DynaTech bastards don't know what they're missing.*

He watches Kev's parents leave for work, one after the other in their matching BMWs. *Definitely lawyers.* He leans over, pats around under the seat and brings his hand out, his fingers wrapping around the cold grip of his Walther. When the coffee's gone he places the paper cup in its holder and turns it so he can read the words *Drum Roaster* printed around the side. He grabs the door handle and steps out of the car, closes the door, careful of the window. He sticks the gun in his waistband at his back and starts toward Kev's house. As he passes along his car, he sees a box in the back and takes the time to carry it to his own front door, where he works the keys and goes in quietly.

In the kitchen, which has been freshly wiped down, he unpacks the smiling pig cookie jar he picked up at Family Pawn. He sets it on the counter where the old one broke. It's ugly, grotesque and folksy, but a close match for the one he shattered. *I owe Lynn that much.* He stuffs the wrapping paper back in the box and returns it to his back seat.

He strides straight to Kev's front door and knocks hard. No response. He rings the bell, hears it chiming inside the house. Still nothing. He jabs the doorbell a few more times.

To Flip's way of thinking, it's not possible Kev is already up and away doing something productive. Though he supposes he could still be out from the previous night. Maybe his band had a gig; but probably not on a Wednesday night. He tests the front door latch: locked.

He's determined not to leave without his father's watch, so he goes around the side of the house, tests the sliding door off the deck. It slides open.

"Hello?" he calls into the kitchen and closes the door behind him. The kitchen is large and impeccably tidy, with black lower cabinets and a matching island, stainless steel appliances and marble countertops. *I should have been an attorney.*

"Hello Kev?" No answer. No movement. The place doesn't feel lived-in, too clean, as if he's broken into a model home. There is a creeping sensation of being the next victim in a horror movie: any moment a maniac with a machete might lunge out of the pantry and chop him into chunks, stuff him, piece by gory piece down the fancy high-capacity waste disposal or into the high end trash compacter. Of course, he knows better. He takes the gun out and holds it in his hand, just to be safe. *Now I'm the dangerous maniac.*

"Kev," he calls again at the bottom of the carpeted steps to the second floor landing. There's no response and the house feels empty. The upstairs has been converted into a giant master suite, complete with His and Hers closets, sitting room, shower with luxury whirlpool jacuzzi and a separate steam room. The only other room on the floor is a dark panelled study.

Back on the first floor, Flip passes a liquor cabinet and takes a squat bottle of Icelandic Vodka. It looks expensive. The blue foil peels back easily and he balls it up into a knob and puts it in his front pocket. The vodka has a bulb-like cork, which takes some effort to pull out. He takes a mouthful and rolls it around, then swallows. It's smooth and clean. *It would be better cold.* He takes another mouthful, pounds the cork back in, leaves the bottle on the kitchen counter and continues his search for a door to the basement. He finds it at the back of the butler's pantry, and calls down ahead of him, "Kev? You down there?"

Flip starts down cautiously. As he nears the base of the stairs a body appears. Flip reflexively raises the gun.

"Whoa whoa whoa man. What the hell?" Kev says, throwing his hands up in surrender and squatting down a bit as if preparing to kneel or spring away. "Is that you Mr. M?" He's shirtless and in jeans that look as if he slept in them. Flip thinks he can see his heart fluttering in his pale, hairless chest.

"It's me." Flip doesn't move the gun away immediately. He just holds Kev there, enjoying the sense of power he wields over the kid. After a long moment, he lets the gun drop to his side.

"Sorry to scare you," Flip says, not sorry at all. "You kinda startled me."

"I startled you, man. How do you think I feel? What the hell you doing creeping down my stairs with a gun?"

"Oh. Sorry. Your folks let me in. I just dropped by to get my watch."

"Right on." He drops his hands and straightens his body. "But what's with the gun, Mr. Mellis?"

"Oh. Don't worry. I was just heading over to the new shooting range for some target practice. That's all." It's a lame excuse, and he knows of no new shooting range, but Kev seems satisfied.

"Right on, man. Come on down and I'll get it for ya. You got my cash?"

"You bet," Flip lies again.

Kev reigns over an impressive, subterranean bachelor pad. The den has a wall mounted flat screen, gaming system, pool table, wet bar and a drum kit in one corner. An attached master suite with a beautifully remodelled bedroom is furnished with what Flip would bet is Kev's parents' previous king size bed, dresser and matching floating side tables. Flip can see the expansive bathroom through the walk-in closet.

"Wow Kev. This beats the hell out of the Lakeside Motor Court."

"Right on, man," he replies as he searches his dresser top for Flip's watch. "My folks did all this in preparation for me moving out, after college. But I fooled them." Kev chuckles a little at his own joke. "Here you go man. Good as new." He passes the watch over.

Flip straps it on and checks the time. *Almost time for my appointment with Dr. Dan.* He jangles his arm and listens for the mechanical wrenching. He hears it and it gives him focus, like the presence of an old friend.

This could be the room where Kev took advantage of his daughter. He imagines the sense of awe Sara might have felt when walking down into Kev's kingdom. How impressed she would be, how attractive Kev would look. A cool, calculated rage starts to well up inside him, and this time, he lets it build.

He switches the gun to his other hand and puts his fist up to bump it with Kev's. The watch makes its mechanical sound and Flip pretends he is imbued with cyborg, super-human augmentations, like a character in a Gibson novel; or like he's Lee Majors.

"Thanks for looking after it," he says.

"Right on," Kev says matter-of-factly.

He wonders about the logistics of shooting Kev. He still has the gun out, so it would be easy enough. Would the sound be heard outside in the neighbourhood? He supposes it would, because he can hear Kev's drums from his own kitchen, next door. He looks around the bedroom, scopes a bong and some Zig Zag papers. Then narrows in on the bed. Could the sound be muffled? Could he use one of those pillows? *Yes*, he decides, *I could.* If he shoots Kev, would he need to dispose of the body? Would he need to immediately shoot himself or could that wait until finishing his appointment with Dr. Hawkins? Because he promised he'd be there. The longer he thinks about it, the heavier the gun feels, the more he wants to set it down. *I don't want to kill anyone, except myself.*

"You got my money?" Kev asks. "Or do you want to pay me later?

"What?"

"I was saying do you want to pay me now or later?"

"I'm not going to pay you Kev. I lied to you. I just needed my dad's watch back."

"What the fuck man," Kev says mildly. "That's not cool."

"You know what's not cool, Kev? Do you want to know? Getting underage girls pregnant. Not taking responsibility for it. Cheating on your girlfriend. That's not cool. Not cool at all. That is what the fuck is up. Man. Right on? You know what I mean, neighbour?"

"Whoa whoa whoa," Kev says. "Now your girl was the aggressor, man. I tried to stop her. But . . ."

Flip balls his fist around the gun's grip and whacks Kev square in his mouth. Kev's bottom lip splits wide open and he goes down on his narrow ass with a hard *thunk*. Sitting on the floor, he cups one hand under his chin to catch the blood and drool, but his howling causes red, slimy strings to dangle onto the carpet.

"Whah tha fush, Man?" Kev asks, his eyes have gone all wild with worry. "My parens will shue your ash."

"When you talk to them, be sure and tell them the good news: You're going to be a daddy. And ask them what kind of jail time you can expect to serve for statutory rape. Then have them give me a call."

Kev lets out another mewling cry, blood bubbles from his nostrils.

Shit. Kev's face is really messed-up.

Flip hustles up the stairs, adrenaline driving his legs like fat pistons pumping in a diesel engine. Upstairs, he runs through the butler's pantry and grabs the vodka bottle on his way through the kitchen, sliding the door so hard he can hear it bounce back open behind him. But he doesn't stop.

He gets to his car and starts the engine. He's winded and thirsty and his hand hurts. He drops the gun in the seat next to him and chugs down more lukewarm vodka. It doesn't satisfy his thirst, but he starts to feel better anyway. *I'm in so much trouble.* He worries he'll be too drunk to drive. His underarms are soaked.

After a few moments and a few more sips he starts laughing, just because he's a stupid motherfucker. But he also feels relieved because he won't have to worry about it much longer.

He takes up the gun. He can't remember how the safety works, and he'll need to know pretty soon. He toggles the switch back and forth with his thumb, looking for a red dot, but there is no red dot. He tests the trigger.

He feels the concussive effect of the explosion as the flash of light and the smell of smoke make him wince and yelp. The violent and unexpected force wrenches the pistol painfully from his casual grip, and he thinks his thumb is broken. He puts his hands over his ears and works his jaw. Moments pass, a breeze from the blasted driver's side window chases some of the smell from the car's interior. His ears start to ring more quietly. He's awed by the sudden absence of window. There's nothing left but glass crumbs piled along the window opening and on the drive-way outside. He brushes most of the crumbs out and waves his hand in front of his face to clear the sharp smell of gunpowder. He glances cautiously at the gun. *So when the switch is toggled down, the safety is off.*

As he backs out, he can hear glass crunchies grinding to dust under his tires.

EVERYTHING WORKS OUT

Adrenaline, having passed through his system, has left him exhausted and sleepy. He considers curling up in a ball in the corner of Dr. Hawkins' waiting room and sleeping, using his workbag as a pillow.

He looks at the yellowed face of his dad's watch, tracking the second hand as it treks past the twelve again. It's seven minutes past the time his appointment is supposed to start. *After all the shit the Doc gave me about being late for my last appointment. I need to piss.*

He stands to leave as Dr. Hawkins swings the door into his waiting room and invites Flip to enter. Flip lugs his workbag past the doctor, nodding a silent greeting. In his soothing office Flip takes a seat across from the doctor. He notices with mild satisfaction that his hips glide easily between the arms of the pretentious chair. Flip finds his legal pad, turns it to his first page of notes and waits.

It takes several moments for Dr. Hawkins to get settled and look over Flip's file. The low lights, calming colours and near silence begin to work on Flip. He could nod off.

"Mr. Mellis," Dr. Hawkins says smooth-jazz-style.

Flip's head snaps up. "Just resting my eyes," he says.

The doctor smirks. Flip liked him better when he was drinking. The doctor still has about four days' worth of beard growth, is still dressed in earth tones, and still has a slightly superior voice. He asks, "How was your week?"

"Do you have a bathroom I could use?"

"No. Mr. Mellis. There is one downstairs at the flower shop. Now let's stay focused, shall we?"

"You're telling me you don't have a bathroom up here?"

"That's what I am telling you. Now, how was your week?"

Flip shifts around in his chair, takes some of the pressure off his bladder. He asks, "Is your middle name Chad," as he reaches into his bag.

"No. It's Christopher. Why do you ask?" a puzzled look on his face.

"No reason really. You just seem like a Chad to me. Forget it, we should stay focused. Right? I made a list," Flip starts to explain, presenting his legal pad.

Dr. Hawkins holds up his hand, "Wait on that please. Let's just talk."

"I have something I need to do, Doc. Can we just get on with this?" He calculates how much time it should take for Kev to call his mommy and daddy, who will in turn call the cops, how long for them to respond. After that, how long to get his name out over the radio. He half expects a SWAT team to come in through the door before he has a chance to get back to his gun and put himself out of his misery once and for all.

"Mr. Mellis, you convinced me to make a questionable and highly unusual deal with you. I was more lax with keeping tabs on you than was strictly professional. The least you could do is bear with me for a few moments. That seems like a reasonable exchange, don't you think?" He speaks to Flip as if he were a simpleton.

Smacking Kev in the face with the side of a gun is not something Flip feels really proud of. But, for a split second, he longs to sucker punch Dr. Hawkins too. Just to see his expression transition from clinically superior to disbelieving shock and then rolling, unceasing pain. *Probably good I left the gun in the car.* He notes how often the Doc admits he isn't doing a great job and is making questionable professional choices. But he needs to keep things moving. So he says, "Yes," with his lips tight.

"So, go ahead. Let's talk about your week. How was it?"

"Very bad. I have the proof right here." Flip pats his notes.

"Yes. No doubt you do, Mr. Mellis. There had to be some high points too. You were called in for a job interview . . ." he says leadingly.

"I was," Flip concedes.

"That seems like progress. How do you feel it went?"

"Good for a while. Then very bad."

"How bad could it have been?"

"I stripped naked in the parking lot while the whole building watched," he replies dryly, feeling comfortable with exaggeration to prove a point. "Then I flipped them the bird and drove across their walking trail."

This gives Dr. Dan a momentary pause. He uses his fancy pen to take notes, he straightens his shirt, and smooths his slacks. "Well. That does sound bad," he admits. "Maybe you should just start at the beginning."

"That's what I tried to tell you," Flip replies.

"Yes. You did, Mr. Mellis. Please proceed."

"I would like to start by saying I lost my job for being too qualified. Then . . ."

Dr. Hawkins puts his hand up again. "Let me stop you there, Mr. Mellis. Let's focus on this past week. Just the time between the last appointment and this. I want hear all about the past too. But that will have to wait for the next session."

Flip turns a yellow page of his legal pad and finds where he wants to start. "Did you know that at Shooters some girl accused me of flashing her?"

"Actually I did know. Kelli said something about it." Flip watches the doctor play with his stubble in a feeble attempt to hide an arrogant grin. *It was Kelli speaking in the background that time on the phone. I knew it.*

Flip checks the next thing on his list, "On the way home that night, a policeman was parked crazy when I stopped to get gas and I scratched his car with my door," Flip explains. Then he slowly goes through a long and expansive list of ridiculous episodes that constitute the past week of his life. He tells about being questioned by D, about his pregnant daughter, the trucker taking a hammer to his car and about the mean old man at the laundromat. He tells about his back pain and his stolen pills, his lying mother, his cancerous father, Dylan's accident, and his mother-in-law's poisonous insinuations about Lynn's social life. He omits his friendship with Dean, the help given by Windle, his growing affection for his father, his gradual weight loss, and the assault on his neighbour, or the German automatic purchased illegally from a High Schooler. He also doesn't mention the pleasant sexual ambush and subsequent emotional beating he suffered from his wife, just because it's none of the Doc's fucking business.

Although he doesn't share the details that might weaken his position or force the doctor to call the authorities, he does roll them around in his head. *Admittedly, there has been some good mixed with the bad.*

To his credit, Dr. Hawkins mostly listens. He asks some questions about Flip's feelings related to his father and mother, he makes a concerned face at the news of Dylan's injuries and he asks what Sara's plans are related to the pregnancy. He suggests the name of a centre that offers support services for teen moms. But he primarily takes notes for fifty minutes and then looks at his watch as if bored when Flip has read through his list.

"Clearly, you've had a bad run. Though you must admit some of it could have been prevented with better impulse control. I could work with you to develop winning strategies for managing your stress, coping with life and better decision-making. You must admit you could use some guidance, you must see that."

"Must I?" Flip asks.

"You seem agitated. And if I'm not mistaken, you might be a little drunk."

"I haven't been drinking," Flip lies, while throwing up a two fingered Boy Scout salute to the edge of his brow.

"Your level of sobriety is immaterial to the subject at hand," the Doc says, putting the issue to rest. "What does matter is if you've convinced me that your life is worth giving up on. And to that, the answer is clearly *No*. You are definitely a work in progress. You have a great deal of potential for personal growth and I simply will not give you my go-ahead to end your life." He folds his hands on his knee in preparation for Flip's inevitable rebuttal.

"Isn't potential for growth," – he makes air quotes and hates himself for it – "a euphemism for saying I'm starting at the bottom?"

"You understand what I said, don't you, Mr. Mellis?" He ignores Flip completely.

"Okay Doc. You're the boss. Whatever you say goes."

"So you will promise not to hurt yourself."

Flip puts his fingers to the edge of his brow again, "I so promise," he says very serious and official. He doesn't bother to tell Dr. Hawkins that he was never a boy scout, so the promise is invalid. In fact, he always suspected Boy Scouts were jackasses. He knows Eagle Scouts are.

"Good," the doctor says, glancing at his notes. "And the abruptly changing moods? The aggressive behaviour? How are they?"

"I'm level. Very centred. I'm beginning to come to terms with the shape of things, thanks to you. Time heals and all that."

"Good. Good to hear," the doctor says, clearly not interested. "Our time is up. But I think it would be best to see you twice a week on an ongoing basis. I checked, and your insurance will allow it. We can reevaluate in six months. Is that agreeable? You need treatment. I will file the appropriate papers with the court and with your insurance, of course."

"Whatever you think is best. You're the professional," Flip says, attempting to keep the facetiousness from his voice.

Sitting in his car, in the parking lot, Flip pulls the gun from his lap and rests it on his knee. It's heavy and some trace memory causes him to jog his knee to give the firearm a horsey ride. When Dylan was smaller, he would hop on Flip's leg every time he sat down and would cackle like a maniac at the slightest motion.

He regrets not being allowed to take a leak in Dr. Hawkins' office. *No bathroom my ass.* He's afraid he'll piss when he shoots himself, as the shrapnel passes through his brainpan. That would be embarrassing. It's a bright day out and he doesn't think he should pee on the side of the flower shop.

The handle of the gun feels good to him, comforting. He doesn't want to move. He thinks he's like a samurai; he shouldn't lift his weapon unless he intends to kill. He weighs the pros and cons of pressing the barrel to his temple and scrambling his grey matter horizontally versus shoving it up under his jaw and blowing the top of his head off. The thought of putting the metal near his trachea makes him gag a bit. So, given the lack of more thorough research on the subject, he decides the temple is the winner. *It's time.*

He looks in all of his mirrors to be certain no one can observe what he's doing, and possibly try to stop him. *All clear.* Traffic sounds from the boulevard behind him come in through the missing window on a warm breeze. He drinks more vodka.

He lifts the gun. It's taken on mass since he pulled it from the glove box. A glance toward the open compartment shows him it's stuffed full of paper, mostly maps, and packets of ketchup. He sets the gun down again and pushes the glove box shut. The scrap paper makes him remember that he needs to leave a note.

His yellow pad is there, in the passenger's seat, but he can't find anything to write with. His pen is still missing. Plus, he finds he doesn't know what to say now any more than he did when he was standing on a bookcase with a noose around his neck.

Realistically, when they find him dead, with a gun in his hand, sitting in a car loaded with all of his possessions, the situation will tell its own story. He thinks of Buck and Dottie's decrepit van, has to admit he's well on his way to a similar fate, if he allows things to continue along the same path. *No time like the present.*

He takes up the gun and sets the barrel to the side of his head. He angles the barrel so the blast will hit as much brain as possible. He inhales. He holds it for a count of four. He begins a slow, calming exhale; careful to keep the barrel of the German-made gun steady. He's scared. The devastating violence that erupted when he applied the slightest pressure to the trigger earlier has left a scar on his psyche. Something hard presses between the finger pad and the trigger, a rough bit of skin or a speck of gravel from his spill in the parking lot. He passes the hard bit back and forth along the crescent-shaped hook, in effect, gently caressing the trigger. He can't hear it scratch with his ears, but can feel it in his body. Then his cellphone rings from the cup holder at his elbow.

He nearly ends up pissing and shooting himself simultaneously. The phone rings again, rattling violently next to his empty paper coffee cup. He puts the gun down, carefully. The phone keeps ringing.

"Hello?"

"Mr. Mellis?" a peppy little voice pipes up.

"Yes."

"Hello, Mr. Mellis. This is Myrna Mays from DynaTech solutions. Do you have a minute?"

"I was kind of in the middle of something."

"Oh," she says, a little dejected.

He hates to make people feel sad, so he says, "But I have a quick moment."

"Great," she says, instantly peppy again. "Mr. Krueger has come to a decision about the position of Director of Internal Communications and he has asked that I let you know we would like you to come in at your earliest convenience to discuss the terms."

"I don't understand," Flip says.

"I should have been more clear. Mr. Krueger would like to make you a job offer. You really left an impression on him, on the whole team. You need to come in to discuss the terms of the offer."

Flip looks over at the gun, he touches the place on his head where the barrel had rested. Then he says, "Myrna. That's good news. I think. I'll have to call you back later to make arrangements. I'm on the road right now, and need to get off the phone. Traffic. You understand."

She says she understands, and they hang up.

He leaves the car with no destination in mind, except farther from the gun, and finds himself stepping into the flower shop. He mills about, not really looking at anything, just letting his heart and his mind slow down.

"Excuse me," Flip says to a woman arranging assorted flowers at a worktable behind the counter. "Is there a bathroom I could use?"

"I wish. It's out of order. A pipe's busted or something. It needs a plumber, but the owner keeps putting it off. Money," she explains. She turns and sets the bouquet next to the cash register.

"I'll take that arrangement. It's nice," he says. He can feel his nose starting to itch. She gives him the damage and he pays with his debit card. Again it goes through.

Outside, he buckles the square vase into the passenger's seat, just as he'd done with Dean's tiki. He will have to call Dean, let him know the good news, ask him about his love life. Maybe he will swing by later. He buckles himself too. *Can't be too careful.* He drives slow and steady all the way to his house.

The first thing he notices is a squad car in front of Kev's house. The next thing is that his driveway and the kerb along the road are full of cars. *Realtors.* There's a sign in his front yard that reads "Open House." It has balloons on it that twist on long strings and beat against one another, agitated by the wind.

Flip turns in his seat and shoves the handgun down into his clothes carton. His ass beeps the horn. He sits quickly and waits to see if he got anyone's attention. No one appears from inside the house, and no one stares out of the windows. He snatches his phone, unbuckles his bouquet and walks toward his house to give Lynn the flowers and deliver the good news.

He can clearly see what is to come. And once he can visualize an outcome, he knows it's only a matter of following through to make the vision manifest:

It's fall, and Dylan is riding on Flip's shoulders. Dyl's fingers are laced together under Flip's chin, and he keeps leaning his weight back too far and choking Flip, cranking his neck out of whack and making his shoulders ache.

"Sit up," Flip says.

Dyl scoots up for a few moments before slumping back into the more painful position. But Flip really doesn't mind. He's slimmed down, feels fit and strong. Plus Dylan isn't so heavy that Flip can't endure a little discomfort.

Flip's wearing his winter boots, newly waterproofed for the season. He listens to the sound of wind in the trees, feet shuffling through fallen leaves and the tiny, cold creek rushing along to his left. He rounds a bend in the tree-lined path and his wife and daughter come into view ahead.

Lynn's legs are in wool leggings and a skirt, curled beside her on the checked blanket as she unloads a thermos filled with hot chocolate and a plate of coffee cake. Sara is on a corner of the blanket, legs crossed and her sweater stretched tight across her round pregnant belly. Her hands absently stroke her stomach, as if smoothing her sweater. He hoists Dyl up and over his head, lets him run on ahead. He stands there, bathed in the glory of nature, of his life. *It's been the harshest year of my life. But finally things are back in order.*

As he imagines it, he knows it's a bit of a stretch, maybe too good to be true. But he feels content with that.

He moves between the cars in his driveway, noticing that someone took the time to sweep the shattered glass from his driver's side window, though he still sees a few pieces.

"Hey," a voice barks behind him.

"Mr. Mellis, I need you to turn around slowly. Keep your hands where I can see them." Flip thinks he recognizes the voice: Officer Steve of the crooked parking. He turns his head to look, his nose rubs across some baby's breath in the bouquet cradled in his arms. He can feel his nostrils pucker, his eyes begin to itch and water.

"Slowly," Officer Steve repeats.

Flip carefully rotates his body. He faces the policeman, can see Steve has a weapon drawn.

"Hey," Flip says, in his most non-confrontational voice. He tries to wave the cellphone in a gregarious, if awkward greeting. The instant he tries to speak though, a huge sneeze rises unbidden, and he pitches forward, spilling water from the arrangement.

"Drop it!" the officer screams.

Flip doesn't want to drop the flowers; they're for Lynn. He wants to say so; draws a breath after the sneeze in order to explain. A gust of wind whips in, twists the balloons on the Open House sign, and two of the balloons burst with a *pop pop*.

"I said drop it!" Officer Steve yells, as he fires at Flip.

Twelve thousand volts of electricity race through Flip's body at 19 pulses per second, all his muscles painfully contract at once, his feet shoot out from under him and he falls on his side, right on his bruised hip. The vase bursts in an explosion of glass, flowers, and water. Flip's head smacks the cement, he releases his over-full bladder. It doesn't seem to make the pain of the electric shock any worse. *Now I know.*

The policeman hustles up and kicks Flip's cellphone away. He's yelling, "Where's the gun?"

Flip's body relaxes, and he notices the shoes of a crowd gathering around him. The realtors stand around, holding paper plates of cookies and Styrofoam cups of coffee.

Officer Steve is clearly upset; he cuffs Flip's wrists behind his back with unnecessary force and yanks him to his feet.

"Aren't you Doctor somebody?" he asks. "You are Mr. Mellis, aren't you? I put gas in your car. I know you. You said you were Doctor someone. Right? Was that you? Are you Mr. Mellis?"

"Yes," Lynn says. "That's Mr. Mellis." The officer looks relieved. He must have worried he'd electrocuted the wrong man.

"Where's the gun?" The officer demands, yelling in Flip's ear and lifting his bound arms so high on one side Flip nearly tips over.

"He doesn't own a gun," Lynn says.

"I saw it. I saw it in his hand. He was carrying a gun."

"Cellphone," Flip says. The crowd of realtors are mumbling and gawking and shovelling down their free food as quick as they can. Coleen is there, shaking her head in clear disapproval, arms crossed over her chest. Lynn stands apart, not coming to his side.

"I brought you flowers," he says, indicating the mash of petals and greenery around him. Room temperature liquid drips down his legs and soaks into his ankle socks. He's truly thankful for the spilled flower water. He hopes it camouflages his circumstantial incontinence.

"I got the job," he says with as much enthusiasm as possible. "At DynaTech. I was coming to tell you. Everything is going to be okay now. Everything is going to work out." Lynn does not appear convinced.

Officer Steve steers Flip toward his cruiser while yelling at him loud enough for the whole neighbourhood to hear, "Mr. Mellis, you've been accused of breaking and entering, assault, possession of a firearm, recklessly discharging a firearm in a public place and resisting arrest."

Before being crunched into the back of the police car Flip sees a prominent gash in the cruiser's fender. *It really looks much worse in broad daylight.*

Lynn steps forward, speaks to the officer. The officer nods and she comes to Flip.

"Flip, What the hell's going on?" She doesn't sound pleased to see him.

"Don't worry baby. Everything will be fine. I got it all under control."

The officer manhandles him into the hard plastic backseat. Before he can close the door Flip calls, "I'm not dead yet." Then the door slams, ending any further conversation. He'd hoped to say more.

Flip's face is in the glare and he closes his eyes against the pain. Blue eyes are the most sensitive to light. Time passes and his worries drain from his heavy body. He feels lighter than he has in years. He's too tired to fight anymore. It feels good to stop struggling. He's visited by the sense of a hard job well done. The sounds of the crowd, the conversations taking place just outside the window seem to drift away, recede into the distance.

Long moments later he feels the sun slide across his face as the squad car backs from the driveway. He moves into shadow as the car glides forward over the slick asphalt. It feels good to let go, to let the car take him where it will. In the comforting embrace of the darkness, in the cool of the backseat, he feels his body passing farther away from his home, and he is perfectly happy to let things follow their natural course.

ACKNOWLEDGEMENTS

Books are long projects that require endurance; at times I feel my writing has as much to do with the shape of my life, and the people I share it with, as it does with putting words on paper. I've been fortunate over the years to meet many smart, creative people who encouraged, inspired, and challenged me. Friedrich Nietzsche wrote, "A good writer possesses not only his own spirit but also the spirit of his friends." If a direct correlation exists between the quality of my writing and the virtues of my friends, this will be a remarkable book indeed.

Through the writing and publishing process I've had the moral support of a vast community of people, a few of which I'll mention here. Good friends like Chris DiStasio, Kelly Kocevar Baldwin, Travis Feldman, Lesley Garretson, Andrea Rose Jones and Marty Hergert. Also Jay and Amy Miller, Dana Hoover, Kelly McCants, Eddie Miles, Bryan Batsell, Paige Hall, Nicholas Dean Beck, Chris Akers, Laura Berman, Inky Bob Atkins, Ana Reinert, Christopher Hoffelt and Julie Wallace, Ian and Laura Wagriech, Jill Wallace and Dave Gorman, Shannon and Tom Quinn, Danielle Morency, and Tracy Bergfeld Cesario.

Artists Joseph Lappie, Anna Pate, Tinameri Turner, Stephen DeSantis, Luan Barros, Kelly Parsell, Karol Shewmaker, Jean Bevier, Meredith R Winer, Mark Moroney, Matthew Aron, Jeffrey Johnson, and the matchless Brad Freeman; each set an example as determined, and talented makers.

Writers Loran Frazier, Wayne Kasper, Rose Marie Kinder, Deron Denton, Jenny Magnus, John Rich, Jason E Hodges, Eric Pietrzak, Janice Deal, Sherry Antonini, and many others generously gave me feedback, camaraderie, commiseration, and a passion for the craft.

Thanks to my first readers, Benjamin Chandler and Jamie Arnold Thome. Also, Patricia Sánchez and Anna Soler-Pont, Karl Sabbagh, and Jacqueline Graham without whom this book would be merely a sheaf of dusty pages hidden under my bed. Especially important to the realization of this novel was the artist and novelist Audrey Niffenegger. The instruction and guidance she offered was exactly the right motivation at a moment when I was ready to embrace it.

The love and support over the years from the Moser family, especially Lester and Lois, Mike and Faye, Mark, Kristin and Layton, Katie, Becky, and Kelli. It means the world to me. My deepest gratitude goes to the many members of the Allee clan.

To my daughter Eliza, and my son Declan, for the endless laughter and hugs.

To my wife, Michelle, since we first spoke you've been a constant source of every good thing in my life. Thank you. I love you.

ABOUT THE AUTHOR

Brandon Graham has worked as a commercial pressman, an adjunct professor, and as a gallery director. He studied in Budapest, Hungary, and Dijon, France, with a summer spent as a barman in Chilham, England. In Chicago, he studied visual and written narrative at Columbia College Center for Book and Paper Arts.

Photo by Mr. King, Chicago

Brandon's first short story was published in the journal *Pleiades* in 1990. Since then he has written for performance, artist's books, zines, book reviews, and web content. His blog, FictionDoldrums, is a firsthand account of his efforts to write and publish this very novel. He has published poems and prose in literary journals, including the recent story, "Razed," published in the experimental journal *Little Bang*. His artist's books are included in several dozen special collections libraries throughout the United States. Currently he is a regular contributor of articles and book reviews to *JAB* (the *Journal of Artists' Books*). He continues to make art and write outside of Chicago where he now lives with his lovely wife and two mostly sweet children, surrounded by an inimitable gang of friends and neighbors.